They were young, ambitious—
and Adamses through and through.
Which meant that marriage and babies weren't
part of their plans. But plans have a way of
changing...especially when love enters the picture!

UNEXPECTED MOMMY

He was determined to get back his share
of the family ranch—even if it meant seducing
his uncle's ornery stepdaughter, Jenny Runningbear,
to do it. And she was equally determined to find the perfect
man. But why, she sighed resignedly, did he have to present
himself in the form of Chance Adams, complete with
hellion son and relentless grudge against her family?

THE COWGIRL & THE UNEXPECTED WEDDING

Ever since she was little, Lizzy Adams had counted on
becoming a doctor. What she *hadn't* counted on:
the charms of handsome rancher Hank Robbins—
and their baby on the way. With a little work,
could Lizzy possibly get her man—and her plan?

NATURAL BORN LAWMAN

en a by-the-book
en he saw a
a bottle of
atsy Langhorn
e rule-obsessed
Jus... ...convinced to throw away the book—for good?

SHERRYL WOODS

The Adams Dynasty

Silhouette Books

Published by Silhouette Books

America's Publisher of Contemporary Romance

SILHOUETTE BOOKS

ISBN 0-373-18505-7

by Request

THE ADAMS DYNASTY

Copyright © 2002 by Harlequin Books S.A.

The publisher acknowledges the copyright holder
of the individual works as follows:

UNEXPECTED MOMMY
Copyright © 1998 by Sherryl Woods

THE COWGIRL & THE UNEXPECTED WEDDING
Copyright © 1998 by Sherryl Woods

NATURAL BORN LAWMAN
Copyright © 1998 by Sherryl Woods

CONTENTS

Dear Reader,

Welcome to the further adventures of those wonderful Adamses of Los Pinos, Texas!

As always, Harlan Adams's influence is deeply felt, especially in the lives of his two daughters—Jenny and Lizzy. One is his by marriage, the other by birth, but both have developed their strong sense of self, thanks to their father. Harlan's influence is no less strong on grandson Justin Adams, whose by-the-book regard for the law is on trial in *Natural Born Lawman*.

In that book, as well as in *Unexpected Mommy* and *The Cowgirl & the Unexpected Wedding,* each of these Adamses will have to balance a deeply ingrained sense of right and wrong with compassion and love. And, as always, Harlan's powerful faith in the importance of family comes into play.

I hope you'll find their stories compelling and that you'll feel as I did when I wrote them—that all the Adamses have found the perfect match for their strong-willed, honorable natures.

All best,

Sherryl Woods

UNEXPECTED MOMMY

Prologue

"It was the prettiest slice of land the good Lord put on this earth," seventy-five-year-old Hank Adams whispered, his voice frail, his eyes glazed over with a faraway look. "Did I ever tell you about White Pines, son?"

Chance held back his impatience and forced a smile. "Only about a million times, Daddy." Seeing his father's disappointment, he quickly added, "But I never tire of hearing about it, you know that."

"Is the heat on?" his father asked, shifting subjects as he often did these days. He shivered and pulled the two layers of blankets a little tighter under his chin. "You sure that danged furnace is working?"

The furnace was pumping out enough heat to sizzle

meat as far as Chance was concerned. The blazing fire only added to the oppressive, stifling atmosphere in his father's small Montana cabin. But ever since Hank Adams's health had begun to fade a few months earlier, it seemed he couldn't stay warm enough. The only thing that seemed to distract him for long was reminiscing about the home he'd left behind decades earlier back in West Texas. The bitterness seemed to Chance to be as fresh now as it must have been on the day his daddy had been chased off by his older brother, Chance's uncle, Harlan Adams.

"The furnace is turned up to near eighty," Chance said. "You'll be warm in a minute, Pop. Tell Petey and me another story about when you were growing up."

"Yeah, Granddad," Petey said enthusiastically. "Start at the beginning. Tell us about how my great-great-granddaddy came all the way from the South after the Civil War and built this big old mansion just like the one he'd left behind."

"You could probably tell that one yourself," Chance said, grinning at his son and ruffling the boy's shaggy sun-streaked hair that so closely resembled his own.

Most of the time lately Petey's moods ranged from difficult to impossible. He'd never been able to sit still for much more than a minute, but recently, ever since his grandfather had come home from the hospital to die, Petey rarely left the old man's side. It was as if he knew there was only a little bit of time left to absorb all the tall tales and family history.

What worried Chance was that he was also latching on to all his grandfather's bitterness and resentment. The fight for a share of White Pines wasn't Petey's. If there was going to be a battle—and that was a mighty big if—it was Chance's to wage.

He glanced at his father and saw that he was settling back, searching his memory for stories to keep Petey entertained or, more likely, to incense him.

"Now let's see," his father began. "That would have been in the spring of eighteen hundred and sixty-nine."

Petey's eyes widened as if he were hearing the date for the first time. "Wow! That's like a hundred years ago, huh?"

"More than that, boy. The war was over and the family's home had been wiped out by them damn Yankees. They plundered it first and then burned the whole place to the ground. That was that hellion Sherman who was responsible," he said, adding a colorful curse or two to emphasize his poor opinion of the man.

Then he went on. "Your great-great-granddaddy was little more than a boy then, not even eighteen, as I recall. He'd been through more at that age than most men live through in a lifetime. He knew things would never be the same for any of them there, so he packed up his mama and his two sisters and headed west to start over."

Hank's voice seemed to fade. It was hard to tell if he'd forgotten the rest or was merely tiring.

"Where was his daddy?" Petey coached.

"Killed in the war."

"Did they have any money?" Petey asked, prompting his grandfather to tell his favorite part of the story.

"Some that his mama hid away, along with some jewelry. They sold that so they'd have a little nest egg for startin' over. They sold it all but a ruby-and-diamond pin."

"The one you brought with you to Montana," Petey proclaimed triumphantly. "Can I see it?"

"It's locked away safe, boy. It's your daddy's to give to his wife, if he ever marries again," he said with a pointed glance at Chance. Then his eyes turned misty again. "Lordy, that pin is something, though. I can remember my mama wearing it when she got all dressed up sometimes. Looked like a little basket of ruby red rosebuds and sparkly diamond baby's breath. There was many a day when your grandma Lottie wanted me to sell it so we'd have a little something in the bank, but I wouldn't do it. That pin was the only legacy I had from my ancestors. Now it's your daddy's and someday it'll be yours."

Chance let his mind wander as the familiar tale washed over him. He knew the story practically word for word. He'd been hearing it since he'd been younger than Petey. Just as his son was now, he'd been enthralled by the adventure of the move from the South all the way to West Texas, by the building of White Pines and the founding of the town of Los Piños. He had a feeling his father had embellished the story a bit over time, inventing a few tussles with Indians and thieves that hadn't actually occurred. Even so, it was a heck of a story.

He could envision the grand house that had been built as an exact replica of the mansion that had been destroyed. He could see the spread of land abloom with bluebonnets and crossed by sparkling streams and shaded by pines and cottonwoods.

"Why'd you ever leave, Granddaddy?" Petey asked. "How come you came to Montana?"

Hank Adams sighed heavily at the question and his eyes darkened with anger. His agitation was as great now as it probably had been decades earlier when he'd been forced from the home he loved. Chance didn't like seeing him get himself so stirred up over something that was long over with.

"Leave it be for now, Petey," Chance said. "Your granddaddy's tired."

"Not tired," the old man said, his chest heaving as he tried to draw in a ragged breath. "Still makes me madder than a wet hen when I think of it, that's all."

"Then don't think of it," Chance advised, regarding him worriedly. "Just rest."

"Can't rest until this is settled," his father retorted. "Should have done it years ago."

"Done what?" Petey asked, clearly sensing a new twist was coming, one they hadn't heard before.

Chance knew it, too. He'd expected something like this his whole life, dreaded it.

"I should have gone home," his father said. "I should have claimed what was mine, instead of letting that low-down scoundrel of a brother of mine take it all."

"You'll go," Chance soothed, knowing it was a lie. If Hank hadn't mustered the gumption for the fight years ago when he'd had his strength, he'd never do it now. As he had with so many things, Hank would want someone else to handle it for him.

"Harrumph," his father responded. "Not me. It's too late for me." He reached out and seized Chance's hand. "You, though, it's not too late for you to go. You and Petey. With your mama and your wife both gone and me breathing my last any day now, there'll be nothing to hold you here."

The mention of his late wife silenced Chance as nothing else could have. The wound of Mary's death was still too raw and painful, even though it had been more than a year now since the flu had turned into pneumonia and a three-day blizzard had prevented them from getting the medical help she desperately needed. It had been his fault. He should have ridden out at the first sign she was sick, instead of listening to her reassurances she'd be fit as a fiddle again in no time.

Losing his sweet, gentle Mary had cost him his soul and hardened his heart. Had it not been for Petey, he might very well have lost his mind. Petey's out-of-control behavior was fair warning that he had to go on living in the here and now. Hank's illness had been the clincher.

What his father said was true enough, though. Chance had come to hate Montana and its bitter winters. He liked ranching, but there were other places he could settle down and start over. If Hank hadn't been too ill and too ornery to move, Chance would have packed them all up and headed off to start over months ago. Once his father died, there really would be nothing left to keep him here. Still, as shiftless and irritating as Hank could be, Chance didn't want to think about not having his father bossing him around and telling his tales.

"You're going to live to be a hundred, you old coot," he said, squeezing his father's callused hand. "You're too stubborn not to."

A terrible racking cough seized his father just then as if to give lie to Chance's prediction. When it was over, his father's brow glistened with sweat. His color was ashen.

"Listen to me," he said, his voice raspy. "You go to Texas. You have as much right to White Pines as anyone who's left there. Maybe Harlan's still alive, maybe he's not, but that house, that land, was my heritage as much as his. He stole it from me. Take it back, Chance. Take it back for me. It's the only way I'll ever rest in peace, knowing that you and Petey have what's due you." His eyes glittered feverishly. "Promise me, son. Promise me."

Chance feared the cost of an argument would be too great. "I promise you, Daddy. Petey and I will go to Los Piños," he said, though he wasn't sure he ever intended to follow through. He wasn't certain he had the strength left to carry on an old family feud.

His father's grip tightened. "Don't say that just to pacify me, son. A promise made on a man's deathbed has to be kept. It's the next thing to making a promise to God. You understand that, don't you?"

Hank had been well into his forties when his only son was born. He'd already been set in his no-account ways. Over the years Chance had fought with his father as often as he'd agreed with him. Their rows had been loud and legendary in these parts, but he loved the old coot.

"I understand," he said softly, reaching for a damp cool cloth to wipe his father's brow.

"Petey?" the old man whispered.

Petey crept closer. "I'm here, Granddaddy."

"You're a good boy, Petey. Wild and spirited, just the way I was, but you have a good heart, same as me. Don't let anybody ever tell you otherwise."

Chance put a hand on his son's shoulder and squeezed. Tears were spilling down Petey's cheeks. It was clear he sensed the end was near.

"Granddaddy, don't die," he pleaded. "Please don't die like Mama did."

Hank Adams gave Chance's hand one last squeeze, then reached out his arms for his grandson. Petey climbed onto the bed and hugged him back fiercely, refusing to let go.

"Shh, boy. Don't cry for me. You have to be brave for your daddy. Make sure he takes you to Texas, okay? I won't be here to see that he does, so you'll have to do it for me."

"Daddy!" Chance warned.

His father shot him a final stubborn look. "Just making sure you keep your promise, son. Now you won't be able to look Petey in the eye if you don't."

Stunned and infuriated by such a sneaky tactic, Chance glared at him. "You're a manipulative old son of a gun. You know that, don't you?"

His father cackled. "Hell, boy, I'm an Adams. That's our heritage as much as White Pines and cattle."

He sighed then and closed his eyes. Chance had to coax a tearful Petey away from the bed.

It was a few more hours before Hank Adams died, but those were his last words, and they echoed in Chance's head in the days to come.

By the time school was out for the year, he'd made up his mind. He put both houses—his and his daddy's—on the market, packed up his and Petey's belongings in the back of his pickup, paid one last visit to the cemetery where Mary and his mother and father had been laid to rest, said goodbye to neighbors he'd known all his life and headed south.

"It's going to be just like it was for my great-great-granddaddy," Petey said, bouncing in his seat with excitement. "We're having a real adventure."

"Yes," Chance agreed with one last look at his past in the rearview mirror. Either they were going to have an incredible adventure, or they were heading straight for disaster. He wasn't quite prepared to lay odds on which was the more likely.

Chapter One

Sweet heaven, it was true. Jenny Runningbear Adams stood just inside the doorway to her fourth-grade classroom and tried very hard not to panic. All around her chaos reigned, which just proved there was always a payback for the sins of the past. Years of childhood misdeeds were returning to haunt her.

If her stepfather could see this, he'd laugh till his sides split. Harlan Adams just loved irony. He'd always told her that one day she'd run across a child as impossible as *she* had been. Apparently this school year she was about to be confronted by a whole class-room of them.

She stared around her in horror and wondered what had possessed her to shift from teaching history and current events to eighth graders. She'd had some idealistic notion that elementary-school students would be more receptive, easier to mold. Obviously she'd lost her mind. The evidence of that was right in front of her.

The opening-day bell had barely rung and already chairs had been upended. Papers were strewn from one end of the dingy room to the other. Graffiti had been scrawled across the blackboard in every shade of chalk. Unfortunately, not even half the words had been spelled correctly. Stacks of textbooks she had neatened herself only yesterday were tumbled in disarray. Pandemonium was in full swing.

A freckle-faced girl was huddled at her desk sobbing as she clutched one fat braid in her hand, while the other bobbed on the left side of her head where it belonged. She looked like a lopsided doll after an encounter with a four-year-old's scissors.

A pack of boys was circling the girl's chair, whooping as if they'd just succeeded in scalping her. It was an image that sent a particularly nasty chill through Jenny's part-Native American blood.

She took in the entire scene, drew a calming breath and prayed for patience, fortitude and maybe just a little divine intervention. At this moment she deeply regretted ever thinking of teaching as a way of giving something back to the community and sticking a little closer to home than she'd been in recent years.

More than one person had warned her that this would not be as simple as dealing with a bunch of hardheaded, shortsighted congressmen or even the eighth graders she'd had the year before. She had scoffed at that. Lobbying on Capitol Hill had been a three-ring circus. Eighth graders had been discovering the power of hormones. Fourth graders were little kids.

Well, that particular horse was out of the barn. She was here, under contract for another school year, nine endlessly long months. The prospect of day after day of *this* made her shudder. The only way around it was to seize control now, right this second.

"That's *enough!*" she said just loudly enough to be heard over the uproar. That particular tone, lethally calm, had quelled many a rioting group in the past, although most of them had been adults caught up in a frenzy of advocacy of some Native American cause or another. She waited with some trepidation to see if it worked with this pint-size mob.

If it didn't, she could always inform the principal that she'd had a sudden mental breakdown and it would no longer be safe for her to be left alone with young children. Patrick Jackson disliked her so much he'd accept the explanation without batting an eye. Besides, teaching was her second career, anyway. She could always find a third. Change was good. In fact, at this precise moment, it struck her as both positive and inevitable.

As she contemplated her future with some enthusiasm, two dozen pairs of eyes turned in her direction, surveying her, sizing her up. The sobbing child with the unfortunate haircut watched her hopefully.

"Everyone find a chair, get it behind a desk and sit," Jenny instructed. When no one moved, she added, "Now!"

Slowly but surely she detected signs of movement. First one chair was scraped into place, then another and another. She caught a couple of guilty looks being exchanged as she crossed the room toward the chubby-cheeked victim of the morning's torment.

She hunkered down in front of her and grasped her trembling hands. "Sweetie, it's going to be okay," she soothed, though she was certain of no such thing.

"No, it's not," the girl said, her voice thick with choked-back tears. "My hair is g-g-g-gone."

"But now you can have a whole new hairdo," Jenny said cheerfully. She smoothed a tendril of hair away from the child's flushed cheek. "Look at my hair. It's short. Takes me two minutes to wash and dry it. No tangles, either. And you have a lovely face. Short hair will show off your beautiful eyes."

The girl blinked owlishly at that. "You think so?" she asked hesitantly.

"I really think so."

"But what is my mom going to say?" she asked miserably. "My hair's been growing practically forever. She'll kill me."

"I'll speak with your mother," Jenny promised. "After all, this wasn't your fault. It's not as if you lopped off that braid yourself. What's your name?"

"Mary," the child said. "Mary Rose Franklin."

"Well, Mary, why don't we go and make a call to your mother right this minute and see what we can do about this." She smiled at her. "Just think how envious all your friends are going to be that you got to miss the first day of school."

Mary sniffed and managed a faltering smile of triumph for her now subdued classmates.

Jenny took the child's hand and led her toward the door, then paused as she recognized the danger in her plan. The class was very likely to erupt into chaos again the instant her back was turned.

She turned slowly back to face the other students. She doubted she would ever learn which student was responsible for this disaster, but maybe she could transform the incident into a lesson for all of them. If she didn't take control of these nine-year-olds today, it would be a very long year.

Or a very short one, if she followed through on seeking new employment. *Any* new employment. Once the principal saw Mary's new haircut, he might very well encourage Jenny's career change. In the meantime, though, she leveled a stern look at her young charges.

"When I get back here, I expect to find you exactly where I left you," she said. "And I expect to find the person responsible for chopping off Mary's hair writing an apology to Mary."

Several boys snickered. Jenny scowled.

"On second thought, perhaps all of you should be

writing that apology," she said firmly. "Even if you didn't cut her hair, you all stood by and watched it happen. That makes you accessories. I'll explain exactly what that is when I get back. Then you can read your letters aloud. They had better ring with sincerity or every one of you will spend the next month in detention. Maybe longer." She scowled. "Maybe the whole semester. Have I made myself clear?"

"Yes, ma'am," a redheaded girl muttered dutifully. Her hands were folded neatly atop her desk and her expression was as solemn and innocent as a saint's.

"Yes, ma'am," several others mimicked.

Jenny sighed and decided to let the taunt pass. "You may start now." She waited until heads were bent and pencils were scratching over paper before taking Mary to the principal's office and explaining the morning's catastrophe.

Patrick Jackson peered at Jenny over the ugly black frames of his thick glasses, then glanced at Mary and sighed heavily. "I just knew something like this was going to happen the minute I heard the board had approved your transfer to this school. I would have fought it, but it would have been a waste of time. Even though you've been trouble ever since you hit town twenty years ago, your family has too much influence for me to win."

She ignored the reference to her family and to her inauspicious beginnings as a resident of Los Piños. Some memories were destined to die hard.

"This is hardly my fault," she protested, instead. "I wasn't even in the classroom yet."

"My point precisely. The bell had rung. Where were you?"

Jenny stared at him incredulously. "In here with you listening to yet another explanation of my duties, along with a few off-the-cuff remarks about my lack of suitability as a teacher," she shot back.

That gave him a moment's pause. He settled for regarding her sourly. "And who's with your class now?"

"No one," she admitted.

"Obviously you learned nothing from what happened this morning." He shook his head. "It's just as I expected. You are not cut out for this."

Jenny barely resisted the urge to utter a curse that would have blistered the man's ears. After all, Mary had been traumatized enough for one morning. She didn't need to see her brand-new teacher lose her temper and punch Mr. Patrick Johnson in his bulbous nose.

She stood a little straighter and said with quiet dignity, "If you will call Mary's mother and explain what happened, I will get back to my other students."

"Go, go," he said, waving her off. "I'll speak to you again at the end of the day."

She beamed at him. "I'll be looking forward to it." He'd have to catch her first, she thought as she gave Mary's hand a last reassuring squeeze and bolted from the office.

As she raced down the hall, she listened for the sounds of renewed chaos erupting in her classroom. Instead, it was absolutely silent as she approached. She found the quiet worrisome, but she was grateful nonetheless.

Inside, Jenny scoured the room for signs of mischief. It appeared, though, that she'd gotten her message across. No one had budged so much as an inch in her absence.

"Is everyone finished writing that apology?" she asked, perching on the edge of her desk and surveying the students.

"Yes, ma'am," the same little redhead replied eagerly.

"Yes, ma'am," the others taunted in a singsong chorus.

"Enough!" Jenny said. "Who'd like to go first?"

Naturally it was that accommodating little redhead who replied.

"Fine," Jenny said. "Your name is?"

"Felicity Jackson."

Jenny winced. "Any relation to our principal?"

"He's my father," the child said proudly.

Of course, he would be, Jenny thought with a sigh. "Okay, then. Thank you, Felicity. You may go first."

Felicity's essay was less of an apology than a well-crafted crime report. Bless her little suck-up heart, she readily mentioned not only the precise details of the insult that had been perpetrated on her classmate, but the name of the boy responsible: Petey Adams.

Before Jenny could say a word, a boy—almost certainly the boy in question—flew out of his seat and aimed straight for Felicity, clearly prepared to knock the breath clean out of her. Jenny stepped in his way with seconds to spare. With one arm looped around his waist, she plucked him off his feet.

"Petey, I presume."

"You can *presume* anything you danged well want to," he said with a defiant tilt to his chin and fire flashing in his startlingly blue eyes.

Something about that chin and those eyes looked disturbingly familiar. Jenny had the uncomfortable feeling she ought to recognize Petey, especially since his last name was Adams, the same as her own.

"Petey, you and I will discuss this incident when the rest of the class goes to recess," she informed him. "In the meantime you have two choices. You can remain in your seat and behave, or you can spend the morning in the principal's office. It's up to you, but I should warn you that Mr. Jackson is very eager to get his hands on the person responsible for Mary's haircut." She smiled at the boy. "What's it going to be?"

The defiance slipped just a notch. "Might's well stay here," he muttered eventually.

"Good choice," she said, and released him to return to his seat. "Perhaps you'd like to read your apology to the class."

"Didn't write one," he said, glaring at her. "You

can keep me here till I'm an old man and I still won't write one.''

The belligerence took her aback. ''You did hear me give the assignment, didn't you?''

''I ain't deaf.''

''Then you are deliberately choosing to defy me?''

He squared his little shoulders and stared straight back at her. ''Yep.''

She had to admire his spunk if not his insubordination. She had a whole new respect for the teachers forced to deal with *her* through the years. How she handled Petey Adams was absolutely critical to gaining the respect of his classmates, with the possible exception of Felicity, who obviously craved the approval of all authority figures more than she wanted the friendship of those her own age. She was definitely her father's child.

''Okay, Petey, we will discuss this matter during recess.''

He shrugged indifferently.

Jenny turned to the other students and called on them one by one to read their apologies. Fortunately there were no further incidents. Still, by the time recess came an hour later, she was so tense her shoulders ached. She made arrangements for the third-grade teacher to supervise her students on the playground, then returned to meet with Petey.

He regarded her with hostility. Jenny sighed. She took a moment to look over his file, which she'd retrieved from the office on her way back from the playground. He was new to Los Piños. His mother had died less than two years before, his grandfather just months ago. He was all alone with his dad, who'd taken a job as foreman of a ranch near White Pines.

Jenny recalled all too vividly her own sense of being lost and alone after her parents' divorce, when her mother had brought her from New York to this strange new place. She kept a tight rein on her sympathy, though, as she looked up and faced the boy seated in front of her.

"You're new this year, aren't you?"

"So?"

Apparently there was to be no such thing as a simple yes or no with this kid. "I remember when I went to a new school," she said. "In this very town, in fact. I wanted to make sure everybody knew they couldn't mess with me."

There was a brief spark of interest in his eyes. Jenny considered that a good sign.

"I got myself into as much trouble as I possibly could," she said, deciding not to tell him the precise nature of that trouble. Explaining that she had stolen Harlan Adams's car and smashed it into a tree when she was barely fourteen might just give this kid the idea that he'd been wasting his time chopping off pigtails.

"What'd you do?" Petey asked.

"Oh, lots of things," she said dismissively. "What I really wanted most of all was to get my mom's attention. She'd been so busy getting us settled and getting set up with her new office that she hadn't had much time for me.''

Petey's eyes brightened. She had clearly caught his interest.

''Did it work?'' he asked eagerly.

Jenny smiled at the memory. ''Oh, it worked, all right. She was furious with me. She made me go to work.''

Petey stared at Jenny, disbelief written all over his face. ''But you were just a kid.''

''True.''

''How old?''

''Fourteen.''

''I'm only nine. My dad would never make me work.''

''That's what I thought about my mom. She was a lawyer, after all. I told her she was violating child labor laws, but she didn't care. She said I had to learn a lesson. She put me to work for the man whose property I damaged.''

Petey considered that, then regarded her with a worried frown. ''Do you think I'm going to have to pay for Mary's haircut?''

''I wouldn't be surprised,'' Jenny said. ''It might even be good if you volunteered to do that. It would show that you're sorry for hurting her and that you know what you did was wrong.''

''But I don't have any money.''

''Then I suppose you'll have to do like I did. You'll have to earn it by doing chores.''

His gaze narrowed. "You mean like doing Mary's homework and stuff?"

She bit back a grin. "No. I think you and Mary should each do your own homework. But maybe you could help out around her house or maybe your dad will give you extra chores at home and you can give the money to Mary's mom."

For the first time Petey squirmed uncomfortably. "You're really going to tell my dad?"

Jenny was fairly sure he'd known that was going to be the outcome from the beginning of this little escapade. Now that it was a certainty, though, he was obviously worried about the consequences.

"Actually I was hoping you would tell him yourself," she said.

"He'll be really really mad, though."

"You should have thought of that before you took those scissors to Mary's hair."

He sighed heavily, then his expression brightened. "I know. Maybe I could do chores for you and you could give the money to Mary's mom. We wouldn't have to tell my dad at all."

"Nice try, but I don't think so. After school you and I are going to go see your dad," she said firmly. "I understand he's working for a rancher right outside of town. It's on my way home. I'll drive you."

"I'm supposed to take the bus," he argued.

"We'll make an exception today."

"I shouldn't ride with a stranger. My dad said so. My granddad, too."

"I'm not a stranger. I'm your teacher."

"I don't think that matters. My dad doesn't know you." His expression brightened. "Maybe you should just write a note and I'll take it home," he suggested hopefully.

And flush it down the toilet, Jenny thought. "Nope. I want to speak to your dad face-to-face."

"Okay," Petey said, his expression sullen again. "But don't blame me if he says it's all your fault."

"My fault?"

"Sure. If you were a better teacher, it would never have happened."

Out of the mouths of babes, she thought wearily. With Petey regarding her triumphantly, she swore that if she survived this day, she was going to think very seriously about choosing another profession. Less than half a day on the job this year and she was already regretting not going into law with her mother or maybe ranching like her adoptive father, Harlan Adams. Heck, maybe even calf roping would have been a better choice. Then again, she'd tried that once at her father's insistence. She hadn't been very good at that, either.

For the rest of the day she pondered what sort of man would have a son as insightful and inventive and troublesome as Petey Adams. Just thinking about facing such a man was almost enough to make her choose to stick around school and square off with Patrick Jackson, instead. Almost, but not quite. Duck-

ing out would irritate the pompous principal, which
was pretty good motivation in and of itself.

In fact, by the time the final bell rang, she was
actually looking forward to meeting Chance Adams.
She was just itching to go toe-to-toe with an adult,
instead of a classroom of pint-size hellions.

Chapter Two

In retrospect, the decision to settle in Los Piños had been easier than Chance had anticipated. Even when he'd driven into town two months earlier, he hadn't been sure he would stay. He'd just meant to keep his promise to his daddy, check out White Pines and then move on if West Texas didn't suit him. In fact, if it hadn't been for Petey, he might have kept on roaming for the rest of his life. He was too restless, too soul-deep exhausted to start over.

As it was, though, he knew his son deserved stability. Petey needed schooling and a real home to come to, his own bed to sleep in. The motel rooms they'd stayed in on the road when they'd first left Montana were fine for a night or two. But they were not the kind of places where he could raise a kid. No matter how sick at heart he was himself, he owed his son a better life than that.

He'd still been wrestling with his conscience when they'd crossed the border into Texas. He'd deliberately taken his time getting to Los Piños. They'd gone to the southeast part of the state first, taken a swim in the Gulf of Mexico, which Petey had declared way more awesome than the creeks back home. Then they'd spent a few days exploring the wonders of Houston, the biggest city Petey had ever seen, before moving on to Dallas, where Petey had wanted to see the stadium where his beloved Cowboys played. Whatever happened, Chance had wanted Petey to have his grand adventure. He'd hoped that would make up for all the grief in his young life. Two devastating losses in as many years were enough to shake up a boy's whole world. A man's, too, for that matter.

At any rate, it had been early July by the time they'd driven into Los Piños. Chance had expected to feel some sort of tug, some kind of connection to the place, but as far as he could see it was no different from any other ranching community in the West. The businesses catered to the cattlemen, nothing fancy, just good solid merchandise at decent prices.

They were just in time for the town's annual Independence Day celebration. Flag-waving families had gathered all along the sidewalks for a parade that was twice the size of the one back home in Montana, even though the town was no more populated, at least as far as Chance could tell.

After the parade there'd been a picnic. Most folks had brought their own baskets of fried chicken, along with blankets to spread on the grass, but there were plenty of food concessions for those who wanted to buy hot dogs and fries and cotton candy.

The celebration was wrapped up that night with fireworks. Chance had choked back bile at the oft-repeated announcements that the lavish display had been donated by none other than Harlan Adams and his sons.

"Y'all be sure and thank 'em when you see 'em," the mayor said.

Petey's eyes had widened at the mention of Harlan Adams. "That's Granddaddy's—"

Fearing he'd be overheard, Chance had put a hand over Petey's mouth, cutting off the blurted remark in midsentence. It was too soon for anyone to know he was connected in any way to the powerful Harlan Adams. He wanted to size things up before he made his presence and his intentions known—if he ever did.

But hearing all that boasting had solidified one thing: he was staying. He wanted to see just how the other half of the family had thrived after running his father off. Resentment he hadn't known he felt simmered all night long.

During the day he had asked around about employment and learned that a rancher named Wilkie Rollins was looking for an experienced foreman.

"It's a small place compared to White Pines," one man told him. "Then, again, most are. White Pines is about the biggest cattle operation in the state, bar none. Harlan's got himself quite a spread out there. That boy of his, Cody, has doubled the size of it these past few years. He's a smart one, all right, every bit as sharp as his daddy."

"Is that right?" Chance said, absorbing the information about his cousin and tucking it away for later consideration. "How do I go about finding this Rollins place?"

"You can't miss it if you head west going out of town. If you come up on them fancy gates at White Pines, you've gone too far."

The directions had been easy enough to follow. The next morning he'd driven out there, talked with Wilkie Rollins and had a job and a new home by the end of the interview. He and Petey had been settled in by sundown. Petey had been ecstatic that they were staying on.

In the weeks since, Chance had been happy enough with the familiar work. Wilkie's spread was smaller than his own had been in Montana, but the man was getting too old to handle it himself. He left most of the decisions to Chance and drove into town every day to hang out with his cronies. Chance had been able to keep up with the work with time to spare to contemplate his next move with Harlan Adams.

Petey was hell-bent on charging over there and introducing themselves and staking their claim. He'd been all but deaf to Chance's admonitions that slower was better. Fortunately, despite being the next-door neighbor, White Pines was too far down the road from Wilkie's for Petey to sneak off there on his own to snoop around.

"Patience, son, patience," Chance said over and over, but he figured he was pretty much wasting his breath. Petey was intent on fulfilling his granddaddy's last request.

Through the years Chance hadn't gotten caught up in his father's bitterness. It had always seemed a waste of energy to him. But now, the more he heard about those paragons of virtue out at White Pines, the more the high praise grated.

He wondered what folks would have to say if they knew that Harlan Adams had stolen half of that ranch right out from under his younger brother. He wondered how they'd react if they knew that Hank Adams had been sent away all but destitute. In the past two months Chance had started working up a pretty good head of steam over it himself.

While he debated the best way to go about making his presence known, he gave Wilkie his money's worth and let the idea of revenge simmer. Some of his plots were subtle and downright sneaky. Some were blatant and outrageous. All of them ended with him and Petey ensconced in that fancy house a few miles up the road from the little foreman's cottage they currently called home.

He was just trying a new scheme on for size when

he glanced up from the wood he'd been chopping and caught sight of a slender dark-haired woman striding in his direction, a purposeful gleam in her eyes. Since she also had his son in tow, he suspected Petey had been up to some sort of mischief again. He'd hoped the start of school today would settle the boy down, but it looked like just the opposite had happened.

The boy was darn near out of control. He managed to find a way to do mischief where Chance would have sworn none was possible. Chance would have tanned the boy's hide, if he'd thought it would help, but his own father's lashings had never done anything except make Chance more defiant than ever. Since Petey had his temper in spades, it seemed likely he'd react the same way.

Chance wiped his brow with the bandanna he'd stuck in his pocket and stood back to watch their approach. Might as well appreciate the sight of a pretty woman while he had the opportunity. In a few minutes they were going to be on opposite sides of something or other. That much was clear from the scowl on that pretty face of hers.

She was tall, five-eight at least, he gauged from a distance, and thin as a poker in her fancy doeskin-colored linen slacks and bright orange blouse. Her black hair was cropped short as a boy's, emphasizing wide cheekbones and eyes as dark as coal. There was a hint of Native American ancestry in her angular features.

He put her age at anywhere from late twenties to

early thirties. She had the brisk no-nonsense stride of a man, but as she neared, he saw that she had the surprisingly ample curves of a woman beneath that clinging silk blouse of hers. His body reacted as if he'd just spotted a primed and waiting sex goddess in his bed.

The reaction, of course, was the result of too many months of celibacy. This woman wasn't at all his type. She was way too skinny, and that determined jut of her chin warned him she'd be a handful of trouble.

"Mr. Adams," she called out as she neared. She sounded way too grim to be dropping by for the sheer pleasure of it.

"That would be me," he confirmed, glancing at Petey. When his son determinedly refused to meet his gaze, Chance looked the woman over from head to toe, hoping to rattle her. The action was as instinctive as breathing. He'd always enjoyed flirting with a pretty woman, no matter the circumstances. If he could distract her from her mission, so much the better. Instead, though, her gaze remained fixed squarely on his face as she patiently withstood the examination.

"Satisfied?" she asked eventually.

There was no hint of color in her cheeks, but Chance felt his own flaming. "Not by a long shot," he said, trying to reclaim the edge he'd lost.

She shrugged. "Let me know when you are. I can wait."

He concluded that trying to best her was a losing cause. "Who are you?" he asked since no one had seen fit to fill him in.

"I'm Petey's teacher."

He'd guessed as much—Petey was coming home from school, after all. And the woman with him had a prim and prissy attitude about her, just like every teacher Chance had ever had, though she was definitely a whole lot sexier than most.

"You have a name?" he asked.

"Jenny Adams."

Chance flinched. This was a turn of events he hadn't anticipated. He'd heard all about Harlan Adams's sons. He hadn't heard a word about any daughters. Then again, Adams was a common enough name. Maybe she wasn't kin at all.

"Adams?" he repeated cautiously. "Any relation to Harlan Adams?"

Her expression brightened. Those great big eyes of hers sparkled like coal well on its way to turning into diamonds.

"He's my father," she said with pride. "My adoptive father, actually. I was Jenny Runningbear before he married my mother and adopted me. Do you know him?"

"Oh, I know him, all right," Chance said coldly. "Or maybe I should say I know all about him, since we haven't exactly been introduced."

"Dad!" Petey protested, tugging urgently on his jeans.

Chance ignored him. Before he could stop himself, he blurted what he'd intended to keep secret for a while longer yet. "Harlan Adams is my uncle. He and my father were brothers."

She gaped at that, clearly stunned. Petey looked equally shocked that his father had done precisely what he'd been warning Petey not to do.

"That's not possible," Ms. Jenny Adams declared.

"Why? Because dear old Dad hasn't mentioned his long-lost brother?" Chance said, surprised at the bitterness in his voice. Apparently Hank's resentments had taken hold, after all. "They haven't been on speaking terms in years, not since he rode my daddy out of town and stole his heritage out from under him."

Genuine bemusement washed across her face. "That's not possible," she repeated, her tone a mixture of shock and outrage. "Obviously you don't know my father at all if you think he's capable of doing something like that."

Chance forced a smile. "Oh, I assure you it's more than possible, cousin Jenny. It's a genuine fact." He regarded her with a touch of defiance. "Unless you're calling me a liar."

He glanced at his son, who was following the exchange with a mixture of shock and relief. Apparently Petey figured this revelation was the next best thing to salvation, since it had served to distract his teacher from whatever she'd been intent on saying about his behavior in school today.

Chance thought Petey's optimism was a bit premature. He doubted that Ms. Adams could be distracted so easily, at least not for long. She struck him as the kind of woman who was all sass and vinegar, the kind who'd needle a man until she got her way or provoke a fight just for the sheer fun of it. It was all there in those flashing black eyes. True, this news had thrown her, but she was visibly gathering her wits as the tense silence dragged on. He found he was looking forward to doing battle with her. Herding cattle wasn't near as much of a challenge as arguing with a pretty woman.

"Well, I must say this is quite a shock," she said eventually. "You've just moved into town, according to Petey's file at the school."

"A couple of months ago," Chance confirmed.

She shook her head. "Daddy has a brother? I just can't get over it."

"*Had* a brother," Chance corrected. "He died a few months back."

Sympathy flared in her eyes at once. "Oh, of course. It was in Petey's file. I'm so sorry."

"No need for you to be sorry. You didn't even know the man."

Her eyes flashed for a second as if she might chastize him for being rude, but then her expression softened, once more sympathetic.

"I'm sorry just the same," she insisted quietly. "I'll have to tell my father you're here. I know he'll

want to get to know you. We'll have you come to
dinner at White Pines.''

The ever-so-polite invitation grated, probably more
than it should have since it was uttered with absolute
sincerity. "No, thanks, darlin'. I'm not the least bit
interested in dropping by for barbecue and coleslaw."

This time her gaze narrowed at his rudeness.
"Oh?" she said. "And why is that?"

She said it in that cool haughty way that might have
tickled him under other circumstances. Chance forced
another smile. "That would make it seem too much
like I was a guest in my own home."

"Excuse me?"

He regarded her with feigned surprise. "Why, darlin', haven't you figured it out yet? I thought for sure
you were quicker than that."

"Figured out what?"

He kept his gaze steady and his voice even. "That
I've moved to Los Piños for the sole purpose of taking that big old ranch away from your daddy."

Jenny felt a lot like kicking dust straight into
Chance Adams's arrogant face. Unfortunately, since
she'd come to his house just to tell him his son required more discipline, she couldn't see that throwing
a temper tantrum herself would accomplish much. It
might give Petey the notion that the only things sep-
arating them were age, height and power. It wouldn't
be a good lesson at all.

However, forcing herself to remain calm in the face

of Chance Adams's outrageous claim required every bit of self-control she possessed.

The whole thing was ridiculous. Of course, he was just confused. It was a case of mistaken identity or something. Harlan had no brother she'd ever heard about. He'd taken a dying ranch left to him by his shiftless daddy and made it pay. If White Pines was legendary in Texas and Harlan was powerful, then he owed it all to the sweat of his own brow. He hadn't stolen anything from anyone. She'd have staked her life on that. She'd never met a more honorable man than the one who'd adopted her when he'd married her mother.

She supposed she ought to tell Chance Adams just how far off base he was, but the angle of that stubborn chin suggested she'd be wasting her breath. She studied that chin for just a moment and concluded there was a distinct resemblance between it and every other male in the entire Adams clan. The discovery shook her a little, because it lent just the tiniest bit of credence to his preposterous claim.

Rather than start an argument over who owned what, she said sweetly, "Perhaps I should leave you to work out those details with my father when you finally meet. I'm actually here to discuss Petey."

The man sighed and some of the arrogance drained right out of him.

"What's he done?" Chance asked as if expecting the worst. He glanced at his son. "Petey?"

Since Petey remained stoically silent, Jenny described that morning's escapade.

"I'll pay for the girl's haircut," Chance said readily enough.

"Perhaps Petey should pay for it," Jenny suggested. She gestured toward the firewood. "Maybe chopping wood, for instance, would work off some of those aggressive tendencies. Physical exertion can be very healthy." She ought to know. Harlan Adams had worked her butt off after she'd stolen and wrecked his pickup.

Chance scowled at her suggestion, clearly resenting it and her.

"I'll deal with Petey the way I see fit," he responded stiffly. "Maybe you should concentrate on getting control of your class. If you can't cope with a bunch of nine-year-olds, maybe it's time to look for other work."

Petey shot her a triumphant look. He'd predicted his father would say that very thing. Jenny refused to concede to either of them that she'd said very much the same thing to herself just a few hours earlier.

She wondered what Chance would think if he discovered that one of the ideas she'd considered was working at White Pines, the very ranch he intended to seize as his own. Maybe she'd tell her father this very afternoon that she wanted to learn everything there was to know about ranching. Then she could flaunt her own claim to White Pines in this man's face. She hadn't had a decent mental and verbal skirmish since she gave up leadership of a Native American rights organization to move back to Los Piños. Something told her that Chance Adams would prove to be a fascinating challenge.

She sighed. Her father, of course, would see straight through her. From the day he'd made her one of his heirs he'd known that what she really wanted to do with her share of White Pines acreage was put a Bloomingdale's on it. Not that she'd ever make good on the threat, but it had been a running joke between them for too many years now for him to believe she'd suddenly developed a taste for ranching.

Her future wasn't the immediate problem, though. Petey's was. She regarded Chance Adams evenly. "It's entirely up to you what you do about your son's behavior," she said. "But I will tell you now that I will not tolerate a repeat of this in my classroom. The next incident will result in a suspension. Have I made myself clear?"

His blue eyes, the exact same shade possessed by every single one of her stepbrothers, sparkled with amusement. That hint of laughter was enough to make her want to spit. Yes, indeed, Chance Adams would be a challenge and then some.

Fortunately for her, Luke, Jordan and Cody had the same kind of arrogance, the identical streak of stubbornness. She'd learned long ago to give as good as she got with the three of them. She'd even learned to do it with words, instead of fists, since not one of them would ever have dared to brawl with their much younger stepsister as they did among themselves.

Chance was once again eyeing her speculatively. "Darlin', you are the cutest little thing when you're mad," he said in a tone clearly calculated to infuriate her. "You sound all prim and fussy. I had an old-maid schoolteacher once who sounded just like that."

Acid churned in her stomach as she fought yet another urge to retaliate with the kind of response that would have been instantaneous only a few years earlier. She was an adult now. A teacher. She was supposed to be setting an example, for goodness' sake, not rolling around in the dirt pummeling a man who'd just insulted her.

Unfortunately Chance Adams was the sort of man who would test the self-control of a saint. She hoped there wouldn't be many more encounters like this one to provoke her, at least not in front of an impressionable boy.

Maybe her desire to belt the man was plain on her face. Or maybe he knew just what the limits of her patience were likely to be, because suddenly out of the blue he sent Petey into the house. The boy scurried off so fast he left dust whirling in his wake.

It was exactly the circumstance Jenny had been hoping for. She could take an unobserved shot right at the man's chin, she thought wistfully, then gave a little sigh of resignation. She wasn't going to do it, of course.

Still regarding her with amusement, Chance Adams

rocked back on his heels and looked her over again. Her skin burned every single place his glance skimmed over.

Well, two could play at that game, she thought with defiance of her own. And he was showing a whole lot more skin.

She fixed her gaze squarely on his bare chest and ogled. She let her gaze drift slowly up to that sexy stubbled jaw, then down to the golden hair arrowing below the waistband of his jeans, then up again to broad shoulders. Looking him over, no matter what her purpose, turned out to be more fascinating than she'd anticipated. Her pulse fluttered, then ran wild. He was quite a specimen.

The technique worked, though. She had a suspicion that not all the perspiration on Chance's gleaming muscular chest was the result of the hot sun and chopping wood. The muscles in his throat worked as if he might just be having the teensiest bit of trouble swallowing. If she'd had some water with her, she would have offered him a cool drink for his parched throat.

Or doused him with it.

When she'd concluded her survey to her satisfaction and his discomfort, she forced herself to look smack-dab into his eyes. "As you can see, I give as good as I get. Shall we declare a truce, Mr. Adams?"

If she'd thought her little challenge was going to end it, she could tell at once from the amusement again sparkling in his eyes that she'd made a terrible mistake. He shook his head very slowly, his gaze locked with hers.

"Not on your life, darlin'," he said slowly. "I'd say the fireworks are just getting started."

Chapter Three

Chance kept a tight rein on his desire to laugh as he watched Ms. Jenny Adams sashay off, her back ramrod straight, her chin tilted at a defiant angle. Darn, but that confrontation had felt good. He hadn't had so much fun in a long time. He couldn't recall the last time a woman had stared at him so boldly and made his blood run quite so hot in the process.

Too bad she was an Adams. Okay, an adopted Adams, technically speaking, but that still made her the enemy. He figured she was tied to his Uncle Harlan by loyalty if not by blood. Sometimes those ties were even stronger than the genetic ones a person didn't have any say over.

The squeaking of the screen-door hinges snapped

his attention back to the matter that had brought the woman here in the first place. He pivoted just in time to see Petey trying to slip off in the direction of the barn to escape Chance's likely wrath.

"Oh, no, you don't, young man. Get back here," Chance commanded.

Petey took his sweet time about complying with the command. When he finally stood in front of Chance, he scuffed the toe of his sneaker in the dirt and refused to look up. He didn't look guilty, though, merely defiant. Chance figured that was an attitude that needed correcting in a hurry.

"Son?"

"Yeah?"

"That's 'Yes, sir.'"

Petey sighed heavily. "Yes, sir."

"That's better. Now look at me."

Another heavy sigh greeted that order. Chance would have smiled, but he figured it would take the edge off the stern displeasure he was trying to convey. "Now," he repeated emphatically.

His son finally darted a glance up at him. The defiance had begun to slip ever so slightly. His eyes shimmered with unshed tears. Chance fought the urge to gather the boy in his arms. It was moments like this that were the hardest tests for a father. He was torn between the discipline he knew needed delivering and the comfort and promise of unshakable love that were also required.

"I'd like an explanation," Chance told him,

pleased with his calm neutral tone when minutes ago he'd wanted to shake the kid for doing something so crazy. Jenny Adams had painted an all-too-vivid picture of that distraught child with a severed braid in her hand, tears spilling down her cheeks. He winced every time he thought about it. He'd been so sure he'd taught Petey girls were to be protected, not taunted or hit. Maybe he'd been remiss in not mentioning that their hair was off-limits, too.

"An explanation 'bout what?" Petey replied.

The innocent act tripped Chance's temper all over again. "About what the dickens possessed you to cut off that girl's braid," he snapped, then sucked in a sharp breath. In a calmer voice, he added, "You had to know it was wrong."

"I suppose."

"Suppose nothing. It was wrong. It was downright cruel, in fact. It's the exact kind of mean-spirited act I've told you to protect girls from, isn't it? Even little girls fuss about their looks. Did you think for one second about how she would feel with her hair all lopsided?" He shook his head. "Obviously not. Now tell me why you did it. You must have had a reason."

Petey still looked as if he was about to cry. Once again Chance had to force himself not to kneel down in the dirt and take the boy in his arms. Mary Rose Franklin was the one deserving of sympathy here, not the perpetrator of the crime. An image of Jenny Adams's disapproving expression stiffened his resolve.

He didn't intend to give her or anyone else the ammunition to accuse him of being a lousy dad.

Keeping his expression stern, he repeated, "Son, I'd like an explanation now."

"Timmy McPherson dared me," Petey said miserably. "He said if I ever wanted to have any friends at all in Los Piños, I'd do it."

I should have guessed as much, Chance told himself. It was all too typical for kids that age to set each other up to take a fall as some sort of test. "I assume you weren't counting on Mary being one of those friends," he said wryly.

Tears leaked out of Petey's eyes and spilled down his cheeks. "I didn't mean to make her cry. Honest, Dad. I just wanted to be friends with Timmy and the other guys. I'm the new kid. I didn't want them to think I was a total geek or something." His chin jutted out. "It's not like her hair won't grow back."

Chance cringed at the logic. "You don't make real friends by doing things you know perfectly well are wrong," he said. "Have you apologized to Mary yet?"

Petey looked even guiltier. "Not really. Ms. Adams assigned us to write an apology in class, but I didn't do it. I told her I wouldn't."

Chance sighed. "Why not?"

"Because it wasn't my fault, not really. It was Timmy's idea," he explained. "And then that Felicity girl ratted on me, just so she could get Ms. Adams to like her."

"Tattling's not the issue here," Chance pointed out. "And Timmy wasn't the one who chopped off Mary's hair, was he? You always have choices, son. You could have found a more sensible way to make new friends. I think maybe you'd better go inside and write that apology now. As soon as I get cleaned up, we're going to take it to Mary and hope and pray that she and her parents will forgive you. And if you ever hope to see a penny of your allowance again, you'd better pray that whoever fixed your classmate's hair did it cheaply."

Petey stared at him in dismay. "You're going to make me go to her house? I have to talk to her parents, too? And give them my allowance?"

"Yes."

"But, Dad—"

"We're going," Chance said with finality. "Have that note ready by the time I'm dressed or I'll start adding days to the week I already intend to ground you."

"Dad!" Petey wailed.

"Save your breath, son. I've let you get away with too much since your mama and granddaddy died. It's going to stop and this is as good a time as any to be sure it does."

"This is all Ms. Adams's fault," Petey grumbled, then added vehemently, "I hate her. If you loved Granddaddy, you'd hate her, too. She's one of *them*. She deserves to have bad things happen in her class.

Maybe they'll even fire her for being a crummy teacher.''

This time Chance did kneel down. He put his hands on Petey's shoulders and forced him to meet his gaze. "I don't want to hear that kind of talk again, okay? One thing has nothing to do with the other," he said, ignoring the fact that only moments earlier he, too, had been thinking of her as the enemy. He didn't want to consider what kind of nightmarish behavior Jenny Adams would have to face in her classroom if he encouraged Petey to make her part of his grandfather's vendetta. No fourth grader in Los Piños would get an education this year.

"But she lives at White Pines," Petey protested.

"For the moment," Chance said grimly, solidifying his resolve to settle things with Harlan Adams the very instant he could come up with a workable plan. Dragging it out would take its toll on all of them.

He looked Petey in the eye. "I repeat, one thing has nothing to do with the other. She is your teacher and you will respect her in the classroom and that is final. Understood?"

"No," Petey said, his chin jutting again. "Her father is a thief. That makes her no good, too. Why should I have to listen to anything she says?"

Obviously Hank had been very thorough in imparting his resentments to Petey. Chance couldn't see any long-term benefit in allowing Petey to grow up with so much hate. If there was a score to be settled, he would be the one to do it.

"Okay, let me put it another way," he said quietly. "I am telling you that you will show respect to her in that classroom. I am your father, and if you don't obey me, there will be hell to pay. Is that clear?"

Petey blinked several times at his father's fierce tone, then bobbed his head once.

"Excuse me. I didn't hear you."

"Yes, sir," Petey mumbled.

"That's better. Now get inside and write that note. We'll be leaving here in twenty minutes."

Petey's expression was sullen, but he did as he was told. Inside, Chance watched him for a moment, his head bent over a piece of paper from his notebook as he began slowly writing the ordered apology. Chance suspected it would be lacking in sincerity, but the point was getting Petey to go through the motions. He had to understand there were consequences for bad behavior.

Chance had learned about consequences at an early age. His father had been tough as nails, impossible to please and erratic about the rules Chance was expected to follow. It had kept Chance in a constant state of turmoil. He wouldn't do the same to Petey. He intended to make sure Petey understood exactly what the boundaries of acceptable behavior were.

When Jenny Adams had been telling him how to discipline his son earlier, he'd been every bit as resentful as Petey was now. But the truth was, her words had been a wake-up call. Petey needed more parenting than Chance had been giving him. Ever since their arrival in Los Piños, he'd been too caught up in this obsession with getting even with Harlan Adams. That was no excuse for neglecting his son or letting him get so carried away with his own brand of retribution. Now that Petey knew his teacher was Harlan Adams's daughter, there was no telling what the boy would try to make her the target of his anger.

Chance resolved then and there that Jenny Adams would never have another reason to question his ability to teach his kid the difference between right and wrong. If they met again—and they surely would—it was going to be because of his plan to ruin Harlan Adams. If a few sparks happened to ignite between them in the process—and they were dead-on certain to—so much the better.

Somehow, though, he intended to keep Petey out of the middle of things. Given how well Hank had primed the boy, though, that was likely easier said than done.

The fireworks between Jenny and Chance were nothing compared to the explosion that night at the dinner table when Jenny repeated Chance's declaration about White Pines. Harlan might have been in his eighties, but he hadn't slowed down and he wasn't inclined to take any threat to the sanctity of his home lightly.

"That darn fool," he said viciously, slamming his fist on the table so hard the dishes bounced. His skin turned an unhealthy shade of red and a sheen of perspiration broke out on his brow. "Obviously Hank spent his whole sorry life filling that boy's head with lies. Now he's dead and the rest of us are left to clean up the mess he's created."

Jenny exchanged a worried look with her mother, Janet, who appeared ready to leap from her chair and go to her husband's side to calm him down. Jenny's younger half sister, Lizzy, stared at him, clearly stunned by their father's outburst.

"Maybe I shouldn't have said anything," Jenny said, regretting her impulsive relating of the entire incident. She should have known it would upset to her father. Being accused of cheating his brother out of an inheritance was not something Harlan Adams would take lightly. "I'm sorry."

He reached out and patted her hand. "Of course you should have told me. No point in keeping quiet about it. Obviously this Chance Adams intends to create a ruckus sooner or later. Leastways now I can be prepared for it. There are plenty of folks in town who were around at the time. They're familiar with the details."

"Then you really did have a brother?" Jenny asked, though that much at least seemed obvious from her father's agitated reaction.

"I did," he said tersely.

"How come you never mentioned him?" Lizzy asked.

"Jenny, Lizzy, leave it be for now," her mother warned. "Can't you see how distraught your father is already without you two stirring the pot? Give him time to absorb all this.''

He waved off her concern. ''I'm not half as upset as I'd be if this Chance Adams had taken me by surprise,'' he declared, pushing away from the table.

Despite his claim, though, he was visibly shaken. Once on his feet, he took a moment to steady himself. This time Jenny was about to rush to assist him, but a sharp look from her mother kept her in her seat.

Finally he squared his shoulders and said, ''I'm going to my office. I've got some thinking to do.''

''Harlan, you haven't even finished your dinner,'' her mother protested.

''I'm not hungry.''

Her mother gave a resigned sigh. ''I'll bring a snack to your office in a bit, then,'' she said, watching him go, her expression filled with concern.

When he was gone, Jenny turned to her mother. ''I'm sorry, Mom.''

''No, Jenny. Harlan's right. It's better to be prepared, I suppose.'' She didn't sound convinced.

''Did you know anything about this brother?'' Jenny asked.

''Nothing. He's never said a word. It's as if the man never existed. I doubt we would ever have heard of him if this Chance Adams hadn't turned up.''

''There's not a single snapshot in the house with him in it, I'm sure of that,'' Jenny said. ''Remember how I used to make Daddy sit down with all the family albums and tell me who everyone was?''

Her mother smiled. "Once he made you an Adams, you went about it with a vengeance. I've never known anyone so anxious to know every little detail about their adoptive ancestors."

"I don't know why that surprised you," Jenny countered. "I was the same way about yours. It's just that you'd been telling me all those stories for years and years. Besides, I wanted to figure out which one of those sneaky Adamses stole Native American land."

She'd made the comment in jest, but her mother looked thoughtful.

"Harlan made you his heir so you'd get your share of that land back," she reminded Jenny. "Do you suppose he'll do the same thing to make things right with Chance Adams?"

"Nephew or not, Daddy didn't sound much like he thought this man had a legitimate claim," Jenny said.

Lizzy agreed with her. "In fact, I'm betting that by tomorrow he'll have the wagons circled. You'd better tell Maritza to count on every family member within shouting distance to be here for dinner. Daddy's probably calling Luke and Cody and Jordan now."

"You're probably right," her mother conceded. "In that case, I'd better take that snack in to him and make sure he eats it. He's going to need all his strength for whatever lies ahead."

By dinnertime the next day, Harlan had, in fact, gathered the whole darn clan. Luke and Jessie had driven over from their ranch. Cody, who ran White

Pines on a day-in day-out basis, was there with Melissa. Even Jordan had flown in from Houston, where he'd been checking on the branch office of his oil operation for the past week. Kelly met him on the porch and they came in together.

The next generation was represented by Jordan's son, Justin, his daughter, Dani and her new husband, and Cody's son, Harlan Patrick. Cody's daughter, Sharon Lynn, was expected as soon as she closed Dolan's for the night, along with her fiancé, Kyle Mason.

Looking at the noisy gathering crowded around the dinner table, Jenny smiled. She was pretty sure Luke's daughter, Angela, and Clint would have flown down from Montana with their son if there had been time. Everyone else was there. That was just the way this family did things. That solidarity and strength was what made them wonderful.

And formidable. She wondered if Chance Adams had any idea what a united front he was about to go up against.

Maritza had reacted to the sudden dinner party with her usual aplomb. The table was filled with platters of the black-bean burritos, the chicken enchiladas and savory beef tacos that everyone loved. There were huge bowls of *pico de gallo* and hot sauce spicy enough to burn the roof of your mouth.

To Jenny's amazement, her father remained absolutely quiet about the reason for the gathering until after Maritza had served the cooling caramel-topped flan for dessert. Maybe he'd figured digesting all that

Mexican food was going to be difficult enough without mixing in stress.

Or maybe he was just putting off the bad news because he feared getting into it at all. Jenny observed him intently all during the meal and noticed he barely touched his food, even though it was something he loved and rarely got a chance to eat since Maritza had taken to keeping a close eye on his diet. Whatever had happened years ago with this long-lost brother was clearly eating away at him now.

"I suppose you're wondering why I insisted on getting all of you together in such a hurry," he began, silencing the small talk and good-natured bickering going on around the table. He cleared his throat. "Something's come up and I felt it couldn't wait till Sunday."

Everyone's expression sobered at once.

"You're not sick, are you, Daddy?" Luke asked worriedly. "You look a little pale."

"Just sick at heart," Harlan said. "Like I said, something's happened and it concerns all of you. You have a right to know what's going on."

Luke exchanged a look with Cody and Jordan. "Whatever it is, Daddy, you can count on us. You know that," Luke said.

"Agreed," the other brothers chimed in.

"You may not be so quick to side with me once you've heard the whole story."

"What story, Grandpa Harlan?" Justin asked.

Jenny watched her father draw a deep breath before he began.

"It all started a long time ago," he said, "around the time I married your grandma Mary." He shook his head as if to clear it, then continued, "No, it began longer ago than that. You see, I had a brother back then, a brother named Henry. Everyone around here called him Hank." He smiled ruefully. "And a lot worse from time to time."

"My God," Jordan's daughter, Dani, murmured, looking shocked. "Betty Lou told me about him months ago when I was out there treating her dog after that hit-and-run. Remember, Duke? You were with me."

"I remember," her new husband said.

Jenny stared at her. "You knew? Why didn't you say anything?"

Dani shrugged. "I meant to, but…" She glanced at her husband and smiled ruefully. "Let's just say a lot of things happened. Anyway, I'd forgotten all about it, partly because I just thought she was mixed up."

"And partly because you and Duke couldn't keep your eyes off each other," Justin taunted his sister.

"Enough, son," Jordan said. "Let's hear what your grandfather has to say."

"I'm afraid Betty Lou was right," Harlan said. "Hank was very real and a handsome enough scoundrel that I'm sure quite a few ladies around town would remember him well."

"Didn't you and Hank get along, Grandpa Harlan?" Justin wanted to know.

Harlan sighed and his expression turned faintly nostalgic. "When we were boys, I suppose we got along well enough, though I was much older. Maybe that was the problem. I didn't pay enough attention when he started getting into trouble. It was little things at first. Shopkeepers would complain to Mama that he was taking a pack of gum or a candy bar. Folks around town caught him smoking when he was barely into his teens."

Justin and Harlan Patrick exchanged guilty glances. Cody scowled at them. "You two will explain those looks later," he said. "Go on, Daddy."

"Then Mama and Daddy died. I was twenty-five, a newlywed. I didn't have time for a brother who was getting into a mess of trouble every time I turned around. Petty thievery got worse. I bailed him out time and time again, feeling guilty because I hadn't tried to stop his mischief."

He paused and rubbed his eyes. To Jenny's shock it almost looked as if he'd been about to cry. She'd rarely seen him this emotional, except perhaps on the day Lizzy had been born.

"Now that I think back," he said, "I suppose his behavior was a cry for attention, but at the time I just wanted him out of my life. I was ashamed of him. I was struggling to get this place back on its feet, and for every step I'd take forward, he'd do something to pull me right back into debt. I was either paying off court costs or paying off neighbors not to press charges.''

"Maybe you should have left him in jail a time or two,'' Jordan said, eyeing his own son in a way that had Justin squirming.

"Maybe I should have,'' her father conceded. "I couldn't do it.''

"What did you do?''

"I sent him away. Actually I got the judge to release him from jail one last time on the condition he would leave West Texas. I gave him some money, enough of a stake to start over someplace, and told him to get out of Los Piños and not come back, that there was nothing for him here—no home, no family. I was cruel.''

"He sounds like he was no good, Daddy. You just did what you had to do,'' Cody said loyally.

"He was my brother,'' Harlan said fiercely. "That should have counted for something, just the way I've always taught all of you to stick by one another through thick and thin. I failed him.''

"He went, then? And stayed away?'' Luke asked.

"Oh, yes, he went,'' Harlan said with little satisfaction. "He stole a piece of valuable antique jewelry, a ruby-and-diamond pin, on his way out the door, but he went.''

"And you never heard from again?'' Jenny asked.

"Not so much as a whisper—until now,'' the old man said wearily. "I didn't know if he was dead or alive.''

"You never looked for him?" Jenny asked.

"Never. I told myself it was for the best to leave things as they were."

"Will you tell Chance the whole story?" she asked. She doubted Chance had ever heard this particular version from his own father.

Harlan sighed. "Only if I have to. It's not the kind of story a man should have to hear about his father. Could be Hank lived an exemplary life from the day he left. If he did, it would be a shame to ruin that memory for his son."

Jenny thought of the bitter, determined man she'd met the day before. He was hell-bent on revenge and enjoying the prospect. He'd never accept platitudes or evasive answers. Eventually Harlan would have to tell him everything. There wasn't a doubt in her mind about that. The only real question was how soon the subject was likely to come up.

"Is there a chance he could make a legitimate claim against White Pines?" Cody asked, looking at Jenny's mother, who practiced law in town.

"Legally he might have some rights," her mother said. "I'd have to check the terms of the will."

Harlan shot a commiserating look at his youngest son. Though everyone in the family would someday own a share of White Pines, they all knew that Cody was the one who'd poured his heart and soul into the running of it. Harlan Patrick was showing every sign of wanting to follow in his daddy's and granddaddy's footsteps.

"No need to look," Harlan said quietly. "Legally there's nothing. The deed's in my name and mine alone. My father made sure of that before he died. He'd already seen that Hank couldn't handle responsibility."

One by one Harlan seared them with a pointed look. "But every single one of you knows there's sometimes a big difference between doing what's legal and doing what's right."

Jenny watched her stepbrother's expression shift from shock to outrage. "You intend to cut him in on the property, give him his half?" Cody demanded, halfway out of his chair.

"Settle down, Cody. I didn't say that," Harlan said. "I haven't decided yet what's fair. The truth is White Pines all but belongs to the whole lot of you now. If a decision has to be made, then all of you are going to have to make it together. From what Jenny tells me, the wolf is only a few miles from the doorstep. I just wanted you to have all the facts before you reach a conclusion about how to face him."

"You're dumping this into our laps?" Cody asked, his expression incredulous. "Is that what you're saying?"

Jenny regarded her father intently. Suddenly he was looking surprisingly pleased with himself.

"That's what I'm saying," he said.

"Well, I'll be damned," Luke murmured. He grinned at his father. "You're a sly old fox, you know that? Not many men get a whopper of a test like this to see how well they've raised their offspring.''

Jenny glanced from one to the other and concluded that Luke had it exactly right. Her father intended to use Chance Adams's threat as a test of some kind to see what the rest of them were made of.

What she couldn't quite figure out, though, was whether he wanted to see them fight to keep White Pines intact or if he wanted them to parcel out a share to his newly discovered nephew. She wondered if he even knew himself, or if, for once in his life, her father was counting on his descendants to show him the way.

Chapter Four

Petey was on his best behavior for the remainder of that first week of school. Chance knew it, because there was no sign of Miss Prim and Prissy on his doorstep. He was forced to admit to being just a little disappointed.

Jenny Adams hadn't been out of his mind for more than a few minutes at a time since they'd met. He wasn't crazy about that fact, but he was honest enough to admit that on some level he'd enjoyed their brief sparring match.

Fortunately for him it wasn't in Petey's nature to stay reformed for long. On Tuesday of the following week there she was again, her face set in a disapproving scowl, her lush lips turned down in a frown and a contradictory blush in her cheeks that Chance suspected had very little to do with addressing his son's sins. Damn, but Ms. Jenny Adams was cute, a description she would no doubt hate.

"Lost control again, did you?" he inquired lightly when she marched down the driveway to stand toe-to-toe with him.

"Three generals and the entire marine corps couldn't control your son," she declared.

Chance hid a grin at her confession. He liked a woman who could admit she didn't have all the answers. He regarded her sympathetically. "Then you see what I'm up against."

She shot a look at Petey, who was regarding them warily, as if they were the last two people on earth in whom he'd want to entrust his life. Chance decided his son didn't need to observe the upcoming negotiations over his fate.

He sent Petey inside with strict instructions to go straight to his room. "No TV," he added, more for effect than any chance the punishment would be followed. Petey would probably have the remote control in hand before the words were out of his father's mouth.

When he was gone, Chance cut straight to the topic that was uppermost in his mind, though clearly not in hers. If he could distract her from Petey's misbehavior for a minute or two, so much the better.

"So, did you pass on the word regarding my intent to get my hands on White Pines?" he asked.

Her frown deepened at the question. "I'm not your messenger," she retorted without missing a beat.

He grinned at the evasion. "No, but you strike me as a dutiful daughter. My bet is you served up the news right along with supper that night. How'd it go over? Did your daddy confirm that I was telling the truth? Did he admit he stole my father's share of the ranch right out from under him?"

The telltale color climbed in her cheeks. It was enough of an admission to suit him. She was still scowling, too, another confirmation of his guesswork. She could fib and evade all she wanted, but he knew the truth.

"Are you deliberately trying to get me to run interference for you?" she inquired testily, deliberately skirting the specifics of his questions. "Forget it, Mr. Adams. Do your own dirty work."

Actually he had wanted to be the one to drop the bombshell in person, but events the last time he and Jenny Adams met had spun out of control too quickly. He'd blurted out the truth before he could stop himself. After that, there'd been no taking it back. He'd just spent the past few days waiting with more than a little impatience to see how events would unfold.

He'd been a little surprised that half the Adams men hadn't dropped by in the days since to tear a strip out of his hide or warn him off or maybe try to convince Wilkie to fire him and send him packing. When none of that happened, he'd been almost disappointed. The possibility that they'd simply dismissed his threat as nonsense hadn't even occurred to him until now.

His gaze narrowed. "Did I get it wrong? Did your father call me a liar? Is that what happened?" he asked. "Did he claim he'd never had a brother?"

She regarded him with exasperation. "Mr. Adams, I told you before—this is something you're going to have to take up personally with my father."

Her refusal to use his first name, her refusal to get involved, irritated him more than it should have. His fight was with Harlan Adams. At the moment, though, he was a whole lot more interested in sparring with the woman standing before him. Obviously that perverse streak of his where she was concerned hadn't gone away. He deliberately locked gazes with her.

"Chance," he instructed softly. More experienced women than Miss Prim and Prissy had come unglued under that direct gaze of his. As he'd expected, she swallowed hard and blinked.

"What?" she murmured, looking a little dazed.

"My name is Chance."

As if she needed to clear her head, she shook it, but she stubbornly refused to give in to his desire to hear his name on her lips. Because he couldn't help himself, he reached out and brushed the pad of his thumb across her lower lip. She trembled at the touch—but so did he. In fact, nothing had shaken him so badly in years. Reacting to Jenny Adams, except for the sheer perverse fun of it, was not a complication he could tolerate.

As a result he was suddenly all too eager to see the last of her. He told himself he'd simply tired of the game, but the truth was she was a potential distraction he didn't need. He'd just realized exactly how dangerous she was to his equilibrium and to his plan.

He allowed himself one last caress of her silken cheek, lingered long enough to feel her skin heat beneath his touch, then withdrew with regret. Confusion and desire were at odds in her flashing eyes. He knew just how she felt. Her expression mirrored his own unexpectedly jittery reaction.

"I've got work to do," he announced abruptly. "Maybe you ought to get to the point of this visit."

The chill in his voice seemed to startle her. "It's, um…" She cleared her throat. "It's Petey."

"I assumed that much."

"He's not paying attention in class."

"Maybe you should make the lessons more interesting," he suggested, enjoying the fresh flood of color in her cheeks. He didn't want Petey challenging his teacher's authority, but that didn't mean Chance couldn't take pleasure in it.

"*Mister Adams,*" she said, drawing it out and using that prim and prissy tone he found so irritating.

"Chance," he corrected again.

"I think I see where your son gets his problems with authority," she retorted.

Chance chuckled. He didn't intend to mention that he'd very firmly instructed his son that he was to show respect for this particular authority figure. He held up his hands.

"Okay, I'm sorry," he apologized. "I know you have a tough job. Tell me what Petey has done to make it more difficult. You said he wasn't paying attention in class. I assume there's more to it."

"There is. If he was reading a book or staring out the window, it would be one thing. Only his grades would suffer. But it's worse than that. He's deliberately distracting the others, drawing them into his mischief. He ignores any attempt I make to silence him. He's setting a terrible example for his classmates. Have you ever considered having him tested for ADD? That's attention deficit disorder."

Chance stared at her, torn between incredulity and outrage. "I know what it is, Ms. Adams. ADD is not Petey's problem. If you've looked at his school records, then you must be aware that he's a very bright boy."

"Many ADD kids are."

"He's received exemplary report cards. Mostly *A*'s and *B*'s. He was never a problem student in any way, shape or form back in Montana. No detentions, no suspensions." Chance regarded her evenly. "I guess that brings us back to you."

She sighed and a little of the spunk seemed to drain out of her. "I was afraid you were going to say that. Maybe I really am no good at this."

Chance was startled by the abrupt turnaround. "You're not giving up, are you?"

"A good teacher would know how to cope with one troubled nine-year-old boy," she said, her expression bleak.

"Petey's not troubled," Chance insisted.

"Of course he is. He's suffered two devastating losses in the last couple of years. Obviously they've taken a toll. He's lashing out at me. I understand that, I really do, but I have no idea what to do about it."

Chance sighed. "He's not lashing out at you because of anything you're doing or not doing," he said. "He's lashing out because of who you are."

She absorbed his statement, then slowly nodded. "An Adams," she concluded. "Of course."

"Exactly. I've told him he was not to let this dispute I have to settle with your father spill over into the classroom, but he's a kid and he's very loyal to his grandfather. He worshiped the old coot and he took to heart all the animosity my father had for Harlan Adams. Now, rightly or wrongly, that hatred extends to you."

"And you've encouraged that, too, I'm sure."

"Just by coming here I suppose I have, but believe me, I did not intend for you to suffer any fallout. I have a lot of respect for teachers. I never meant to make your job more difficult. My problem's with your father, not you."

Jenny sighed again and sank onto the stump he'd been using the week before as a chopping block. When she gazed up at him with those huge, despairing eyes, his stomach turned flip-flops.

"What are we going to do about this mess?" she asked. "There's nothing I can do about being Harlan Adams's daughter. I wouldn't even if I could. I'm very proud of it."

Chance found he liked this softer more vulnerable side to her almost as much as he enjoyed the sass and vinegar. "You mean to tell me you don't have all the answers?"

"Not half of them," she conceded.

Chance was struck by an inspiration. Of course, it was just the teensiest bit self-serving, but so what? The point was to get Petey to behave in school. His son needed to stop thinking of Jenny Adams as the enemy, right?

"Go out with me," he suggested impulsively. At her stunned expression, he promptly amended the idea. "I meant with us. To dinner. Petey's been dying to try that Italian restaurant in town. We could all go. He's basically a friendly, loving kid. If he sees I'm not treating you like a bad guy, maybe he'll get the message. I've told him of course, but actions speak louder than words."

"Has it also occurred to you that this could backfire? Maybe he'll conclude that means I'll give him good grades just because you and I are friends."

Chance grinned. "Yeah, but you're tougher than that, so it's not a problem. A couple of *F*'s and he should get the message."

Jenny regarded him skeptically. "We're talking one dinner here, right? Just a pleasant evening so Petey can get to know me informally and conclude I'm an okay person, maybe separate me from the feud with my father.''

''Exactly.''

''There's a flaw in here somewhere, but for the life of me I can't figure out what it is. Besides, I'm a desperate woman. I'll try anything.''

Chance wasn't exactly crazy about the implication that only a desperate woman would be willing to have dinner with him, but he was too relieved by the acceptance to bother questioning the reasoning behind it. As for his own logic in asking, that didn't bear any scrutiny at all. Not ten minutes earlier he'd been warning himself to stay the hell away from her.

''Do you want to go now or do you need to go home first?'' he asked.

''Now is fine. Except for Petey, it was actually one of the better days at school. No one threw food or paint, so I'm still looking halfway respectable.''

Chance took a lazy, deliberate survey from head to toe and nodded. ''More than halfway,'' he said approvingly. ''I'll get Petey.''

To his annoyance Petey was less than enthusiastic about the plan, despite the promise of pizza.

''I'm not going,'' he declared, folding his arms across his little chest and glaring up at Chance.

''Excuse me?''

''I'm not,'' Petey repeated.

''Oh, but you are,'' Chance countered. ''You have exactly five seconds to get those shoes on and that shirt tucked in.'' He studied his son more carefully. ''And another sixty seconds to get in the bathroom and wash your face.''

Petey wasted a good many of those seconds glaring back at his father. Chance returned the gaze evenly and slowly started counting. Finally Petey jammed his feet into his sneakers without bothering to untie them and stomped off to the bathroom. Chance considered it a small victory.

When Petey returned, his face was scrubbed clean and even his hair was combed more neatly. He looked up into Chance's eyes. ''I just don't get it, Dad. Why are you being so nice to her? What do you care if she hates our guts now or after we take back White Pines?''

''Because none of this is her fault,'' Chance said. ''Harlan Adams adopted her when she was only a little older than you are now. Why blame her for something he did years and years before that?''

Petey stared at Chance incredulously. ''You sound like you even like her a little bit. You don't, do you, Dad? I mean not like a guy likes a girl or something.''

''No, of course not,'' Chance said a little too quickly. Anyone with the least bit of understanding of the battle of the sexes would have seen straight through the sharp denial. Fortunately, as bright as he was, Petey wasn't savvy enough to guess the truth—that Chance was growing more intrigued with Jenny Adams by the minute.

Before all was said and done, he had a feeling one

of them was going to be hurt. Given his avowed mission in Los Piños, it was clear to him which one of them it was going to be.

Before he could suffer too many pangs of regret over that, Petey's expression brightened.

"Hey, I get it," he said. "You're, like, sneaking into the enemy camp. You're gonna use Ms. Adams to find out what's going on with her dad, huh?"

Chance didn't want to acknowledge that the very same reprehensible idea had occurred to him. It sounded so low-down and sleazy when Petey said it that he found himself denying the possibility.

"Son, we're going to dinner, nothing more. You've been wanting to try the Italian place to see what their pizza's like. I figured it wouldn't hurt to have some feminine company so we don't forget our table manners."

"Yeah, sure."

"That's all," Chance insisted.

Petey shot him a look of pure disgust, either because he didn't like the idea of Ms. Adams telling him which fork to use or because he'd concluded that Chance was a very bad liar. Either way it appeared they were in for an interesting dinner.

Jenny should have known better than to accept Chance's invitation. Oh, sure, his intentions were probably honorable enough. They both wanted to improve her relationship with Petey so they could survive the school year.

But agreeing to go to the Italian restaurant in town was as much as begging for trouble. Half her relatives showed up there for meals at least once a week. With as many relatives as she had, she and Chance were pretty much destined to run into somebody from the family.

Thankfully it was Dani and Duke tonight, she thought as she hurriedly surveyed the crowded tables from the doorway. Those two were still so besotted with each other maybe neither of them would notice her. The twins weren't with them, either, so they were busy gazing into each other's eyes. Maybe they wouldn't waste this rare night out alone by sticking their noses into Jenny's business.

"That booth in the corner is open," Jenny said, practically bolting for it before Chance could choose another table. She slid in so that her back was toward Dani and Duke. When she was settled snugly into a corner, she glanced up into Chance's amused eyes.

"Hiding from someone you know?"

She couldn't think of a good reason not to tell him the truth. In a town the size of Los Piños, sooner or later he would get to know the whole family whether he made good on his threat to go after White Pines or not.

"My niece, actually. My stepbrother Jordan's adopted daughter. She's the town vet. She just married Duke Jenkins. He works for her father's oil company."

"How cozy," Chance said with a surprising touch

of sarcasm. "Any particular reason you're trying to avoid them?"

Jenny swallowed hard and admitted, "I'm not exactly sure how I'd explain this."

"You mean being here with Petey and me?"

She nodded.

"How about the truth? I asked. You said yes."

"It's more complicated than that and you know it."

Petey sat patiently enough through most of their conversation, but judging from his expression, he'd finally tired of it. "Are we ever gonna eat?" he asked.

Jenny smiled at him. "Right now in fact. I'm starved," she confided. "And this place has the very best pizza I've ever tasted."

"Not as good as we used to get back in Montana, I'll bet," Petey declared.

"Better even than what I used to get in New York City," she countered. "What do you like on yours?"

He directed a belligerent look at her and said, "Anchovies."

Jenny managed not to gag. Instead, she beamed back at him. "Me, too."

Chance chuckled. "Okay, son, now what?"

Jenny regarded Petey innocently. "You mean you don't really like anchovies?"

Petey sighed heavily. "Not really." He eyed her warily. "Do you? Are we gonna have to get 'em?"

"No, I can live without anchovies this once. How about pepperoni, instead?"

"And sausage," Petey added.

She glanced over at Chance. "Okay with you?"

"Hey, I'm at your mercy. Whatever you two decide."

Jenny grinned. "Then pepperoni and sausage it is."

The harried waitress, Maria, finally rushed over to take their order. "I don't know what's going on in here tonight. It's the middle of the week and every table's taken. Doesn't anybody cook at home anymore?"

"I'm the wrong person to ask," Jenny said. "From the moment I left New York years ago, I've been suffering withdrawal symptoms from the lack of takeout. Until I came here at fourteen I thought that was how dinner was served in most homes. Chinese takeout was my favorite and I had at least a half-dozen restaurants in the neighborhood to choose from."

"Don't tell Maritza that," Maria said. "She'll go on strike out at White Pines if she thinks you'd rather have Chinese takeout than her home cooking."

Jenny held up her hands. "No, no, don't misunderstand. Maritza was my salvation. If it had been up to my mom, we'd have lived on burned toast and tuna salad with an occasional boiled egg tossed in. And before Mom married Harlan, I'd have starved if it hadn't been for this place." She glanced at Petey and explained, "My mother is a truly terrible cook. Maritza, the housekeeper at White Pines, cringes whenever Mom comes near the kitchen. She shoos her right back out again."

"Hey, that sounds like dad," Petey said.

"Watch it, kid," Chance warned.

"Your dad's not a very good cook?" Jenny asked, amused by this bit of information. Chance Adams had struck her as the kind of man who'd be very very good at whatever he put his mind to.

"If it doesn't come frozen, we don't eat it," Petey said.

"That's not true," Chance said indignantly. "I can open cans, too."

The waitress grinned. "Well, you're in for a treat tonight, then. The food here's the best in town. I highly recommend the pizza and the lasagna. The lasagna's my mom's old family recipe from Italy." She looked at Jenny. "Hey, did you see Dani and Duke on your way in? Want me to tell 'em you're here?"

"No, that's okay. They think they're still on their honeymoon. Let 'em pretend a while longer."

When the waitress had left, Chance regarded her quizzically. "Honeymoon? When were they married?"

"Right after Valentine's Day."

"That's more than six months ago."

"But they only get about fifteen minutes a week alone. Duke has twin boys and a high-pressure job that takes him out of town from time to time. Dani's a vet. She gets calls at all hours of the night."

"Ah, I see. Exactly how many people are we talking about in your family?"

"It depends on whether you count all of us who've been adopted in or married in."

"Let's say I do."

"Okay, there would be Harlan and my mother, me and my half sister, Lizzy. Lizzy's the baby. Then there are my three older stepbrothers and their wives, Dani and Duke, Sharon Lynn and her fiancé, Justin and Harlan Patrick, Angela and Clint, plus Duke's boys and Angie and Clint's baby. You do the math."

She shot him a belligerent look. "And no matter where we actually live, we all consider White Pines home."

Chance chuckled. "Is that supposed to be a warning, darlin'?"

"They do say there's strength in numbers, but you take it any way you like."

"I think I'll just consider it a challenge, then." He glanced past her shoulder. "And don't look now, but we're about to have company. Get ready to do some explaining."

Jenny bit back a sigh and turned to watch Dani and Duke approach.

"We're just on our way out," Dani said, leaning down to give Jenny a kiss on the cheek. "We stopped by to say hi." She regarded Chance curiously. "Hi. We haven't met."

"Dani and Duke, this is Chance Adams," Jenny said with reluctance. "And his son, Petey."

Dani's extended hand halted in midair and her expression froze. ''Mr. Adams,'' she said with a curt nod.

The chilliness in her voice startled Jenny. She'd never known Dani to be impolite to anyone.

''Mrs. Jenkins,'' Chance said quietly, ignoring the snub. He shook Duke's hand as if he hadn't even noticed that Dani's had been withdrawn. ''A pleasure to meet you both.''

''Same here,'' Duke said, his tone neutral.

Dani turned a speculative gaze on Jenny. ''We'll talk tomorrow. How about Dolan's at four-thirty?''

There was no question it was a command performance for Dani and Sharon Lynn, who ran the place. Jenny could have wriggled off the hook, but it would only have been delaying the inevitable. If she didn't show up, Dani and Sharon Lynn would probably invade her classroom at midday and demand answers.

''I'll do my best to make it,'' she said.

Dani did grin ever so slightly at that. ''Yes, I imagine you will.''

''Good night,'' Duke said, giving Jenny's shoulder a supportive squeeze. He leaned down to whisper, ''Give 'em hell, kiddo.''

Jenny wasn't exactly sure whether he'd misinterpreted her presence here with Chance as an infiltration of the enemy camp or whether he was referring to her upcoming meeting with his wife and Sharon Lynn. She managed a halfhearted smile in response.

After they'd gone Chance regarded her intently. ''I gather you're not looking forward to this little get-together tomorrow.''

"Hardly. If I was an evil person, I'd insist you go in my place," she said in a dire tone. "You're the one with the answers they really want."

"I could join you," he offered readily. "It might be interesting."

Jenny tried to imagine her nieces' reaction to that and concluded she was better off facing them alone. "Never mind," she said wearily. "I know enough of their secrets to keep them in line."

"Oh, really?" Chance said, obviously fascinated. "Care to share?"

"Not on your life. If you intend to blackmail this family, you'll have to find your own means to do it."

"There'll be no blackmail, darlin'. Sooner or later I'll just claim what's rightfully mine."

"Yeah," Petey chimed in. "Nobody's going to stop us."

Jenny admired their confidence if not their intentions. "Simple as that, huh?"

"Simple as that," Chance concurred.

Jenny shook her head and thought of the formidable lineup of foes he faced. "You poor deluded man."

Rather than taking offense, he smiled. "We'll see."

Something in his tone raised the hairs on her arms. For the briefest of instants she wondered if she hadn't been a little too quick to dismiss him. Chance Adams suddenly struck her as an astonishingly formidable force himself.

Chapter Five

As things turned out, Chance was glad he'd persuaded Jenny to leave her car at his place when they came into town for dinner. If he hadn't, he was very much afraid she would have bolted from the dinner table after the encounter with Duke and Dani Jenkins.

Whether Jenny cared to admit it or not, she had been deeply shaken by her niece's reaction to finding the two of them together. Even though she had clearly expected it, had even tried to prevent their being seen, Dani's shocked response to the introduction to Harlan's avowed enemy had taken Jenny by surprise.

He could understand her worry, could even sympathize with it on an objective level. No doubt she had felt like a traitor. Chance wondered if her father would consider her one, as well, when he learned of the dinner they'd shared.

"How's Harlan going to react when he finds out we were out together?" he asked, drawing a startled look.

Jenny had been concentrating very hard on the slice of pizza she'd been toying with for the past few minutes. She hadn't swallowed more than a couple of bites. Petey, oblivious to the tension and the undercurrents, had been gobbling up more than his share.

"I'm not sure," she confessed, her expression bleak. "I mean, it's not a big deal, right? It's dinner."

"That would certainly be the tack I'd take," he said, deliberately insinuating there were other less innocuous explanations.

She stared at him. "Meaning?"

He regarded her with pure innocence. "Meaning that I'd kiss it off as a simple uncomplicated meal. Who could make anything out of that?"

"It *is* an innocent meal."

"If you say so. Obviously, though, your niece didn't think so. Whose version do you think the rest of the family will believe? My hunch is they're all prepared to think the worst of me."

Clearly agitated by the question, she glanced at Petey, dug in her purse and handed him a handful of quarters. "There are some video games in that alcove over there. Why don't you go try them?"

"I'm not finished eating," Petey protested.

"Please," Jenny said.

When Petey glanced at him, Chance knew Petey was hoping for a reprieve. Instead, he gestured toward the games. "Go. You know you love video games."

Pete's turned-down mouth indicated his displeasure, but he slid out of the booth. "Okay, but you'd better leave the last slice of pizza for me," he warned. "I've only had two and I'm still hungry."

"You've had three, but you'll get another piece," Chance promised, eager to send him on his way and see just what Jenny had on her mind. "And thank Ms. Adams for the change."

"Yeah, sure," he grumbled ungraciously. "Thanks."

When Petey was gone, Chance directed a solemn look at the woman across the table. "I take it you had something you wanted to say in private."

She lifted her gaze and met his evenly. "I just wanted to make sure we were clear about something."

"What's that?"

"You and I..." She waved her hand dismissively as if no other words were necessary.

Chance got the message, but he wanted her to spell it out just the same. "Yes?" he prodded.

"There is no you and I, no us, no anything, correct? We established that before we ever left your house."

She was so darned determined to tidy up the situation, to establish the limits of their friendship, that he couldn't help giving her a difficult time. He returned her look with a perfectly bland expression. "If you say so, darlin'."

"I do," she said firmly.

Chance grinned. "Last time I heard those two words said with so much passion I was standing in a church."

She scowled at him. "Chance!"

"Yes, darlin'?"

She sighed heavily. "Oh, never mind."

"Tell me. You can tell me anything, you know."

"And you'll find a way to use it against my father, no doubt."

"Not all my motives are ulterior. In fact, I think I'm developing a case of straightforward lust where you're concerned."

She frowned, creating an endearing little furrow between her brows. He wanted to kiss it away.

"Blast it, Chance!" she said. "Stop looking at me like that and stop saying things like that. This situation is complicated enough without you suggesting that there's some sort of chemistry between us."

"There is," he said. "It might be a tad inconvenient under the circumstances, but life is messy. I've learned it's best to go with the flow."

She regarded him incredulously. "Oh, really. You don't strike me as a go-with-the-flow kind of guy. Not many men who claim to be hell-bent on revenge would even try to pass themselves off as laid-back."

He shrugged. "Contradictions are a part of life."

"Oh, save your dime-store philosophy. This dinner

was about me trying to get Petey's respect so he'll settle down in class. That's absolutely all it was about. I would never have agreed to it otherwise.''

''Maybe for you that's all it was,'' he taunted, and allowed his own interpretation to remain unspoken. In fact, Chance was enjoying himself too much to stop teasing her now. Besides, there was more than a little truth behind his taunts. He could easily get addicted to watching that blossoming of pink in her cheeks, that rise of indignation that darkened her eyes. He sat back and enjoyed the predictable return of both.

She leaped to her feet, then leaned across the table until she was in his face.

''Stop that this instant,'' she demanded.

Chance couldn't help himself. He chuckled. Big mistake. Her eyes flashed with pure fire. It was a little like staring into a bed of flaming coals. It was downright mesmerizing.

''Damn you, Chance Adams!'' she shouted, oblivious to the stares she was drawing.

Aware that she intended to say a whole lot more at full volume, he stood up, too, a move that forced her to take a quick step back until the booth's bench caught the back of her knees and trapped her where she was. Even though the table still separated them, he could feel the heat radiating from every furious fiber of her being.

He reached over and cupped her face in his hands,

then murmured only half apologetically, "Darlin', this is for your own good."

Before she could guess his intentions, he kissed her. The position was awkward, the stares disconcerting, the table an impossible barrier, but Chance gave his all to that kiss. The instant his lips touched hers, all that mattered was the wildfire it set off in his veins and making sure it never stopped.

Jenny trembled, quite possibly with fury. He was quaking for another reason entirely. The sensual feel of her mouth under his, the taste of her, the scent of her spicy, sexy perfume all combined to scare the daylights out of him. He'd begun by teasing, but what was happening right now, with Jenny's mouth surrendering to his, was deadly serious. He backed off as if he'd inadvertently touched an open flame.

Jenny remained exactly where he'd left her, hands braced on the table, eyes dazed. When she realized he'd released her, she sank back onto the bench as if her knees would no longer support her. She stared at him, blinked several times, then ran her tongue slowly over her lips.

That last unthinking gesture almost cost Chance his very fragile grip on sanity. If she'd done it again, he might have picked her up caveman-style and carried her out of the restaurant and off to the nearest bed… or floor…or hayloft.

"What…?" She began, but her voice trailed off. She swallowed hard and tried again. "Why…?"

Chance searched for any explanation besides the

truth. He wasn't about to admit he'd impulsively and thoroughly kissed her solely because he'd no longer been able to resist. In fact, he dimly recalled that there'd been another reason entirely at the outset.

"You were about to cause a scene," he said, remembering. "I figured it would be better if people thought it was a lovers' tiff."

"Why?"

For one halfway honorable instant, he'd had some crazy notion about protecting her reputation, but he supposed a case could be made that the very public kiss hadn't done much for that, either. In fact, when the truth came out about the reason he'd come to Los Piños, more folks than Dani Jenkins would be labeling Jenny a traitor, especially if they'd seen that kiss. Unexpected guilt made him edgy, so he skirted the truth with lighthearted banter.

"I'm an impulsive man. It seemed like the right thing to do at the time."

"Impulsive? Go with the flow?" Her skepticism was plain in her tone and in her expression. "These are not words I would use to describe you," she said.

"Maybe you just don't know me all that well."

"No," she conceded, "I probably don't, but some things it doesn't take more than a few minutes to figure out."

He regarded her speculatively. "We could work on changing that so you know the real me, all of it."

Alarm flared in her eyes. "Oh, no. No way. You're

not dragging me into the middle of this mess. It's complicated enough already.''

"You're already in the middle," he pointed out.

"No, I'm not. I'm Harlan Adams's daughter, period."

"And my son's teacher."

"That part's not a problem," she claimed.

"That part is what brought us here tonight," he reminded her.

"Well, it won't happen again, that's all. Either Petey learns to behave in class or…" Her voice trailed off.

He wasn't crazy about that unspoken threat. "Or what?" he demanded quietly.

Her chin jutted. Her gaze clashed with his. "Or I'll see he's suspended."

The threat, about what he'd expected, had Chance's hackles rising. "And I'll tell the principal you're taking your displeasure with me out on my son." Chance kept his tone even and friendly, but he was pretty sure she got the message he was seething.

"That's blackmail," she accused, clearly not the least bit intimidated.

"If you're going to use that label for me, I might as well live up to it. Besides, I call it protecting my boy. You don't want to be caught in the middle. I don't want him to be caught in the middle. I'd say we're at an impasse."

"Why don't you just come out to White Pines,

have it out with my father and get it over with?'' she asked a little plaintively.

It was an approach Chance had considered and then dismissed. He shrugged. ''Too easy. I figure I ought to let you all stew for a while wondering when I'll make my move and what form it'll take.''

''Don't wait too long,'' she warned in a somber tone. ''My father's in his eighties. He's got a softer, more forgiving heart than the rest of us. You'd do better to make peace with him than to wait around and risk having to deal with his sons and daughters. And if there's so much as a hint that stress was behind something happening to him, there'd be hell to pay.''

Chance thought about that grim warning long after he'd taken Jenny back to her car and watched her drive away. The only problem was, he didn't want to make peace with Harlan Adams. He'd become more and more dedicated to making him pay for what he'd done to his younger brother. Chance wanted him to suffer during whatever time he had left here on earth, and then he wanted him to rot in hell. White Pines might not hold the same mystique for Chance that it had for his father, but getting his hands on it was the least he owed Hank.

Jenny would have preferred being pilloried to walking into Dolan's drugstore the next afternoon to face Sharon Lynn and Dani. Although technically she was their stepaunt, they were close enough in age that they'd always treated one another more like very tight-knit cousins, maybe even sisters. Jenny had a feeling this afternoon they were going to be regarding her more like a traitor.

The irony, of course, was that going out with Chance and Petey had stirred up all this trouble and accomplished absolutely nothing. If anything, Petey had been even more impossible in class today.

As she'd feared, he seemed to think their dinner the night before implied she'd be lax in disciplining him. He'd seemed stunned when she'd hauled him out of the classroom and planted his little butt on a chair in the hall and told him to stay there and think about whether he wanted an education or if he'd prefer to go through life ignorant.

"I'm going to tell my dad about this," he'd threatened. "And he will never, ever kiss you again."

"I can live with that," Jenny had muttered, determined to ignore the terrible sinking sensation the threat stirred in the pit of her stomach. She had liked kissing Chance Adams entirely too much.

"Yeah, well, you're gonna have to," Petey shot back.

All in all it had been a rotten day. And there was more to come, she thought as she glanced around Dolan's.

At four-thirty the soda-fountain counter was mostly empty. Two teenage boys, who had a crush on the older and very out-of-their-reach Sharon Lynn, were finishing their soft drinks when Jenny came in. Dani wasn't there yet.

Jenny breathed a sigh of relief. Maybe Dani hadn't even filled Sharon Lynn in on what she'd seen the night before.

Her hopes were dashed when she saw Sharon Lynn's speculative expression. If Dani hadn't spread the word, then someone else surely had. Los Piños thrived on gossip, especially when it concerned a member of the Adams clan. Some folks in Los Piños thought the family had been born and bred purely to provide them with titillating entertainment.

"Hi," she said as she slid onto a stool. "I gather you've been expecting me."

"Dani mentioned she was meeting you here," Sharon Lynn said neutrally.

"Did she also mention why?"

"Something about you being out with Chance Adams last night."

Jenny sighed. Sharon Lynn grinned and took her sweet time pouring a soda for her.

"Of course a few other folks in town have had a far more fascinating tale to tell," Sharon Lynn said as she set the drink on the counter. "One I don't think Dani knows about yet."

"Oh?"

"The word is, he planted a kiss on you that had half the women in town swooning. True or false?"

"I can't attest to whether or not anyone swooned," Jenny said evasively.

"But he did kiss you?"

"Yes," she admitted reluctantly. "He claimed it

was to keep me from slugging him and causing a scene."

Sharon Lynn chuckled. "An interesting approach." She peered closely at Jenny. "So how was it?"

"What?"

"The kiss?"

"Is that all you care about, that the man kissed me?" Jenny demanded, then recalled that Sharon Lynn's own parents had been responsible for many a steamy scene right here in Dolan's. Maybe a lack of restraint and a streak of incurable romanticism ran through the lot of them.

"You have to admit it's the most interesting part of the story," Sharon Lynn said.

"I suppose that depends on who's telling it."

"Are you saying you didn't enjoy it?"

Jenny considered lying and claiming that Chance's kiss hadn't affected her one way or the other. Other men had kissed her. It wasn't as if one kiss from Chance was anything special. For the past twenty hours or so she'd been trying to convince herself of precisely that. Sooner or later she was going to need someone to confide in. Sharon Lynn didn't seem to be judging her too harshly so far. Maybe she could tell her the truth and put the whole thing into perspective.

"My knees went weak," she admitted ruefully.

Sharon Lynn grinned. "All right!"

Jenny studied her warily. "Aren't you furious?"

"Why should I be?"

"Because of who he is. Goodness knows, I'm furious. It's an impossible situation."

Sharon Lynn waved off the obvious problem. "This may be the best for everyone concerned. You can mediate. You're very good at that. Ask those people on Capitol Hill you used to badger all the time."

Jenny groaned at Sharon Lynn's lack of understanding of her skills. She wasn't in the habit of making nice just to keep peace. More often than not, she was the one touching off dynamite, though not in the literal sense.

"I am not good at mediating," she corrected. "I am good at waking people up, stirring up controversy. My initial impression is that this time I've already stirred up a veritable hornets' nest."

"That would certainly be my impression, too," Dani said, slipping onto the stool next to her. She glared at Jenny. "What the heck were you thinking last night when you decided to go out with Chance Adams?"

Feeling defensive already, Jenny returned Dani's scowl with one of her own. "Not that I owe you an explanation, but I was thinking that I had an out-of-control student on my hands and that spending a little time with him and his father outside the classroom might help the situation."

"So that led to playing kissy-face with a sworn enemy of Harlan's?" Dani demanded, her expression incredulous. "Parent-teacher conferences with you must really be something."

Jenny winced, upset not so much by the pointed barb but by its implication. She had really really hoped that Dani hadn't heard about the kiss. It had happened after she'd gone, but obviously Dani had heard every steamy little detail. Of course half the people in the restaurant had probably made it their business to take a pet in to see Dani. Those who hadn't gone there had apparently stopped by Dolan's for a soda first thing this morning to fill Sharon Lynn in.

"I didn't kiss him. He kissed me," Jenny protested in self-defense. It wasn't much of an argument, but it was the only one she had.

"The way I heard it you didn't exactly shove him away," Dani countered. "Most people had the impression that you two were giving off more heat than the pizza oven."

Jenny hated fighting with someone she'd always loved like a sister. Because they weren't sisters, they'd rarely had cause for any of the usual sibling spats. Besides, Dani had always been even tempered and rational. She'd been a calming influence on Jenny's more fiery personality. Now she seemed hell-bent on inflaming it herself.

"Dammit, Dani, whether or not I kiss Chance Adams really isn't anyone's business but mine," Jenny all but shouted.

Dani faced her defiantly. "It is when it hurts the family."

"Who, pray tell, was hurt by my kissing a man?"

"Not just a man," Dani contradicted. "Chance Adams."

"Okay, okay, you two, settle down," Sharon Lynn soothed. "Fighting among ourselves won't help anything." She turned to Dani. "Does Grandpa Harlan known about this?"

"I haven't told him, but I can't speak for any of the direct witnesses or participants," Dani said. She glared at Jenny again. "If I were you, I'd fill him in before someone else does."

"That was my plan," Jenny said. "I would have last night, but he was already in bed when I got home."

Dani regarded her worriedly. "Were you that late or did he go to bed much earlier than usual?"

"It was early. Mom said he spent most of the day out riding. He was tired. He went to his room right after dinner."

"He was probably taking a last nostalgic look at the property this jerk intends to try to steal from him," Dani said. "How could you, Jenny? How could you consort with the enemy?"

"I've explained that. I'm not going to do it again. And for the record, I'm just as upset about Chance's threats as anyone else. Don't forget, a share of that property is going to be mine one day. My ancestors on my mother's side were robbed of it or land very much like it generations ago by white men."

"Maybe if you signed over your share to Chance, it would satisfy him," Dani suggested with an edge of bitterness. "Then Grandpa Harlan could stop worrying himself sick and Uncle Cody wouldn't be afraid that the ranch he loves is going to get carved up like a Thanksgiving turkey to satisfy some old grudge."

"No," Sharon Lynn said sharply, startling them both. "Jenny shouldn't have to give up one single acre she's entitled to. We all need to stick together on this. That's what Grandpa Harlan wants. As for whether or not Jenny spends time with Chance, that's up to her. Maybe it'll be a good thing to have a spy in this man's camp."

Jenny had had enough. First they called her a traitor. Now they wanted her to become a spy. The whole mess was rapidly getting out of hand. She slid off her stool and tossed a dollar on the counter to pay for her soda. "I am not in his camp. I am not spying. I am going home."

"Enjoy it while you can," Dani said. "Unless, of course, you figure you've got an in with the prospective new owner."

"Dani!" Sharon Lynn protested.

"Well, I can't help it. I agree with you that we should all stick together and present a united front, so cozying up to Chance Adams over pizza strikes me as being pretty darned close to treason."

Jenny sighed. "You're entitled to your opinion." Dani's judgment hurt her more than she'd expected. She forced a smile for Sharon Lynn. "Bye. Stop in on your way home if you have the time."

Sharon Lynn shot a worried look at Dani, but nodded. "I think I will."

Dani frowned at both of them. "Well, isn't that just peachy. Doesn't anybody but me see how ludicrous this budding romance is?"

"There is no romance," Jenny said impatiently. "None, zip. *Nada.*"

Dani shook her head. "Try telling that to Grandpa Harlan and see how well it flies."

Jenny intended to do just that. Her father was the only person in the family to whom she owed any explanation at all. Somehow she would have to make him see that she hadn't betrayed him last night and that she didn't intend to in the future. Harlan would believe her. He was much more reasonable than Dani.

Most of the time, Jenny thought with a sigh.

If last night had been a disaster, tonight was already showing promise of being a full-scale calamity. And like it or not, thanks to her decision to take on the fourth grade this year, instead of sticking with eighth-grade history, she was smack-dab in the middle of it.

Chapter Six

Jenny was so distracted when she walked out of Dolan's she slammed right into what felt like a brick wall. The unexpected encounter rocked her back on her heels. Large calloused hands clamped her arms to keep her upright. She promptly felt the sizzle of the contact right down to her toes.

In fact, that sizzle was her first clue to the identity of the solid wall of muscle she'd run into. Only one man had ever made such a devastating impact on her senses with little more than a touch: Chance Adams.

Her startled gaze flew up and clashed with his. He seemed amused. Come to think of it, he usually did around her, which was darned irritating. She had not been put on this earth to provide him with entertainment. Obviously Petey hadn't reported in yet about being banished to the hall, or Chance's mood wouldn't be quite so lighthearted.

"What are you doing here?" she demanded, taking her annoyance with Dani and Sharon Lynn out on him. It was his fault she'd fought with them in the first place. And the timing of his arrival today struck her as particularly suspicious. He probably intended to add to the impression that they were newly inseparable, thereby widening the rift between her and her family.

"It's a public sidewalk," he said blandly.

"And you just happened to be strolling by at this precise moment?"

"It is possible, you know."

She shook her head. "No way. I don't believe it."

"If you don't believe in coincidence, what do you think I'm doing here?"

"You came by intentionally because you knew I was going to be here with Dani and Sharon Lynn," she accused. "Even though I specifically told you to stay away."

"Why would I want to do that?" he asked.

A baby couldn't have looked more innocent. Jenny wasn't buying his act for a second.

"To stir up trouble," she said flatly.

He gestured toward the drugstore. "Is that what happened in there? The three of you had a fight?"

Still stinging from her nieces' verbal assault, she admitted, "Actually it was primarily the two of us, me and Dani. Sharon Lynn pretty much tried to mediate, but it was a lost cause. Dani's got her dander up. There's no one on earth fiercer than an Adams who's all riled up.''

''I'm sorry.''

The soft-spoken, sincere-sounding apology was the last thing she'd expected. She stared into his eyes and thought she recognized a genuine flash of sympathy.

''Are you really?'' she asked, unable to hide her skepticism. He was probably getting exactly the results he wanted: chaos in the Adams ranks.

''Yes,'' he replied emphatically. ''Believe it or not, family is every bit as important to me as it is to you. After all, why would I waste my time coming here to settle an old score between my father and his brother if it wasn't? I'd never seen White Pines. I'd never met your father. It wasn't my grudge to start with. It was my father's. He asked me to come here on his deathbed.''

''You would never have come here on your own?'' Jenny asked skeptically. ''Are you sure about that?''

''Nope. This was all my father's idea.'' His expression turned vaguely rueful. ''As a matter of fact, he manipulated me into it. He pulled out all the stops, including filling Petey's head with tales of his ancestors and the way both Petey and I had been cheated out of our heritage right along with him. Petey would never have forgiven me for not doing as his granddaddy asked.''

Chance regarded her evenly. ''It wasn't until I got

here that I turned it into my own battle. I suppose I'd always thought Daddy was exaggerating about what had been taken from him. Once I saw White Pines and heard about Harlan Adams and his power, I realized Daddy's bitterness was justified.''

Jenny could have enlightened him a bit on that point, but she figured that was her father's story to tell if he ever chose to.

''Okay,'' she said, instead. ''So you're just a loyal son. That doesn't mean you're not also just a greedy bastard who saw an easy way to make a claim on some valuable land.''

Chance's expression darkened and his eyes glittered dangerously. ''Maybe you ought to take a minute one of these days and look at this from my perspective.''

It was a reasonable suggestion, but Jenny wasn't feeling particularly reasonable. ''Why would I want to do that?'' she asked.

''Because my situation isn't all that different from the one you were in when you first came to town.''

The mild comment startled her. Jenny thought back to that tumultuous period of her life. She'd been an angry teenager, bent on getting into trouble and resentful of every adult, especially those who were rich and powerful like the Adamses. It was so long in the past, so wildly different from her attitude now, that she'd virtually forgotten that time in her life.

She'd also thought it forgotten by everyone else in

Los Piños. Her gaze narrowed. "What do you know about that?"

Chance grinned and settled one hip against the fender of his truck. He hooked the heel of his boot on the bumper. No one on earth could have looked more at ease or more inclined to let her simmer for a bit and wonder who'd been filling his head with tales of her misadventures.

Jenny wished she could convey the same sort of calm. She suspected her churning emotions were plain on her face. She'd never been able to hide what she was feeling. Not for more than a minute, anyway.

When she'd first arrived in Los Piños at fourteen, everyone had known exactly how angry and bitter she was about her parents' divorce, about the move from New York, about the sins she felt had been committed against her Native American ancestors. All that rage had taken the form of some very stupid actions. She really hoped Chance hadn't heard all the sordid details.

"Forget it," she said finally, tiring of whatever game he was playing to torment her. "It doesn't matter what you think you know."

"Oh, I know quite a bit," he taunted. "Wilkie was feeling talkative when I got home last night."

"Really?" Jenny said, fighting to keep her tone neutral.

"Yep. He told me about how you and your mama came here all worked up about righting old injustices to your Native American ancestors. He said you'd even told Harlan that his land had really belonged to your granddaddy and that, by rights, it should be yours.'' He regarded her speculatively. ''Was he telling the truth about all that?''

''I suppose,'' she muttered, seeing now why he'd drawn the comparison between the two of them.

Chance grinned. ''Thought so. Wilkie's not prone to telling tall tales. So how did you and Harlan work it out? The way I have it figured, your mama took the easy way of assuring she got what she wanted. She married Harlan to make sure she got your ancestors' land back, right?''

''Of all the twisted, outrageous accusations,'' Jenny sputtered. ''How could you even think such a thing without ever having met her or having seen the two of them together? She married him because she loves him. She's not getting one acre of his land.''

''And you? What's your stake in White Pines?''

She hesitated for a moment, then admitted, ''I'm entitled to the same share as Luke, Cody, Jordan and Lizzy—one-fifth of the land. I never even asked for that, by the way. It was Harlan's idea. He drew up the papers and gave them to my mom on their wedding day. Cody's the one who actually gets the ranching operation, though. We've all agreed he's entitled to it after all the work he's done over the years. His son, Harlan Patrick, will probably take it over after him, if he can stop chasing girls long enough to concentrate on learning the business side of things.''

''I see.''

Something in his tone alerted Jenny that she'd just blabbed an important piece of family business. Not that the division of White Pines was much of a secret. Everybody in town had probably guessed the terms of Harlan's will, including the chatty Wilkie. Some were purely speculating. Others had probably wrangled insider information from one Adams or another. They all knew exactly how Harlan's estate had been set up. He thought each of them had a right to know where they stood so there would be no wrangling among themselves after he was gone.

That didn't mean she had to confirm all the details for this man who was so intent on disrupting everyone's lives. That was her problem—she was impulsive. She tended to open her mouth and say whatever was on her mind without thinking about the consequences. Add the fact that Chance could probably charm a spiteful old spinster out of her life's savings, and she was bound to blab way too much sooner or later.

"I have to be going," she said, backing away. She didn't like the fact that she had a hard time doing it. It was as if there were an invisible force pulling them toward each other. She actually had to consciously fight to escape it.

"Scared of getting caught with me again?" he asked, amusement twinkling in his eyes as he glanced toward the drugstore.

"I'm not scared of much," she retorted.

Despite her claim, she followed his gaze toward the

window just the same to be sure that Dani and Sharon Lynn weren't peering out. If they were, Jenny would never hear the end of it. They might not be able to make out the words being exchanged, but Chance's presence alone would be enough to stir them up, especially Dani.

Assured that the two women were still at the soda fountain, she added, "Most folks around here know I'm a risk taker."

"Really?" His tone was filled with disbelief. He trailed a finger down her cheek, his eyes fastened on hers. "What kind of risks are you in the habit of taking, Jenny?"

She felt the heat climbing into her face. A quick little shiver danced down her spine. She prayed Chance wasn't aware of either, but the quirk of his lips suggested otherwise. He knew he affected her. He knew he scared her more than the prospect of tripping over a rattler in the desert.

"Have dinner with me again," he suggested softly, still caressing her cheek. "Just the two of us. Two grown-ups with an attraction that needs exploring."

"I don't think so," Jenny said, exasperated at being barely able to get the words past the yearning clogging her throat.

"Must be scared, after all," Chance said.

"I am not scared," Jenny insisted. "It just doesn't make sense for you and me to spend a whole lot of time together. It's asking for trouble."

"Why? Because you're afraid you'll stop fighting me one of these days and we'll wind up in bed?"

"Absolutely not," she replied at once, probably with a little too much vehemence. "Why would I be afraid of something that I would never in a million years allow to happen?"

Chance grinned. "A simple no would have been sufficient."

"I doubt it," she said defensively. "The word doesn't seem to register with you. Maybe you haven't heard it enough."

"I understand the concept," he said dryly. "I can also tell the difference between conviction and desperation. You, sweet thing, sounded just a trifle desperate."

Jenny stared at him in disbelief. "What on earth would I have to be desperate about?"

"Oh, I think you're downright panicky that you won't be able to persuade me to back off, and that one of these days you'll just give in to what you're feeling."

"That is absolutely ridiculous," she declared, despite the fact that he was right on the money. She didn't like the wickedly sensual feelings that came over her when he so much as grazed her cheek with his finger, much less the heart-stopping breathlessness stirred up by his kiss. She couldn't control them and she really liked being in control of herself and her destiny. Always had, ever since she'd been uprooted from New York all those years ago without any say in the matter.

"We'll see," he said, his voice low and husky.

"We will not see. I am not changing my mind."

"I'll give you a few days to think it over," he said, clearly pleased with himself for the magnanimous gesture.

Exasperated, Jenny poked a finger into the middle of his chest. "Save your breath. Ask anyone around town just how stubborn an Adams can be."

He laughed at that. "Darlin', that's just the point. You might have the name. You might have latched on to the habit of being contrary. But I'm the one with Adams blood running through my veins. When it comes to stubborn, I'd say you've met your match."

He was still chuckling when Jenny whirled away and took off as if a herd of cattle was stampeding down the road behind her.

Jenny broke every speed limit between Los Piños and the gates at White Pines, cussing a blue streak the entire way. Chance Adams figured at the center of that blue streak. Low-down sneaky scoundrel was one of the milder labels she pinned on him.

The truth was, he had shaken her. In fact, she couldn't recall the last time any man had shaken her so badly. She had stood on the sidewalk in front of Dolan's caught in the grip of emotions so powerful and so conflicting it had taken her the entire trip home to sort them out.

More than once she had wanted to slug the man, to land a shot to that handsome square jaw that would prove to him once and for all she was not a woman to be messed with.

Then, an equal number of times, she had felt very much like throwing herself into his arms and kissing him again. Only the nearby presence of Dani and Sharon Lynn, not good judgment, had kept her from acting on the almost irresistible desire to discover if his kisses were consistently bone melting, or if the one she'd experienced had been a once-in-a-lifetime aberration.

How was it possible for a man to stir such contradictory reactions, especially in the space of a few heartbeats? How was it possible she could feel anything but contempt for a man who threatened the happiness of her family? Was she simply edging toward middle-aged desperation, after all? Was she subconsciously feeling the ticking of her biological clock? Or was it specifically Chance who had the ability to turn her inside out?

Not that for one single instant the thought of marriage had entered her head, she told herself staunchly. Chance didn't make her think about marriage or babies or growing old together. He made her think about sex. Big difference. *Huge* difference. She sighed. Intolerable difference.

She bounded up the front steps and stormed

through the front door, slamming it behind her with enough force to rattle it on its hinges.

Naturally, because he was the last person she wanted to see, her father was standing at the foot of the stairs, staring at her with a thoroughly bemused expression.

"Bad day?" he inquired lightly.

"You could say that."

"Want to talk about it?"

"Not especially," she said, then recalled her vow to fill her father in on the dinner she'd had with Chance. Now she had today's encounter to add to the confession. She forced a rueful smile. "I take it back. Do you feel like going for a walk?"

"Sure."

Jenny turned around and headed back outside, taming her pace to suit her father's slower gait.

"Where to?" he asked when they reached the bottom of the front steps.

Jenny shrugged. "Doesn't matter."

"Then let's head out to the stables. I want to take a look at the new broodmare Cody paid an arm and a leg for."

She slanted an amused look at him. "Cody's throwing your money around again?"

Her father chuckled. "There's nothing he enjoys more. Not that he's made a bad investment yet," he conceded. "Just don't tell him I said that."

"Don't you think maybe it's time to let him know you approve of the way he runs things around here?"

Her father gave her a startled look. "You think he doesn't know?"

"I think it wouldn't hurt to remind him every once in a while just in case he takes your constant grumbling to heart."

Harlan nodded slowly. "You could have a point," he conceded. "Now why don't you tell me what's on your mind? Who's been picking on you? Do I need to get out my shotgun and wave it around?"

She looked at his fierce expression and smiled. "You would, too, wouldn't you?"

"If somebody hurt one of my kids or my grand-babies, you bet I would."

Impulsively Jenny stopped and hugged him, then planted a kiss on his weathered cheek. "Thank you."

He seemed startled by the gesture, but clearly it pleased him. "What was that for?"

"For treating me like one of your kids."

"Great heavenly days, you *are* one of my kids, Jenny, my girl. I've never thought of you any other way."

His emphatic response warmed her heart, but it also deepened her fear she was the worst sort of traitor. "How would you feel if one of your kids betrayed you?" she asked, her tone barely above a whisper.

This time he was the one who halted. He searched her face intently. "You think that's what you've done?"

"Some people in the family think I have."

"That's not the same as you believing it, is it?"

''No.''

''Why don't you just tell me what happened and let me decide for myself?''

She forced a smile. ''Easier said than done. I'm scared you'll agree with them.''

''And do what? Hate you? Disown you? It won't happen, Jenny, my girl. You're family. We'll work it out. You being straight with me now will go a long way toward fixing things, assuming they even need repair in the first place.''

Reassured by that promise, she described her dinner with Chance and all the events that had led up to it. ''Then today, not two seconds after leaving Dani and Sharon Lynn, I ran smack into him again and there we were, in plain view of everyone, talking.''

''Talking, huh? On a public sidewalk? To a man who happened along?'' Her father's eyes twinkled with amusement. ''Now that is cause for concern. I declare, I've never heard such goings-on.''

''You're making fun of me,'' she accused. ''I'm serious.''

''I can see that,'' he said, his expression turning more somber. ''But, darlin' girl, I am not going to lose any sleep because you spent a little time with Chance Adams. The truth is, I'd like to meet the man myself.''

Stunned, she stared at him. ''You would?''

''Don't look so shocked. Of course I would. I might not agree with what he intends to do, but he's my brother's son. And that son of his, Petey, sounds like Luke and Cody when they were boys. Seems to me they'd both probably fit right in with the rest of us if we gave them the opportunity. Chance is the one who wants to turn White Pines into a battleground and me into the enemy. It's not the other way around."

"But no matter which one starts it, isn't it all the same in the end?" Jenny asked. "If he's determined to claim what he thinks is his, then we *are* pitted against each other, like it or not."

"I suppose that depends on what you and the others determine is the right thing to do under the circumstances. I gave all of you the choice of how to handle this."

"Well, obviously Dani, at least, is gearing up for a fight. She must be getting that from Jordan."

He seemed surprised by her uncertainty over the views of the rest of the family. "Haven't you talked to any of the others?"

"Not since they were here for dinner."

"Maybe it's time you all sat down and thrashed it out. We could get this settled once and for all."

"Maybe so," she agreed with a sigh.

He regarded her intently. "Let me ask you something. Aside from this battle over White Pines, what do you think of Chance?"

She thought about the question, determined to answer it as honestly as she could. "He seems like a decent man. He's a good father and, from what I gather, he's a loyal son. He's also arrogant and handsome and stubborn.''

Her father chuckled. ''Sound like anyone else you've ever met?''

''Every Adams man on earth,'' she conceded.

''Then he can't be all bad, can he?'' Harlan pressed his callused palm to her cheek and gazed directly into her eyes. ''Darlin' girl, you make up your own mind about Chance Adams, and you decide what sort of relationship you want to have with him. Trust your own judgment.''

''I can't bear the thought of everyone in the family thinking I'm betraying you. You're the most important person in the world to me, besides mom.''

''Well, when it comes to that, I'm the only one you have to worry about,'' he reminded her. ''And I've just told you where I stand. If anyone else wants to make a fuss, send 'em to me. I'll set 'em straight.''

''Somehow I don't think even you will be able to appease Dani and the others.''

''Then you do want to spend more time with the man?''

''Yes,'' she said impulsively, then promptly retracted it. ''I mean no. It's just…I'm sure we're going to be thrown together from time to time because of Petey.''

''Is that all you're worried about?''

''Yes,'' she insisted.

''Okay, then. You're a teacher. It's your job to deal with the parents of your students. You can't treat

Chance Adams any differently than you would any other parent in town. If anybody in the family questions you, just tell them that. Then tell 'em to go to blazes.''

Jenny grinned. ''Who'll pick me up off the ground when they punch my lights out?''

''I will.''

''Thank you,'' she said, hugging him again.

Her father wrapped his arms around her and held her tightly. Then he stood back and gazed warmly into her eyes. ''If you should change your mind and decide that your interest in this man is personal, that would be okay, too,'' he said quietly.

When Jenny would have moved away to argue, he held her in place. ''Just listen to me for once,'' he commanded. ''Real love's a scarce commodity in this life. When it comes along, only a fool turns his back on it.''

''I never said anything about love,'' Jenny protested. She wasn't in love with Chance. She still wasn't sure if she even liked him very much.

Her father chuckled. ''You didn't have to.''

This time she did pull away. ''Don't you dare go getting any ideas about me and Chance Adams,'' she ordered, realizing exactly where his thoughts were headed. ''I am not going to become one of your little matchmaking projects.''

''Of course not,'' he said agreeably. ''You're a grown woman. You can pick and choose your own friends, settle on your own husband. I'm just saying, if you were to settle on Chance, it would be okay.''

"Oh, for goodness' sake," she began, then decided to save the protest. He clearly wouldn't believe anything she had to say about Chance meaning absolutely nothing to her. Once Harlan Adams's romantic fantasies stirred to life, no one was more dedicated to the promotion of a good love story. Anything she said would only encourage him.

"I'm going back to the house," she said.

"I'll say it again, darlin' girl. Don't turn your back on your heart. Listen to what it has to say."

"I know exactly what my heart is saying," she retorted. "And it is not saying anything about Chance Adams."

"Maybe it's just not saying anything you want to hear."

"Pardon me for saying this, Daddy, but go to blazes."

He stared at her for an instant, then threw back his head and laughed. "Whoo-ee! It's about to get real interesting around here."

As she walked away, Jenny realized it was the second time that day she had provided a man with so much entertainment. Adams men! Darned if they weren't all alike.

Chapter Seven

Wilkie Rollins's books were a disgrace. Chance had spent every evening for the past two months trying to untangle the mess the old man had made of his ranch finances. Wilkie claimed the details didn't matter to him, as long as he had money in the bank at the end of the month.

The disorder made Chance edgy. He'd insisted on setting them right so Wilkie would know how Chance's management of the place was going.

"Son, I can see the kind of job you're doing by looking around," Wilkie had countered. "I don't need to see the books to get an answer."

Chance had been appalled. "Wilkie, you can't run a ranch like that. How will you ever know if you're being cheated?"

His boss had looked him up and down. "You intend on cheating me?"

Chance had waved off the ridiculous question. "No, of course not. If I'd intended to, I never would have brought up the books in the first place."

"Well, then, I don't see that we've got a problem."

Chance had given up after that. He was still intent on straightening out the bookkeeping, but he was doing it more for his own satisfaction than for Wilkie's. Besides, he liked making order out of chaos. He'd been doing that most of his life. Hank hadn't exactly been a paragon of orderliness, and Chance's mother had been more eager to please Hank than keep the household running smoothly.

From the time he could reach the stove, Chance had done most of the cooking, albeit even then it had been limited mostly to frozen dinners and fresh vegetables. He'd also done a good bit of the cleaning, in addition to whatever chores Hank had allotted him. It had given him a sense of structure that hadn't been forthcoming from his parents. He'd always prided himself on seeing that Petey had rules and routine, even if Hank had taken equal pride in seeing that his grandson broke most of them.

Chance was trying to make sense of a column of receipts when he realized Petey was standing beside him. He glanced up from the accounting ledger into solemn blue eyes.

"Hey, what's up?"

"You busy?" Petey asked.

"It's nothing that can't wait. You got something on your mind?"

"Sort of."

"What?"

"It's school."

One simple word—school—and Chance's blood surged as if he'd been shown an album of erotica. Images of Miss Prim and Prissy looking all mussed and kissable lit up in his mind like neon.

"Did something happen today?" he asked when he thought he could get the words out without sounding ridiculously breathless.

"Something happened all right. That lady punished me!" Petey blurted, his little body radiating indignation. "I thought she was supposed to be your friend. I told you she wasn't. I told you she was that bad man's daughter and that made her bad, too, but you didn't believe me."

Chance sighed. He should have known one dinner would not build a bridge between those two, not with Petey so determinedly loyal to his grandfather. He couldn't help wondering why he'd heard none of this from Jenny herself this afternoon. Had her silence on the topic been deliberate or had she simply been distracted by her session with Dani and Sharon Lynn? Maybe she'd just been rattled by his presence. That possibility brought him a very large measure of satisfaction.

"Dad," Petey complained, "you're not paying attention."

"Okay. Sorry. Why don't you tell me exactly what happened?" he suggested, keeping his tone neutral.

"She yelled at me in front of the whole class," Petey began, then drew a deep breath as he gathered momentum. "And then she made me go into the hall and told me I was going to grow up and be ignorant."

Chance bristled on his son's behalf, but reason told him Petey was only relaying part of the story. "Why did she yell at you in the first place?"

Petey stared down at the floor. "I don't know."

"Excuse me?" Chance said. "You have absolutely no idea why your teacher was yelling at you? Was it just out of the blue? Did she jump up and pick you out of a whole roomful of kids to humiliate?"

"What's humiliate?"

"Never mind. The point is, I can't help thinking that Ms. Adams must have had a good reason for yelling. I'm also thinking I'd rather hear that reason from you. You might prefer that as well, because if I get an explanation from her, it will probably irritate the dickens out of me and I might be inclined to yell at you, too."

Petey stared back at him with a wide innocent look. Tears pooled in the corners of his eyes. Chance felt like a louse, but he refused to back down. He was beginning to get an idea of just what Jenny was up against. He wasn't quite ready to be sympathetic, but a few more incidents and he might be forced to shift his allegiance.

"I'm waiting," he said quietly.

"It wasn't anything really bad," Petey said finally. "It wasn't like I chopped off a girl's braid or something."

"I'm relieved. What was it, then?"

"I put some glue down," he mumbled.

Chance had a sinking sensation in the pit of his stomach. Glue and Petey were a dangerous combination. He could tell already that he wasn't going to like the rest of the story. "Where?"

"On some papers."

"What papers?"

"The math test papers."

Chance stared at his son in stunned disbelief. "You glued the math test papers together? Is that what you're telling me?" he demanded, his voice climbing.

"It's not like she couldn't make more copies," Petey said defensively.

"Then this was a test you hadn't taken yet, correct?"

"Yeah, I mean, it was just a joke. You can see that, can't you?" Petey asked, his tone pleading. "She can always give the test tomorrow when she has more copies, right?"

Chance was tempted to send Petey straight to his room and ground him until he reached puberty, but he figured there were a couple of additional things he needed to know first.

"Why did you do this?"

"What do you mean, why?"

"I mean what the dickens were you thinking?" Chance shouted.

Petey's expression faltered. "Now you're yelling at me, too."

"For good reason," Chance said, but he managed to lower his voice. "Did you glue these papers together, by any chance, because you hadn't studied for the test?"

"Not exactly. Besides, math's my best subject. You know that. I could have passed it, anyway."

"Then why?" An idea began taking shape, an idea that made all too much sense. "Wait, let me guess. Timmy McPherson hadn't studied for the math test, had he?"

"Jeez, Dad, you know I can't tell you that," Petey exclaimed. "That would be, like, tattling."

"Okay, we'll let that pass," Chance said, concluding it would be a waste of time to deliver another lecture on the folly of protecting a kid who appeared to be dedicated to destroying Petey's life. "I think I know the answer. Besides, the important thing here is that you did something you knew was wrong. Again," he added. "What was Ms. Adams's punishment?"

"I told you, she made me go into the hall and she told me I was gonna grow up ignorant."

"I'd say she let you off lightly." Chance looked directly into his son's eyes, then added pointedly, "Way more lightly than I intend to let you off."

Petey stared back at him in horror. "You're gonna punish me, too?"

"Oh, yeah," Chance said grimly. "You will get off the school bus every afternoon for the next week and go directly to your room. You will double your homework assignments. If Ms. Adams gives you five math problems, you'll do ten. If she assigns ten pages in your history book, you will read twenty. I want her to send me a written list of your assignments so I can sign off that you've done the work. Got it?"

"No way," Petey said, clearly shaken. "I'll be up all night."

"Missing a little sleep won't hurt you. Besides, you'll have all weekend to get ahead."

"What are you saying? I can't even go outside this weekend?"

"You've got it, pal."

Petey shot him a rebellious look. "Who's gonna make me stay in my room?"

"I will. If I'm not here, I'll hire a baby-sitter."

Petey looked doubly horrified. "A baby-sitter? You can't. I'm too old. I'll never be able to show my face in school again if anyone finds out you've hired some girl to baby-sit me."

"Then I guess you'll think long and hard before you misbehave in school again, won't you?"

"But, Dad—"

Chance shook his head. "No buts, pal. You brought this one on yourself."

"It's not fair!" Petey protested. "You're siding with the enemy!"

"Ms. Adams is not the enemy, not in the classroom. She's in charge there. We've been over this before."

"But—"

"There's no point in arguing. Go to your room now. I'm sure you have a lot of homework left to do."

"I hate you!" Petey yelled as he raced from the room. "And Granddad would hate you, too, if he knew you were picking her over your own kid!"

Maybe so, Chance conceded to himself when Petey was gone. But Hank wasn't the one trying to get a kid through school without winding up in juvenile court.

He had to bear some of the responsibility for this. He obviously hadn't made his displeasure over the hair-chopping incident plain enough to his son. Even after their dinner together Petey clearly thought making Jenny Adams's life a living hell was within bounds.

Well, it had to stop. No one was going to find some way to say he wasn't a fit parent. He'd get Petey under control.

Besides, if anybody in this family was going to keep Jenny all riled up, it was going to be him. He was already enjoying it way more than he ought to.

Chance wasn't certain exactly what drew him to White Pines on Saturday. He was still feeling guilty about Petey's misbehavior, and maybe on some level he wanted to make amends. Or it might have been the simple desire to catch his first up-close look at the ranch his father had been obsessed with most of his life. Maybe he'd just run out of the willpower he needed to stay away.

More than likely, though, it had something to do with his need to butt heads with Jenny. Clashing with her just on general principle made him feel more alive than he'd imagined possible a few short months ago when he'd been grieving the loss of Mary and his father.

With Petey settled in for the day and the dreaded teenage baby-sitter keeping guard, Chance took the highway in front of Wilkie's and headed west in the direction of the family ranch. He'd traveled the same road at least a dozen times since arriving in town a few months back, but he'd always stopped well short of the gate to White Pines. He'd vowed he wouldn't set foot on the land until it belonged to him.

Today, however, he broke that vow. He turned in and drove slowly down the long winding lane, absorbing his first impression of the land around him. It was ruggedly beautiful, as he'd known it would be. His father had described it endlessly, his voice thick with emotion. And Wilkie's neighboring property gave a hint of what he could expect. It was just that White Pines had more of it. Acres and acres more. The endless view was awesome.

Chance's first sight of the house, though, had him hitting the brakes and wondering if he'd taken a wrong turn. Apparently his father's memory had failed him here, or else Harlan Adams had spent a small fortune restoring the place to its original glory.

Chance cut the truck's engine eventually, but he couldn't stop staring. There was a strong hint of the old South to the house. That much his father had recalled. But in his stories, the house had been virtually tumbling down, a mere shadow of the dream home his ancestors had built when they'd come west after the Civil War. Hank had talked of grand rooms from which the furnishings had been sold off piece by piece to pay the bills. He had described ragged drapes and scarred paint.

The house certainly wasn't suffering from such inattention now. Freshly painted a pristine white, its pillars impressive, if out of place in West Texas, its gardens a riot of color, the mansion could have been transported back to the South and not suffered by comparison to its neighbors.

The sweep of the porch—he supposed it ought to be called a veranda or some such—was such a far cry from the tiny two-rocker porch on Hank's cabin back in Montana that it left Chance awestruck. He wondered if the family sat out here at sunset, watching the changing colors on the horizon, or if they just took the wonder of it all for granted.

There had to be twenty rooms inside, he thought as he continued to sit and stare, trying to absorb the grandeur of it. More, probably. For just an instant he wondered what the devil he'd do with twenty rooms—or even ten, if they split the place down the middle. Then he banished the thought as irrelevant. Half of White Pines—house and land—was his. That was all that mattered. He could close off every room but one if he wanted to. The point was, it would be his choice to make.

Pushing aside an unexpected surge of uncertainty, he climbed out of his pickup, settled his hat on his head and strode up the front steps, steeled for the bitter confrontation that was bound to come, especially if anyone other than Jenny answered the door.

He hadn't exactly considered what he was going to say to whichever stranger answered his forceful knock on that heavy, carved front door. The sound of footsteps slowed his pulse to a dull thud. Maybe he was making a terrible mistake by coming. He should have thought this moment through, planned more carefully for it.

It was too late now, though. The door swung wide and he was suddenly face-to-face with a silver-haired, stoop-shouldered, yet still impressive man who had to be Harlan Adams. The family resemblance between him and Hank was stunning. In recent years Hank had been thinner, but both men had the same clear blue eyes, the same square jaw.

Chance stared at Harlan Adams, suddenly feeling oddly tongue-tied. He told himself it was fury that silenced him, but it was more. Much more. It was history and family and pride, all kicking in with a swell of contradictory emotions.

His uncle, however, had no such reticence. "You must be Chance," he said quietly, his gaze even and unblinking. If he was thrown by the surprise arrival of his nephew, he hid it well. He held out his hand, closed it in a firm grip around Chance's. "I'm Harlan Adams, your uncle."

"I'm surprised you recognize me," Chance said stiffly, returning the handshake he'd been too startled to ignore.

The comment drew a broad smile. "Come on in," Harlan said with what appeared to be unforced graciousness. "I'll show you why."

Chance followed his uncle into a living room that was three times as big as his own and filled with comfortable furniture that was obviously expensive but surprisingly unpretentious. Harlan followed his gaze and said, "The place used to be filled with antiques, but Jenny got tired of tippytoeing around in here. Next thing I knew, her mama had redecorated. This suits us. It's a room you can live in without being scared of breaking something every time you move. When Jenny was a teenager, that was especially important. She tended to be rambunctious."

"I can imagine," Chance said wryly, wishing for just an instant that he had known her then, that their relationship could have started off in some uncomplicated way. He suspected she would have made his heart pound and his mouth go dry even then.

Harlan led the way to a piano sitting in front of a huge bay window. Sunlight spilled through the window and glinted off the glass on literally dozens of formal photographs and snapshots. For Chance, looking at some of those pictures was like looking in a mirror.

But the absence of one picture in particular stuck in his craw. There was no snapshot of Hank Adams, no formal portrait of his grandparents with Hank and Harlan. It was as if his father had never existed, as if he'd been cut out of the universe as easily as he'd been cut out of the will.

Harlan took first one picture in hand, then another, explaining who was in each, proudly showing off his family, right down through the grandchildren, most of whom were now too darned grown-up to suit him, he claimed.

"I'm starting with great-grandbabies now, though," he said, showing off another half-dozen snapshots of a squalling newborn and a couple of boys who looked like twins and didn't look at all like Adamses.

"These two belong to Duke Jenkins," Harlan said, apparently seeing Chance's confusion. "He just married my granddaughter Dani, so, of course, now they're family, too. Born, adopted, it doesn't matter. They're all family."

The pride, the love shining in his eyes, all of it was too much for Chance. He wanted to smash every single one of those pictures. Harlan Adams thought more of these great-grandchildren who hadn't even been born to an Adams than he did of his own brother.

Instead of saying that, though, instead of railing against the injustice of it, Chance kept his cool and solidified his determination. This little exhibition had fueled his determination for battle just when he might have been tempted by his fascination with Jenny into tempering it. That didn't mean he would leave here today without catching a glimpse of her.

"Is Jenny around?" he asked eventually.

Harlan regarded him speculatively. "Is that why you really came? To see Jenny?"

Chance nodded. "I need to talk to her about my boy. He's been giving her a rough time in school."

"So I've heard," Harlan said, chuckling. "I'd like to meet him. He sounds like my sons way back when. They were up to mischief all the time."

"That's Petey, all right."

"Why don't you bring him along next time you come?"

Surprised by the invitation, Chance nodded. "Maybe I will—if there is a next time."

"Why wouldn't there be?"

"I just thought…" Chance shrugged. "Never mind. You never did say if Jenny was around."

"She's gone for a ride with her sister," Harlan said. "They should be back soon. Or if you'd like, we could saddle up and go out and find them. It would give you a chance to look the place over."

Even more startled by this invitation, Chance had

to wonder if Harlan realized what he was offering. He was giving the enemy a chance to size up the potential spoils of this family war. His uncle's bland expression, however, gave nothing away.

"I'm surprised," Chance confessed.

"By?"

"The fact that you didn't kick me off the property. Most men would have."

His uncle seemed genuinely puzzled by the suggestion. "Why would I do that?" he asked, then added simply, "You're my brother's boy."

"A brother you ran off," Chance retorted bitterly.

"Something I will regret to my dying day," Harlan said with apparent sincerity. "I was sorry to hear he'd passed away. I wish we'd had a chance for me to make amends. Someday, if you like, we can talk about that."

"I don't need to talk about it. I know the details."

"From your father's perspective," his uncle said. "There are two sides to every story. A wise man listens to both before making up his mind. Whether you do or not, though, you'll always be welcome here."

Chance stared at him in amazement. "Even though I intend to do everything in my power to take it away from you?" he asked.

Harlan actually had the audacity to smile at that. "Give it your best shot, son. Nothing gets the blood to flowing like a good brawl."

Chance's respect for the man deepened in that instant. Under other conditions he had a feeling he could actually like Harlan Adams.

But there were no other conditions. History stood between them, just as it did between him and Jenny. Not that it was stopping him where she was concerned, he thought ruefully.

"I think I'd like to ride out with you," he said.

Harlan gave a brisk nod of satisfaction. "Good. I'll get my coat. There's a chill in the air today, and these old bones of mine don't take to the cold they way they once did."

"Maybe you'd rather just point the way."

"No, indeed. I go for a ride every day just to see the beauty of this land. I've got the time to appreciate it now, and I never let a day pass without letting the good Lord know I'm grateful." His expression turned wistful. "Can't go quite as far as I once could, though. Hopefully we'll come across Jenny and Lizzy before I tire out, and then Jenny can show you what I can't."

"Thank you," Chance felt compelled to say, though it grated at him to thank this man for anything. "You've been very kind."

Harlan squeezed his shoulder. "No reason not to be." His gaze narrowed. "One word of warning, though. I'll fight you fair and square over White Pines, but you do one single thing to hurt Jenny and you'll live to regret it."

Chance nodded, not surprised at all that Harlan Adams had intuitively sensed that his interest in Jenny was dangerous. ''Fair enough.''

The line had been drawn in the sand, so to speak. It suited Chance's need for order. It also told him that Harlan Adams was a man with clear priorities. He might love his land, he might even fight for it if forced to, but his children were his life. In that instant Chance wondered for the first time how a man who felt that strongly about family could have turned his back on his younger brother.

Maybe, just maybe, his father hadn't told him the whole story, after all.

Chapter Eight

In the midst of spreading a blanket on the ground for the picnic she and Lizzy had brought with them on their ride, Jenny thought she heard the sound of hooves. She glanced toward the southeast and spotted two men on horseback heading their way at a leisurely pace. She recognized her father at once, but the man beside him almost looked like Chance, which, of course, was impossible. He would never show up at White Pines. Nor was her father likely to welcome him, except maybe with a shotgun blast or dueling pistols.

Then again, he had said just a few nights ago that he wanted to meet his brother's son.

"Lizzy, can you see who's riding with Daddy?" Jenny asked.

Her younger sister looked up from the picnic basket Maritza had packed and stared in the direction Jenny indicated. "I've never seen him before, which is too bad, because he is one hundred percent gorgeous," Lizzy declared breathlessly. She automatically reached up to tidy her naturally curly black hair, which she'd scooped into a careless ponytail.

Jenny fought back amusement. Lizzy was at the age when her fascination with men was increasing by the same leaps and bounds as her hormones. Jenny couldn't recall ever being quite so over-the-top about the opposite sex in general and only once about a specific man. The latter had occurred all too recently. She was still trying very hard to pretend that it was nothing more than a wild fantasy taking control of her body.

Lizzy's brow wrinkled as she peered more intently at the riders. "He looks a little like Cody, don't you think, only younger?"

Jenny sighed heavily at the description. It was Chance. It had to be. He was the only man she knew who might be mistaken for Cody. Not even Cody's own son resembled him as closely. Harlan Patrick was still gangly, while Cody, like Chance, was solid muscle.

Lizzy stared at her worriedly. "What's wrong? Do you know who it is?"

"Possibly."

"Who?"

"My hunch is you're about to meet Chance Adams."

Her sister's eyes widened. "Our long-lost cousin? The man who wants White Pines?"

"The one and only."

"Oh, dear. What do you suppose he's doing with Daddy?"

"Scoping out the property, I imagine," Jenny said wryly.

"Daddy looks okay from here. You don't suppose they fought or something, do you? Maybe Chance kidnapped him and forced him to take him on a tour."

Jenny had briefly considered the very same scenario, but it was ridiculous of course. Chance was perfectly civilized, if misguided in his intentions. Besides, from this distance, both men looked unbloodied, which must mean this first meeting had gone passably well. She would have expected as much of her father. He was an amazingly tolerant man and he'd flat out told her he was anxious to meet his nephew.

Chance, though, was another story. He was just itching for a fight. From the moment he'd explained what he was doing in Los Piños, it had been clear he wouldn't be happy until he'd paid his uncle back for the sins he believed had been committed against his father.

So what was he doing here today? Jenny wondered. Was it as simple as taking a look around? Or was he setting his plan into motion finally? And why was his gaze fixed so avidly on her as they neared? The intensity of it could have set off a forest fire from a hundred yards back. It certainly set off a lickety-split pace of her pulse.

Before Jenny could reach any conclusions about what his presence might mean, Lizzy gave an exuberant shout and raced off to meet their father. At least she was still one part little girl, Jenny thought, watching her race across the open field. Because looking at Chance unsettled her, she kept her gaze fixed on Lizzy.

Harlan bent low and gave Lizzy a hand up onto his horse, settling her on the saddle in front of him. Jenny had seen her father do the same thing a hundred times over the years, but she never failed to feel a trace of envy as she watched their rapport. Harlan might love her, might love all of them deeply, but even at twenty, Lizzy was his precious baby.

"Don't look now, but jealousy is gnawing at you," Chance observed, dismounting right beside her.

Startled by his insight and by the fact that he'd managed to sneak up on her, Jenny scowled at him. "You don't know what you're talking about."

"Oh, I think I do. You got to be queen of the roost for how long? A year, maybe two, before baby sister came along and stole your daddy's heart."

"Don't be ridiculous. I was fifteen when she was born. I was thrilled to have a baby in the house. I had no cause to be jealous."

"Maybe no cause," he said, "but jealousy's a

funny thing. It gets under the skin and eats away at logic.''

Refusing to concede he might be at least partially right, Jenny slanted a defiant look at him. ''Why are you out here today, anyway? Is this another of your less-than-subtle attempts to stir up trouble?''

''Not really. I just thought it was time to pay a friendly visit.''

''Since you claimed not to be interested in coleslaw and barbecue,'' she said, reminding him of his taunt, ''shall I assume you've come to scope out the territory for the invasion you have planned?''

He grinned at that. Jenny's traitorous heart turned an unexpected flip. For a good many years now she'd thought herself immune to a man's charms. Maybe she just hadn't met one who was half this gorgeous when he smiled. She didn't need to remind herself that this particular man was also as dangerous as a dozen rattlers. His motives were as suspect as a reformed burglar's asking to see the silver.

Harlan closed in just then. ''You two mind if I take off with Lizzy and leave you to your own devices?''

Jenny shot a panicky look at her sister. ''What about the picnic? We were just getting the food out.''

''You and Chance can have it,'' Lizzy said as she dismounted from her father's horse and climbed into the saddle on her own. ''I'd rather take a ride with Daddy. I'll eat when I get back to the house.''

''That okay with you, Chance?'' her father asked. ''I promise I'm leaving you in good hands. Jenny knows every inch of this land. She can show you anything you want to see.''

''Perfect,'' Chance said, just as Jenny prepared to utter another desperate protest.

''I really don't think—'' she tried again.

Chance cut her off. ''Cousin Jenny and I will spend the time getting to know each other,'' he said, looping an arm over her shoulder in a display of friendliness that had Lizzy smirking and their father looking a little too pleased with himself.

''I am not your cousin,'' she reminded Chance fiercely under her breath.

She promptly regretted the quick retort when she saw that it stirred a suspicious gleam in Harlan's eyes. That all-too-familiar glint confirmed her worst fears. The sneaky old matchmaker really was scheming to light a spark between her and Chance. What the devil was wrong with him? That would be like inviting the wolf to make himself at home in the henhouse and then sitting back with a glass of bourbon to watch the feathers fly.

Though he'd accepted the suggestion readily enough, Chance seemed to be wondering about his uncle's motivation, too. He followed Harlan's departure with a puzzled expression on his face. When he turned back to Jenny, though, the gleam in his eyes suggested he was far more fascinated with her than he was with Harlan's behavior.

Jenny recognized that gleam for exactly what it was. She might be living on a ranch in the middle of some half-baked deserted part of Texas, but she'd spent her first fourteen years on the streets of New York. She'd spent most of the past ten years lobbying in Washington, where the halls of Congress were every bit as mean as the streets of Manhattan. She wasn't naive. She wasn't anybody's fool. And she wasn't about to become some pawn in the war between Chance Adams and his uncle.

"Forget it," she said as firmly as if she were in the classroom and Chance were a mischievous student. She deliberately turned her back on him and busied herself with setting out the food Maritza had prepared. If it had been up to her, she would have packed it up again and headed straight for home, but she knew exactly how Chance would interpret that. He'd love to have more evidence that he disconcerted her.

"Forget what?" he inquired in a lazy way that was about as innocent as pure sin. He took a step closer, casting a shadow over her.

Jenny shivered. Her heart fluttered. Despite the unexpected chill that had come over her when he'd blocked out the sun, her skin heated. Her throat dried up like the desert in the middle of a drought.

"Whatever," she barely managed to choke out.

"You mean this?" he asked quietly as he hunkered down beside her and tucked a finger under her chin to tilt it up. He lowered his head without warning. His lips skimmed lightly over hers, teasing, taunting, until her knees felt weak and her resolve turned to mush. It was a good thing that she was already kneeling. That way, it didn't look quite so obvious when she sank spinelessly onto the blanket. Chance followed her down, his lips still firmly locked with hers.

The kiss was greedy and all-consuming. Pretty soon, with her resolve long since in tatters, Jenny lost herself in it. With a sense of wonder she discovered that his mouth felt like cool satin and tasted like peppermint. His cheeks were rough with just a hint of stubble, and his thick sun-streaked hair slid through her fingers like strands of silk. She breathed deeply and drank in the masculine scent of him, all musky heat and soap with just a hint of coconut. She smiled when she recognized that the last was sunscreen lotion.

"You smell like summer at the beach," she murmured without thinking.

A lazy smile broke over his face. "That must bring back good memories. You're actually smiling at me for a change."

Startled and furious with herself for yielding to temptation, she backed away until the width of the blanket was between them.

"It's not going to work," she declared staunchly when she finally managed to drag some air back into her lungs.

"Sure it is, darlin'," he declared with absolute confidence in his powers of persuasion.

"A kiss doesn't mean anything," she insisted.

"Maybe not one, but sometimes they start to add

up.'' He was still grinning. ''That's when things begin to get interesting.''

The comment scared her to death. She could understand exactly how that could happen. She was already growing addicted to the feel of Chance's mouth on hers. A giddy sort of anticipation rushed through her now every time she saw him. There wasn't a doubt in her mind that it could whirl out of control in no time at all.

That meant restraint was critical, she realized, her thoughts scrambling frantically in search of a plan. No more accidental encounters, though she had no idea how to go about preventing them. No more shared meals, especially not just the two of them. And absolutely positively no more kisses. That was essential.

Of course here she was, unexpectedly alone with him, an entire meal spread out on a blanket no less, and her mouth scant inches away from his and still warm from their last kiss. He looked as if he might be one breath away from stealing another.

''You're thinking too much. What's going on in that head of yours now?'' Chance asked, reaching out and brushing a strand of hair back from her cheek.

The light caress sent a jolt of pure yearning slamming through her. ''Nothing,'' she murmured shakily.

Chance sighed. ''Darlin', you are a terrible liar. Now tell me the truth. What's got you worrying? Surely it's not being out here all alone with me.''

Jenny debated attempting another lie, but in the end

she couldn't see the point to it. Obviously she was no good at it. Maybe Chance was the kind of man who would appreciate straightforward honesty. Maybe he would even respect her enough to back off and leave her alone.

"Okay, here it is. You, me, this," she said, gesturing at the blanket with an all-encompassing wave. "This is a very bad idea. Nothing can come of it, but something will."

"Not unless you want it to," Chance countered, sketching a cross over the region of his heart.

"Oh, really," she said doubtfully. "I didn't want to kiss you, but I did, not just once but...how many times now?"

"Not nearly enough."

She shot an impatient look at him. "Stop it! Aren't you hearing anything I'm saying? The way we're begging for trouble, we might as well go into the middle of the street and wait for a speeding car to knock us down."

He frowned. "I'm not sure I like the analogy."

"Then pick one of your own," she retorted. "The point is, we have absolutely no business spending even five minutes alone together."

"Because we can't keep our hands off each other?"

"Exactly. Or at least that's part of it."

"Doesn't that tell you something?" he inquired reasonably.

"It tells me we are fools. We don't want the same things in life at all."

"Of course we do."

"How can you say that?"

"We both want White Pines, don't we? Can't you think of it this way? We're just two outsiders uniting to claim what ought to be ours."

So that was his game! Jenny backed away furiously at the suggestion that somehow the two of them were alike or that they had the same underhanded mission. She stood up, towering over him as he reclined on the blanket and watched her with that knowing amused gleam still in his eyes.

"I don't have to claim a damn thing," she practically shouted, figuring it was the only way to get anything through that thick head of his. "This is my land we're on. Mine and Lizzy's and Cody's and Jordan's and Luke's. The only way you'll get so much as an inch of it is by destroying the whole lot of us."

The tirade didn't seem to upset him at all. Without missing a beat he said, "I can think of an easier, more pleasant way to accomplish my goal." His gaze swept over her, lingering on her curves with an intensity she knew was meant to rattle her.

The tactic worked. Her insides were in turmoil. Jenny's gaze narrowed. "How?"

"Marry me."

If he'd declared his intention to stage a night raid with a band of thieves at his side, she couldn't have been more shocked. "Are you out of your mind?" she demanded in a voice that shook with indignation.

He went on as if she hadn't said a word, "I'll settle for a fifth of the land, instead of half. Your fifth. You'll be protecting the interests of all the others."

"You *have* lost your mind," she said. "That's it, isn't it? You've flipped out, gone round the bend."

He shook his head. "Nope. I don't think so. In fact, I think I'm seeing things clearly for the first time in a very long time."

Jenny took a minute to grapple with his outrageous proposal. "How can you possibly think I'd marry you and turn over my share of White Pines to you?" she asked eventually.

"Simple. You love your father and this family he brought you into. Marrying me will solve all their problems. In essence I'll no longer be a threat. Everyone, especially your daddy, can rest easy again."

There was an insane kind of logic to it. Obviously he knew how much she loved her father, how desperately she wanted these last years of his life to be carefree. Yet the two of them, married? It was impossible.

"Have you actually thought about this?" she asked quietly, trying to inject a note of rationality into the conversation. "You don't even know me, much less love me. Your son hates my guts or thinks he does. I am rapidly reaching the point where I can't stand the sight of you. Besides which, it is more than likely my father would change his will and cut me out of it before the ink was dry on our wedding license.''

"That would never happen. He obviously loves you. I could see that watching and listening to the two of you just a moment ago."

"It would be a marriage made in hell," Jenny said, trying to get through to him how preposterous his idea was.

"That's what you say. I prefer to believe the evidence I discover every time you're in my arms. I think we're compatible. We'll get along."

"In bed maybe," she conceded. "But nobody spends every minute of every day in bed."

Chanced grinned. "Newlyweds do. We'll work out the rest after the honeymoon."

Jenny stared at him, waiting for the flash of humor in his eyes or the twitching of his lips to indicate he'd been teasing her. When neither happened, she whispered, "You're serious, aren't you?"

Chance hesitated, his expression thoughtful, then nodded. "It would be a solution."

"It would be a nightmare."

He reached over and folded her hand in his, then brushed a kiss across the knuckles. "Look, I'll admit the proposal was impulsive. It took me by surprise, the same as it did you. But it makes sense. Take some time to think it through. You'll agree with me. I'm certain of it."

"How long?" she asked, feeling desperate.

"Forty-eight hours. We'll go to dinner on Monday,

someplace fancy so I can order the best bottle of champagne in the house. I'll bring along an engagement ring, something big and sparkly so you can show it off to the family.''

"Save your money," Jenny responded.

"Darlin', that is not an indication of open-mindedness," Chance chided.

"The family would be appalled if I came in and announced we were getting married. They'd never believe we'd fallen in love."

"Then I guess we'll just have to figure out some way to convince them," he said, his expression unrelenting. "Your father strikes me as the kind of man who believes in love at first sight. He'll buy it. The rest will accept it because it solves a problem."

With her heart thumping unsteadily in her chest, Jenny felt as if her world was spinning wildly out of control. It was just as she'd feared. Her fate was out of her hands.

That made Chance's thoroughly relaxed demeanor all the more irritating. She needed some space. She also needed time, but he'd given her only forty-eight hours. She could have used a couple of years at least.

"I'm going home," she said abruptly.

"Before lunch?" He looked surprised. "Did something ruin your appetite?"

"You don't really want me to answer that, do you?"

"Come on, darlin'. Sit back down." He patted the space on the blanket right beside him. "Nibble at a piece of chicken at least. You don't want the house-keeper getting the idea that you and I were out here all alone and occupied with something besides lunch, do you?''

"I don't give two hoots about the food. Leave it. You eat it. Whatever. I'll make something up to tell Maritza.''

"Such as?''

"I don't know," she said impatiently. "I'll tell her a storm blew up.''

Chance gestured at the clear blue sky. "Not a cloud in sight. Come on," he coaxed. "It would be a shame to waste a perfect fall day like this.''

He held out a barbecued chicken leg. "Looks delicious." When she didn't budge, he grabbed a package of brownies and waved it under her nose. "Chocolate. Don't tell me you can resist that. Something tells me you love the stuff." He unwrapped the brownies and took a bite of one. "Moist, rich. Best I've ever had, as a matter of fact. Sure you don't want one?''

Chocolate had always been her worst weakness, at least until she'd discovered Chance's kisses.

"Oh, for goodness' sake, give me one," she said irritably, snatching a brownie out of his hand. She sat down as far from him as she could possibly get on a blanket no bigger than a twin-size bed. Her blood raced at the inadvertently provocative image. Why had she made that comparison? Why was it when she looked at Chance all she thought about was tumbling into bed with him? She finished the brownie in half a dozen bites and reached for another one.

"Settled down yet?" he inquired when she was idly picking up the last crumbs.

Her gaze snapped up and clashed with his. "I don't know what you mean."

"Sure you do, darlin'. You've been in a dither ever since I rode up. I disconcert you."

"What do you expect? You propose to me out of the blue. I think it's perfectly normal to be a little unsettled."

"Then you do admit it?"

"Okay, fine. I admit it. So what?"

"Maybe we should change the subject for a minute, talk about something that doesn't get your drawers in a knot."

"Such as?"

"This latest incident with Petey."

Jenny grinned, despite herself. "I thought you wanted to talk about something that wouldn't irritate me."

"I was just going to say that I'm on your side with this one. He told me what happened. He's being punished for it. In fact, at this very moment, he's shut up in his room with a baby-sitter standing guard."

"Oh, boy, he must hate that." Jenny could almost imagine his indignation.

"That's putting it mildly."

"You can't keep him locked up forever," Jenny said, trying not to sound too wistful.

"I suspect just this once will be enough to make my point."

The words were barely out of his mouth when a rider appeared once again from the southeast. Jenny saw at once that it was Lizzy. She'd lost her hat along the way and her black hair was streaking out behind her.

"Chance!" she shouted as soon as she was close enough. "You've got to get home right away."

Even without an explanation, her tone was so urgent they were both on their feet before the words were out of Lizzy's mouth. Chance glanced at the food containers, clearly torn.

"Go," Jenny said. "I'll take care of this."

"What happened?" he asked, picking up his horse's reins as Lizzy finally reached them.

"Your baby-sitter called. Your son's disappeared."

"Oh, no," Jenny whispered as the color washed out of Chance's face. He dumped everything into the center of the blanket and tied it into a knot, then headed for her horse. "I'm coming with you," she said as she mounted.

"This isn't your problem," Chance retorted.

"It started in my classroom. Besides, if you and I go through with this crazy notion of marrying, then Petey will be my son, too. I need to help." She rode up beside her openmouthed sister and held out the picnic blanket. "Lizzy, can you take care of this for me?"

"Sure, but…married? Did you say the two of you are getting married?"

"It's a possibility," Jenny confirmed grimly. "Keep it to yourself, though. This is one piece of news I think I'd better spread around in my own good time."

"Are you coming?" Chance demanded impatiently, his horse dancing nervously in place. "You know the way back better than I do."

"Let's go," she said, kicking her horse into a gallop.

With the wind rushing in her face, the ride could have been exhilarating. Instead, Jenny kept feeling as if she was trying to outrun her destiny. Glancing over her shoulder into Chance's anxious face, she realized it was too late. For better or worse, it had already caught up with her.

Chapter Nine

Chance was cursing himself six ways from Sunday all the way back to Wilkie's place. He should have known Petey would pull a stunt like this. The kid was developing a mile-wide rebellious streak. Chance should have stuck around himself to enforce Petey's grounding, rather than deliberately fueling the boy's unhappiness by hiring a sitter.

Not that he was about to excuse what his son had done now. He'd never struck his kid, but he was very much tempted to tan his hide for sneaking off and scaring them half to death.

The baby-sitter must be beside herself. She was Wilkie's niece and she'd been hanging around the ranch ever since Chance had been hired to run the place. He suspected from some things Wilkie had said that Leesa had a crush on him. He knew very little about teenage girls, but he did know that, aside from worrying about Petey, Leesa would be distraught over having failed him.

He hit the accelerator and pushed the truck past seventy. A glance in his rearview mirror told him Jenny was right behind him. She'd insisted on bringing her own car in case they needed to expand their search and spread out in different directions. Chance hadn't wasted time arguing with her, even though he couldn't imagine how a boy on foot could get too far. Then, again, he'd never envisioned Petey slipping out of the house undetected in the first place.

Chance made the turn into Wilkie's driveway on two wheels, spewing dirt and gravel every which way. At his first glimpse of Leesa, he pulled to a stop in front of the main house. The girl was sobbing her heart out and muttering that it was all her fault. Wilkie was making a futile attempt to comfort her and assure her that nothing she could have done would have stopped Petey from sneaking out if he was of a mind to.

Chance was out of the truck before the engine stopped rumbling and heard most of the exchange. He suspected it had become repetitive by now. Wilkie stared at him helplessly over the girl's head.

"What happened?" Chance demanded. His sharp tone brought on more tears, plus a glare from Wilkie.

Chance apologized. "I'm sorry, darlin'. Just try to fill me in, okay?"

"I...I don't know," Leesa finally said between sobs. "One minute he was there and the next—" she held up her hands "—he was gone. I thought for sure he was still in his room, but when I went up with a snack for him, he just wasn't there."

"How long had it been since you'd seen him?"

"A half hour at the most, I swear it. I was on the phone with one of my friends and he came down and asked for the snack. You'd told me he wasn't to be out of his room, so I said I'd bring it up to him. I got off the phone right away."

Which obviously meant nearly thirty minutes later, Chance guessed.

"And you didn't see him slip past you or hear anything that could have been him climbing out the window in his room?"

Leesa shook her head. "No. And the window wasn't open. I checked."

"Well, how the hell—" Chance stopped when Jenny shot him a warning glance.

Chance waited impatiently as Jenny took the girl in her arms and soothed her, while Wilkie looked on uncomfortably. Obviously he was no more at ease around a crying woman than Chance was. Leesa's sobs finally began to abate. Jenny glanced at him over her head and nodded.

"You searched the house?" Chance asked, forcing himself to remain calm.

"High and low," Wilkie said, appearing relieved that they'd finally gotten to a question he could answer. "The minute Leesa called me I went right over. Thought maybe the boy was playing some sort of game with her. You know how kids his age do. I've gone through every building on the property since I put out that call to you, but there's not a trace of him."

Wilkie's worried expression suggested there was more. "What else?" Chance asked.

"I think he took Golden Boy," the old man said. "The horse is missing from his stall, and no one recalls seeing him in the pasture, either."

"Well, isn't that just dandy!" Chance exploded. When Leesa burst into a fresh bout of tears, he reined in his temper. "Sorry, darlin', none of this is your fault. It's mine. I shouldn't have gone off today. I knew he resented being left with a baby-sitter and I did it, anyway, to make a point. I guess he's making one, too."

He drew a deep breath and tried to think. If Petey was on horseback, where would he head? He didn't know Los Piños all that well yet. How far could he venture before he became lost and confused?

"Chance?"

Jenny's soft voice snapped him back to reality. "What? Do you have an idea?" he asked.

"Does he know the way to White Pines?"

"Of course he does," he said as the obvious answer dawned on him. "And you're right. That's more than likely exactly where he'd head, because I've forbidden him to go over there.''

"Then it's even more likely he'd go if he knew that's where you'd intended to go today," she suggested. "He wouldn't want to miss the opportunity to see the ranch he'd heard so much about from his grandfather."

Chance wasn't sure if Petey had guessed his destination or not. He hadn't told him. In fact, if Petey had figured it out, then he might go anywhere except the family ranch. Chance preferred to count on the likelihood that Petey was intent on defying him. In that case, the forbidden White Pines would be the first place he'd go.

"He wasn't on the road," Chance said thoughtfully. "We'd have spotted him."

"Maybe I can help with that. He's been asking about where the White Pines property butts up against this ranch," Wilkie explained. "He seemed to know they connected somewhere. I didn't think much about it at the time, but I'll bet he was storing the information away for an occasion just like this. He probably decided that with you out of the house it would be a good time to sneak off and go exploring on the land his granddaddy had been telling him about."

"I'm sorry," Leesa whispered again. "I should have been paying closer attention."

"Don't you worry about it, princess," Wilkie said. "A boy intent on mischief will always find some way of getting into it. Isn't that right, Chance?"

"You bet." He glanced at Jenny. "You willing to ride with me to look for him?"

"Of course."

"Wilkie, can we borrow a couple of horses?"

"You bet. I'll come, too. I can show you the direction he's likely to have gone in."

"Can I help?" Leesa asked. "Please? I have to do something."

"No, you stay here in case he calls or turns up," her uncle said. "I'll stick the cell phone in my pocket so you can reach us if something happens here. You might want to call your mama and tell her what's going on so she won't worry if you're late getting back home. Tell her I'll bring you as soon as we find the boy."

The teenager looked disappointed at not being included in the search party, but she nodded. "Should I wait in his house or yours, Uncle Wilkie?"

Wilkie glanced at Chance, who nodded. "You go on back to Chance's and stay there until you hear from us."

"I'll call White Pines," Jenny said. "Daddy and Cody can round up a few men to start searching."

"Thanks," Chance said, surprised once more by the realization that his uncle probably wouldn't hesitate to offer assistance, despite their strained relationship.

"We've only got a couple of hours before dark," Wilkie said when they'd all saddled up and mounted.

"We're going to have to spread out so we can cover more ground in a hurry."

They rode over Wilkie's land toward the White Pines property line in silence. Chance was lost in thought, trying to imagine what his son had been thinking. It wasn't all that difficult to figure out really. Petey had been wanting to see White Pines. Chance had forbidden it. So, angry at his father already, he'd taken the first chance he had and gone exploring.

Chance doubted Petey would care all that much about the land or even the herds of cattle. He'd be far more interested in the house.

"Wilkie, did you specifically point the way toward the house from here?" Chance asked when they reached the fence dividing the property.

"Sure did," he said, then grinned. "I reckon the boy had a million questions about it, too. He asked if I'd ever been inside. Then he wanted to know what every single room looked like and how many outbuildings there were. Wouldn't be at all surprised if he didn't go home and map it out for himself, he was that fascinated by it."

Exactly what Chance had suspected. "Jenny, let your father know that Petey is probably peeking in his windows about now or trying to slip in the back door."

She looked over at him, then chuckled. "I'll bet you're right. That sounds exactly like what he'd do." She borrowed Wilkie's cell phone and made the call.

While they waited for word back from White Pines,

they rode at a gallop over the flat pastures. When they came to a rain-swollen stream, Jenny led them to its narrowest point and took them across. On the other side Chance reined in his horse and glanced upstream and down at the churning water.

"Stop it," Jenny said, obviously guessing the dire direction of his thoughts. "Petey's a smart kid. He would have looked for a safe place to cross. Besides, we would have spotted some sign of him if he'd tried to cross sooner than this and run into any trouble."

Chance's hand shook as he reached for a bandanna and wiped his brow. "I want to believe that."

"Then believe it. We're going to find him safe and sound at White Pines."

"Why haven't we heard something, then? Surely your father's had a chance to look around."

"There are a lot of good hiding places," Jenny said. "Especially for a kid who doesn't want to get caught."

"I agree with Jenny," Wilkie said. "You two ride on. Keep the phone with you. Just to make certain we haven't missed something, though, I'll ride along the stream for a ways."

Chance darted a worried look at the old man. "Maybe that's what I should be doing."

"No," Wilkie said firmly. "You go where it's most likely he'll be. This is just a precaution. I'll catch up with you at White Pines."

"Thanks, Wilkie," Chance said sincerely. "This means a lot to me."

"No need to thank me. Let's just find the boy safe and sound. I'm getting right fond of that rascal myself. Never realized how much I missed having kids and grandkids of my own until I started spending a little time with your boy. Leesa and her sisters are sweet girls. Their mama sees that they're real attentive to me, but it's not the same as having a child that's your own flesh and blood. And it's sure not the same as having a boy who's up to something every second."

"That's for sure," Chance said. "Petey's definitely up to something all the time."

As Wilkie headed upstream, Chance and Jenny continued on in silence.

"It's going to be okay," she said eventually.

"I know," Chance said grimly, wishing he felt more conviction.

"We'll all laugh about it someday," she promised.

"By the time I finish with him, Petey may not feel like laughing for a very long time." He slanted a look at Jenny and saw she was smiling. "I mean it," he insisted.

"I'm sure you do," she said, "now."

Chance ignored her skepticism. "Is there anywhere between here and the house he could hide?"

"No," she said with certainty. "Cody's place is in the other direction. There's not a line shack for miles. I'll lay odds he's already somewhere around the main house. If he is, Daddy or Cody will find him."

Right on cue, the cell phone rang. "Yes," Chance said tersely.

"Son, your boy's here," Harlan Adams said. "Found him poking around outside the stable trying to find a place to hide that horse of Wilkie's. He's fine. Good little cowboy, too. He saw to it his horse was fed and watered."

"Don't let him out of your sight," Chance muttered.

His uncle chuckled. "Not much chance of that. He's been pestering me with questions since he walked in the door. Soon as I get off the phone, the boy wants a top-to-bottom tour of the house."

Chance laughed, despite himself. "Watch the silverware. I wouldn't put anything past him."

"Don't you worry. I've got my eye on him."

Chance clicked the phone off and uttered a heartfelt sigh of relief.

"He's there?" Jenny asked.

"Oh, yes, and taking over, from what I gather."

"He's in good hands. Daddy's had a lot of experience with out-of-control kids."

"All those sons of his, huh?"

"Actually I was thinking about me," she admitted. "Remind me to tell you sometime about how we met."

"Tell me now," he said.

She shook her head. "Not now," she said, spurring her horse to a gallop. "I want to get to White Pines and see who's in charge."

A few months ago, even a few days ago, Chance would have said there'd be no doubt. His power-hungry uncle would never cede control to another living soul. Today's events had shaken his beliefs more than a little. For the second time since morning, he was wondering just how far his daddy had stretched the truth about what had happened all those years ago.

Jenny had seen the genuine worry etched in Chance's face while they'd searched for Petey. From the moment Wilkie had told them of Petey's questions about White Pines, she'd been less concerned, even though she knew there was a lot of room for mishaps along the route Petey had most likely taken.

Now, knowing that the boy was safely ensconced in her home with her father, she couldn't help thinking about Chance's earlier proposal. If she accepted, in no time at all Petey would be her full-time responsibility, too. Could she cope with him? Her experience with trying to control him in a classroom wasn't especially reassuring.

Far more important, though, could she deal with his father?

Riding hard after tossing that taunt at Chance, she could almost believe that the future would take care of itself. The rush of air washed the cobwebs out of her head and left her thinking more clearly. She would be able to talk Chance out of this insanity. He just needed some time to see how ridiculous a marriage between them would be.

In fact, his first clue was likely to appear any minute. She doubted Petey was going to react favorably to her arrival at White Pines. Surely one look at the two of them together would convince Chance that she was not mother material. He already had plenty of evidence of her inabilities in the classroom. All together, it ought to be enough to doom a relationship that had no business getting off the ground in the first place.

Feeling more confident, she slowed her horse as they approached the house. One of the stablehands was waiting. "I'll take care of the horses, miss. We'll trailer 'em back over to Wilkie's once he turns up."

"Thanks, Roddy. He shouldn't be too far behind us. He was going to ride downstream for a bit, then head this way."

Without a word Chance handed over the reins to his horse and bolted past her to the house. He didn't bother knocking. He just opened the front door and dashed inside. She followed at a more leisurely pace. She could hear the bursts of childish laughter even before she crossed the threshold. Obviously Petey was totally unaware or unconcerned that he was about to be at the center of a big-time fuss.

She found Chance standing at the doorway into the kitchen, mouth gaping. She slipped up beside him and peered inside.

Petey and her father were seated at the kitchen table, huge sundaes in front of them. They'd been topped with hot fudge, nuts and a mountain of whipped cream. Obviously neither Maritza nor her mother were at home, or her father would never have attempted sneaking such a high-cholesterol snack.

"Enjoying yourselves?" she asked wryly, drawing a guilty look from her father and a disgusted one from Petey.

"I thought you weren't home," the boy said accusingly as if she'd deliberately arrived just to spoil his fun. Before she could respond to that, he caught sight of his father and the color washed out of his face. "Uh-oh," he murmured.

Chance scowled. "I hope you have a whole lot more to say than uh-oh."

Petey glanced up at his great-uncle. "He's gonna kill me."

Harlan nodded, his expression bland. "That would be my guess."

"Aren't you gonna stop him?"

"I never interfere in matters between a father and his son," he claimed piously.

Jenny gave a snort of disbelief at that. Her father interfered in whatever struck his fancy. He shot her a warning look, however, that suggested she consider keeping her big mouth shut.

"Let's go, son," Chance said. "Now."

"But I haven't finished my sundae," Petey protested.

"I said now," Chance repeated emphatically. He glanced at Jenny. "Can we get somebody to drive us all back to my place so you can get your car?"

"Roddy will take us when he takes the horses," Jenny said. "As soon as Wilkie turns up."

"Wilkie's looking for me, too?" Petey asked worriedly. "How come?"

"Because you took off without telling anyone where you were headed," Chance informed him. "Leesa's half out of her mind with worry." He turned to Jenny. "Can I use a phone? I should give her a call."

"There's one on the counter over there." She pointed to it just as Wilkie walked in. He took one look at the melting sundaes in front of Petey and her father and sat down at the table.

"How 'bout fixing me up one of those? Missed my dinner riding all over the countryside."

Jenny got the distinct impression he wouldn't be budging until he had one. Her father started to get up, but she put a hand on his shoulder. "I'll do it." As Chance returned from making the phone call to Leesa, she said to him, "Wilkie wants a sundae. How about you?"

"This isn't a blasted ice-cream social," he muttered.

"Try telling Wilkie that."

Chance sighed. "Okay, okay, fix me one, too."

"Extra hot fudge, I'll bet."

He hesitated, then winked. "Make it extra whipped cream," he said, lowering his voice. "I've always thought there was something downright sensual about whipped cream."

Jenny trembled at the images he'd deliberately evoked. She'd wanted him distracted for a moment from his fury with Petey, but she hadn't intended that he focus his attention on her.

She turned her back on him and pulled the half-gallon of ice cream from the freezer. She was dishing scoops into three more bowls when Lizzy came in. She halted in the doorway and surveyed the scene before her, her gaze locked with Jenny's.

"Is this a celebration?" she asked cautiously.

Jenny knew exactly the sort of celebration Lizzy thought it might be. "Sure," she said hurriedly. "We're celebrating finding Petey safe and sound."

Lizzy nodded slowly. "I see. Nothing else?"

Jenny scowled at her sister. "Nothing," she said firmly.

Chance chuckled. "Come on, darlin'. Now that everybody's here, you might as well spill the news."

"What news?" her father said eagerly. "You two have something you want to tell the rest of us?"

"No," Jenny said flatly just as Chance said, "Yes."

"Well, which is it?" Wilkie asked.

"This is not a good time to get into it," Jenny said with a meaningful glance in Petey's direction.

Chance looked disappointed, but he backed off. "I suppose you're right. It can wait."

Petey regarded them both suspiciously. "What's going on?"

"Nothing that needs to concern you right now,"

Chance said. "In fact, if I were you, I'd be concentrating on coming up with an explanation for your behavior that'll keep me from grounding you until you graduate from high school."

Petey turned a sly look at his great-uncle. "Maybe you'd better let me move in here," he said. "I don't think it's gonna be safe for me to go home."

"Oh, I imagine you'll be safe enough," Harlan said. "But if you ever get released from your grounding, maybe your dad will let you come back to spend the night in your grandfather's old room."

Petey's eyes lit up. "You'd let me do that?"

"Of course I would."

"You should see it, Dad. It's really cool. It has posters of cowboys and stuff in it."

Jenny regarded her father with surprise. "I've never seen a room like that here." Then the explanation dawned on her. "That's the room on the third floor we were never allowed to go into, isn't it?"

Her father looked uncomfortable. "I kept it the way Hank left it. Mama tried and tried to get him to stay in one of the larger rooms on the second floor with the rest of us, but he liked being way up high. Said the housekeeper didn't like to climb all the way up there, so she never messed with his things."

Jenny heard the catch in his voice and wondered if Chance did. "You never stopped regretting that he left, did you?" she asked quietly just to be sure Chance got the message.

Her father shook his head. "In the back of my mind

I suppose I was hoping that one day he'd come home again.''

Jenny did glance at Chance then and saw that his hand shook as he put his spoon back on the table.

''It's time to go,'' he said tersely.

This time when he stood up and moved toward the door, no one argued.

Chapter Ten

Back at Wilkie's Chance saw to it that Petey apologized for worrying Leesa and then went straight to his room. Once he was assured Petey was settled in for the night, he walked Jenny to her car.

"Don't be too rough on him tomorrow," she said.

"Now that's surprising advice coming from you," he said. "I expected you to be praying I'd hog-tie him and set him up for home schooling."

A flash of humor lit her eyes. "Yes, well, that is a thought."

Her expression sympathetic, she reached up and almost put her hand on his cheek. Chance felt his heart go still as he waited for the caress that never came. She was about to pull away, when he captured her hand in his and placed it against his jaw. The reluctant touch soothed him even as it set his blood on fire.

"You'll be okay driving home?" he asked more to keep her with him than because of worry she wouldn't be perfectly safe. For reasons he hadn't had time to examine too closely, he liked being around her. It must just be the sexual attraction, he thought as she grinned and his entire body reacted.

"Chance, I've been driving these roads longer than you can possibly imagine," she assured him.

His gaze narrowed suspiciously at her amused tone. "Meaning?"

She winked at him. "I think I'll let you ponder that for a while."

"I'd stand here and try to wrangle it out of you, but I have to go in and make sure Petey is staying where I left him," he said with regret.

"I know."

"See you tomorrow?" he asked impulsively, uncertain why Monday's planned dinner suddenly seemed way too far away.

"I don't think so. We have church in the morning. The whole family comes afterward for dinner." She hesitated, then said, "You and Petey could come, too."

Chance thought about it. It would ease the family into the possibility that there was a relationship growing between him and Jenny, but he wasn't sure he wanted that to happen until he was certain what her answer to his proposal was going to be. Besides, Petey didn't deserve a return visit to the ranch so soon after today's escapade.

Nor was Chance entirely certain he was ready to butt heads with Luke, Cody and Jordan. He had a feeling they were not going to be as easily won over or as trusting as Harlan Adams appeared to be.

"Another time," he said eventually. "But you and I have a date for Monday night. Don't forget."

"I'm not likely to," she said dryly, then regarded him thoughtfully. "Of course, you probably shouldn't leave Petey with another baby-sitter."

"Nice try," he said, amused by her attempt to put off giving him an answer. "Of course, you could answer me now and get your worrying over with and save me having to lock the doors and bar the windows to keep Petey inside while we're gone."

"Maybe you ought to leave him with my father, instead. He can be an impressive disciplinarian when he puts his mind to it."

"Yeah, I noticed that tonight when he and Petey were loading up on hot-fudge sundaes. You let me take care of Petey. You concentrate on planning our wedding."

"Don't get overly confident. You gave me forty-eight hours," she reminded him. "I'm taking every one of them."

He shrugged. "Suit yourself, but in the end the answer's going to be the same. You're going to say yes."

As soon as the teasing words were out of his

mouth, Chance regretted them. Jenny was as stubborn as any Adams, and if the rest of them were anything like him, they hated being backed into a corner.

"Sorry," he said. "I didn't mean to push."

"Yes, you did, but it's okay. You come by it naturally. Fortunately I know how to push back."

He regarded her speculatively. "Will you push back if I get the notion into my head that I have to have a kiss before you drive off?"

Alarm flared briefly in her eyes, then shifted into something that might have been longing. He waited to see which turned up in her response.

"Try me," she suggested quietly.

Oddly shaken by her acquiescence, Chance didn't give her time to change her mind. He drew her at once into his arms. After taking one long, lingering look deep into her eyes, he lowered his mouth to hers. The contact sent a surge of pure adrenaline rushing through him. He was fairly certain a live wire couldn't have jolted him more.

Then Jenny was melting against him, molding her body to his and making soft little whimpering sounds in her throat. With her here in his arms, there wasn't a doubt in his mind that she wanted him as desperately as he wanted her. Every time he let her go, though, rational thought intruded, certainly for her, and, more often than not, for him.

What was he doing? The barrier between them, the one that history dictated, was growing indistinct. His proposal had been totally impulsive, an instantaneous reaction to his body's need and his obsession for White Pines. It was an incendiary combination.

He had always wondered exactly how he was going to manage to stake his claim on the ranch. This afternoon the answer had come to him like a bolt from the blue. If even so much as an acre of that land was destined to be Jenny's, then he was going to claim her—and the land right along with her.

What worried him was the increasingly distinct and totally unexpected possibility that he wasn't going to come through this maneuver unscathed. She was staking a tight-gripped claim on his heart at the same time.

No sooner had Jenny walked in the front door of White Pines after leaving Chance than whirlwind Lizzy confronted her with a barrage of questions that proved she'd inherited their mother's interrogating skills. Apparently, though, Lizzy at least kept her word about remaining silent about the possibility of Jenny's marrying Chance. Otherwise their mother would have been blasting Jenny with her share of questions.

"Would you mind telling me what the heck is going on?" her sister demanded.

Jenny deliberately misunderstood the question. "Petey ran away, he turned up here and we just took him home," she replied blandly. "Now I'm back. You knew most of that, so why are you asking?"

Lizzy impatiently waved off the evasive response. ''Not that. What about this engagement?''

Jenny sighed. ''Not now, please. You know the basics. That'll have to satisfy your curiosity. I'm tired. I'm going to bed.''

''Not until we talk. This isn't just idle curiosity,'' her sister retorted. ''A lot's at stake for all of us.''

Her chin was jutting and her eyes were flashing with determination. She might be only twenty, but she had a highly developed stubborn streak. In fact, evidence suggested she might be the most willful Adams yet, which was a very scary thought. It ought to have the men in Los Piños, maybe even in all of Texas, trembling in their boots, especially a certain rancher named Hank Robbins. Lizzy had eyes for him and she always got what she went after.

''Lizzy, please. Can't it wait?'' Jenny pleaded.

''Until when?'' Lizzy countered. ''You can't drop a bombshell like you did and then wave it off as inconsequential. Do you expect me to sit back and wait until you make an announcement to the whole family? Somebody has to try and talk some sense into you. Either you listen to me or I'll call Dani and Sharon Lynn and get them involved. We'll gang up on you.''

That threat was enough to force Jenny to detour into the living room. She sank onto a chair and held up her hands in a gesture of surrender. ''Please, leave them out of it, at least for the time being.''

''Okay, fine,'' Lizzy agreed. ''Then you can talk to me. What on earth do you think Daddy's going to say if you suddenly tell him you're going to marry Chance Adams?''

"First of all I haven't given Chance a definite answer yet. Second I have no idea what Daddy's going to say." Jenny rubbed her temples where a throbbing headache was making its presence felt. "He's unpredictable at the best of times. You saw the two of them tonight, along with Petey. Didn't it strike you that they're only a minute or two away from being thick as thieves?''

Lizzy hesitated, her expression thoughtful. "Daddy did seem to accept the two of them, didn't he?''

"Accept them? He practically invited them to move in. Maybe he figures with a couple more guys around the house, the odds will shift back in his favor and he'll get to sneak in a few more snacks.''

"Not if Mama and Maritza ever find out about tonight," Lizzy said dryly. "They'll padlock the refrigerator.'' Her gaze narrowed. "How did we get away from this marriage business? What exactly happened after Daddy and I rode off and left the two of you? Don't leave out any of the details, either. I'd have laid odds you were going to throttle each other, not get all lovey-dovey.''

"That would have been my choice," Jenny admitted. "Chance had other ideas.''

"Details," Lizzy reminded her.

"Are you sure you're not just being nosy?''

"Jenny!''

"Okay, okay. We were talking and then, out of

nowhere, he asked me to marry him. It's as simple as that." And as complicated, Jenny thought. She knew the proposal had nothing to do with love and everything to do with a backdoor way for Chance to get exactly what he wanted.

Unfortunately she could also see that it was the safest way to ensure that he caused her father the least amount of stress. She couldn't tell Lizzy or anyone else any of that. If she agreed to this idiotic scheme, everyone had to believe it was because she'd fallen head over heels in love with the man. Just thinking of the lies she was going to have to tell made her headache throb harder.

"Jenny, what is it?" Lizzy asked worriedly.

Jenny managed a smile. There was no point in upsetting her sister, an idealistic young woman who still had stars in her eyes when it came to romance.

"Nothing," she assured Lizzy.

"It doesn't look like nothing," her sister insisted. "A marriage proposal, especially from a certified hunk like Chance Adams, ought to make you deliriously happy. I've never seen you look sadder."

And possibly wiser, Jenny thought. In all of her thirty-five years she had never once fallen madly in love. Now when her skittering pulse told her she might be on the verge of it, the man turned out to be one who could never truly love her back.

Jenny hadn't slept a wink the past two nights. Sunday, with all the family gathered around and bursting with questions about Chance and Petey, had been filled with tension. She was so on edge she was afraid her nerves would snap like old rubber bands.

Nor could she manage to concentrate for more than a minute at a time in class on Monday. Naturally the kids spotted the weakness right away and set out to exploit it. She'd lost all semblance of control by lunchtime.

Fortunately one of the other teachers was scheduled to supervise the cafeteria. Jenny, however, refused to subject her to these pint-size terrors. They were going to be on their best behavior or she was going to quit her job and find a cabin in the wilderness to hide out in until she could restore her self-respect. Preferably it would be a cabin that Chance would never in a million years be able to find.

Clinging to her sanity by a thread, she looked at the restless students and managed to demand quiet in a tone that suggested a definite lack of tolerance for disobedience. It took several minutes, but they eventually settled down.

She regarded them evenly. "If I so much as hear a whisper about any of you misbehaving during lunch," she said quietly, "you'll have enough homework this week to keep you glued to your books at home until bedtime. Got it?"

"Yes, ma'am," Felicity said dutifully.

"Oh, stuff a sock in it," Petey muttered to the little redhead.

"Yeah, stuff a sock in it," several others chimed in.

Jenny sincerely wanted to echo the thought, but it would set a very bad example, one that would more than likely be dutifully reported to Felicity's father, the principal from hell.

Instead, she said mildly, "We're not getting off to a very good start here." She directed a stern look straight at Petey, who turned red, but remained silent.

"That's better. Petey, why don't you lead the line to the cafeteria?"

"Huh?" He stared at her, clearly amazed that he was being chosen for this important role.

She stood up and moved to the door. "Right here, okay?"

He glanced at Timmy McPherson, who was making faces, but he eventually joined her. She nodded. "Good. Now everyone else. A nice straight line, if you please. Timmy, you be last so you can make sure everyone is together."

That ought to keep enough distance between her two worst troublemakers, she thought, pleased with the ingenuity of her plan.

She actually managed to get them into the cafeteria without further mishap. When they were all settled at tables, she turned to Megan Richards, the sixth-grade teacher. "They're all yours."

Megan chuckled. "You sound relieved. Bad morning?"

"You'll never know how bad."

"Oh, I think I will. There are some days it just doesn't pay to get out of bed."

Jenny grinned. "And some that are worse."

She spent the next half hour praying the aspirin she'd taken would kick in and relieve the headache that had started two nights before and continued unabated. Naturally the pills didn't help at all, and before she knew it she was back in the classroom with twenty-five kids who'd all had too much sugar for lunch. If she'd had the strength herself, she would have taken them for a long brisk walk to burn off a little of their energy.

Instead, she gave them a very long reading assignment and then sank into the chair behind her desk. She was so grateful for the blessed silence that followed that she let the students keep on reading until the final bell rang. Eager faces turned to her expectantly. She grinned. At least she'd accomplished one thing this year. They no longer bolted for the door at the first sound of the bell. It gave her the illusion of control. It was a reassuring way to end the day.

"You may be excused," she said, trying not to cover her ears to block out the ensuing sounds of chaos.

Everyone was gone in a matter of minutes. Except Petey, she realized, who was still lurking in the doorway.

"You'd better hurry, Petey. You'll miss your bus."

"Dad said you'd give me a ride."

Jenny stared. "He what?"

"If you don't want to or something, it's okay," he said a little too eagerly. "Like you said, I can still catch the bus."

What on earth was Chance up to now? Jenny wondered. He must have a reason for manipulating the two of them together like this. Maybe he wanted to ensure that Petey made it home and didn't trust him to take the bus. Or maybe he was simply hoping they'd find some way to get along. That did make sense, though she couldn't help resenting him for making the decision without consulting her. What if she'd had other plans this afternoon? What if, for instance, she'd been in a rush to get home and get ready for the most important date of her life?

"I can take you," she said, as much to prove she wasn't anxious to get dressed for the evening as anything else. "I'll just be a minute."

She gathered up the papers she intended to grade later that night after her command dinner date, along with her purse and coat, and headed for the door. Petey trailed behind her until they were well out of sight of the kids still lingering in front of the building.

"How did you enjoy visiting White Pines Saturday?" she asked when they were settled in her car.

"It's cool," Petey said, then immediately looked guilty as if he shouldn't admit he'd enjoyed himself.

"I think my dad really liked showing you around," Jenny said. "He thinks you're a pretty terrific kid."

Petey looked at her with surprise. "He said that?"

"Sure. He told me so first thing on Sunday. Besides, why wouldn't he like you?"

"I dunno. I just thought, you know, because of my granddad and everything, that he'd be mad I came over."

"Did he seem mad?"

Petey paused, his expression thoughtful. "No, not really."

"There, you see?"

"Could I ask you something?"

"Of course."

He regarded her worriedly. "Do you think my granddad would be mad that I, you know, ate ice cream there and kinda hung out with your dad?"

Jenny hesitated. "Well, I never knew your granddad, but it seems to me it's always best if people get to know each other and try to understand each other. I think he'd be proud you did that."

The concept seemed to startle Petey. "Really?"

"Absolutely. I think it was good that you came, although it might have been better if you'd had your dad's permission."

"Yeah, no kidding," Petey said. "He was really mad at me."

"Because you scared Leesa and him and all the rest of us."

He glanced at her in astonishment. "You, too?"

"Of course, me, too."

"Why?"

The question stymied Jenny. Obviously Petey was

smart enough to realize he'd caused her nothing but trouble. He also knew it wasn't likely to endear him to her. "Because you are a terrific kid," she said eventually. "Even if you've done everything in your power to hide that fact from me."

"I don't get it," he said, clearly confused by her reaction. "I figured you must hate me."

"No way. I may not like some of the things you've done, but I've tried to understand why you've done them. I'm still working on that part. Maybe you could explain it to me."

"You mean like why I cut off Mary's hair?"

"Uh-huh. We could start with that."

"It was a dare, kinda." He slanted a look at her. "Pretty dumb, huh?"

"Pretty dumb," Jenny agreed.

"That's what Dad said. I did apologize, though." He made a face. "Now Mary has a crush on me."

Jenny grinned. "I noticed."

"She's been following me around and stuff and she's always asking me to do things with her, like come over to her house or go out for pizza with her mom and dad."

"Would that be so terrible? Mary seems like a nice girl."

Petey looked horrified. "But that's just it. She's a *girl*."

"Someday you'll be grateful for that," Jenny promised as they turned into the driveway at Wilkie's. She saw Chance come out of the barn and start toward them. Petey bounded out of the car and headed for the house with no more than a wave the instant the car rolled to a stop.

"He must be anxious to get to his homework," Chance said dryly.

"Or away from me," Jenny countered. "How come you didn't let him ride the bus? Were you hoping we'd get to know each other better?"

"That's one possible outcome," he agreed. "But I was also hoping it would give me a chance to catch a glimpse of you before tonight."

His heated gaze seemed to burn straight through her. "Really?" she asked, sounding disgustingly breathless.

"In fact, forget about later," he said, moving closer to the car and reaching through the window to cup her face between his hands. "I think maybe I'll just steal a kiss right now—you know, to tide me over."

Jenny decided it was way past time to show a little of her old familiar spunk. As he ducked his head in the window, she twisted just beyond his reach. His kiss landed in the air near her ear. His expression of astonishment was worth every bit of awkward maneuvering.

"You're getting just a little too full of yourself," she told him, extraordinarily pleased with herself for the first time in weeks. She'd always had gumption to spare. It was about time she demonstrated it.

Chance's gaze narrowed. "Meaning?"

"You're a bright man. Figure it out." She put the

car into gear and inched it away from him. He stared after her in openmouthed astonishment.

"I'll pick you up at six," he called after her.

Feeling downright giddy from her first tiny victory, Jenny shook her head. "I'll meet you at seven."

"Do I at least get to pick the place?" he asked, visibly irritated.

Given the amazingly limited number of choices, Jenny figured she could allow him that much. "Sure. Why not?"

"Chandler's Steak 'n' Ribs?"

That was perfect, she thought. No one in the family ever went there. They preferred their steaks from their own cattle and cooked on a backyard grill. Chandler's was forty miles away, but it boasted the only fancy meals to be had without going all the way to Fort Worth. For just an instant Jenny regretted that they wouldn't be making the trip in one car.

"Want to change your mind about going with me?" he asked as if he'd read her mind.

"I don't think so. In this part of the country, that's just around the corner," she said.

He grinned. "Suit yourself."

Jenny gave a little nod. "From now on that's exactly what I intend to do."

Chance tilted his head and regarded her quizzically. "Darlin', that almost sounds like a warning."

She grinned. "Good ear."

"You're playing with fire. You know that, don't you?"

"Of course," she said airily. "What fun is life if you're not living on the edge?"

Chance chuckled. "Don't look now, but you're about to topple over."

"Is that supposed to scare me?"

"It should."

"It doesn't. How about you?"

"Darlin', I've been flat out terrified from the minute we met."

The heartfelt admission had Jenny humming all the way to White Pines. This evening might just turn out a whole lot better than she'd anticipated.

Chapter Eleven

Something about Jenny had changed, Chance thought. It wasn't just that she'd deliberately avoided his kiss, although that had been disconcerting enough. It was her whole attitude. It had undergone a radical shift. It was as if she'd discovered she held some sort of power over him.

Had he been that transparent? Had she guessed that his feelings for her weren't based entirely on his obsession with the family ranch? Or had the implications of the obsession itself finally registered? Had she concluded that she had something he wanted and that she might as well make that work to her advantage? Maybe she knew more about power and control than he'd realized.

Whichever it was, dinner promised to be darned interesting. He was looking forward to it.

Ironically, after this afternoon he wasn't nearly as certain that the outcome would be what he'd imagined. While that would be disappointing in the short term, it presented him with an absolutely fascinating long-term challenge.

If Jenny turned him down, he'd just have to figure out another way to get what he wanted. What confused him was that he was no longer quite as sure whether that was Jenny or White Pines.

He was still trying to figure out what to make of the change in Jenny as he followed the directions Wilkie had given him to the steakhouse. After thirty minutes or so, he spotted the neon sign and turned into the huge parking lot that was already crowded with cars and a few tractor trailers, hinting that not only was the food superb, but that the atmosphere wasn't pretentious. To his way of thinking that was an ideal combination.

He glanced around the parking lot but didn't immediately spot Jenny's impractical little sports car. Disappointed, he headed toward the door to wait for her inside. Before he could get it open, though, he heard the familiar roar of her engine and the squeal of her tires as she braked none too gently less than a half-dozen spaces away from the entrance. There was absolutely nothing prim and prissy about the way the woman drove, he thought, smiling. Just more evi-

dence of the passion churning inside her, waiting to
be unleashed by the right man.

A moment later the sight of her wiped the smile
off his face. In fact, it was all he could do to breathe.

When she exited the car, her legs bared by an
astonishingly short skirt and emphasized by very
slinky high heels, Chance's mouth gaped and his
heart thundered in his chest. As desperately as he
wanted to survey those long shapely legs, he also
wanted to get her inside where they would be safely
tucked under a table and out of view of every other
male.

With her high cheekbones touched by blush and
framed by wisps of black hair, and her lipstick a
brighter shade than she usually wore, she was dev-
astatingly beautiful and stunningly sexy, the kind of
sexy that no twenty-year-old understood. It came with
maturity and experience and confidence.

How had he ever thought of her as prim and prissy?
he wondered. If someone had slapped a picture of her
on a calendar, men around the world would have been
panting over her.

As she walked up beside him, she patted his cheek
gently. "Don't look now, but you're practically
drooling," she said, then sashayed straight on past
with a provocative sway of her hips.

Obviously she was aware of the effect she'd created, he thought. It appeared, in fact, that she'd
worked on this new image just to unnerve him.

"What have you done to yourself?" he asked, his

tone grim as he followed her, his gaze locked on her backside. He was tempted to strip off his jacket and drape it around her waist to prevent others from seeing that tempting little behind.

She glanced over her shoulder. Eyes wide, she stared at him innocently. "It's an important night, isn't it? And this is a nice restaurant. I thought I'd dress up for the occasion."

"You barely dressed at all," he muttered, suddenly aware that the dazzling hot pink top she'd chosen to wear with that thigh-skimming skirt barely reached her waist. With every move she made an inch or more of flesh was displayed. Forget the jacket. He was sorely tempted to throw his arms around her to cover her up. Unfortunately he wasn't at all certain his motives were entirely pure. He wanted to touch that silken skin very very badly.

He was so busy fighting his own base desire that the hostess had to ask twice if they had a reservation before her question registered. He nodded mutely.

"Adams," Jenny supplied, looking highly amused.

"Oh, of course. Right this way," the woman said, looking Chance over approvingly.

He hardly noticed. Mouth dry and heart hammering, his gaze was glued to the sensual sway of Jenny's backside as she walked to the table. Women should be banned from wearing heels that high, he concluded, at least out in public. It did something to them, to the way they moved, that was downright indecent. His blood was humming so fast and furiously and he was so close to being fully aroused it was embarrassing.

"You did this on purpose, didn't you?" he demanded when the hostess had gone.

"Did what?"

"Wore that outfit."

She regarded him innocently. "I bought this outfit on my last trip to New York. I found it in a perfectly respectable department store. I've worn it before and no one's complained. What's wrong with it?"

"There's not enough of it."

Her laugh was low and throaty and sexy. Was that new, too? Had she set out to torment him tonight? If so, she was doing a fine job of it. He fingered the ring he'd tucked in his pocket and wondered if he truly had lost his mind to even consider marrying this woman. She was entirely too disconcerting. She'd keep him tied in knots.

"You look uneasy," she observed, that amused glint flashing in her eyes again.

"Do I?" He barely resisted the need to lick his suddenly parched lips.

"Is there some problem I don't know about?"

"Problem?" he echoed. "No, there's no problem." He sucked in a deep breath and deliberately opened the menu. Maybe if he focused his attention on T-bones and porterhouses, he'd regain his equilibrium.

Suddenly he felt the skim of a stocking-clad foot up his calf and almost bolted from his chair. A light sweat broke out on his brow as he tried to pretend he'd noticed nothing. The amused smirk on Jenny's face suggested that she knew exactly how she was affecting him and that she was enjoying the heck out of it.

Of all the times for the woman to discover the power of her own sensuality, he thought despondently. As he knew all too well, power was a heady thing.

All he'd ever wanted was a simple little marriage of convenience, maybe a little revenge. There was no longer anything remotely simple about this. As for revenge, at the moment Jenny was having the last laugh.

Okay, he thought, trying to adjust to her unexpected new tactics. Two could play at this game. He was willing to bet he'd had a whole lot more experience.

He slid one hand beneath the table and reached for her thigh. He brushed a light caress from her kneecap to the hem of her skirt, all the while keeping his gaze fixed on the menu selections. Her sharp gasp and sudden shift indicated he'd made his point. Retaliation could be rather sweet, he concluded, repeating the caress just for the sheer fun of it.

"Have you found anything that appeals to you?" he inquired lightly.

She swallowed hard and avoided his gaze. Chance grinned and deliberately gave her knee a last little squeeze. Check and checkmate.

A small country band started to play just then, a

provocative slow song about lost love and second chances. Chance figured the opportunity was too good to pass up. He'd managed to turn the tables and disconcert her a little. Maybe he could actually manage to recapture the edge he'd lost.

"Care to dance?"

Her gaze flew to his. Her panicky expression suggested she'd rather be buried in mud and left to swelter in the noonday sun.

"We haven't even ordered," she protested.

"There's no rush. I hate to waste a song as pretty as this one. Makes me think of slow lovin' and long nights," he whispered, his gaze locked with hers. He stood up and held out a hand. "Come on, darlin'. Let's see how you move on a dance floor."

Apparently he put a little too much challenge into his tone, because her eyes suddenly flashed fire. She slapped her hand in his and rose gracefully, slipping her foot back into her shoe before following him into the middle of the handful of couples already dancing.

With those heels on, she was only an inch or two shorter than he was. Chance slid his arms around her waist. Jenny hesitated a beat, then tucked her head into his shoulder. She looped her hands behind his neck. Her warm breath feathered against the V of bare skin where his shirt collar was open. That whisper of air stirred him as effectively as a caress.

In no time he was surrounded by the daring come-hither scent of her perfume. No rose garden had ever smelled so inviting. Her body heat beckoned to him.

In a matter of seconds she was fitted to him as intimately as if they'd been carved from a single piece of wood and were destined to link up curve to curve like an interlocking puzzle.

He was no longer sure which of them had started the game or whether it even mattered. All he knew was the desperate hunger to finish it, in bed, her arms and legs wrapped tightly around him. If he'd been convinced she would agree to it, he would have made a dash for the nearest motel room and to hell with dinner. But he wasn't feeling quite that confident.

The music came to a slow sensual conclusion. For an instant Chance couldn't bring himself to release her. He had the feeling he'd just glimpsed heaven, but it was elusive yet. Another minute, maybe two, and he was all but certain it would be his.

"Chance?" she murmured.

"Hmm?"

"The music's over." There was a breathless catch in her voice.

He grinned, aware she couldn't see it. "I know."

"Shouldn't we go back to the table? People are staring."

"Don't tell me the infamous Jenny Adams is scared of being the talk of the town."

She sighed and her breath feathered against his throat. "Being talked about is the least of my concerns."

"Oh?"

She tilted her head and gazed at him innocently.

"It's just that I'm getting a really desperate need to strip naked and have my way with you."

Chance fought the urge to shout, "Hallelujah!" and bolt from the restaurant with Jenny in his arms. Instead, he met her gaze and said, "If that's a genuine offer, darlin', we can be out of here before the next tune starts."

A trace of worry skittered across her face, but she never lowered her gaze. "Without dinner?" she asked, then added in a tone usually reserved for seduction, "I'm starved."

Very brave, very cool, he thought. Only a faint tremor in her voice suggested she was at all fearful about his possible response. He grinned. This tit-for-tat banter was escalating nicely. It would be interesting to see which of them backed out of the game first. His money was on Ms. Adams. She was good, but it was clear to him she was new to the technique. He doubted she'd have the nerve to stay the course.

"Now that you mention it, sustenance is probably a good idea," he said softly, "especially if this evening's destined to end the way you've been hinting."

Turning, he kept one hand clasped firmly in his and led the way back to their table. As he seated her, he bent down and brushed a kiss across the nape of her neck. She gave a start as if he'd touched her with a branding iron.

"You're a little jumpy, darlin'. Anything wrong?"

She swallowed hard. "Not a thing," she said, her voice breathless.

"Good. I'd suggest you go for a nice big steak. That ought to tide you over till morning, no matter how much activity the night holds."

"I'll have a salad," she said, her expression defiant. "A small house salad."

"At the rate things are going, that won't sustain you through foreplay."

"It will sustain me just fine," she insisted stubbornly.

He shrugged. "Suit yourself. How about an appetizer at least? Maybe some oysters?" he suggested. "I hear they have some interesting side effects."

"Don't you ever think about anything except sex?" she muttered.

"Not when someone's signaling the way you've been tonight," he replied blandly. "Once that track's been laid down, I'm more than willing to ride it to the end." He regarded her innocently. "Unless, of course, you've been playing some sort of game here. Have you?"

"No, of course not," she said firmly.

He gave her an encouraging smile. "Good."

She met his gaze boldly. "Have you?"

"Absolutely not."

"Fine."

When their waiter came, Chance ordered a beer for himself and white wine for Jenny. While they waited for the drinks, he let the silence linger and swell. He wanted her to sit and worry about just what she'd gotten herself into. In truth he could use the time to try to figure out just how far he was going to press this game she'd started.

On a purely physical level he wanted her so badly he ached. That much was straightforward and clear-cut. On an emotional level it was a hell of a lot more complicated. Why? Because something told him that once he slept with Jenny Adams, nothing would ever be simple again.

Jenny had recognized the mistake she'd made the minute she'd seen the flare of heat in Chance's eyes as she'd walked across the parking lot. Everything that had happened since pretty much proved she had dangerously miscalculated.

All she'd intended was to throw the man off-kilter, maybe get the upper hand for the first time since they'd met. She'd planned on engaging in a little light flirtation, a little blatant seduction, maybe even indulging in a breath-stealing kiss or two just for the pure exhilaration of it.

It had stopped being fun and started throwing up very serious warning signals the minute she'd seen that avid look in his eyes. He was a whole lot better at flirtation and seduction than she was. She'd turned weak-kneed and muddle-brained the minute he'd touched her. It had required every ounce of willpower she possessed and then some to insist on having dinner, rather than racing him to the nearest bed.

And then, out of pure cussedness, she'd ordered an itty-bitty house salad. How long could it possibly take to eat a handful of lettuce leaves and a couple of cherry tomatoes? Fifteen minutes if she dragged it out? She should have ordered a half-dozen courses, starting with an appetizer and going all the way through to dessert and coffee.

Well, there was still time to insist on looking over the dessert cart. Maybe she'd order a huge bowl of fresh strawberries with whipped cream and linger over them for at least an hour. She glanced up at Chance and noted that he was watching her with his usual amused expression. Forget the whipped cream, she thought, as a vision of Chance slowly licking it off her surfaced and shot her temperature up several degrees.

"Something worrying you?" he inquired.

Jenny smiled brightly. "Not a thing." She lifted her wineglass, the only one she intended to allow herself all evening. "Nice wine."

"We should have ordered a bottle," Chance said.

"One glass is plenty. I'll nurse it."

"You've already finished all of it but the last swallow," he pointed out.

Jenny stared at the glass in astonishment. The wine was gone. She must have tossed back most of it when her throat went dry under Chance's intense scrutiny.

"Oh, well," she said with a shrug. "I guess it's water for me for the rest of the meal." She picked up her glass and drained it, then glanced around desperately for a waitress to refill it with lots and lots of ice.

"You're sure?" he asked.

"Absolutely. I never drink more than one when I'm driving."

He nodded. "Smart thinking. Too bad we didn't come together. Then I could be the designated driver. Maybe, though, if you had another glass of wine, you'd relax."

Relax? No way. In fact, Jenny thought, coming separately might have been the one bright decision she'd made all day. Surely whatever amorous notions either of them entertained would die out on the long lonely drive back home. That was her safety net, her one guarantee that no matter how far she went flirting, she could get home without giving in to his lust and her increasingly persistent hormones.

He sat back in his chair and observed her with that all-too-familiar irritatingly smug expression. Jenny resisted the urge to squirm.

"Okay," she finally said. "Just spit it out."

"What?"

"Whatever's on your mind. You're the one who insisted on getting together for dinner."

"And you're the one who was supposed to come prepared to answer a question," he reminded her. "Have you thought about it?"

Jenny decided to be deliberately dense. She'd thought about his proposal until her head was spinning. She hadn't come up with an answer she could live with, not without feeling as if she was betraying someone, either her family or herself.

"What question?" she asked.

He shook his head, his expression sorrowful. "Oh, darlin, you can do better than that."

"No," she said stubbornly. "I think you ought to repeat the question just so I'm sure you haven't changed your mind or something. Spell out all the terms so we're clear on what sort of arrangement you're making."

"Arrangement? I suppose that's one word for it," he said. "Okay. Whatever you say, darlin'."

Before she realized what he intended, he was out of his chair and down on one knee next to her. He had a small jewelry box in one hand. When he flipped open the lid, the most gorgeous diamond ring she'd ever seen was displayed. The sight of its glittering beauty took her breath away. The implication of it left her speechless. She had never really expected him to carry things this far. She'd all but convinced herself he'd been teasing her.

She sighed at the folly of her thinking. That ring was no joke.

"Jenny Adams, will you marry me?" he asked loudly enough to draw attention.

Jenny could feel at least a dozen pairs of eyes turn toward the two of them expectantly. Silence fell in their corner of the restaurant. She wasn't absolutely certain, but she was relatively confident this was the most humiliating moment of her life. She'd been at the center of a fair amount of gossip over the years, but this scene promised to be the story that lingered.

"Get up," she hissed under her breath.

"Not until you give me an answer."

"Please," she begged.

"Only if you take the ring and try it on," he said.

"That's blackmail."

He grinned. "Yep. As you've reminded me more than once, I'm good at it."

Jenny debated doing absolutely nothing and seeing how long Chance would stay right where he was. This had to be humiliating for him, too.

Apparently not, she realized when he still hadn't budged a couple of minutes later. Unfortunately she wasn't made of the same stuff. The attention from all the other diners was way too embarrassing. She wanted to get this farce over with. Her left hand trembled, but she held it out.

Chance took the ring out of the box and slowly slid it onto her finger. The contrast of cool metal and his warm skin set off gooseflesh. His gaze locked with hers and she found she couldn't quite bring herself to look away. Chance, however, did. He gazed at the ring, which sparkled brightly even in the dimly lit restaurant.

"A perfect fit," he murmured.

Jenny choked back a bubble of panic deep in her throat and followed the direction of his gaze. The ring was spectacular and fit as if it had been made for her hand. She recalled how many times as a girl she'd taken out the engagement ring her mother had put away after her divorce from Jenny's father. She had slipped it on and imagined the day when she would have a ring of her own, given to her by a man who worshiped her. Now that moment was here, and the man cared more about her prospective inheritance than he did about her. Rather than the ecstasy she'd once imagined feeling, she wanted to cry.

Before she could make a complete fool of herself by bursting into tears, everyone surrounding them assumed that her decision had been given. They all broke into applause. A bottle of champagne arrived at the table, a gift from the management. Jenny felt like the worst kind of fraud, but at least Chance made good on his promise. He went back to his seat. He just didn't release her hand. For some reason, the warmth of his grip felt reassuring.

Now that she'd gotten her way, Jenny was almost tempted to rip the ring from her finger before she became too comfortable wearing it. Something in Chance's expression stopped her. He looked almost shaken, as if he, too, was being torn by unexpected emotions.

"Don't take it off," he said quietly as if he'd guessed her intentions.

"Chance—"

"Please. Think it over at least."

"I've *been* thinking it over."

"Doesn't the fact that you couldn't say no outright tell you something?"

"It tells me that I love my family, that I would do almost anything in the world to prevent them from being hurt.'' Her voice broke as she again fought back tears.

''Is that all?'' he asked doubtfully.

She stared back at him defiantly. ''What else could it be?''

''Maybe, just maybe, there's a part of you that wants to marry me for your own sake.''

''Marry a man who's blackmailing me?'' she asked incredulously. ''You must be crazy.''

''I don't think so. The attraction's there, darlin'. If you're honest with yourself, you can't deny it.''

''Attraction's not a reason to get married. Attraction can burn itself out way too fast.''

''You want love, then? I'm surprised. I didn't peg you as a romantic.''

''Every woman's a romantic.''

''I don't know. I've met a few who were driven more by ambition and greed. Their matches weren't made in heaven. They were mergers. That's what ours could be. We'd be great partners, Jenny.''

Her heart sank at the cool assessment of their future, the bland definition of their relationship. She didn't want a partner, at least not a business partner. She wanted a man in her life who loved her. She wanted passion and excitement.

Chance could give her the passion. She had very little doubt about that, but would it be enough if there was no love behind it? No matter how desperately she wanted to help her family, she couldn't compromise on that. Deep in her heart, she knew her father would understand and forgive her.

She took one last longing look at the ring Chance had given her, then slowly twisted it off and held it out in the palm of her hand. "I can't accept it," she said quietly.

"Not even to save White Pines," he said, clearly stunned.

With tears in her eyes she shook her head. "God help me, not even for that."

SHERRYL WOODS   210

must on that idepath in her head, she knew her only
would understand and forgive her.
She took one last lingering look at the man Chance
had given her, then slowly dropped it off and held it
in the palm of her hand. "Then I accepted," she
said quietly.
"I've even so said. Whoa? Then?" he said, almost
stunned.
Mila tears in her face she shook her head. "She
said the, just even for him.

Chapter Twelve

Chance watched in stunned silence as Jenny picked up her purse and left the steakhouse. One part of him wanted desperately to stop her. Another part told him he'd escaped disaster by the skin of his teeth. The contrary forces kept him immobilized as she walked away.

"Sir, is there anything I can get you?" the waitress inquired solicitously. Her tone held just a hint that she could cure all his ills.

Chance tried to work up some enthusiasm for that possibility, but he couldn't. Mindless mutually satisfying sex wasn't the answer to what ailed him. Nor was alcohol, though he did gaze longingly at the row of liquor bottles behind the bar.

"Just the check," he told the obviously disappointed waitress. He read her name tag for the first time. "Thanks, Thelma."

"You bet, handsome. If you change your mind, let me know. I know all about making a man feel better."

Responding automatically, Chance grinned. "I'll bet you do, sweetheart, but it would be wasted on me tonight."

Thelma left and returned in minutes with his check, then asked, "Mind if I give you some advice?"

Chance figured he was at such a low point he'd take advice from wherever it came. "Go right ahead."

"Forget about her. She looks a little stuck-up to me, like she's better than the rest of us."

Chance thought about Jenny turning down marriage and a chance to save her family's ranch, all because she still believed in the happily-ever-after kind of love.

"Maybe she is," he said quietly.

Maybe his priorities were the ones that were all messed up. There'd been a time when he'd been lucky enough to love a woman and have her love him back, heart and soul. With his beloved Mary he'd known the joy of that kind of marriage firsthand. What kind of man would trade that for a piece of land he'd never set eyes on until a few months back? What kind of man expected a woman to sacrifice such deep emotions? He wasn't crazy about the answer that came to him.

He tossed a handful of bills on the table. "See you," he said to Thelma as he slid away from the table.

"Anytime, lover. You know where to find me."

Chance appreciated the invitation, but he knew he'd never take her up on it. Unfortunately the woman who'd taken him totally by surprise and managed to get under his skin had just walked out on him. And he had some long hard thinking to do before he made up his mind what—if anything—to do about it.

"How was your date with Chance?" Lizzy demanded before Jenny was even through the front door.

Jenny frowned. She really didn't want to do a postmortem of the evening, not with her curious younger sister. She didn't want advice or pity or sympathy. She didn't want to have to explain her decision, not when she wasn't entirely sure she understood it herself.

"Were you waiting up for me?" she asked testily. "Don't you have better things to do?"

"Who's waiting up?" Lizzy retorted, instantly defensive. "It's barely ten o'clock." She studied Jenny worriedly. "Didn't it go well? Did you two fight? Or did you finally come to your senses?"

Jenny thought back over the evening, from its promising, even stimulating beginning, all the way to the disastrous ending when she had made her decision and walked out on Chance. She could still remember the way that diamond ring had felt on her finger and the husky note in Chance's voice when he'd slid it on. If only...

She brought herself up short. There were no *if onlys* here. Chance wanted White Pines, not her, and she wasn't about to become a pawn in his game. That was that. Sooner or later she would have to tell her father what had happened. She would have to warn him that Chance might be more vindictive than ever since she'd thwarted his scheme.

Just not tonight. Tonight she didn't want to think any more about Chance Adams at all. She wanted to sink into the oblivion of sleep. Maybe if she slept deeply enough, she wouldn't dream about the promise and hope that ring could have represented if their lives had been different and both their last names hadn't been Adams.

"I'm going to bed," she told Lizzy.

"But—"

"Good night," Jenny said firmly. "I'll see you tomorrow."

Lizzy seemed about to protest, but Jenny's expression must have warned her to save it. Instead, she pulled Jenny into a fierce hug.

"I love you. Remember that. And so does everyone else in the family. It's not up to you to save us all by yourself. It never has been."

Jenny smiled wanly. "I know." She only wondered how sorely tested that love was going to be when the others learned the truth about what she'd done tonight, when they realized she could have protected White Pines and hadn't done so.

Jenny hadn't thought it possible, but Tuesday turned out to be an even worse nightmare than Monday had been. Petey was so completely out of control, so totally defiant, that by noon she'd marched him down to the principal's office and left him there, ignoring Patrick Jackson's expression of triumph. Obviously the principal was pleased she'd lost control again.

Petey looked slightly chagrined when she went to get him after lunch. In fact, he even apologized, albeit halfheartedly.

"I didn't mean to make Felicity cry," he told her as they walked back to the classroom together. "But she's such a little suck-up." He slanted a look at Jenny. "I told Mr. Jackson that, too. I guess I sort of forgot he's her dad. I thought for sure he was gonna have a stroke."

Jenny had to work very hard not to laugh. "I can imagine," she said.

Jenny actually shared Petey's opinion of Felicity, but that didn't excuse Petey's tormenting the child earlier by stealing her homework and making all her answers incorrect. Felicity, who prided herself on her neatness, had been humiliated not just by the inexplicable mistakes on her papers, but by the sloppiness of the work. She'd been in tears when Jenny had insisted she hand the paper in or get an *F* on the assignment.

One look at the messy work and Jenny had guessed what had happened. One look at Petey's smug expression and Timmy McPherson's triumphant one had confirmed it. Getting Petey to admit he was responsible had been traumatic for all the students, every one of whom she'd threatened with detention if someone didn't confess.

She glanced at Petey. "Why did you do it? I don't want to hear that stuff about Felicity being a teacher's pet. I can see why that might make her an easy target. Why did you feel that you had to do something you knew I would punish you for?"

"I dunno," he whispered, looking miserable.

"I don't buy that. Come on, Petey. Tell me why. Did this have something to do with Timmy again?"

"No."

"What, then?"

He sighed heavily. "Do I have to tell?"

"Yes," she said firmly. "I want the whole truth this time."

"I guess it's because you pay attention to me when I do stuff," he said, avoiding her gaze.

She stared at him incredulously. "Petey, I'd pay attention to you if you were good, too."

"But you wouldn't come to the house and stuff."

"I'm confused. I thought you didn't like me coming around. I thought you didn't like me at all because of who I am.''

''That was before.''

''Before what?''

''Before I figured out you were kinda okay and you made Dad laugh sometimes, the way he used to.''

Jenny saw that for the supreme compliment it was. Coming from Petey, who'd been raised to dislike anyone connected to Harlan Adams, it was high praise, indeed. As for her ability to make Chance smile, that was yesterday's news, but apparently Petey didn't know it yet.

''I'm glad you think I'm okay,'' she said quietly. ''I think you're pretty okay, too.'' She regarded him soberly. ''But I'd like you even more if you'd stop doing these terrible things to your classmates just to get my attention.''

''But I want you to keep coming to the house. I think Dad does, too.''

''I'm not so sure about that,'' Jenny protested. In fact, she was fairly confident she wouldn't be seeing any more of Chance Adams than was absolutely necessary from now on. ''Look, maybe you and I can get a soda at Dolan's after school once in a while. Or maybe you can come over to White Pines and go riding with me.''

His eyes widened and he gazed at her hopefully. ''Really?''

''I'll try to work it out. I promise.'' She stared at

him intently. "But only if you're on your best behavior in class from now on, okay?"

He grinned. "Okay." He raised his hand to give her a high five.

"Since we're on a roll here," she said, "maybe you should work on getting those grades up, too. You're a whole lot smarter than you've been letting on."

He shrugged. "Maybe a little."

Jenny chuckled. "*A*'s and *B*'s. I won't settle for anything less."

"Okay, okay. You're worse than Dad. It's way too much pressure for a little kid like me."

"Oh, I think you can handle it," she said with confidence. After all, he'd just manipulated her into doing exactly what he'd wanted. He had those Adams genes in spades.

As they reached the door to the classroom, Petey hung back. "Can I ask you something? It's something I can't really talk to my dad about."

"Of course," she said at once. His tone alerted her that whatever was on his mind was something very serious to him. "But I'll bet you could talk to your dad about it if you wanted to. He cares about you, Petey. You know that."

"I know. It's just that this is about Mom, and sometimes talking about her makes him real sad."

Jenny's heart seemed to stop. She'd never considered that Chance might still harbor feelings for the wife he'd lost two years earlier. "What about your mom?" she asked quietly.

Petey gazed up at her with tear-filled eyes. "Do you think it's terrible that sometimes it's real hard for me to remember her?"

Jenny knelt down and gathered him close, oblivious to the possibility that someone might come along and see her comforting one of her students, especially one she'd banished to the principal's office only a couple of hours earlier.

"Oh, sweetie, it's perfectly normal to forget sometimes. You were very young when she died."

"But she was my mom," he protested. "I should remember what she looked like and not have to stare at some old picture to get it right."

"I know." She tapped the center of his chest gently. "I'll bet you never forget the way you felt about her right here, in your heart."

His expression brightened a little. "Yeah," he said slowly. "That's true."

"It's not the details that are important, not the color of her eyes or the shape of her nose, but the times you shared and the way she made you feel. Those memories will never go away."

Petey regarded her worriedly. "Not even if I got a new mom someday?"

Jenny grinned and tried not to turn weepy at the realization that she wouldn't be that new mom. "Not even then," she assured him.

His expression turned sly. "Then I guess I'll tell Dad it's okay if he decides to marry you."

Jenny winced. The kid truly did have lousy timing. "Maybe you'd better not tell him that just now."

"How come? I think he wants to."

What the heck was she supposed to do now? she wondered. Tell him she'd turned down his father's proposal? That was news best delivered by Chance. She suspected he was going to be stunned that Petey had even been thinking along those lines.

"Sweetie, marriage is a very grown-up decision," she explained. "Maybe you'd better just leave that up to your dad."

"Are you sure? Sometimes he can be real mule-headed about stuff. At least that's what Grandpa used to say. He said when Dad gets that way, he needs a good shove."

"I doubt he meant for you to do the shoving," Jenny said. "Now let's get back to class, okay?"

"Yeah, I guess."

Jenny grinned. "You don't have to sound so over-joyed about it."

"Hey," he said, "it's school. I'm a kid. What do you expect?"

Jenny sighed. There were days, she was forced to concede, when she felt pretty much the same way.

Still, it had been a good conversation, if ever so slightly disconcerting. In fact, her relationship with Chance aside, she'd begun to feel fairly hopeful about life in general by the time she drove home that afternoon.

The feeling didn't last. The sight of all the cars and trucks in front of the house brought her spirits crashing right back down. Something was wrong if everyone in the family had turned up in the middle of the afternoon on a weekday.

Jenny took the front steps two at a time and burst into the living room where everyone was gathered, their expressions as somber as if a major illness had struck.

"Daddy?" she asked at once. "Is he—"

"I'm just fine, darlin' girl," he said quietly, coming up behind her and giving her shoulder a squeeze. "I was just in the kitchen getting something to drink. It's the rest of 'em. They've all got their feathers ruffled."

Relief washed over her, only to vanish as she studied the somber faces in the living room. "What now?" she asked.

To her surprise it was her mother who answered.

"I had a call today from an attorney in Dallas, a big-shot partner at a firm with a dozen names on the masthead," Janet said.

Jenny felt her stomach clench. Only one piece of legal business she could think of would draw everyone in the family together on the spur of the moment. "About?" she asked reluctantly.

"That mean-spirited snake of a cousin of ours is suing for half of White Pines," Cody snapped.

Jenny reached for the back of a chair to brace herself. He couldn't have. It hadn't even been twenty-four hours since she'd turned down his marriage proposal. Had he made all the arrangements ahead of time just in case she said no? Or had he planned to do it all along no matter what she said? Maybe he'd just been playing a sick game with her.

"Damn him," she muttered.

"My sentiments exactly," Luke chimed in bitterly. "I don't know where the hell he gets off waltzing into town after all these years and stirring up trouble."

"Maybe if you all had done the thinking I asked you to do and settled on a solution, it wouldn't have come to this," her father said quietly.

Jenny swallowed hard and said, "I could have stopped it. I'm sorry." With that she burst into tears and ran from the room, leaving everyone except Lizzy gaping after her.

"I'll talk to her," Janet said.

Jenny heard her mother hurrying up the stairs behind her, but she didn't slow down. She just wanted to get to her room and throw herself on the bed and cry until she had no more tears left.

How could she possibly have gone and fallen in love with a man capable of hurting everyone she cared about? And that *was* what she had done. She'd realized it the night before when she'd had so much trouble taking off that beautiful ring he'd bought for her for all the wrong reasons. The sad truth had echoed in her head just that afternoon when Petey had talked about her becoming his mom.

She made it as far as the bed, but the hot angry tears had barely begun to spill when her mother sat down next to her and pulled her into her arms.

"Okay, why don't you tell me what's going on?" Janet asked.

Her gentle reasonable tone had a calming effect on Jenny's distress. "I've made a real mess of things," Jenny said, sniffing. "I thought I could work it out with Chance, keep him from doing this, but I've only made it worse."

"How?"

She took a deep breath, then blurted, "He said if I'd marry him, he'd settle for my share of the ranch and forget about suing."

Her mother stared at her in shock. "He what?"

Jenny regarded her ruefully. "You heard me. He was trying to blackmail me into marrying him."

"Why, that rotten low-down scoundrel!" her mother exclaimed. "How could he put you in such a terrible position?" Holding Jenny's shoulders, she searched her face. "You turned him down, didn't you? You told him to taking a flying leap, right?"

Jenny nodded. "More or less."

"When?"

"Last night."

"Well, good. The whole idea is absolutely ridiculous." She paused and studied Jenny's face again. "It is, isn't it?"

"Of course," Jenny said, then sighed.

"Oh, no," her mother whispered. "You've fallen in love with him, haven't you? Harlan told me he'd seen all the signs of it, but I thought it was just wishful thinking."

"I don't know, maybe," Jenny admitted brokenly. "God, what a mess!"

Janet stood up and began to pace. "Maybe not," she said thoughtfully.

"Mother, I know that tone of voice. What are you thinking?"

"I'm thinking that Chance Adams would never have made such an outrageous proposal if he wasn't at least half in love with you, too."

"No," Jenny said bleakly. "I think this was just part of his revenge. He got me all tied up in knots when he intended all along to sue for half of everything we owned. If I'd said yes, he probably would have abandoned me at the altar just to make his revenge complete."

"He didn't sue until today," her mother reminded her. "After you'd said no. Maybe he's simply trying to force your hand, show you he means business."

"This isn't about me," Jenny said adamantly. "It's about White Pines. It always has been. He came to town to get revenge and now he has, or at least he's put the wheels in motion."

"I'm not convinced of that," her mother insisted. "I think there's more to it. Do you mind if I go down and tell the others what's been going on?"

Jenny resisted the idea. She knew, though, they had to be told. In the end she was forced to admit as much, but she didn't want her mother stuck with the dirty work.

"Give me a few minutes to get my act together and I'll tell them," she said finally. "They might as well hear straight from the horse's mouth just how big a fool I've been."

Her mother chuckled. "You tell them like that and they're liable to go over there and lynch the guy."

"Why?"

"For hurting you."

The prospect held a certain sick appeal. "Do you really think they would do that for me?"

"These are Adams men you're talking about," Janet reminded her dryly. "Protecting those they love is what they do best."

"So telling them this will stir up a real hornets' nest," Jenny said thoughtfully.

"It's what Chance deserves, don't you think?"

Jenny sank back down on the edge of the bed. "Wait a minute, though. What will it solve in the long run?"

"It may not solve anything," her mother conceded. "But right now I'd like to see him with a bloody lip and a couple of black eyes, wouldn't you?"

"No," Jenny said at once, then changed her mind. "Yes." She sighed. "Maybe."

Her mother chuckled at her indecision. "Well, as much as you and I would take satisfaction in that, I think maybe if we all put our heads together, we can come up with something a whole lot more devious.''

''To save White Pines?''

''Of course not,'' her mother said, waving off the suggestion as if the ranch was the least important issue on earth. ''To get the man to admit he loves you.''

Jenny's mouth gaped. ''Weren't you listening? He doesn't love me.''

''Oh, I think he does,'' her mother countered. ''But if he's like most men, he just might not realize it yet.''

Chapter Thirteen

Chance walked out of Wilkie's barn after feeding the horses for the night and came to a dead halt. There was a parade of pick-ups coming up the driveway, and unless his eyesight was going bad, each one was driven by an Adams. He guessed they'd gotten the word about his suit.

The decision to file it had been impulsive, made in the middle of the night when Jenny's rejection had cut deep into his heart. He'd put it together first thing this morning after a flurry of phone calls and faxes to an attorney in Dallas Wilkie had recommended.

He kept his gaze fixed warily on the approaching trucks. Despite the implications of that convoy, he felt more exhilarated than frightened. It was all finally going to come to a head right here and now. He'd suspected they wouldn't wait around to settle things in court.

He walked toward the fence around the corral, propped a booted foot on the bottom rail and waited. His pulse hammered in his ears.

All his planning and scheming had come to this. The irony, of course, was that with every scheme he'd mentally concocted he'd found himself losing just a smidgen of his heart to a prim and prissy school-teacher of all things. An Adams.

And that wasn't the way it was supposed to be at all. He was supposed to be immune to all these con-niving Texas relations. He was supposed to be com-pletely focused on his goal.

And for a brief while he had actually been able to view Jenny purely as a means to an end, but some-thing had happened in recent weeks that scared the dickens out of him. She was rattling him, leaving him tongue-tied and sweating and aching so damned badly, he needed a dozen cold showers to relieve the tension. Last night had been the worst.

Petey wasn't helping matters, either. For some rea-son or other, his son had fallen under Jenny's spell, too. Last night of all nights he had talked about her nonstop and actually had the audacity to offer the two of them his blessing.

In the middle of the night, aching for her, Chance had realized he couldn't have gone through with using her to get the ranch even if she'd said yes. He hoped he'd have the chance to tell her that. A look up the road suggested that his prospects for living long enough were iffy at best.

Seven men, all bearing shotguns, emerged from those trucks. He recognized Harlan and Duke and guessed that the others were Luke, Cody, Jordan and a couple of the grandsons. What were their names? Harlan Patrick and Justin. They were young enough to look both eager and uncertain at the same time. It was a dangerous combination in a man armed with a gun. Chance kept his gaze fixed on the two of them as he waited to see who in the group would speak first. Naturally it was Harlan who stepped forward.

"Chance," he said, regarding him with obvious regret, "I'm mighty sorry to be here under these conditions."

Chance tried to ignore the vague sense that he'd disappointed someone whose respect he'd wanted. "It was something I owed my daddy. I made him a promise the day he died," he explained. "I had no choice."

"We always have a choice, son."

"Yeah, right. Were you going to sit down with me over dinner one night and work out some arrangement to turn over some of your land?"

Harlan shook his head, his expression filled with sorrow. "Sooner or later we would have done exactly that. We'd have talked, worked something out to rectify the injustice you believe was done to your father.

But we're not here about White Pines, boy. This is more important.''

Chance swallowed hard. An uneasy feeling began nagging at him. What could be more important between them than the fate of the ranch? ''If you're not here about White Pines or the suit, what's this about?''

''It's about Jenny,'' Harlan told him.

Chance's heart slammed against his ribs. Had she told them about his proposal? Had they made the obvious link between her refusal and his initiating the lawsuit? He never would have done it if he hadn't spent all night stewing over her rejection. He'd wanted to get her attention, not punish her. He'd wanted her over here today herself, shouting and fussing and making a deal. Judging from the glares of the men standing before him, he'd gotten not just her attention, but the whole damn family's. He'd miscalculated once again. Just as it had been years ago, all the power and the decision making rested with Harlan Adams.

Well, there was nothing Chance could do now except face the music. He brought his chin up a defiant notch.

''What about her?''

''You hurt her,'' Harlan said coldly. ''You tried to use her in a fight with me. I warned you about that. Nobody hurts my girl. Nobody.''

Chance could have tried to explain, tried to appease

him. Instead, he responded with pure bravado. "What do you intend to do about it, old man? Shoot me?"

"That's mighty tempting, but it'd be too easy," one of the sons said.

"Cody..." Harlan warned in a low voice.

"Sorry, Daddy. I just wanted to make sure he realized we weren't here as window dressing."

Harlan almost smiled at that. "Chance is a smart man. I doubt he'd make a mistake like that."

"If he's so smart, why'd he go and hurt Jenny?" one of the younger boys demanded, his trigger finger moving nervously. "He made her cry. I've never seen her cry before." He sounded both awed and dismayed.

"Now that's a good question, Justin," Harlan said. He looked at Chance. "Care to give us an answer?"

Chance figured his best shot was to try to bluster his way through. "Are you sure you've got all the facts straight about this? I asked the woman to marry me, didn't I? She's the one who turned me down."

"You were using her," Harlan reminded him coldly. "What did you expect?"

Something about this whole situation didn't feel quite right to Chance. He could understand these men being furious about being served with legal papers. He could even see them getting bent out of shape if he'd deliberately hurt Jenny, but she hadn't been hurt when she'd walked away from him the night before. She'd had the upper hand all evening long. It had been her decision to go.

Or had he missed something? He'd convinced himself during the night that he didn't have the capacity to touch her in any way. She'd been willing to walk away, hadn't she? If she'd cared for him at all, wouldn't she have taken a risk on the future by accepting his proposal and working on the details of their relationship later?

"You know, men, as much as I respect the fact that you all stick by Jenny, it seems to me that what goes on between the two of us is just that—between the two of us."

"Not anymore," Harlan said grimly. "You turned it into a battle that drew the rest of us in when you dangled a marriage proposal in front of her as a way of getting a share of the ranch. It stopped being personal right then and became business."

"What exactly does that mean?"

"It means I want you to steer clear of her and settle this ranch thing with me, Luke, Cody and Jordan. I want you to stay so faraway from her you'll only be a dim memory."

Chance stared at him incredulously. "You're forbidding me to see her?"

Harlan shrugged. "That shouldn't be a problem, should it? After all, you were just playing games with her head, weren't you?"

There was no way to answer that question without landing in even hotter water. Chance, however, really hated being told who he could and couldn't see. He especially hated the prospect of not seeing Jenny again. If he'd had to choose between her and the land... Well, thank goodness, it hadn't come to that. Not yet, anyway.

"What if I tell you to forget it?" he asked. "What if I tell you that I'll see her when and if I choose to?"

His uncle didn't look nearly as distraught at those words as Chance had anticipated. In fact, he almost looked as if he'd been expecting it.

"Then I'll go back into court with a response to this suit that will destroy forever any good impressions you had of your daddy," Harlan said.

Chance swallowed hard at the implacable note in his uncle's voice. There wasn't a doubt in his mind that Harlan would do exactly as he'd threatened. Nor, at last, was there a doubt in his mind that the old man had the ammunition to do it. Oddly enough, none of that mattered anymore, not as much as working things out with Jenny. He doubted, though, she would ever trust his motives or him. He supposed she even had a right to hate his guts, but it was her right, not her daddy's to dictate.

"Well?" Harlan asked. "What's it going to be?"

"I'll stay away from her," Chance said at last. Then he allowed himself a slow confident smile. "But only if Jenny tells me herself that's the way she wants it."

"We're telling you," Cody said. "And we're the ones you need to listen to."

"Sorry," Chance said. "It has to come from Jenny."

His uncle met his gaze evenly. "Fine. You follow us on back to White Pines and she'll tell you to your face."

Chance wasn't sure he wanted to risk it just now, especially not with the entire family looking on, but he couldn't see he had much choice.

"I'll be right behind you," he said.

They actually waited until he'd climbed behind the wheel of his truck before they got into their own pickups and headed back down the driveway. He noticed that one of the trucks, the one with the two boys, waited and fell into place behind him. No prisoner had ever been more carefully escorted.

On the short drive to White Pines, Chance wondered just what he was going to say to Jenny or why the heck it mattered to him so much that she not push him out of her life forever. All he knew was that the prospect of never seeing her again left a huge empty space inside him.

"It's not going to work," Jenny declared for the hundredth time since her father and the rest of the men had left to confront Chance. "Telling him he's to leave me alone won't exactly break his heart. All he cares about is the ranch."

"If that's so, we'll know soon enough," her mother said calmly.

Jenny sighed. "Tell me again exactly how we'll know."

"Sweetie, just count the trucks coming up the

driveway. My hunch is there'll be one more than the number that left here.''

"And that will mean?" Jenny asked.

"That Chance insisted on hearing straight from you that you never want to see him again."

"Well, if you ask me, all that proves is that he doesn't like to lose," Lizzy piped up.

"My sentiments exactly," Jenny murmured.

"Wait and see, you two. I think this plan Harlan came up with is ingenious.''

Lizzy groaned. "Mom, you think everything Daddy does is ingenious. You're prejudiced.''

Their mother did not appear to be the slightest bit annoyed by the accusation.

"Wait and see," she said again with quiet confidence.

"Well, I just hope and pray Daddy has all his meddling out of his system by the time I'm ready to find a man and settle down," Lizzy announced. "I'd like to handle the details of my courtship myself.''

"Then you were born into the wrong family," Jenny said dryly.

She crossed the living room to the window and peered outside again, searching for a stirring of dust on the long winding driveway that would indicate that the confrontation with Chance was over and the troops were returning home. Lizzy came up beside her.

"Daddy won't let you down," she said softly.

"I know." Jenny nodded. The only real question

was whether or not Chance would let her down, whether he would choose the ranch over her. She'd been so sure on more than one occasion that her feelings for him were reciprocated.

"Isn't that Daddy's truck?" Lizzy asked urgently, pointing to a tiny moving speck in the distance.

Jenny's heart skipped a beat. "Looks like it," she said. "And there are Luke's, Cody's and Jordan's behind it."

"Damn, I wish I'd thought to get those binoculars from Daddy's office," Lizzy said. "Isn't that another truck behind them?"

"It's probably Justin's," Jenny said.

"No, no, his is behind the one I'm talking about." She turned and grinned at Jenny. "It's Chance. It has to be."

Jenny pressed her nose against the windowpane to get a better look.

"Jenny, you're fogging up the glass. In a minute we won't be able to see anything," Lizzy complained.

"Have either of you considered just going out on the porch to meet them?" their mother inquired.

"And look anxious? Are you kidding?" Jenny snorted. "That would defeat the whole purpose of this crazy stunt. Chance has to be convinced I don't care if I ever see him again."

Lizzy rolled her eyes. "Do the words straightforward and honest mean anything to anyone in this room?"

"Of course," her mother said. "But when it comes

to men, sometimes a winding road will get you to the destination a whole lot faster than a straight line."

"Whatever that means," Lizzy said.

"It means you shouldn't put all your cards on the table at once," Jenny explained. "Keep them guessing."

"And you—Miss Direct and to the Point—subscribe to this?"

Jenny grinned. "Not really, but I have been persuaded today to listen to my elders and learn from their wisdom."

"You'll see," her mother said. "Very soon, I suspect."

Sure enough, within minutes the pickups were slamming to a stop in front of the house, and sure enough, Chance's was among them. It looked as if he'd been surrounded by a posse. He didn't appear overjoyed.

"Mama," Jenny said worriedly, "what if they just kidnapped him?"

Janet chuckled at her concern. "Does anyone look bloodied? Any shotguns raised?"

"No, but Chance does look as if he'd like to murder someone," Jenny concluded after studying his grim expression. "I think maybe I'll just slip out the back door and head for..." She shrugged. "I don't know, any place but here."

"Jenny Runningbear Adams, don't you dare leave this room," her mother commanded, getting gracefully to her feet. "I think I'll tell Maritza that our guest is here and she can serve tea now."

Jenny and Lizzy exchanged glances as their mother left the room.

"Tea?" Lizzy said. "Since when do we have tea?"

Jenny chuckled. "Maybe that was another lesson we missed. Maybe it goes with bulldozing a man into admitting he's in love with you."

Before her sister could respond, booted footsteps sounded in the foyer. Jenny glanced nervously at the door.

"Go on in, son," her father was saying. "Ask her what she wants."

"Is it vital I do it with an audience?" Chance asked.

The low rumble of his voice raised goose bumps on Jenny's arms.

"What do you think, Luke? Cody?" That was Harlan again.

"I suppose he can be trusted to be alone with her in her own house," Luke responded.

"Besides, Jenny's got better aim than half of us," Cody said. "I ought to know. I taught her to shoot."

After that things happened very quickly. Maritza brought in a tray with teacups, a teapot and tiny sandwiches and cakes. Her mother shooed Lizzy from the room, and then Jenny was alone with Chance. The gaze he fixed on her was hot enough to brand cattle. She forced a bright smile.

"What brings you by?" she asked.

"As if you didn't know."

"I have no idea. Last I heard, you failed to convince me to go along with your scheme to get a chunk of White Pines, so you were suing for half the ranch." She gestured toward the tray Maritza had left. "Care for some tea?"

He eyed the china cups suspiciously, as if he expected them to shatter at first touch. "I don't think so."

Jenny shrugged and poured herself a cup, more for something to do than out of any desire for tea. She added several lumps of sugar and a splash of milk for the same reason. She would have tossed in a shot of liquor if any had been nearby.

Chance's scrutiny turned speculative. "You nervous about something, darlin'?"

"Why would I be nervous?"

"I thought maybe you didn't feel so good about having to lie to me."

"What lie? Why on earth would I lie to you?"

"If you tell me you never want to see me again, that would be a lie. You know it and I know it."

She returned his gaze blandly. "Is that so?"

He'd been standing behind her father's favorite wing chair, but now he moved toward her and sat next to her on the love seat, thigh to thigh. No wonder they called them love seats, Jenny thought. A man and woman crowded next to each other on one of these were forced into a certain intimacy. She could feel his heat reaching out to her. It took all her restraint to keep from pitching herself straight into his arms.

Which, of course, was exactly what he intended.

"Say it," he instructed quietly, his gaze locked with hers.

"Say what?" she murmured.

"That you never want to see me again." He reached out and brushed a strand of hair away from her face, then trailed his finger along her jaw.

Jenny couldn't have spoken two intelligent words, much less the whole lie she was expected to spit out. Her heartbeat was so fast, so unsteady, a cardiac monitor would have labeled it unhealthy—or love.

"Well?" he encouraged.

"Chance…"

"Yes, darlin'. I'm waiting."

Jenny shot to her feet and raced for the safety of the spot he'd vacated behind the wing chair. She clamped her hands on the back so he wouldn't see them trembling.

"I want you to go," she said even as her heart cried out for him to stay.

For a fraction of a second he looked stunned. Then he was on his feet and moving toward her again. A cougar stalking its prey couldn't have looked any more intense.

"Okay," he said softly, "I'll go, but only after one last kiss."

Her pulse ricocheted wildly at the suggestion. "Absolutely not," she said breathlessly.

"Why not? You've kissed me before. This won't be any different. Just a little goodbye kiss between acquaintances if that's the way you want it."

That, of course, was the trouble. He wasn't just an acquaintance and that wasn't the way she wanted it. She wanted him to plunder her mouth. She wanted him to make mad passionate love to her right on that infernal love seat. One little kiss was more dangerous than he could possibly imagine. It would never be enough.

"No," she said emphatically.

His eyes glittered. "Too risky?"

"Of course not."

"Then prove it. Prove you can kiss me and then tell me to go away."

"Why? What difference does it make whether or not I kiss you? The game's over, Chance. You'll go into court and take your best shot. Maybe you'll win, maybe you'll lose, but you'll have done what your father wanted. You can get on with the business of living your life, instead of his."

"This kiss isn't about White Pines," he told her. "It's about you and me."

"There is no you and me. The fight over the ranch has made sure of that."

"Then I'll give up the fight for the ranch," he said.

Jenny wasn't sure which of them was more stunned by his statement. Chance looked as if he couldn't believe he'd uttered the words. Jenny wasn't sure she'd heard them.

"Damn," he muttered, raking a hand through his hair. "I should have known I couldn't do it."

Jenny smiled, more relieved than she'd ever admit. "Couldn't do what?" she asked innocently.

"Use you to get the ranch."

She shrugged as if that was no surprise. "Never thought you could."

He stared. "Why not?"

"Because it's not the kind of man you are," she said confidently. "I knew you'd never go through with it. It was just a matter of waiting you out until you saw what I knew all along."

"Which is?"

"That you could never do anything to hurt someone you love."

Chance started at the mention of love. "What makes you think I love you?"

"You're giving up on White Pines, aren't you? Why else would a man give up something he wants so badly?"

"Is there anything else you think you know about me, Miss Smarty-Pants?"

"That you're going to ask me to marry you," she suggested, but she couldn't keep a hint of hesitation out of her voice. What if she was wrong? What if he didn't want to marry her? She held her breath as she waited for his response.

"And what would your answer be if I did?"

She grinned. Naturally he couldn't have made a straightforward reply, not a man like Chance.

"Oh, no, you don't, Chance Adams. If I'm going to be saddled with a couple of hellions like you and Petey, you're going to have to do it the old-fashioned way. I want a brand-new, genuine, from-the-heart proposal."

"Will you marry me, Jenny Runningbear Adams? It's you I want."

"Say that again," she said softly.

He hesitated for one long endless beat of her heart, then said, "Marry me and I'll forget about White Pines."

"Why?"

"Because you're more important," he said, and now he spoke without any hesitation at all. "It's a funny thing about land. One piece is pretty much the same as another. It's the people who make the difference. I can make a home wherever you are. I can't make one anywhere without you."

Tears welled up in Jenny's eyes halfway through this pretty speech. "Why?" she asked again, this time in a whisper.

"Because you were right. Somewhere along the way I've gone and fallen in love with you."

"You're sure?" she asked, not quite daring to believe it.

"I'm sure," he said emphatically. "What about you, darlin'? I haven't heard you say a word about what you feel."

Jenny's throat was so clogged with emotion she couldn't manage to squeak out so much as a single word. She settled for rounding the chair and throwing herself into Chance's waiting arms and peppering his face with the kisses he'd demanded and she'd withheld. She added a few more for good measure.

"I can't hear anything," they heard Lizzy whisper from the other side of the door.

"Get away from the door," her mother said. "You, too, Harlan."

"How the heck are we supposed to know what's going on if we don't listen in?" he demanded, sounding thoroughly disgruntled. His voice faded a bit, though, suggesting that her mother had gotten him to move.

Chance chuckled. "It's always going to be like this, isn't it?"

"Worse," Jenny confirmed. "If we get married, you'll be switching from outsider to family member, which means Daddy will assume a God-given right to meddle in your life."

"If?"

"Okay, when."

"That's more like it," he said solemnly. "Petey told me last night he was giving us his blessing. I figure that's too precious to waste."

Jenny smiled. "He mentioned the same thing to me."

"Smart kid," Chance said.

"The brightest," Jenny agreed.

Chance shook his head, his expression one of disbelief. "You sound a whole lot like a proud mama."

"Isn't it amazing what a difference a few weeks makes?"

"A few weeks and the love of a good man," he said.

"That, too." She wound her arms around his waist and fit her body to his.

There were more whispers outside the door, then a thump as if someone had bumped against it. Jenny sighed.

"We might as well put them out of their misery before someone out there gets hurt," she said.

Chance glanced over her shoulder toward the door, then grinned. "Nah," he said. "Let 'em sweat. I have more fascinating things in mind than satisfying your daddy's curiosity."

He edged over to the door and flipped the lock to assure their privacy, then grinned at her. "Come here, darlin'."

Jenny heard the indignant muttering on the other side of the door that indicated her father was aware he'd just been locked out of his own living room. She chuckled.

"That bought us maybe five minutes," she warned. "Daddy has a key in his office."

"Then I guess we'd best make the most of it," Chance said, and angled his mouth over hers.

Jenny lost track of time, lost track of everything except the feel of Chance's lips, the hard warmth of his body. She was about to suggest a test run of the love seat when she heard the spare key rattle in the lock over her mother's protests.

Chance kept his arms looped around her waist from behind and faced the door as her father burst through. Jenny couldn't see Chance's face, but she saw the expression of satisfaction on her father's.

"I guess she didn't tell you to get lost," Harlan said dryly.

"To the contrary, she's agreed to marry me," Chance told him.

"I see."

"Do we have your blessing?" Chance asked, then held up a hand. "No, wait, don't answer that yet. Do you have those legal papers anywhere around here?"

"Right here, snug in my pocket," her father said, pulling them out.

Chance took them from him and ripped them in half. Jenny recalled another legal agreement that had been shredded on another wedding day years before. Her gaze flew to her mother, whose nostalgic smile suggested she was recalling the very same thing.

"Now do we have your blessing?" Chance asked.

Harlan grinned at him. "It was never in doubt, son. Jenny has a way of getting what she wants."

Jenny reached for her father's hand. "Of course I do. I'm an Adams."

"Always will be, too," Chance said. "It's a proud name, don't you think?"

"That it is," her father replied. "That it is."

Epilogue

Jenny had never envisioned herself in a fancy white wedding gown. She wasn't sure why. Maybe it was for the same reason she'd never played with dolls or makeup and had climbed trees and painted graffiti on her daddy's old shed, instead. As a kid, it had been pure rebellion. Standing in the Fort Worth bridal shop, it was pure gut-deep panic.

"I'll look ridiculous," she muttered, even as she fingered the delicate lace and the smooth satin of the samples the shop owner had supplied.

"You'll look beautiful," her mother corrected. "All women look radiant on their wedding day."

"But me? In frills? I don't think so."

Her mother grinned. "Forget the frills, then. Go for simplicity."

Simplicity turned out to be more outrageously expensive than frills, but Jenny stood in front of the mirror in a slim gown that hugged her breasts and flowed to the floor in endless yards of satin, and her breath caught in her throat.

"Oh, my," she whispered.

"I guess you're not a tomboy anymore," her mother said, brushing her cheek with a kiss and squeezing her hand. "You're all woman."

"Do you think Chance will like it?"

"I think you could wear a terry-cloth robe and Chance would like it."

"Mother!"

"Okay, okay, Chance will love it. He'd be a fool not to."

Lizzy grinned. "What Chance will love most is getting you out of it. It has a nice simple zipper down the back, instead of all those tiny impossible buttons."

"Careful, sis. We still have your dress to pick out. I could decide I want you in pink tulle."

"Then you'd have to get yourself another maid of honor," Lizzy shot back. "And all those bridesmaids you're planning on would wind up hating you because they'd have to wear mauve or something to coordinate with me."

"Pink and mauve, the perfect colors for the day before Mother's Day, wouldn't you say, Mama?" Jenny asked.

Janet chuckled. "I think pink and baby blue would be even more appropriate."

"You two are awful," Lizzy declared. "How did I survive growing up around you and turn out so good?"

"You can thank Daddy for that!" Jenny said, laughing. "You're one hundred percent Daddy's little girl."

"Oh, go to—"

"Mary Elizabeth Adams," their mother said. When Lizzy fell dutifully silent, Janet fiddled with the train on Jenny's dress. "I think this is the one, don't you?"

Jenny gazed at herself once more in the triple mirror and slowly nodded. "Oh, yes," she said softly. "This is the one."

For one day in her life, she was going to look every inch a lady. Of course, more than likely, no one in town would recognize her.

"Daddy, did you wear a tuxedo when you married Mama?" Petey asked.

Chance ran a finger around the too-tight collar of his white shirt and cursed the day he'd agreed to wear one for this wedding. "No, son, and don't ever let a woman talk you into wearing one, either."

"But I think you look real handsome. I'll bet Jenny's going to think so, too."

She'd better, Chance thought grimly. He'd put on this monkey suit for her and her alone. Of course, when he thought of the grumbling she'd done when she'd had to go shopping for a wedding dress, he'd figured it was worth it.

It still astounded him how things had turned out. Coming to Los Piños had been the best decision of his life, even if it had shattered forever his impression of his daddy being wronged by a cheating older brother. He'd forced Harlan to tell him the whole story one night when they'd been sipping bourbon and talking about life's astonishing twists and turns. Chance had been saddened by what he'd heard, but at last he'd understood his father. Some of the old Hank had lived on in his father until the very end, enough that Chance had recognized the truth in his uncle's story.

He reached into his pocket and fingered the ruby-and-diamond pin his father had stolen all those years ago. Tonight he would give it to Jenny. Tonight it would be back where it belonged as part of the Adams-family heritage.

"Daddy, I hear the music," Petey said, his voice quivering with excitement.

"Then I guess it's time." He hunkered down in front of his son and straightened his tie. "Looks to me like you were made for a tux yourself, young man. A few years from now every girl in Los Piños will be chasing you."

"Oh, yuck!" Petey declared with a grimace.

Chance laughed. "You'll change your mind." He tapped Petey's pocket. "You have the ring?"

"Dad! You've asked me that a million times."

"So what? Things have a habit of disappearing around you. Give me an answer one more time."

"It's right here," Petey said, dragging it out of his pocket. "See. I'm not going to mess up, Dad. That's why I'm called the best man."

Chance grinned and ruffled his son's hair, which had been slicked back a little too neatly to suit him. There, he thought. Now Petey looked more like the pint-size scoundrel he was.

"You are happy about this wedding, aren't you?" he asked, also for the millionth time.

"Dad!"

"Okay, okay, I was just checking."

"Can we please go get married now?" Petey asked.

Chance looked at him and grinned. "Yes, son. Yes, we can."

The wedding had gone off without a hitch. In fact, it was the first thing in Jenny's entire life that had.

When she'd spotted Chance and Petey waiting in the front of the church, her heart had climbed into her throat. She'd thought for a minute she was going to burst into tears from sheer happiness. Then she'd looked up into her father's sparkling eyes.

"Ready, darlin' girl?"

"Oh, yes," she'd whispered.

Lizzy, Sharon Lynn and Angela had started the procession. He'd grinned at her and said, "Just one last thing before we walk down that aisle. I may be giving you away to Chance today, but you will always be my darlin' girl. Don't ever forget that.''

Tears had spilled down her cheeks and she'd dabbed them away. "Look what you've done," she chided. "You've made me cry. I thought it was only the bride's mother who was supposed to cry."

"In this family we've never done anything according to the rule book," he said. He glanced toward the front of the church. "Looks like your groom might be getting a mite anxious. Shall we put him out of his misery?"

"There are some who'd say his misery will start the minute we finish saying I do," Jenny said.

"Not around me, they won't," Harlan said, tucking her arm through his and taking the first step down the aisle....

Now Jenny was standing in the middle of the honeymoon suite at a very fancy Dallas hotel. In the morning they would fly off to an undisclosed destination for their honeymoon. To her exasperation, Chance had been adamant about keeping the details a secret.

"A man's got to find an edge wherever he can," he'd told her repeatedly. "Something tells me I'll never get one with you again."

Smiling to herself, she resolved to wrangle the secret out of him before the night was over.

"What are you grinning about?" Chance asked,

coming back into the suite's expansive living-room area wearing only his tuxedo pants.

"Nothing in particular," Jenny claimed as her gaze zeroed in on his bare chest. How could she possibly think about anything except how desperately she wanted to touch him, to be touched by him? She'd waited so long for this moment, her entire life, it seemed.

He crossed the room slowly. "Have I mentioned that you're the most beautiful bride I've ever seen?"

"Once or twice," she teased, hoping he'd tell her again. She liked hearing it, loved the way his gaze heated when he said it.

He moved closer, close enough for his scent to surround her, but to her deep regret, he didn't touch her. Instead, his gaze locked with hers.

"You are the most beautiful bride I have ever seen, Jenny Runningbear Adams."

"Really?" she whispered.

"Absolutely."

His hands settled on her shoulders, his thumbs touching bare skin at the edge of her gown. Jenny trembled from that oh-so-slight caress.

"You know what, though?"

Jenny swallowed hard. "What?"

"Lovely as it is, I really want you out of this dress."

Her lips curved into a smile. "I would have been out of it hours ago if you hadn't insisted on scooping me up while I was still wearing it and carting me off to Daddy's plane for the trip to Dallas. I had a very expensive, very prim going-away suit I was supposed to change into back at the house.''

''Forget prim. It doesn't suit you, at least not around me. You can show it off some other time. I was too anxious to get you to myself.''

She touched his face, felt the way his skin burned. ''You've got me. Now what?''

He took a step back and Jenny felt suddenly bereft.

''Champagne?'' he asked lightly.

This time she was the anxious one. She shook her head. ''No champagne.''

''A late supper?''

''No food.''

He grinned. ''What then?''

She shrugged and feigned a yawn. ''I suppose we should get some sleep.''

''Oh, no, you don't,'' he said. ''I've waited way too long to get you in my arms and in my bed.''

''Actually the bed doesn't belong to you,'' she teased.

''Funny.'' His gaze locked with hers again. ''Come here, darlin'. Turn around.''

Heart hammering in her chest, Jenny moved closer, then turned her back to Chance. She felt the skim of his fingers as he found the zipper and tugged it smoothly down. His knuckles burned a path down her spine.

She felt the bodice of the gown fall loose. And

then, as the zipper dipped below her waist, all those yards of satin slid into a pool at her feet.

"Sweet heaven," Chance murmured as he turned her around to face him.

The adoration Jenny saw in his eyes in that instant took her breath away. For one long endless moment time stood still. The power of love shimmered in the air, as pure and radiant as anything she'd ever felt in her entire life.

Then, with a single touch of his hand on her breast, it exploded like fireworks into a spectacular barrage of sensation. His mouth was everywhere, tasting, teasing, magical.

And his hands, oh, his wonderful, gentle, persuasive hands slid over her, lingering, tormenting, magical.

The last of the clothes—her lacy lingerie, his slacks and shorts—disappeared in a trail as they worked their way toward the bedroom. It took an eternity to get there. With each step, with each scattered piece of clothing, there was something new to explore, a new sensation to rock them both.

By the time they reached the bed, Jenny's knees were shaking and her heart was thundering like a summer storm.

"I love you," Chance murmured as he settled her in the middle of the huge soft mattress and stretched out beside her. He began exploring her body all over again, as if it were a brand-new experience to be savored.

Jenny thought she was going to shatter into a million pieces from the wonder of it. When Chance finally kneeled above her, when he slowly entered her, filling her, then withdrawing until a scream of protest formed on her lips, only to die with the next thrust, she felt as if she'd finally found what she'd been seeking her entire life. She felt whole, a part of something larger than herself. She felt as if she'd come home.

Much much later, with Chance's arms wrapped tightly around her, she tried to express to him what he'd given her. The words eluded her.

"I feel complete," she finally said. "That's what you've done for me. You've given me my own family and made me whole."

"You've always had a family," Chance said, clearly not understanding. "Your mother, your sister, all those brothers. And no father could love a daughter more than Uncle Harlan loves you."

"I know that. It's just that it was something I had no control over. He didn't choose me to be his daughter. He didn't father me biologically. I was part of the package that came with Mom."

"That doesn't mean he loves you any less."

"No, of course not," she said impatiently. "But you chose me, just me."

He shook his head. "You're wrong about that, darlin'. There was never any choice to make. What I feel for you just is. It's there in my heart and I couldn't deny it."

He reached across her in a movement that brought

bare skin brushing provocatively across bare skin again. Jenny's body vibrated with awareness and shivery desire, but Chance had something other than making love on his mind.

"This is for you," he said, and opened his hand.

Jenny stared at the dazzling ruby-and-diamond pin. It looked old and delicate and more beautiful than any piece of jewelry she'd ever seen.

"Oh, Chance," she whispered. "It's gorgeous."

"It's the pin my daddy took when he left White Pines, the one that came from our Adams ancestors. I want you to have it. I asked Uncle Harlan and he agrees it belongs with you."

Tears welled up in her eyes as he put the pin into her hand. It was yet more evidence of belonging.

"Sorry, there's no place for me to pin it at the moment," he said dryly.

"I don't want to wear it, anyway. I just want to look at it." She stared at the sparkling gems, then met Chance's gaze. "It's like it's come full circle, isn't it?"

"I think nothing on earth would have made my father happier than knowing it was back where it belonged. As much as he treasured this pin and the memories attached to it, I think he regretted taking it away from Los Piños. I've thought about it a lot lately. I'm not as sure as I once was that he truly wanted revenge. I think maybe he just desperately wanted some part of him to come home again to

White Pines. I think that's why he was so insistent that Petey and I come here.''

Jenny touched his cheek. "Maybe he knew somehow that this was where you'd find your destiny."

Chance smiled. "Maybe he did at that."

* * * * *

THE COWGIRL & THE
UNEXPECTED WEDDING

Prologue

Lizzy gazed at the grades posted for her anatomy exam and sighed. A lousy *C*. In all of her twenty-four years, she'd never gotten below a B on any test. Studying was second nature to her, cramming for exams as natural as breathing. She'd known the material inside out, but on the day of the test her mind had been somewhere else, not on bones and body parts.

Nothing, *nothing* about the past weeks of her first year in medical school had gone right. The classes had been the most challenging and fascinating she had ever taken, but she'd faltered more than once on exams she should have aced, like this one. It was a lack of concentration, pure and simple, and she knew why.

Her roommate regarded her with a sympathetic expression. "It's only because you've been worried about your dad," Kelsey said. "You'll do better once you've seen for yourself that he's doing okay."

That was part of it, Lizzy agreed. When she should have been memorizing anatomical details, instead her thoughts had been straying to her father.

Harlan Adams had had a mild heart attack the week before, too mild to require her to come back to Texas, too serious to let her concentrate on her studies. All she could think about was the upcoming spring break and her scheduled visit to the family ranch so she could see for herself exactly what shape her father was in. She wouldn't put it past him or her mother to keep the truth from her, if they thought it would worry her when there was nothing she could do to change it.

The huge Adams family revolved around her father. Though he was in his eighties now, none of them could imagine life without him. This heart attack had been a warning that he wasn't invincible. She'd heard the stunned shock in the voices of each of her older brothers when she'd spoken to them. Her older half sister, Jenny, had been even more transparent. Jenny, who wasn't afraid of anything, was clearly terrified at the prospect of losing their father.

In the end, despite his irksome meddling, Harlan Adams was the force that guided all their lives. And even though he'd hated seeing his youngest—the surprise of his life, he liked to say—go off to Miami to medical school, he'd done what needed to be done to pave the way. Lizzy would always be grateful to him for that, for letting her go her own way.

He hadn't been so easy on his sons or even on Jenny, who'd been fourteen and hell-bent on self-destruction when he'd married her mother. He'd forced Luke, Jordan, Cody and Jenny to fight for their chosen careers, putting up roadblocks and hurdles that would have daunted them had they been less determined. Lizzy had been prepared to do the same.

She'd begun by using her wiles as his "baby girl" and then dug in her heels as a typical Adams. Not even the formidable Harlan Adams had had the strength to stand in her way. As much as she loved ranching and despite a whole rebellious year during which she'd experimented on the rodeo circuit, medicine had always held a special place in her heart.

Maybe it had something to do with all those TV shows she'd devoured—reruns of the old *Marcus Welby, M.D.* and *Ben Casey* series, hot new series like *ER* and *Chicago Hope*—shows that had made medicine seem every bit as thrilling as a few seconds on a bucking, bareback horse. She'd thought about medicine all through her undergraduate days at the University of Texas, volunteered at a nearby hospital to soak up the atmosphere, and taken a premed program, just to prove to herself that she'd chosen wisely.

Only one man could have made her change her mind, she thought with a predictable surge of very complicated emotions. Rancher Hank Robbins had had the power to sway her decision way back when she'd first left for college, but he hadn't. He'd wished her well and waved goodbye as if she'd been no more than a casual acquaintance.

Even now, years later, tears threatened as she thought of how easily that particular man had let her go even after the impulsive, passionate kiss she had initiated had proved just how badly he wanted her to stay. Maybe he'd only meant to do the honorable thing, but rejection was rejection and it had hurt more than she could say.

And yet, if she was to be totally honest, she couldn't help feeling at least a trace of gratitude that he, like her father, hadn't stood between her and her dream. He'd been twenty-four then, the same age she was now, and already he'd been wise enough to see she needed to test her wings.

Still, in all the years since, she'd been careful to avoid Hank. Embarrassment over that kiss was only part of it. Stubborn pride had kicked in, too. But the bottom line was something else entirely. She was afraid, a flat-out coward, in fact. To be honest, though, she wasn't sure what she feared most; that he might not let her go a second time...or that he would.

Yet she couldn't be back home for long without wondering about him. She was pathetically eager for any mention of him, any hint of gossip about his activities. And every time his name came up in conversation, she was terrified that it would be in connection with a wedding announcement. She'd found she could accept with relative calm the news of his being seen with this woman or that. It was only the repeat of the same woman's name that stirred a wellspring of anxiety deep inside her.

It was all ridiculous, of course. In almost five years away, she'd dated dozens of men herself. After the first couple of years when she'd stared at an old snapshot for hours on end, lately she'd gone for entire weeks without once picturing Hank's rugged features or wishing she could hear the low, seductive sound of his voice.

Eventually, she had buried the snapshot in the bottom of a dresser drawer and rarely took it out deliberately. When she stumbled across it, though, her heart always lurched, the pain as fresh as it had been five years ago. Schoolgirl crush or not, she had idolized the cowboy next door.

And all it ever took to resurrect the memories of that long-ago and very much unrequited love was the thought of going home. She'd been thinking about Hank nonstop for the past few days, ever since her mother had called to tell her about her father's heart attack.

The two men were so much alike, despite the decades of difference in their ages. Stubborn, strong men, both of them. Men with staying power. Men capable of powerful emotions and guided by a deep-rooted sense of honor.

So, the truth was, Kelsey was only partially right about Lizzy's thoughts being on her father, instead of concentrating on her exams. In addition, she'd been wrestling with the thorny question of what to do about Hank Robbins, how to—or even if she could—shake the hold he had on her. She'd finally concluded that there was only one way to get Hank permanently out of her thoughts. She had to swallow her pride and see him again. This time she wouldn't avoid him. This time she'd discover if the attraction was still alive.

Maybe then she would be able to put Hank Robbins behind her once and for all, get her medical degree and begin practicing in some big city so far away that she'd never be reminded of him at all. Maybe then she would be able to stop comparing every man she met to the one who'd gotten away.

Or maybe things would get a whole lot more complicated, she conceded candidly. More fascinating, yes. She recalled the way his lips had felt on hers, the way his arms had felt around her. Definitely fascinating. But there was a price for fascination, a whole Pandora's box of complications.

"Lizzy, are you okay?" Kelsey asked, her brow over her thick horn-rimmed glasses knitted with concern. "You're not really worried about this grade, are you? It's a tiny blip on your academic record."

Lizzy forced a smile. "I'm fine," she insisted, setting out for the chemistry lab. "One more exam to go, and then I'm out of here."

Unfortunately, the chemistry exam had nothing to do with the hormonal tug-of-war between a man and a woman. In her current state of mind, she could have written lengthy essays on that particular subject.

On a more optimistic note, it was a written test, rather than a practical exam. The way her mind was wandering, if she'd had to conduct experiments, she very likely would have blown up the whole blasted building.

Chapter One

"Lizzy's coming home," Cody Adams said casually as he and Hank sat on a fence rail between their properties.

Hank had no difficulty at all keeping his expression impassive. He'd had lots of practice over the years at pretending that he had no interest whatsoever in Lizzy's comings and goings. Unfortunately, Lizzy's big brother had his own opinion of Hank's fascination with his baby sister and he used almost any opportunity to taunt Hank about it.

"For how long this time?" Hank inquired, keeping his tone every bit as neutral as Cody's. Most of Lizzy's visits had been whirlwind affairs during which he'd never once caught a glimpse of her. He suspected that was deliberate on her part. He also had no reason to think this time would be any different.

In fact, he'd long since come to terms with the fact that keeping his distance from Mary Elizabeth Adams was the wisest thing he could do. The woman had a way of clouding his thinking, of making him want things he had no business wanting if he expected to turn the run-down ranch he'd bought into a respectable neighbor for the Adamses' White Pines operation. Besides, Lizzy wasn't interested in being a rancher's wife. She had her own dreams.

"A couple of weeks, I suppose. Whatever spring break is these days," Cody said.

"I see. I imagine she's been anxious about Harlan."

"That's part of it, I'm sure." Cody grinned. "Then again, I don't think Daddy's the only reason she's coming."

"I'm sure she misses all of you," Hank said, ignoring the blatant innuendo in Cody's remark.

Cody chuckled. "Give it up, Hank. You're not fooling anyone. Why don't you ask what's really on your mind?"

"Which would be?"

"When she's coming home for good."

"She's not," Hank said flatly. "She made that clear way back. She's going to be a hotshot, big-city doc. From the day I bought this place, all she talked about was her fancy office and her fancy patients."

Cody shook his head. "For a smart man, you are the dumbest son of a gun I've ever met."

Hank refused to take offense. "Thanks," he said dryly. "I've always held you in high regard, too."

"Can't you see that all that talk about setting up practice far away from Los Piños was so much nonsense? All she wanted was for you to ask her to stay. One little sign from you, and she'd be back here in a flash."

Hank wished he could believe his friend, but Cody was every bit as capable as his daddy of wishful thinking. "Did she ever once say that?" he demanded. "Or are you into mind reading now?"

"It's as plain as day," Cody insisted. "Always has been. Don't you think it's time you did something about it?"

"Me? Not a chance. I don't intend to tangle with a woman who's got her mind set on a certain path for her life, especially when that path takes her far away from Los Piños. I chose to be here. She couldn't wait to get away. She'd just end up resenting me, and then where would we be?" He shook his head. "No. This is for the best. Lizzy's smart and ambitious. She'll get the life she wants."

"Paths have a way of coming to a fork," Cody advised him. "Leastways that's what Daddy always says. Maybe when Lizzy hits that crossroads, you could help her decide which way to go. It's always been plain that you have more influence over her than the rest of us. Even Daddy admits that, though it clearly pains him to think that he can't control her.''

''I don't think so,'' Hank said. ''That's just Harlan dreaming up a new way to get what he wants and using me in the process.''

Cody regarded him knowingly. ''Are you saying you aren't already half crazy in love with Lizzy?''

''I'm saying that it doesn't matter whether I am or I'm not,'' Hank said impatiently. ''I'm not what she wants.''

''A hundred bucks says otherwise,'' Cody taunted.

Hank stared at the older man, whose own kids were about the same age as his baby sister. He wasn't sure he'd heard Cody right. It had sounded an awful lot like he was actually daring Hank to make a pass at Lizzy.

''You're betting me to do what?'' he asked cautiously.

''See Lizzy, flirt with her, see where it leads. If she blows you off, I'm wrong and you win.''

''And just how far am I supposed to carry things to win this bet?'' Hank asked. ''I don't want you and Luke and Jordan chasing after me with a shotgun.''

''Not that far,'' Cody retorted with a hard glint in his eyes and a harder edge to his voice.

''See what I mean. You all would have my hide if I actually pursued your baby sister. You chased off every other man around these parts who was interested in dating her.''

''It wasn't the dating we were concerned about,''

Cody said, his temper visibly cooling. "Besides, even though you're too stubborn to admit it, I know you care too much to ever hurt her."

"I'd say your logic is twisted," Hank retorted, torn between anger and laughter at the pure foolhardiness of Cody's plan. "You want me to put my heart on the line, then be glad of the hundred bucks you'll give me if your sister tells me to take a hike?"

"Then you're admitting your heart would be at stake," Cody said with a hoot of triumph. "I knew it. Daddy said so, too."

"I suppose he put you up to this, too. Well, it's wishful thinking on your part and Harlan's. I'm not admitting a damned thing," Hank corrected. He allowed the weight of his words to linger, before adding impulsively, "But what the heck, you're on."

He wasn't going to admit it to Cody, but he'd been looking for an excuse for a very long time to see Lizzy Adams again. Maybe there'd be fireworks. Maybe there wouldn't. But it sure would break up the monotony of his unceasing thoughts on the subject of the pretty little gal he'd let get away.

"Will you get that danged stethoscope away from me?" Harlan shouted at Lizzy. "You're my daughter, not my doctor."

"I just want to see for myself how you're doing," Lizzy protested.

She'd been home less than a half hour and so far she was no closer to knowing exactly how her father was doing than she had been back in Miami. The only certainty was that he was every bit as cantankerous as ever.

He scowled at her, daring her to put the stethoscope anywhere near his chest again. "You got a degree yet?"

"No."

"Then keep that thing away from me."

Lizzy sighed and put the stethoscope back in her medical bag. "I don't suppose you'll let me take your pulse, either."

"You think I don't know why you've been clutching my wrist every few minutes since you walked in the door?" Harlan grumbled. "If you haven't found the pulse by now, I must be dead."

Lizzy resigned herself to getting a complete picture of her father's medical condition from his doctor and not firsthand. She leaned over his bed and hugged him, relieved by the strength with which he hugged her back.

"What're you checking for now?" he grumbled as he released her.

"That was a daughterly hug, nothing more," she reassured him.

He regarded her warily. "You sure about that?"

"Absolutely."

"Okay, then. Sit down here and tell me what you've been up to. Don't leave out any of the juicy stuff, either. Have you found yourself a man yet?"

She should have known it wouldn't take long to

get to the subject nearest and dearest to his heart. "Daddy, not every woman needs a man in her life," she explained for the thousandth time, even though she knew she was wasting her breath.

"Don't give me that feminist hogwash. How're you going to give me any grandbabies if you don't find a man?"

"Maybe I'll just have them on my own," she taunted because she knew it would irritate him. Clearly, he was well enough to argue. He was probably well enough to be out of bed, too. His wife Janet had hinted that he was playing invalid just to entice his baby to stay around a little longer. If his doctor confirmed that, Lizzy was going to drag him out of bed by force and put him on a regimen of exercise that would have him pleading for mercy.

She shot him a deliberately innocent look and added, "I think I'd make a terrific single mom, don't you?"

"Over my dead body!" he shouted.

"You keep losing your cool like that, and you will be dead," she informed him mildly.

His gaze narrowed. "You said that on purpose, didn't you?"

Lizzy grinned. "Yep."

"Daggone it, girl. You know my heart's weak."

"I don't know that," she reminded him plaintively. "You won't let me check it."

He scowled at her, then said casually, "Cody saw Hank Robbins the other day."

"Really?" Getting that word out without betraying any emotion was harder than tangling with her daddy over the state of his health.

"He said Hank was asking about you."

Lizzy's heart did a little tap dance of its own. "Oh? How is he?"

"Getting along right good," Harlan said. He shot her a sly look. "Cody says he's thinking of getting married and settling down."

This time her heart plummeted straight to her toes. "Married?"

"You sound surprised. Ranch life's a whole lot easier if there's a woman you love by your side. Besides, he's not getting any younger. I'm sure he wants kids."

"I suppose," she said as her heart thudded dully. "Who's he marrying?"

"I didn't say he had anyone special in mind, just that he was thinking of it."

Lizzy stared at her father's innocent expression and chuckled. She should have known he was up to something. "You did that on purpose, didn't you?"

He grinned. "Yep. Worked, too." His expression sobered. "Why don't you just break down and see the man, Lizzy my girl? You know you want to. You were always crazy about him. For a few years there, you were thick as thieves. It made me hope that you'd settle down right next door. I never did figure out what happened between the two of you."

"Nothing happened." Which, of course, was the

whole point. She stood up and leaned down to kiss her father's weathered cheek. "Stop manipulating, Daddy. I'd already planned to see Hank while I'm here."

His expression brightened. "Whooee! It's about time you showed some sense."

"Daddy! Don't make too much of this."

"Okay, okay. You going to see him today?"

"I don't know when I'm going to see him."

"Don't waste too much time. Spring break's short." He regarded her wistfully. "Or were you thinking of sticking around?"

"Daddy," she pleaded.

"Okay, okay," he said again. "I'm an old man. I'm allowed to indulge in a little wishful thinking."

"Don't pull that old-man garbage with me. You're going to outlive all of us. You're too ornery not to."

"Sooner or later, age catches up with all of us." He caught her hand in his and clung to it. "Don't let life pass you by, Lizzy. I know you love medicine, but I know something else, too. You've always had a soft spot in your heart for that man up the road. Don't pretend you don't, not with me. I'm just saying whatever you do, don't wake up one day with regrets."

"I told you I was going to see him, didn't I?"

"No need to get defensive, darling girl. I can't help doing a little prodding. It's my nature."

Lizzy sighed. "It surely is." She leaned down and

planted a kiss on his forehead. "Now, get some rest and leave Hank Robbins to me."

Harlan Adams grinned, the color in his cheeks getting better every second. "Something tells me the poor man doesn't stand a chance."

"Maybe you're overestimating my charm. Hank didn't have a bit of trouble saying goodbye when I went off to Austin to college or down to Miami for med school."

"Maybe he was just wise enough to let you go after what you wanted. That's not the kind of thing you should blame a man for. In fact, maybe you ought to take a good hard look at what it cost him to let you leave."

Lizzy touched a finger to his lips to silence him. "You're overselling, Daddy. I already know what a paragon of virtue Hank Robbins is. I fell for the man when I was sixteen years old and he bought the old Simmons place. Nothing's changed in the eight years since."

"Then what are you waiting for, girl? Go find him and tell him straight-out what you want."

"I suppose you know what that is, too," she said, wishing she had so few doubts. Loving Hank had been complex enough years ago. Now, with medical school convincing her that she'd chosen exactly the right career for herself, loving him had gotten a whole lot more complicated.

"You want a husband and babies," her father said without hesitation.

"If only it were that simple," Lizzy murmured.

"What was that?"

"You left out medicine, Daddy. I want to be a doctor, too."

"So? You won't be the first doctor to get married and have babies."

"You seem to forget that I have to finish medical school, an internship and my residency. Do you think Hank's going to wait all that time? You've already said he's in a hurry to have a family."

"Darlin' girl, that's what compromise is all about."

Lizzy hooted at that. "What do you know about compromise?"

"Hey, your mama and I don't agree on every little thing. We work things out."

"I'll remind you of that the next time you're trying to bully her into letting you have your way." She squeezed his hand again. "Now get some sleep. I'll be back to see you later."

"After you've seen Hank, right?"

Lizzy rolled her eyes and left the room without answering. She found her mother lurking in the hallway.

"How much did you hear?" Lizzy asked.

"Enough to know that he's trying to marry you off before you go back to school," her mother said with a rueful smile. "Thank you for not arguing with him too ferociously."

"What would be the point? He knows I want to

see Hank. He's just trying to make sure I do it on his timetable. There's nothing new about that."

"No, that's your father, all right. When he gets an idea into his head, he can't wait to set it into motion."

"That's how he got you to marry him, isn't it?" Lizzy reminded her. "He wheedled and cajoled and finally wore you down."

Janet Runningbear Adams chuckled. "It wasn't a case of wearing me down," she insisted. "I fell in love with him too quick for that to be necessary. I just held out to keep him on his toes."

"That's not the way Jenny tells it," Lizzy said. "She says the two of them had to conspire to get you to walk down the aisle."

Janet winked. "And I've always let them think that. It gives me a good bit of leverage around here. Now come on into the living room and tell me all about school and Miami. Did you know I went there a couple of times when I was married the first time and living in New York? Jenny's father liked to go there on vacation, but from all I've read, it's changed a lot over the years. In those days, there were still old people rocking on the porches of those hotels in South Beach. Now, if the pictures I see are to be believed, the place has been overrun with sexy models in bathing suits and in-line skates."

Lizzy grinned. "That's not so far off, but can we talk about it at supper? I'd like to go for a ride. It's been way too long since I've been on a horse."

"Of course it can wait. Are you going to see Hank?"

"You, too?"

"Sorry." Her mother studied her intently. "Well, are you?"

Lizzy shrugged. "I'm not sure. I suppose I'll make up my mind while I'm riding."

"Well, in case you decide that the answer's yes, Cody tells me Hank is working in his south pasture today. You know, the one that conveniently butts up against ours. I believe he's replacing a fence that Cody swears was just fine the last time he checked it."

"I'll remember that."

"Be back by suppertime," her mother reminded her. "The whole family's coming for dinner to welcome you home."

"I'll be back," Lizzy promised.

"Bring Hank, if you like."

"If I see him."

"Oh, something tells me you'll see him," her mother said. "Can I just add one piece of advice to whatever your daddy's been telling you?"

Lizzy paused in the doorway. "What?"

"This isn't a game, Mary Elizabeth. While you've been gone, the rest of us have been left to watch Hank. The man's been miserable without you, but he's gotten by. Unless you're really sure about what you want, don't start something up with him."

Lizzy looked her mother squarely in the eye. "I

was never the one who was unsure, Mom. Hank didn't just let me go. He practically pushed me out the door. You all seem so all-fired sure that he wants me, but he's never once given me any evidence of that. How come nobody seems worried that I'm the one who's going to wind up hurt?"

"Because you've always been able to pick yourself up and dust yourself off, just the way the song says. And maybe because you're the one who's going to walk away in a couple of weeks." She gave Lizzy a penetrating look. "Aren't you?"

"Yes," Lizzy said quietly. No matter how things turned out when she saw Hank Robbins again, she was going to be on that flight back to Miami. She sighed heavily. "Maybe I won't go for that ride this afternoon, after all. I think I'll go on up to my room and unpack. I've got some thinking to do."

"The answers aren't in your room," her mother argued. "Something tells me they're out in Hank's south pasture."

Lizzy grinned at her beautiful mother. Janet Runningbear Adams's Native American ancestry had grown more pronounced as the years lined her face. Her straight black hair was streaked with gray now, but her eyes sparkled with intelligence and wisdom.

"Now who's trying to manipulate me?" Lizzy teased. "You've been with Daddy way too long." Her expression sobered. "He really is going to be all right, isn't he?"

Her mother met her gaze evenly. "If he takes it

easy and stops sneaking into the kitchen for ice cream when I'm not looking. I'm thinking of having the refrigerator padlocked.''

''It won't do a bit of good. He'll just find somebody in the family who'll sneak things in for him.''

''You're probably right. I caught Harlan Patrick taking cigars up to him the other day. He swore he'd just forgotten to take them out of his pocket, but Cody's boy never could lie worth a darn. You should have heard your daddy when he found out I'd confiscated the things.''

''When did Daddy start smoking cigars?''

''When he found out he shouldn't. He puffs on one every now and again just because he knows it makes me furious.''

Lizzy chuckled. ''He does know how to rile you, doesn't he?''

''Oh my, yes.''

''Mom, I'm sorry I wasn't here when he got sick and that I couldn't get back right away.''

''Oh, sweetie, don't feel bad about that. You have a right to live your life. And neither of us wanted you to take time off from your studies when we knew everything was going to turn out fine. Of course, your father and I both wish you were closer to home and that we could see you more often, but we're proud of you. Taking on medical school is a big deal. We know you're going to be a fine doctor.''

Lizzy thought of the grades she'd gotten on her last exams. ''I wish I had your confidence.''

Her mother regarded her with concern. "Troubles with your classes?"

"Nothing to worry about," Lizzy reassured her. "I'll get a grip on things once I get back."

"I'm sure you will. Now, go. If you're not going for a ride, get some rest before supper. You'll need it to fend off all the nosy questions. Your brothers and Jenny may complain about Harlan's meddling ways, but they've inherited the tendency."

Lizzy retreated to her room, which remained exactly as she had left it, with the ruffled curtains and rodeo posters, an admittedly incongruous mix that pretty much summed up her personality.

Instead of unpacking, though, she went straight to the window seat and settled back against the mound of pillows, staring out across the rugged terrain, imagining Hank out there somewhere, his skin bronzed by the sun and glistening with sweat.

Tomorrow, she thought. Tomorrow she would face him and find out if anything at all had changed between them. With luck she wouldn't be able to stand the sight of him. She sighed at the improbability of that. With better luck, he would sweep her into his arms and tell her he couldn't live without her. Now that, probable or not, was something worth waiting for.

Chapter Two

A man could only mend the same fence so many times without looking like a darned fool, Hank thought as the sun beat down on his bare back. Cody Adams had passed by twice the day before just to get in a few taunts about the obviousness of his activity and to keep him updated on Lizzy's whereabouts.

Even if Cody hadn't told him, though, Hank was pretty sure he would have known the precise instant Lizzy was back at White Pines. He could feel her presence. The air seemed to crackle with the electricity of it. And that old familiar ache in the region of his heart started up again.

"Just come to dinner at White Pines tonight," Cody had suggested. "You know you'd be welcome. The whole family will be there."

"I know that," Hank said.

He liked the whole Adams clan, from Harlan on down. They'd always made him feel like one of them. The littlest rascals in the family were so used to his presence, they had even taken to calling him Uncle Hank. He'd liked the feeling of belonging and he'd enjoyed spending many an evening with them since buying his ranch, but this was different. This time Lizzy would be there, and he didn't know what kind of welcome to predict from her, not when they'd parted on such uneasy terms.

"Another time," he said, covering his regret.

"She won't be here forever," Cody had reminded him. "And we have a bet."

"It's her first day home. There will be time for me to make good on that ridiculous bet."

Call it masculine pride or sheer muleheadedness, but what he didn't say was that he wanted Lizzy to come to him, that he wanted to know that she'd missed him at least enough to finally seek him out.

Oh, he knew as sure as shooting that she'd been avoiding him all these years. He'd seen the flush of embarrassment in her cheeks after she'd kissed him on the eve of her departure for college. He'd also seen the quick rise of anger and pride when he hadn't tried to stop her from leaving. She'd been so sure he would, so confident that that kiss would make a difference. He'd seen that, too.

Little did she know what letting her go had cost him. That unexpected kiss had turned him inside out.

No woman had ever made him want so much. And no woman had ever been so far out of reach. The distance was far greater than the miles between Los Piños and Austin or even the miles between home and Miami. They were separated by their dreams.

His were simple. He wanted a wife and children and a small ranching operation that he could take pride in having built from the ground up. The Triple Bar was his. There was no history or conditions tied to it, the way there would have been if he'd stayed at his daddy's place. In that, he was a whole lot like Luke Adams, the oldest of Harlan's sons.

Lizzy's hopes and ambitions were more complex and all-encompassing. Harlan Adams had laid the world at the feet of his baby daughter, and she had embraced it all. Hank wasn't sure she could ever be happy with a life as quiet and self-contained as the one he could offer.

He knew—he had always known—that he wanted more from her than a brief, passionate fling. And for that, she had to come to him in her own time, on her own terms. He'd long ago accepted the fact that she might never come at all.

Knowing that, he'd turned Cody's invitation down, then spent a miserable night back at his own ranch, cursing the day he'd ever met the pretty little sixteen-year-old who'd gone and grown up into a beautiful, willful woman who'd twisted his heart into knots. No man should have to contend with loving a woman like that and watching her walk away.

Today he was back in the same pasture, doing the same work all over again, hoping to catch at least a glimpse of her. What kind of fool did that make him? He'd been asking himself that since sunup and he didn't like the answer any better now than he had hours ago.

Hopefully, Cody wasn't spreading the word about what a pitiful spectacle Hank was making of himself. When he glanced up a few moments later, he thought he was seeing things. There was Lizzy Adams strolling across his pasture looking very much at home and pretty as a picture in her snug jeans and bright red shirt, her black hair streaming down her back under a big black Stetson. Right at this second, with that long, athletic stride of hers, she was a cowgirl through and through. He could almost make himself believe she hadn't changed at all.

Nor, unfortunately, had his reaction to her. His blood heated as if she'd done a whole lot more than offer him a smile and a wave. He was glad then that he'd waited to see her, glad that this first meeting wasn't taking place in front of all those prying, hopeful Adams eyes.

She looked confident and sassy and so damned tempting that Hank clutched the posthole digger a little tighter to keep from dragging her straight into his arms and giving her a proper—well, improper, actually—welcome.

Lizzy didn't seem inclined to show the same restraint. Her pace never even slowed as she sashayed toward him, lifted her hands to his cheeks, gazed straight into his eyes and planted a kiss on him guaranteed to fell a saint. The woman never had hesitated to take what she wanted. Her daddy had always led her to believe that it was her due.

There was hunger and passion and maybe even a little greedy desperation in that kiss on his part and hers. She smelled of sunshine and some kind of exotic flower and she tasted just the way he'd remembered with a hint of mint on her breath. They were both trembling and breathless by the time she pulled away.

"Damn," she murmured, her expression shaken.

Hank grinned. He knew precisely how she felt, as if the ground had shifted under their feet when everyone had declared the earthquake safely past. He dredged up his sense of humor to keep from revealing how shaken he, too, had been, how eager he was for more.

"Was it everything you remembered?" he taunted.

She scowled up at him. "Oh, go to hell."

"Now, that's a fine way to greet an old neighbor."

"The kiss was the greeting. The rest was regrets."

He laughed at that. "I know exactly what you mean."

She regarded him suspiciously. "You do?"

"I was kinda hoping I'd gotten it all wrong, too. Care to try again, just in case the first time was an accident?" The question had nothing to do with his bet with Cody and everything to do with his longing for further experimentation. He'd spent too many restless nights dreaming of having this woman back in his arms. The discovery that she still fit him like the other half of a carved piece of wood was too tempting to resist.

Lizzy shook her head as if to clear it. "No, please. Once was enough to prove the point."

"Coward."

"Me?" she protested. "If you thought the last kiss was all that great, where have you been for the past five years?"

He liked the disgruntled attitude and decided to spur it on. "Comparison shopping," he said.

She frowned at that.

Hank clung to the tiny hint of jealousy. "According to your family, you haven't exactly been living in a cocoon," he accused, immediately proving that he was just as capable of envy. Every mention of a man in Lizzy's life had set acid to churning in his gut, though until now he'd been good at hiding it.

"True."

He studied her speculatively. "So, Miss Lizzy, what do we do now? Wait another five years before we try it again?"

She considered that, her expression thoughtful as her gaze locked with his. Heat sizzled in the air. Finally she shook her head. "Pick me up at six."

Hank's pulse kicked up like an unbroken horse at the touch of a saddle. "For?"

"I wish I knew," she said with a sigh. "Trouble, more than likely."

"Now, Miss Lizzy, I do like the sound of that," he retorted.

"Don't go getting any wild ideas, cowboy," she said, and started to clamber back over the fence.

Hank wasn't ready to see her go. Not yet, not even with the promise of a whole evening ahead of him. "Lizzy?"

"Yes?"

"If you're not busy," he said oh so casually, "why don't you stick around?"

"Why?" she asked bluntly. "You need some help with this fence? Word is it was just fine before you started tampering with it."

He winced at the direct hit, but pressed on. "Actually, I was hoping you'd join me for lunch. I brought a couple of extra sandwiches, just in case you happened by."

Her expression brightened. "Ham and cheese?" she asked, eyeing his saddlebags with a gleam in her eyes.

"On Mrs. Wyndham's home-baked pumpernickel bread," he said, knowing she would find that—if not him—irresistible.

"Did you bring pickles, too?"

"A whole jar."

She was pawing through the saddlebags in an instant. When she'd plucked the thick, foil-wrapped sandwiches from them, her face lit up.

"I've dreamed of Mrs. Wyndham's sandwiches," she admitted as she moved to a spot in the shade of a huge old cottonwood. "I've been in a lot of delis the past few years, but none of them has gotten it quite right. Your housekeeper ought to be declared a national treasure."

"It's the bread," Hank said, taking a spot beside her and stretching his legs out in front of him. "I don't know what she puts in it, but the taste can't be matched."

"How'd you remember that I loved these so much?"

If only she knew how many times he'd sifted through the memories of every moment they'd ever shared. After all, she'd trailed after him for years, pestering him with questions and as time passed and she grew into a woman, blistering him with looks hot enough to sizzle steak.

"I remember a lot of things," he said quietly, his hat low so she couldn't read his expression.

"Such as?"

He could pretend, as he had done so many times in the past, treat the question dismissively, or he could tell the truth. Maybe it was time for a little straight-forward honesty between them.

"For one thing, the way your eyes light up with golden sparks when you take the first bite," he said, tilting the hat back and keeping his gaze on her steady. "The way your tongue darts out to lick the mustard from your lips. The way you always save one bite as if you can't quite bear to finish."

She blinked and swallowed hard, but it was Hank

who looked away first. If he started cataloging all the rest of the things he remembered about Lizzy, they'd waste the whole afternoon and his blood would be in a heated frenzy.

"How's med school?" he asked, forcing a neutral tone into his voice. This was safer ground, turf that would remind him of all that stood between them still.

"Okay."

"Still getting straight *As*?"

"Not this quarter," she said.

He heard the rare insecurity in her voice and wondered at it. "How come? Is it tougher than you expected?"

Even as he asked it, he wondered if he wanted the answer to be yes, wanted med school to be so tough that she'd give up on it and come home. But of course, Lizzy was no quitter and coming home a failure wouldn't sit well with her. That was no way to get what he wanted, and he knew it.

"Not so tough. I just haven't been able to keep my mind on my studies the way I should the past few weeks."

"Since Harlan's heart attack?" he guessed, knowing how that would have thrown her. He'd almost called her then to offer support or sympathy or, just as likely, to finally hear the sound of her voice again. That was what had held him back. He hadn't fully understood his own motives, and that was dangerous with a woman like Lizzy.

She nodded, then faced him, her green eyes with

those dazzling flecks of gold now clouded with worry. "Do you know how he is?" she asked. "I keep getting the feeling that nobody's telling me the whole truth."

He wanted to smooth away her frown, but settled for a teasing comment intended to do the same job. "Hey, you're the budding doctor. Couldn't you tell by looking at him that he's doing okay?"

"He looks good," she admitted. "But he wouldn't let me examine him."

Hank chuckled at her disgruntled tone. "I'm surprised you didn't wrestle him down and do it anyway."

"Believe me, I was tempted." She regarded him thoughtfully. "And you haven't answered my question, either. How is he?"

"What did your mother say?"

"Hank, you're being as evasive as the rest of them," she accused.

"I'm just saying if you want answers, the best people to ask are those around him, not me. Your mother doesn't lie to you, does she?"

"No, but—"

"No *but*s. What does she say?"

"That he's recuperating nicely and he'll be fine if he takes it easy."

"Well, then, that's your answer."

"No," she said, clearly unconvinced. "He should be up and about by now. You know Daddy. He never was one for sitting still for more than a minute."

"Maybe he's just hoping to get a little sympathy from his baby girl."

"Maybe."

He could tell that she still wasn't reassured. "You're really worried, aren't you?"

"Not worried," she said slowly, lifting her gaze to his. "Scared."

He saw now what he should have seen all along. "You're scared of losing him?"

Tears welled up in her eyes and came close to breaking his heart. She nodded.

"The others have all had him for a long time," she said in a choked voice. "Not me. Twenty-four years isn't nearly long enough."

Hank reached out and brushed away the tear that was tracking down her cheek, barely resisting the temptation to pull her into his embrace and comfort her. "Something tells me Harlan will be around a long time yet."

"Is that guesswork or wishful thinking?"

"Oh, I don't think he's going anywhere until he's had a chance to dance at your wedding. It wouldn't be like him to give up before getting his way."

A smile trembled on her lips. "He does seem to be fixated on getting me married off and pregnant. You'd think all those grandbabies and great-grandbabies already overrunning the place would be enough to suit him."

"But none of them belong to his precious baby girl," Hank countered. "You were the surprise and the blessing of his life. Naturally, he wants to see you settled."

"Whose side are you on?"

"Yours, of course. Always have been."

She regarded him with an unblinking gaze. "You have, haven't you? Even when you thought I'd lost my mind for running off and getting on the rodeo circuit."

"Now, that one did take a few years off my life," he said, recalling the heart-in-his-throat moments she'd put him through every time she'd climbed onto a bucking horse. "But nobody's ever been able to change your mind once you got something into your head. I figured it made more sense to make sure you could stay on a horse than to fight you."

"If it had been up to Cody, Jordan and Luke, they would have locked me in my room until I came to my senses," she recalled, grinning. "You and Daddy were the only ones who didn't try to stop me."

"What would have been the point? You'd have climbed out the window."

She leaned back against the trunk of the tree and gazed around, then sighed. "Do you have any idea how much I've missed all of this?"

"Not enough to come home for more than a minute at a time the last five years," he retorted.

Her gaze locked with his. "You noticed? I'd wondered if you had."

"I noticed," he said.

"You didn't exactly burn up the phone lines between here and Austin or here and Miami."

"Did you want me to? I thought the whole point of going away was so you could try your wings away from all the overprotectiveness around here, mine included."

"Maybe it was, at the beginning," she conceded. "Rebellion seems to be one of those Adams traits." Her lips curved. "But I missed this. I missed—"

Hank held his breath.

"—you," she said softly, as if she were testing it. "I missed you."

Damn, but it was good to finally hear her say the words. But missing wasn't loving. It wasn't saying that this time she'd stay and make a life with him. He couldn't put his heart on the line for that. "I missed you, too, kid."

She glared at him, just as he'd known she would. "Kid?"

Hank winked. "You're still younger than me."

"Oh, yeah. What are you now? Pushing sixty, right?"

"Not even half that, smart aleck."

"Twenty-nine isn't all that old, Hank." She looked him over with a deliberately provocative gleam in her eyes. "Looks as if you have a few good years left in you, if you'd work a little to get yourself in shape."

"What's wrong with the shape I'm in?" he demanded. "It can't be all that bad. You've been ogling me since you came out here."

"Have not."

"Have, too."

She chuckled. "Listen to us. We're back to bickering the way we used to."

"Some things never change."

"I wish nothing had to change," she said with a sigh.

He sensed the shift in mood went beyond the bickering of two old friends. "You're thinking of your father again, aren't you?"

She nodded, then forced a smile. "But all the worrying and wishing in the world won't change things."

"Have you talked to his doctor?"

"Not yet."

"Then go. Do that this afternoon. Maybe it'll put your mind at ease." He touched a finger to her cheek, watched the color bloom at the light caress. For an instant, her gaze clashed with his and he thought for sure she was going to turn her face ever so slightly and press a kiss to his palm.

But she drew in a deep breath and shot to her feet instead. "I think I will go see the doctor."

"Still want me to pick you up at six?"

She gave him a sassy grin. "Unless you're having second thoughts."

"Oh, no, darlin'. Where you're concerned, I've always had a one-track mind."

Hank's words lingered in Lizzy's head for the rest of the afternoon. There'd been a challenge there, no doubt about it. The man had actually been flirting with her, which had to be a first. She couldn't help wondering whether that was because he'd finally seen that she was all grown up or whether something else was going on. Living with a houseful of manipulators had made her wary of sudden shifts in attitude.

Of course, wariness wasn't enough to keep her home. She was curious to see just where this brand-new attitude would lead them. In fact, now that she'd been reassured by her father's doctor that his heart had suffered no permanent damage, she could devote all of her attention to Hank and figuring out just how much he really mattered to her.

Cody wandered in as she was pacing in the living room, awaiting Hank's arrival.

"Going someplace?" he asked, looking her over, then scowling at the short skirt she'd chosen.

"I have a date."

"With?"

"Hank."

His gaze narrowed. "Is that right?"

"Do you disapprove?"

"Of Hank? Of course not. But you might want to consider adding a couple of more inches to that skirt before you walk out the door."

Lizzy glanced down. "Why? Don't you think he'll like it?"

"Oh, he'll like it. A little too much would be my guess."

She grinned. "Then I got it just right, I think."

Her brother studied her worriedly. "Lizzy, what are you up to?"

"Up to?" she repeated innocently. "I have no idea what you mean."

"Oh, yes, you do. You've got that sneaky-female look in your eyes."

Lizzy laughed. "And what would you know about sneaky-female looks?"

"I'm married, aren't I? Melissa always gets a look just like that in her eyes right before she pulls the rug out from under me. I've watched my own daughter use it on every man she's ever dated, too. Now that Sharon Lynn's engaged, poor old Kyle Mason spends most of his life looking thoroughly bewildered by her. I actually feel sorry for him."

Lizzy gave a little nod of satisfaction. "Then I suppose I've finally got that right, too."

Something that might have been panic flared in her brother's eyes. "Lizzy, I will not have you going out with Hank and doing something you're going to regret."

"Regrets are for people who never took any risks," she retorted.

"Risks?" Cody demanded, his voice escalating. "Just what risks are you intending to take?"

Lizzy heard Hank's car outside and decided Cody had had about all he could take of her teasing. She reached up and patted his cheek. "Don't worry about a thing, big brother. I've got everything under control."

Cody moaned.

Lizzy walked out on him before he could get it into his head to try to run Hank off the property. That was not the sort of trouble she'd intended when she'd made this date. No, if there was going to be trouble tonight, it was going to be between her and Hank Robbins.

She could hardly wait.

Chapter Three

When Lizzy got outside, Hank was exiting his pickup. He almost stumbled at his first glimpse of her. His stunned expression was everything she'd hoped for when she'd chosen the skirt of which Cody so vehemently disapproved.

"Too anxious to wait for me to come in and get you?" Hank inquired, giving her a lazy, purely masculine once-over that raised goose bumps.

"Protecting your sorry hide," she declared, refusing to rise to the taunt. "Cody's into his big-brother mode. If he'd seen you looking me over like that, there's no telling what he'd do."

His gaze strayed to the midthigh hem of her skirt. "I can imagine. That skirt ought to be banned in most parts of the world."

"You don't like it?"

"Oh, I like it," he conceded. "It just changes my plans for the evening."

"In what way?"

"I don't think we'll be dining out in town, after all."

Lizzy chuckled. "Suddenly can't wait to get me alone, huh?" she taunted. She had deliberately—and successfully—provoked one reaction out of him. Now she was working on one far more dangerous.

"Not exactly," he retorted. "I'm just afraid I'd have to strangle half the men in town for salivating over you. Fortunately, Mrs. Wyndham hasn't left yet. I'll call her from the truck and tell her to fix something."

"Sounds good to me," Lizzy said, thinking the evening couldn't have looked more promising.

"You haven't gone and turned into a vegetarian, have you?"

"And have Daddy disown me? I don't think so."

"Then I'll tell Mrs. Wyndham to leave a chicken roasting or defrost a steak or something," he said, still sounding as if he'd been poleaxed.

Lizzy gave him a knowing look, then turned toward the truck and hesitated as she contemplated the long step up to get inside. It was the one thing she hadn't considered when she'd chosen her outfit for the evening. Obviously, she'd been living in the city too long, where flashy cars, not practical trucks, were the norm among the men she'd dated.

"An interesting quandary, isn't it?" Hank inquired, laughter threading through his voice. "Either you ask for help or you scramble up on your own and expose yourself—" he chuckled "—to humiliation."

"A gentleman wouldn't need to be asked," Lizzy declared.

Before the words were out of her mouth, he slipped up behind her. She felt his hands circle her waist and the next thing she knew she had been lifted off her feet and settled snugly into the passenger seat of the 4×4. But Hank wasn't half as quick to release her as he had been to lift her up. His work-roughened hands slid from her waist to settle briefly on her thighs. Her suddenly all too bare thighs.

Lizzy's breath caught in her throat, and heat climbed into her cheeks. Her pulse ricocheted wildly as Hank leaned closer and closer still until his lips were almost on hers. She waited impatiently for him to close the distance between them.

The man had impeccable timing. She'd give him that. Just when she thought her heart was going to burst with longing, his mouth settled over hers, soft and gentle and coaxing. It was nothing like their greedy, frantic kiss that morning. This one was all about subtle nuances and pure temptation.

The kiss lasted an eternity, or maybe it only seemed that way because it stole her breath and left her reeling. If she was over the man, his kisses shouldn't have any potency at all. One should have been pretty much like another.

Instead, they seemed to get more and more devastating. That morning, Lizzy had been thoroughly shaken by the discovery that time hadn't dimmed the power of Hank's kiss to rattle her completely. She was even more shaken by this one, in part at least because he had initiated it. It only confirmed the risk she was taking in seeing him tonight. Somewhere along the way, he'd gone and changed the rules on her.

First he'd openly flirted with her, and now this kiss. Whatever restraints he'd placed on his actions years ago seemed to be a thing of the past. The turnaround was unexpected and dangerous, but it played nicely into her own plans. For once she wasn't going to worry about risks or consequences. She was dedicated only to discovering whether old dreams could be turned into reality.

She suspected they both knew where this date was going to end up. Heck, she'd wanted to throw him down on the ground out in that pasture and make love to him right there. Discovering after all this time that he was not nearly as indifferent to her as he'd always pretended had only heightened her desire. At this rate, they'd be lucky if they made it to the end of the very long White Pines driveway before they started ripping each other's clothes off.

"Hank?"

"Hmm?" he murmured, clearly reluctant to release her.

"Cody's inside. He's probably been watching

every move we've made. My hunch is he's halfway between the living room and the gun cabinet.''

Hank pulled away and sighed. "I suppose you have a point.''

"Believe me, no one wishes it were otherwise more than I do.''

"Then I suppose I'll have to be satisfied with the fact that we're only twenty minutes down the road from my ranch.''

"We could make it in five, if we took the horses, instead of driving the long way around,'' Lizzy argued.

He studied her intently. "Surely you can hold the thought a few extra minutes.''

Lizzy refused to admit that she'd been clinging to the same thought for years. "I'm not sure. You might have to remind me.''

"Not a problem,'' he said, regarding her with a look every bit as hot as a branding iron. "Not a problem at all.''

Hank was pretty sure he was in way over his head. One look into Lizzy's sparkling, expectant eyes, and rational thought fled. He'd always known she wanted him, always forced himself to ignore the blatant desire in her eyes.

Tonight, though, there would be no ignoring the obvious. He had the distinct impression if he tried to exercise a little restraint, Lizzy would take matters into her own hands. Clearly, the woman was out of patience, and he was darned sure out of willpower.

Hank doubted Cody had intended him to seduce Lizzy the first chance he got. He also figured it was none of her big brother's damned business what they did. Lizzy was twenty-four now and certainly knew her own mind, and this had been a long time coming. Not that Lizzy's desires would enter into it for Cody—or any other Adams. If their protectiveness kicked in, Hank was done for.

For once, though, Hank was only going to worry about one Adams, the woman seated beside him with her eyes on the road and her hand resting less than subtly at the top of his thigh.

Lizzy's touch was so intimate, so disturbing that he forgot completely about the call he'd intended to make to his housekeeper. He had to concentrate very hard to keep his eyes on the road or they'd end up in a ditch.

Because of that, they walked into the ranch to find the lights on, but the oven cold and not so much as a whiff of Lizzy's favorite bread in the air, much less the scent of dinner.

"Damn," Hank muttered, gazing around in dismay at the tidied room and bare table. "Mrs. Wyndham's gone."

"Were you feeling the need for a chaperone?" Lizzy inquired.

"Actually, I was more concerned about the dinner I promised you."

She stepped up close and slid her hands up his chest. "Oh, I think we can improvise. I'll bet you know your way around a kitchen."

She might have been talking about cooking, but Hank got the distinct impression that dinner was the last thing on Lizzy's mind.

Still, he made a valiant attempt to get her to focus. He extricated himself from her clever, wandering hands and aimed for the refrigerator. Maybe a quick blast of chilly air would cool him off sufficiently to keep his wits about him. After all these years of waiting, he didn't want to hurry things along too much. There was something to be said for anticipation, though he'd thought until now that he'd had his fill of it.

"Hank?"

"Yes?"

"Am I making you nervous?"

"Sweetheart, a tornado makes me nervous. You scare the daylights out of me."

She seemed surprised and just a little fascinated by that. "I do? Why?"

Hank grinned at her. "Oh, no. I'm not giving you any ammunition to use against me. You're way too sure of yourself as it is." He deliberately turned back to study the contents of the refrigerator. "How about baked ham?"

Instead of a response, he felt the glide of a hand up his back. His body jolted at the touch.

"Lizzy." It came out in a choked voice, part plea, part protest.

"Yes, Hank."

She sounded amused. Obviously, Lizzy had learned a lot about seduction since she'd been away. Hank wanted to murder the man who'd taught her. He swallowed hard and forced a nice, neutral tone into his voice.

"I asked if you wanted baked ham."

"I want you."

Well, hell. The game was pretty much up now, Hank thought desperately. He slowly closed the refrigerator door and turned to face her. "Lizzy..." he began, intending to be rational and very, very careful in what he said next.

She cut him off by slanting her mouth over his and snuggling up so tight that his entire body went on red alert. He locked his fingers around her elbows, intending to push her away, but a moan of pure pleasure escaped instead.

She tasted like mint and felt like satin and fire. Hank's ability to fight the potent combination pretty much wilted on the spot. Years of pent-up hunger rampaged through him. There was a brief moment— no more than an instant—when he could have backed away, but as if she sensed it intuitively, Lizzy chose that precise second to slide her tongue into his mouth, to rock her hips against his already throbbing arousal.

Hank was lost. He'd wanted her for so long, dreamed of having her in his arms, in his bed, hot and willing and filled with just this kind of urgency. He broke off the kiss and scooped her into his arms, then headed for the master suite. At the door, he locked gazes with her.

"Are you sure?" he asked, because it was the right and honorable thing to do. Even so, he prayed he already knew her answer, because if she said no now, he was pretty sure his body would shatter into a thousand pieces.

She touched a finger to his lips and smiled. "Stop fretting, cowboy. I've been sure forever."

Hank believed her because he was desperate to. He carried her into the suite and kicked the door closed behind him. Slowly, he lowered her to the king-size bed, then went to pull the drapes across the wall-to-wall glass with its view of the wildflower-bright fields at sunset.

"No," Lizzy protested. "It's beautiful. It will be like making love outdoors." She grinned at him impishly. "Just the way I wanted to earlier today."

"Making love was on your mind this afternoon?"

"Yep," she said without the slightest trace of embarrassment. "How about you? Did it cross your mind when you saw me?"

All this straight-out talk about making love was making Hank nervous, but he couldn't deny the truth. "Oh, yeah, darlin'. It crossed my mind."

She gave a very feminine nod of satisfaction. "Good."

Hank sank down beside her. She had always had a

tart tongue and willful nature, but he got the distinct impression that the past few years had given her a new level of confidence to go along with that. Add in the discovery of her own sexuality, and she might very well be more than any sane man ought to tangle with.

"Lizzy—" he began, only to be interrupted before he could get the thought out.

"Hank, surely we did not come into your bedroom to chat," she said, reaching over to fiddle with the buttons on his shirt.

Hank brushed her hands away and tried one more time to focus on having a sensible discussion. "Lizzy, just how experienced are you?"

Her hands, already back at work on his buttons, stilled. She met his gaze evenly. "You want to talk about my track record with men?"

Hank detected a dangerous note in her voice, but he plunged on. "I think we should. Not how many or anything like that. That's none of my business, actually."

"I'm glad you can see that much at least."

He swallowed hard. "I was just wondering…have there been any?"

"I'm twenty-four, Hank. What do you think?"

He thought if she'd run across a man she wanted since leaving Los Piños, she wouldn't have hesitated to sleep with him. The gleam in her eye suggested it would be wise not to suggest that.

"I think," he said softly, "that a straight answer

is called for. Your experience or lack of it makes a difference in where we go from here.''

"Is this one of those technical discussions, then?'' she inquired ever so politely. "To determine if delicate, virgin-appropriate behavior is warranted?''

Heat flooded into Hank's cheeks. "Something like that.''

To his astonishment, a smile suddenly broke across her face and she flung herself into his lap.

"If that isn't the sweetest, most caring thing anyone has ever done,'' she said, peppering kisses across his face. "Next you're going to want to talk about birth control, aren't you?''

Hank sighed. "Yes.''

She knelt and straddled his thighs, framing his face with her hands. "Okay, here it is. I have never, ever slept with a man. I am taking birth-control pills. It seemed like the sensible, responsible thing to do. Does that cover everything?''

"Sensible?'' He seized on her choice of words. It wasn't a word he would have associated with the impetuous Lizzy. "Were you anticipating—'' he hesitated and chose his words carefully "—something like this?''

"I'm twenty-four,'' she reminded him again. "You never know when the right man might come along.''

"I see.''

"Hank?''

"Yes?''

"How much longer is this conversation going to last?"

He heard the thread of impatience in her voice, recognized the flare of fire in her eyes. "Oh, I'd say we're pretty much at the end of it."

"And you're not backing out or anything?"

He pulled her to him. "No, darlin'. Not if my life depended on it."

He covered her mouth with his and wondered at the way the taste and feel of her made his pulse jump and his blood heat. Surely other women had had the same effect, but at the moment he couldn't think of a single one who had. Maybe that's what truly scared the daylights out of him. He knew—had always known—that once a woman like Lizzy got into a man's blood, she'd be there forever.

Yet there was no way at all, no way in hell, he could walk away from her now without ever knowing the way her body would come alive at his touch, without tasting for the first time the pebble-hard nipple of her breast, without feeling the slick, moist heat of her surrounding him.

One by one, he stripped away her clothes, allowing himself to feast on the sight of her. He'd seen her in the skimpiest of bikinis, but it wasn't the same as watching her blouse slowly slither away to reveal a lacy, sexy bra in purest virginal white. It wasn't at all like watching her shimmy out of that scrap of a skirt to reveal lacy bikini panties in startling, come-hither red.

Sweet heaven, she was perfect, with her full breasts and narrow waist and hips that flared just enough to entice a man to bury himself inside her. Her skin, when he reached for her, was burning hot to his touch, a wonderfully alluring mix of silk and dangerous fire.

But it was the look in her eyes that captivated him. Part saucy wanton, part innocent, it was the look of a woman with no second thoughts and anticipation very much on her mind. She was his for tonight at least, and he would never forget the precious gift she was bestowing on him.

"You are so beautiful," he said, his voice low and husky. "So very beautiful."

"Am I?" she asked, sounding surprised.

"As if you didn't know."

"Okay, you're not the first person to say it," she admitted. "Just the first one who mattered."

Hank was awed by the implication of that and by the trust she was placing in him. "I've always thought you were beautiful," he told her. "I just wouldn't allow myself to think about it."

"I was so afraid you would never look at me as a woman, that I'd always be the pesky kid next door."

Hank chuckled. "Lizzy, I think you were born grown-up. I never thought of you as a kid—that was the scary part. I used to be terrified someone would take advantage of that."

"But never you," she said softly.

"No," he agreed. "Never me."

"Hank?"

"Mm-hmm."

"I think we've waited long enough."

"Yes, darlin', I think we most assuredly have," he agreed as he removed the last of her clothes and set out to teach her everything he knew about making love.

He was slow and patient and dedicated with his caresses, until the fire burning inside her had her writhing beneath him, her body coated with a sheen of perspiration and jolting with his every touch as she strained toward a first-ever climax.

"Not just yet," he whispered as he knelt above her. "We're going on this ride together."

He entered her then, taking care to be sure that the pain was quick and over almost before she knew it.

"Oh!" she protested, then "Oh, my" as he eased deep inside.

Hank couldn't seem to tear his gaze away from her face as emotions raced across it, from anxiousness to anticipation to pure, ecstatic delight. Then when he was sure that her pleasure was at its peak, he allowed his own to build until they both shattered with soul-rocking climaxes, first hers, then his.

Slowly, slowly, their breathing returned to normal. Hank's heart began to pump at a steadier beat. But, he realized, his desire hadn't waned at all. He knew in that instant that he would never get enough of Lizzy Adams, that the attraction would never wane, only deepen.

Maybe if this night had never happened, eventually

he would have found another woman to love, another woman to share his life. Now, though, he knew for fact what he'd always suspected: his life would never be complete without Lizzy in it. Just how in hell they were going to accomplish that was something to contemplate another time, without the distraction of having her curled up next to him, her sweet breath feathering across his chest.

"Lizzy?"

"Hmm?" she murmured.

"Are you okay?"

"Oh my, yes."

He smiled at the disingenuous reply. "Hungry?"

"You mean for food?"

"Yes, for food. It's getting late, and we missed dinner completely."

She sat up and stretched, the unselfconscious movement stirring him all over again. He couldn't seem to drag his gaze away from her body. She looked over at him, noticed his state of arousal and grinned.

"Are you absolutely certain dinner is what you're hungry for?" she inquired.

"I suppose I could wait a little longer," he conceded, reaching for her again.

It was an hour later before they finally left his bed and traipsed into the kitchen. He'd insisted Lizzy wear one of his shirts. "Otherwise we never will get dinner."

"No willpower, huh?" she inquired lightly.

"I think I've displayed amazing willpower over the years. Today's lapse is hardly inexcusable."

Her expression sobered. "Hank?"

He stilled and gazed into her upturned face. "What, darlin'?"

"What happens now?"

The topic was way too heavy and way too complicated for a midnight discussion. Hank sidestepped it.

"Now we get out eggs and scramble them, add a little ham and cheese and have ourselves a midnight snack."

"That's not what I meant and you know it."

He sighed. "I know it. I think maybe that's a question we both need to sleep on before we get into it."

"Which raises another subject," she said. "Am I sleeping here tonight or are you taking me home?"

Hank had given the matter some thought already. "Much as I would like to have you stay right here with me all night long, I think the smart thing to do is get you back to White Pines."

"Why?"

"The obvious answer is to keep your brothers from hunting me down with a shotgun, but it's more than that."

"Such as...?"

"I'm not sure we want to stir up a lot of questions before you and I are ready with the answers. Beyond that, I respect your father and mother too much to want to flaunt this in front of them."

She nodded slowly. "I suppose you're right." She regarded him with a hint of uncertainty. "You're not regretting this, are you?"

He cupped her head in his hand and planted a lingering kiss on her lips. "There is no way I could ever regret this. You and I have had this date with destiny a long time now." He studied her closely. "What about you, though? Any second thoughts?"

"Not a one."

"Well, then, let's get out a bottle of champagne and have a toast with our meal."

"Champagne?"

He grinned. "Would you prefer hot chocolate?"

"As a matter of fact, yes," she said, eyeing him with a touch of defiance. "So I'm not a world-class sophisticate. Sue me."

"Hey, there's nothing I like better than a little hot chocolate with marshmallows on top."

"You manage to make that sound incredibly sexy."

"It is. When all that gooey marshmallow winds up on your lips, I get to lick it off."

Lizzy's eyes brightened. "Now, there's an idea. Where are the marshmallows?"

"Over the stove."

He couldn't help noticing that when she reached for them, his shirt rose to an indecent level that distracted him from the eggs he was supposed to be fixing.

"Hank, is that the scrambled eggs I smell burning?"

He glanced down and yanked the frying pan off the burner. "Damn."

Lizzy peered into the ruined mess.

"Maybe you'd better let me fix them this time. You don't seem to be able to stay focused."

"If you had on a few more clothes, it wouldn't be a problem."

She spun around in an exaggerated pirouette. "I don't know. I'm growing rather fond of this look. It makes a definite fashion statement."

"Exactly. It says 'I've just been in bed with a man and I'm going back there at the first opportunity.'"

She chuckled. "Can you think of a better marketing slogan than that?"

"I don't think they need to market sex. It does just fine on its own."

"I was talking about shirts."

"Sure, you were."

"Not everything is about sex."

"It is in this room," he observed. "Now sit down over there and behave. The eggs will be ready in a minute."

She sat, but she bounced right back up. "How about toast? Want me to make toast?"

He scowled with mock ferocity. "Sit."

She grinned knowingly, but she sat once more, only to pop right back up. "Juice. I'd love some orange juice. How about you? Aren't the glasses up on the top shelf? I'll just stretch a little and—''

Hank gave up on the eggs, the meal, everything except Lizzy. He turned off the stove, then scooped her up.

''Whoops,'' she exclaimed when he swept her off her feet and headed back to the bedroom.

It was 3:00 a.m. when he finally dropped her off at White Pines. Neither one of them seemed to give a darn that they never had had dinner.

Chapter Four

Lizzy would have slept until noon, but the pounding on her bedroom door had her jolting awake at barely seven. The incessant noise pretty much destroyed the good mood she'd been in when she'd crawled under the covers after coming home from Hank's.

"Who the devil is it?" she shouted.

"Justin."

"And Harlan Patrick."

Her nephews, who were virtually the same age she was, had better have a very good reason for hauling her out of bed at this ungodly hour or she was going to scalp the pair of them.

"What do you want?" she demanded, hauling the covers up to her neck and considering whether to bury her head under a pillow to drown out the noise.

"We thought you might want to go for a ride," Justin said, sounding innocent as a lamb. "Unless you've turned into too much of a city girl and forgotten how."

"It's a beautiful morning," Harlan Patrick added.

Neither of the two young men had ever been particularly inspired by the weather before. Lizzy's suspicions were promptly aroused. They had been sent, no doubt by their respective fathers—her big brothers—to pump her for information about her date with Hank.

"Go away."

"You sound sleepy," Justin noted. "Must have been a late date."

"She got home after three this morning," her father chimed in from his suite of rooms across the hall.

Oh, sweet heaven, Lizzy thought, moaning. The whole blasted family was in on the act. Thank goodness she *had* come home, instead of staying at Hank's as she'd desperately wanted to do. He'd been very wise to insist on it.

Obviously, going back to sleep was out of the question. She climbed out of bed and yanked on a robe. Without bothering to wash her face or run a brush through her hair, she yanked open her bedroom door and padded out to join the fray.

"Are you two happy now?" she inquired testily. "Now the whole household's wide-awake and knows the details of my date."

Justin grinned. "Sounds to me like Grandpa Harlan already knows more than we do."

She poked her head in her father's room to find him out of his bed and reading the morning paper in a chair by the window in the sitting room next door. He wasn't even trying to look innocent. She aimed a suspicious look in his direction.

"Which brings up an interesting point," she said. "What were you doing up at 3:00 a.m.? You're supposed to be a sick man."

He winked at his grandsons, then turned to Lizzy. "I'm a light sleeper. You ought to remember that next time you come in humming some cheerful little ditty. Of course, your mama and I certainly did enjoy the entertainment."

"I'll bet it was a love song," Harlan Patrick, Cody's son, taunted with a wicked gleam in his eyes.

"And I'll bet you never inspire a woman to hum a love song, you sorry excuse for a male," Lizzy retorted.

"Children, children," her father chided.

Justin's expression sobered at once. "How're you feeling, Grandpa Harlan?"

"Better now that I've got a doctor in the house."

"That's nonsense," Lizzy countered. "You don't even trust me enough to let me take your pulse."

Harlan Patrick winked at her. "Is that what you were doing till three in the morning? Playing doctor with Hank?"

A fiery blush bloomed on her cheeks. "You are such a pain. You know that, don't you?"

"But I'm handsome and sexy and lovable."

"I can't imagine who ever told you that," she said.

"Laurie Jensen, that's who," Justin retorted, giving his cousin a wink. "Laurie thinks Harlan Patrick hung the moon. And for your information, she has been writing songs about him. She claims one day she's going to make him famous with a Grammy-winning country-music song."

"She'll do it, too," Harlan Patrick said with obvious pride. "The woman does have a way with words."

"She ain't half-bad-looking, either," Justin noted appreciatively. "Wait till you meet her, Lizzy. You won't be able to imagine what she sees in a poor old cowboy like this one."

"Hey, watch it," Harlan Patrick warned. "Just because you don't have a woman in your life doesn't mean you get to pay close attention to mine."

"Would *you all* stop your fussing?" Harlan grumbled. "A man can't get any peace in his own house anymore."

Lizzy dropped a kiss on her father's cheek. "I thought you were sick of peace and quiet."

"I'm just beginning to recognize its advantages," he retorted. "Now, get along with you, all of you. Breakfast's getting cold downstairs." He shot a look at his namesake. "I don't suppose you could slip one of those blueberry muffins up to me."

"No, he could not," Lizzy declared, even as Harlan Patrick gave his granddaddy a conspiratorial wink. She whirled on her nephew. "You will not bring a muffin up here."

"Oh, don't go getting your drawers in a knot, Doc," Harlan Patrick responded. "They're fat free. Everything around here these days is fat free and cholesterol free—"

"And downright boring," her father concluded.

"You mean healthy," Lizzy corrected.

"No, I mean boring. If you knew what I'd pay for some eggs and bacon and home fries, you'd haul it up here yourself."

"Not if I was destitute," she countered. "Now read your paper and rest. It's good to see you out of bed."

"Then you'll be downright thrilled when you find me downstairs at lunchtime," he retorted. "It's about time I had me a face-to-face talk with that housekeeper of mine. Janet won't let Maritza near me because she's afraid I'll pull rank and make the old woman fix me something edible."

That said, he turned his attention back to the paper, dismissing the lot of them.

With her father's bedroom door closed again, Lizzy turned to her nephews. "I'll see the two of you downstairs."

"Don't take too long primping," Justin warned. "Hank's probably getting restless."

"Besides, something tells me the man's so smitten

already, he won't care if you're all dolled up or not," Harlan Patrick chimed in.

"What does Hank have to do with this ride we're taking?" she inquired warily.

Both men grinned.

"What would be the fun of going if it didn't give us a chance to see the fireworks going off the minute the two of you get into close proximity?" Harlan Patrick said.

Justin added, "And something tells me the show's going to be better than ever this morning."

"Daddy told me Hank planned to work up by the creek today," Harlan Patrick added. "Funny how that immediately brought to mind what a lovely spot that would be for a romantic little picnic should anyone special happen to come along."

"Hasn't anyone ever taught you guys the old expression that two's company and three's a crowd?" Lizzy muttered, slamming her bedroom door in their faces.

Despite their admonition to hurry, she took her time and primped. She told herself it was just to spite Harlan Patrick and Justin, but the truth was she wanted Hank to take one look at her and remember every steamy, sexy minute they had spent together the night before. She didn't want that famous noble streak of his to go kicking in and call a halt to this relationship before it got off the ground. He'd already been worrying something fierce by the time he brought her home. She'd felt it in the distracted, halfhearted way he'd kissed her good-night.

Thinking about that, she concluded she didn't especially want an audience when she saw Hank this morning. She wanted to be able to indulge in all of her powers of persuasion, which she certainly didn't want reported back to the rest of the family as the kind of gleeful gossip Justin and Harlan Patrick were prone to. The pair of them had spent their teenage years tormenting her about her crush on Hank and about every other date she had. They considered it their duty to be their grandfather's eyes and ears on his baby girl's love life.

She slipped down the back stairs, intending to sneak out through the kitchen, only to find Harlan Patrick and Justin sitting at the kitchen table talking to the housekeeper as they drank their coffee.

"Took you long enough," Justin grumbled.

"Typical woman," Harlan Patrick said.

"Actually, I was hoping you two would be long gone by now."

"And miss out on watching you and Hank dance around each other in some sort of bizarre mating ritual?" Harlan Patrick said. "Not a chance. I can't recall ever seeing two people spend so much time pretending not to be crazy about each other, when it was plain to everyone else how they really felt."

"Boys, stop teasing your aunt," Maritza chided. "In matters of the heart, only the people involved can decide what's for the best."

"But some of them are pitifully slow about figuring it out," Justin commented.

"I wasn't aware there was a timetable," Lizzy retorted. "Maritza, is there any coffee left or have these two finished the entire pot?"

"I have coffee in a thermos for you and saddlebags packed with warm coffee cake. Enough for two."

Lizzy grinned. "Not four?" She looked at the two men as she took the thermos and headed for the door. "Sorry, guys."

"They have had their share," the housekeeper said. "Along with eggs and toast and home fries and ham."

She paused with the screen door half-open. "Neither of them slipped away during breakfast and carried that same menu upstairs, did they?"

"Never," Maritza insisted. "That is why I made them eat in here, where I could keep a close eye on the two of them. I know they are the ones responsible for sneaking things to your father."

"Uh-oh," Justin said. "We've been busted."

"Hope word doesn't get around when you go off to the police academy," Harlan Patrick said. "You'll never get an undercover assignment."

Stunned by the taunt, Lizzy stared at the older of the two. "Justin?"

He shot her a defiant look. "What?"

"Since when are you not going into the oil business with your father?"

"I decided a while ago," he admitted.

"But he just got around to telling Jordan last week," Harlan Patrick said. "Be glad you weren't around for that explosion."

"I can imagine," Lizzy said. "He always dreamed of turning the business over to you."

"So, he'll turn it over to Dani's husband instead," Justin said, referring to his older half sister. "Duke loves the oil business. He's good at it. Let him sit around and push papers for the rest of his life. I want to be a cop."

Lizzy wasn't sure which startled her more, Justin's choice of a career or his daring to defy his father.

"Even when we were kids, you always wanted to play the good guy," she recalled thoughtfully. "I suppose it makes sense. If Jordan calms down long enough to think about it, maybe he'll see that you came by the notion naturally. He was always a real straight arrow, too."

"Maybe you could mention that to him next time you see him," Justin said. "Not that I need his approval, but it sure would be nice not to walk into an armed camp every time I go through the front door. Poor Mom's caught in the middle."

"How does she feel about you becoming a cop?"

"She's pretty much okay with it, as long as I come back here to work, instead of going to some big city like Dallas or Houston. That scares her to death."

"Will you do that?" Lizzy asked. "Will you come back to Los Piños?"

Justin nodded. "That's the plan."

"He seems to think he knows all the laws around here real well," Harlan Patrick teased, "especially since he broke so many of them."

Ignoring the taunt, Lizzy came back into the room and hugged Justin. "I'm glad for you. Fighting the plans this family makes for us isn't the easiest thing in the world to do." She turned to Harlan Patrick. "You're lucky. You've always wanted to follow in your daddy's footsteps and run White Pines someday. Ranching is in your blood."

"That and Laurie Jensen," Justin taunted.

"Okay, enough," Harlan Patrick said, heading for the door. "Are you two coming or not? I don't have all day to waste sitting around here gossiping like an old woman."

"Oh?" Lizzy retorted. "But you have enough time to come along and spy on Hank and me?"

He grinned. "Yep. I always make time for the important things. Besides, I promised Grandpa Harlan I'd come back with a full report."

With that, he took off running, Lizzy right on his heels. "You'd better be darned glad your legs are longer than mine," she shouted after him. "Because if I catch up with you, Harlan Patrick Adams, you are a dead man."

"Big talk for a city girl," he shouted right back as he mounted his horse.

The two men had saddled Lizzy's horse before she came downstairs so she was able to mount the pretty little mare and take off after Harlan Patrick at a full gallop. Justin muttered a curse, then raced after them.

After the first ten minutes of the high-spirited chase, Harlan Patrick slowed his horse and allowed Lizzy and Justin to catch up. He winked at her.

"Truce?"

She debated making it so easy on him, then nodded. "Truce."

"Thank goodness," Justin muttered. "I really wasn't ready for my first homicide investigation."

"But just think what a reputation you would have gotten if your first arrest had been Lizzy," Harlan Patrick noted. "Ordinary folks would have trembled in fear at the sight of you in uniform."

"Okay, okay, fellows, let's not get carried away," Lizzy said. "Nobody's going to die." She gave him a pointed look and added, "Leastways not this morning. And nobody's going to jail. Now fill me in on the rest of the news around here."

"You heard it all at supper your first night back," Justin declared. He shot a sly look over her head at Harlan Patrick. "Of course, there was that one rumor about Hank that nobody mentioned."

Lizzy's gaze narrowed. "What rumor about Hank?"

"That he's got a woman over in Garden City, one he's been seeing real regular."

"Yeah, I hear she's hot, too," Harlan Patrick said.

Lizzy's temper began to heat. "Is that so?" she said softly.

"Now, I ain't saying it's fact," Justin said. "Just that it's a rumor. Of course, you know how talk can get started around here. All it takes is somebody blabbing about something totally innocent, and the next thing you know, trouble's brewing."

"Oh, trouble's brewing, all right," Lizzy said just as Hank came into sight. He was taking a break from whatever work he'd been doing. He'd stripped off his shirt in the morning heat and was leaning back against a tree, his Stetson tilted low over his face.

Lizzy dismounted, stalked straight over to the creek and filled her own hat with icy water, then took it and dumped it squarely over the two-timing sneak. Drenched, he jolted upright to the sound of masculine laughter and hoofbeats. Lizzy whirled and saw that her nephews had taken off, kicking up a storm of dust in their wake.

When she turned slowly back, Hank was regarding her warily. "Mind telling me what that was all about?"

She winced as she watched the water tracking down all that bare flesh.

"If I had to guess, I'd say it was a little practical joke courtesy of Harlan Patrick and Justin."

"Where's the guesswork? You're the one who soaked me. Don't you know why the hell you did it?"

"I did it because of something they told me," she confessed, watching him uneasily. "But judging from the way they took off, I'd have to say now that they probably made the whole wild tale up.''

''And what wild tale would that be?''

She would have preferred to avoid getting into that, but Hank's expression warned her not to try dancing around the subject. ''Something about you and a woman in Garden City,'' she admitted reluctantly. ''A very hot woman.''

Hank nodded soberly. ''I see. And you were what? Jealous, maybe?''

''Never,'' she denied instinctively.

''Oh, really? Then why am I soaking wet?''

''Because...'' Her voice trailed off for lack of a plausible explanation.

''Because you were mad as hell that I might be seeing another woman,'' he teased. ''Well, hallelujah!''

''I'm glad you're enjoying yourself so much.''

''It's just that I have waited for a very long time for some sign that you gave two figs about what I did with my time. Do you know how many rumors I planted at White Pines every time you were due home?''

She stared at him incredulously. ''You planted rumors,'' she repeated slowly. ''To make me jealous?''

He nodded, grinning. ''If you counted up, I have supposedly dated at least a dozen women since you left town. I came darned close to playing the wedding march as background music every time I casually dropped a hint about one of them. You have no idea what it did to my ego to have you ignore every single rumor.''

Lizzy walked up and jabbed a finger in his chest. ''Why you, low-down, sneaky, lying devil,'' she said as she began backing him up. She came up with a satisfyingly long list of comparisons to reptiles and other forms of lowlife. With each step, an unsuspecting, defensive Hank came closer and closer to the bank of the creek. In the end, all it took was a gentle nudge to topple him straight into the icy water.

The shocked expression on his face was priceless, but she didn't have much time to enjoy it. The glint in his eyes suggested she just might have overplayed her hand.

''Gotta go,'' she announced, and raced for her horse.

Just as she loosened the reins she'd looped around a low-hanging branch, Hank gave a sharp whistle and the mare bolted.

''Uh-oh,'' Lizzy murmured as a dripping Hank strode toward her.

''Uh-oh is right,'' he said in a silky voice that was more dangerous than a shout.

''Now, Hank,'' she soothed.

''Don't worry, darlin'. This will be painless,'' he replied as he reached for her.

''You're all wet,'' she protested.

''Now, whose fault is that?'' He dragged her close, then slanted his mouth over hers, swallowing her screech of dismay.

Then she concluded that it didn't matter that Hank was soaking wet or that the creek had been like ice. Between them, there was enough heat to warm an entire cabin in a blizzard. She was pretty sure there had to be a fog of steam around them.

"Now, then," Hank murmured slowly when he pulled away. "You won't ever, ever try anything like that again, will you?"

Lizzy grinned. "If it's going to turn out like this, I might."

He chuckled. "Obviously, the punishment did not suit the crime. My mistake."

With that, he scooped her up and headed straight into the creek, not slowing until he was waist high and Lizzy was every bit as soaked as he was.

She was sputtering by the time he carried her back to shore. "That was…"

"Yes?"

She heard the dare in his voice. "Memorable," she said finally. "Definitely memorable."

"Good."

"Just one thing."

"What's that?"

"Is there a woman in Garden City?"

Hank hooted. "If there were, do you think I'd tell you?"

Lizzy regarded him suspiciously. "Whose hide would you be protecting? Hers or yours?"

"Doesn't matter. When you get riled, you are a force to be reckoned with."

She gave a little nod of satisfaction. "You'd do well to remember that."

"Duly warned," he agreed, then gave her a once-over that raised goose bumps. "Now, then, why don't we get out of these wet clothes and lay them in the sun to dry?"

"That could take a long time," she noted, her pulse already pounding.

"Indeed, it could."

"What will we do to make the time pass?"

"Oh, I have a few ideas."

She grinned at his expression. "Oh, I'll just bet you do. I have some nice hot coffee. We could drink that. And have some of Maritza's coffee cake."

"That wasn't by any chance in your saddlebags, was it?"

She glanced over to where she'd had her horse tethered and remembered the beast's defection. "Never mind."

"Don't look so sad, darlin'. I think I can make you forget all about that coffee cake."

"You'll have to work very hard at it."

"Oh, I intend to," he said, beginning to undo the buttons on her blouse. "In a couple of minutes, you won't even remember how we got into this fix."

His knuckles skimmed across her nipple as he removed her soggy bra. Desire shimmered through her. By the time her clothes were spread out in the sun and his were scattered beside them, there was absolutely nothing on Lizzy's mind but the way Hank's body fit so perfectly with her own.

Chapter Five

For Hank and Lizzy, the pattern established itself quickly and continued for the next several days—a few hours apart, then long, leisurely evenings indulging in the passion they had denied themselves for far too long.

They discovered a lot about each other during those nights. She realized that his feelings for her weren't new at all. Years ago they had been powerful enough for him to understand her dream and to let her go. He recognized that she had grown into a woman capable of giving every bit as much as she took. She was dedicated to the profession she'd chosen, but she was capable of being just as committed to a man.

None of that changed the fact that she was going

to leave, that in a few days she would go back to Miami and back to medical school.

And he would stay behind.

It made their time together bittersweet, but this time Hank clung to the possibilities instead of the doubts. He set out to court her, to show her all of the thousand and one ways he needed her.

He was selfish about it, too. He didn't want to share her for a minute. Their trips into town for dinner were always cut short by the quick flaring of passion, the hunger to be alone and in each other's arms.

Even though he understood the necessity for her going back to White Pines each night, even if it was barely before the crack of dawn, he hated losing even those few sweet hours when they might have been together. To his gratification, she hated it more.

But no matter what arguments she tried, he was adamant. Part of it was respect for her parents. Some of it was a way of clinging to a shred of distance, a way of pretending to himself and to her that their relationship wasn't as all-consuming as they both knew it was.

And some of it, he conceded ruefully, was a way of staving off exhaustion. In bed together, there wasn't a chance in hell either of them would get a wink of sleep.

"Will you be having dinner in tonight?" Mrs. Wyndham asked as Lizzy drove up outside as she had been doing every afternoon by three, the time when Hank cut short whatever work he'd been doing and came inside to shower and change for their time together.

Hank watched Lizzy emerge from the car and managed to draw his attention away from the sight of that slim, lithe body long enough to murmur assent.

"Anything in particular you'd like me to fix?"

"Whatever you think."

"I doubt either one of you will notice," the housekeeper muttered, but there was a smile on her face when Hank jerked around to look at her.

"You're probably right, Mrs. Wyndham," he admitted sheepishly. "But just in case, fix something decadent for dessert. Lizzy has a sweet tooth."

He'd discovered that about her, that and her ready laughter, her razor-sharp wit and the surprising grasp she had of ranching. Why hadn't he realized that being Harlan Adams's daughter meant ranching was in her blood? It allowed him to believe that she would be suited to life here with him, even if it meant foregoing her medical career. He prayed he wasn't deluding himself about that.

She'd certainly seemed contented enough the past few days. The subject of school hadn't cropped up once. He sighed and wondered if maybe it should. A big part of her life had been declared off limits by silent, mutual consent.

Yet when she came rushing through the front door, a smile on her face, Hank didn't have the stomach for hard truths.

"Hey, darlin'," he said, opening his arms to welcome her.

Lizzy fit against him snugly, generating enough heat that only Mrs. Wyndham's presence nearby kept him from making love to her smack-dab in the middle of the foyer. Eyes shining, she met his gaze.

"So, cowboy, what are we going to do tonight?"

"I thought we'd stay in. Do you mind?"

"Are you kidding? There's no place I'd rather be, nothing I'd rather do."

He searched her face intently. "You sure about that?"

"Absolutely."

"There must be friends you've been wanting to catch up with," he suggested. "And your family must be wondering where you've disappeared to."

"I've caught up with all my friends in the mornings, when you've been busy. As for my family, they have a pretty good idea where I've been spending my time."

"And they don't object?"

"Not when you're making me so incredibly happy."

He grinned at that. "I'm sure if it were otherwise, I'd have heard from those overprotective big brothers of yours."

"Exactly right," she said, then gave him a wide-eyed look. "What are you planning to do to keep me happy?"

"I think I'll start with this," he said, lowering his head to steal a kiss.

He meant it to be no more than a teasing brush of his lips, but kissing Lizzy never quite turned out the way he expected. She had a sneaky way of luring him into doing things he'd never intended. He was hot and hard and breathless by the time they broke apart. Not that it took a lot of doing, but she could make him want her with a fierce desperation just by skimming her mouth over his.

Wanting that badly should have terrified him, but he ignored all the warning signs. All he felt was gratitude that she wanted him back. Today, this minute were the only things that mattered. Tomorrow would just have to take care of itself.

"If we don't slow down, we're going to shock Mrs. Wyndham," he said.

"Give her the rest of the day off," Lizzy suggested.

"She's fixing our dinner."

"We can finish," Lizzy said as she unbuttoned a few more buttons on his shirt. "Later."

Hank groaned as her lips touched bare skin. "Much later."

She had worked most of his shirt free when he struggled to regain his composure. "Wait," he murmured with regret.

"Wait? Why?"

"Because I still haven't made it to the kitchen to tell Mrs. Wyndham she can leave."

"Oh. Right." Her gaze locked with his. "Maybe I'll just wait for you in your room."

Hank swallowed hard. "That would be good."

He watched her sashay off down the hall, then shook himself. What was he supposed to be doing? Oh, yeah, giving his housekeeper the night off.

At the doorway to the kitchen, he checked to make sure all his clothes were back in place, then opened the door. Suddenly, he felt like a schoolboy again, trying to put something over on a teacher.

"Mrs. Wyndham."

She glanced up from the pie crust she was rolling out. "Yes, sir."

Hank searched for an explanation that sounded innocent, but not one single word came to mind. "Um, how's dinner coming?"

"It'll be a while yet. It's not even four. I was figuring on getting it on the table at six, like always. Is that okay? Are the two of your hungry now? I could fix a snack."

The kind of hunger troubling them could not be sated with cheese and crackers, Hank thought. Still, he nodded. "Sure, a snack would be great." He glanced around for something that didn't require preparation. "Maybe some fruit," he said, seizing on the sight of a huge pottery bowl of apples, oranges and bananas. "I'll just take this."

He grabbed the bowl and headed for the door. Only when he was on the other side did he realize that the woman was chuckling. So much for discretion. Obviously, he was totally, disgustingly transparent.

When he walked into the bedroom with the fruit, he found Lizzy in the middle of his bed without a stitch of clothes on. The bowl slipped from his grasp, and fruit tumbled every which way. He barely noticed. Thankfully, the pottery was cushioned by the carpet or he'd have been walking over shards of it to get to the woman before him. He quickly shut the door behind him and turned the lock.

"Got a little ahead of me, didn't you?" he asked, his gaze fastened on her bare breasts.

"You looked as if you could use a surprise."

"Honey, a birthday cake is a surprise. This is a shock."

"A shock?" she repeated, sounding suddenly uncertain.

"Not a bad shock," he said hurriedly. "It's just that Mrs. Wyndham is still here."

"You didn't tell her to go home?"

He shook his head. "Afraid not."

"How come?"

"Because it would have been like telling my mother to go away so I could have sex." He shuddered at the thought. His mother was a lovely woman, but she did have her rules about propriety. This situation definitely did not fall within the guidelines. He figured his housekeeper would agree.

Lizzy chuckled. "Hank Robbins, you are shy."

"Not shy, just discreet."

"Which explains all those apples and oranges. Somehow your housekeeper got the idea that we were hungry."

"Starving, in fact."

"Then I suppose you'd better gather them up and bring 'em over here. You can peel the oranges and feed them to me." She winked. "With any luck, the juice will trickle into all sorts of interesting places."

"Right," Hank said, though he was having difficulty tearing his gaze away from the sight before him on the bed. "Just one thing."

"What's that?"

"Do you suppose you could put your clothes back on? I'm having a really hard time concentrating." He forced himself to begin the search for apples and oranges. When he had most of the elusive fruit back in the bowl, he backed toward the door. "I'll just be in my office when you're dressed."

"I could just slide under the covers and wait until Mrs. Wyndham leaves."

"Bad idea," Hank said.

"You afraid she'll check the room before she goes?"

"No, I'm very much afraid I'll throw caution to the wind and join you. The whole orange-juice image you stirred up was damned inviting."

"I could live with that."

He grinned at the declaration. "Sure. You're leaving town. I'm the one who'd have to live down send-

344 THE COWGIRL & THE UNEXPECTED WEDDING

ing my housekeeper into cardiac arrest when she found the two of us.''

She studied him thoughtfully. ''Maybe it wouldn't be such a bad idea. At least the gossip would warn all the predatory females in town that you're mine.''

''Darlin', there are no females in town you need to worry about,'' he assured her.

''What about Garden City?''

Amused by her continued fascination with the mysterious woman in the next town, he shrugged. ''I doubt the gossip would spread that far.''

Her gaze narrowed. ''Then you're admitting there is a woman there?''

''I'm not admitting to a thing.''

''Why won't you tell me?''

''Because not knowing for sure will give you a reason to hurry home.''

''Oh, I'll be back in June, all right. And I'd better not hear that you've been roaming over to the next county.''

''Or what?''

''Or I'll just have to go over there myself and tear her hair out.''

Lizzy sounded so fierce that Hank was very relieved that no such woman existed. He also couldn't help feeling just a bit of smug satisfaction that Lizzy Adams was finally, at long last, pea green with jealousy.

Except for her morning visits with her father over his much-hated bran cereal, Lizzy was beginning to resent every second she had to spend away from Hank. These first days of loving him openly were so precious, she didn't want to waste a minute of them.

Still, there were those times when Hank had to work, anyway. She used those hours to visit with her sister, Jenny, and her nieces, Dani and Sharon Lynn, both of whom were a few years older than she was. Sharon Lynn was happily planning an oft-delayed, midsummer wedding to longtime fiancé Kyle Mason. This time the two of them were determined to pull off the event. Every previous attempt had been postponed due to one crisis or another. Lizzy had her own opinion about the real reason for the delays, but she would never in a million years have shared them with Sharon Lynn. As long as her cousin was determined to go through with this wedding, come what may, then Lizzy was behind her a hundred percent.

Now, with the absolutely, positively, last-chance, final date practically upon her, Sharon Lynn was so distracted that most of the customers at Dolan's Drugstore were at high risk when they ordered lunch at the counter Sharon Lynn had been running for the past few years. Lizzy walked in just as her niece was about to serve a raw hamburger to the local sheriff.

"I'll take that," she said, swooping in and grabbing the plate before her niece could put it down.

Sharon Lynn gazed at the plate blankly. "Was something wrong?"

Lizzy winked at Tate Owens. "Even old Tate here

likes his meat cooked before he eats it," she said as she slapped the burger on the grill. "Why don't you have a seat at the counter, sweetie? I'll rustle up a sandwich for you, too."

"But it's my job," Sharon Lynn protested.

"Which won't last much longer if you keep running off the customers with your offbeat recipes."

Sharon Lynn looked puzzled. "Offbeat recipes? I don't understand."

"You gave Millicent ketchup with her pancakes yesterday and tried to pour soda over Mr. Lincoln's cornflakes," Lizzy said, mentioning only the latest two episodes of forgetfulness that had been described by her father that morning. He was taking great delight in the tales Harlan Patrick was spreading about his sister.

"Then there was the notorious tuna-salad incident," the sheriff chimed in cheerfully. "Jake Conroy's still trying to figure out the sweet taste of that sandwich you served up on a sliced doughnut. Fortunately for you, Jake's eyesight ain't what it used to be."

Sharon Lynn sank down on a stool. "Good heavens. It's gotten that bad?"

"Worse, actually, but nobody's blaming you yet," Lizzy said. "Everybody knows your mind's on your wedding."

"Do you suppose that's why Kyle thought the last milk shake I fixed him tasted like grapefruit juice?"

Lizzy exchanged an amused glance with Tate as

she gave him his medium-rare burger. "Could be," she agreed. "I'm surprised he noticed. Word is that he's every bit as muddleheaded these days as you are."

"And I suppose you've never done anything absentminded," Sharon Lynn grumbled. "Just wait. The way things are going with you and Hank, one of these days you're going to walk out of the house without your shoes or with your hair in curlers and wonder why everybody's staring."

"Lordy, I hope not. If I get that distracted, I'll be downright dangerous with a flu shot."

Tate studied her intently. "So, it's true, then? You're going to be a doctor?"

Lizzy nodded. "That's the plan. Of course, I have a long way to go yet. I have to finish med school, an internship and a residency."

"Old Hank must be a patient man," the sheriff noted. He winked at her. "But a darned lucky one. Hope you'll be coming back here and hanging out your shingle one of these days."

His words sent a chill through her. That wasn't the plan at all. And yet, what had she thought was going to happen? Did she expect Hank to abandon his ranch and move to some city with her? Of course not. Which meant either she had to come back to Los Piños eventually or she had to give up the man she loved.

"Well, damn," she murmured, sinking down onto the stool next to Sharon Lynn.

"What is it?" her niece demanded. "Lizzy, what on earth is wrong? Are you sick?"

"Not sick, just stunned."

"Am I supposed to understand what you're talking about?"

"No, of course not." She forced a smile. "I guess I just butted headlong into some hard truths."

"Such as?"

"The fact that Daddy's been fibbing to me all these years."

Sharon Lynn looked shocked. Like the rest of the family, she was convinced her granddaddy Harlan hung the moon. "How so?" she asked in a voice barely above a whisper.

"He's always told me I could have it all. Now I'm not so sure."

"Why on earth would you say that?"

"Because in order to have Hank, I'd have to give up medicine."

"Don't be ridiculous. You heard Tate. You could practice right here in Los Piños."

"There's not a trauma center anywhere near here."

"Trauma center? Since when did you decide you wanted to do emergency medicine?" She regarded Lizzy intently. "Is it because of that cute actor on *ER*?"

"Don't be absurd," Lizzy said, though her words were belied by the defensive note in her voice.

Sharon Lynn began to laugh. "It is, isn't it? You wouldn't sound so irritated if that weren't it."

"It's because of the volunteering I did in the emergency room when I was in college," Lizzy retorted.

"If you say so."

"I do."

Just then Hank walked up behind her. "Now, there's a phrase I've been longing to hear."

Lizzy whirled around so fast she almost spun herself right off the stool. "What phrase?"

"I do."

She studied his face, searching for a trace of humor, some sign that he was only teasing. His expression was sober as could be. "Careful what you wish for, cowboy."

"Do you want to put my sincerity to the test?"

Lizzy thought about the terrible quandary she'd been pondering just before his arrival and shook her head. "No," she said ruefully.

There was the slightest flaring of disappointment in Hank's eyes, but it vanished almost before she could be sure it was there. He slid onto the stool next to her, then glanced around.

"Who's working around here? Or have you turned this place into a self-service restaurant, Sharon Lynn?"

"It might be better if I had," Sharon Lynn replied as she moved behind the counter. "Apparently, I'm getting to be downright dangerous back here. I'd suggest you stick to something simple, like a soda."

"How about a grilled cheese and fries with it?"

"Don't say you weren't warned," she retorted, and went to work fixing his order.

Hank swiveled to study Lizzy. She winced under the intense scrutiny.

"What's up with you, darlin'?"

"Nothing," she denied.

"You're going to have to do better than that."

She forced an indifferent shrug. "Oh, just thinking about this and that."

"Which one am I, this or that?"

"What makes you think you've been on my mind at all?" She paused. "Wait a second. What are you doing here in the first place? Shouldn't you be working?"

"I'm the boss. I left Pete in charge and gave myself the day off. Then I came looking for you. Your father said you'd come into town. Your mother reported you were over here pestering Sharon Lynn."

"With those tracking skills, you could become a private eye."

"I don't think so. You're the only person I'm the least bit interested in finding."

She regarded him with fascination. "Is that so?"

"That's the honest-to-God truth."

"Interesting. You do realize, of course, that you've just given me an amazing amount of power over you?"

"No, darlin'. The power's always been there." He winked. "You're just now figuring out how to exercise it."

Chapter Six

Hank was pretty sure life didn't get any better than this. His ranch was thriving, but more importantly, the woman he'd been crazy about as far back as he could remember almost seemed to be within reach.

Lizzy was amazing, every bit as surprising and delightful in bed as she was in the other parts of her life. The way she'd taken him on at the creek, when she'd thought he had a lover in another town, brought a smile to his lips every time he recalled it. Okay, it had been fair warning never to cross her, but more importantly, it had also been proof positive that she cared.

That didn't mean he wasn't going to have a thing or two to say to Justin and Harlan Patrick next time he saw them. They'd been careful to steer clear of him ever since their practical joke.

Those two were entirely too full of themselves. They'd always been capable of getting into mischief, but now these were grown-up games they were playing. Once he'd had his say, they wouldn't be pulling any pranks on him again anytime soon.

Then there'd been the eager way Lizzy had fallen in with his afternoon of playing hooky from the ranch. After leaving the drugstore and Sharon Lynn the day before, they'd gone riding, taking along the picnic dinner his housekeeper had prepared for them. They'd eaten on a ridge overlooking his land and hers and watched the sunset splash a golden glow over everything.

Then they'd made love, out there in the open with the sky turning dark and filling up with stars. Just the memory of it was enough to stir his blood.

He was sitting in his office taking care of the monthly bills, when he heard a car skidding to a halt outside, followed by the slamming of a door. His body promptly concluded it had to be Lizzy, even though she wasn't due for a half hour yet. His hormones reacted with predictable anticipation. Just to prove to himself he still had a little self-control, he left it to Mrs. Wyndham to answer the door.

To his deep regret, it was a man's voice he heard talking with his housekeeper.

"Hank, it's Pete," she said, even though his foreman was by then standing right beside her.

"Hey, Pete. I thought you were going to move the cattle today."

"I was, but we've got a problem."

Looking at the older man's face, Hank could see a rare hint of despair. He was on his feet at once and already heading for the door, his heart pounding.

"What's going on?" he demanded. "What's happened?"

"The new man, Billy-Clyde, he got in between that new prize bull of yours and that beast's current love interest. Billy-Clyde's gored pretty bad. I think his leg might even be broke. He needs better care than what he can get here in town. I'd like to get him airlifted over to Fort Worth."

"Do it. Why are you wasting time talking to me? I'll make the arrangements. Where is he now?"

"In the back of the pickup. I thought it would save time. We were real careful moving him, made sure to stabilize his neck and back before we got him off the ground."

Just then Lizzy came rushing into the room. "What is it? I saw the truck outside and all the men hovering around it."

"It's one of the men," Hank said, already reaching for the phone. "He's been gored pretty bad."

Lizzy didn't ask a lot of questions after that. To his astonishment, she began barking orders like the head of a big-city trauma team. Hank made the call for a chopper to fly Billy-Clyde out. By the time he got outside, Lizzy was up in the bed of the truck, blood all over her as she worked to stop the bleeding. Billy-Clyde was passed out cold.

"It's going to be okay," she kept soothing the man anyway. "We'll just get this tourniquet a little tighter." She gave a little nod of satisfaction. "There now, that ought to do it." Looking around, she shouted, "Hank, where the hell's that chopper?"

"On its way," he promised, just as he heard the whir of the medevac unit, then felt the sting of stirred-up dust as it settled into place fifty yards away. The team inside raced for the truck and replaced Lizzy at Billy-Clyde's side. They listened carefully to her report, then went to work on the unconscious man.

Within minutes, Billy-Clyde was loaded into the chopper, ready to be flown toward a Fort Worth trauma center. Pete looked to Hank for permission, then climbed aboard to go with them.

Only after they'd gone and the rest of the men had dispersed to finish herding the cattle onto new grazing land did Hank take a good, long look at Lizzy. She was covered with blood and trembling.

He walked over and touched a finger to her chin. "Hey, you okay?"

Her head bobbed, but she was still shivering as if she'd been doused in creek water again.

"Inside," he said, prodding her toward the front door.

She glanced down at her clothes. "But I'm a mess."

"Doesn't matter," he insisted. Inside, he bellowed

for the housekeeper. Mrs. Wyndham took one look at Lizzy and began to cluck.

"Oh, you darling girl, come with me. I'll have you all cleaned up and changed in no time. Then I'll fix you some soup and some hot tea."

Lizzy went along with the older woman with surprising docility. Hank watched them go with a sinking sensation in the pit of his stomach. Watching Lizzy take command outside had shaken him more than he'd realized. For the first time, he'd seen exactly what kind of doctor she was going to be—skilled, quick thinking, patient and compassionate.

For some reason, even though it had kept them apart all these years, he'd never taken this medical-school thing seriously. It hadn't seemed to matter that she'd declared it her dream or that she'd gone chasing off after it. He'd always assumed it was just another passing fancy, sort of like that year on the rodeo circuit.

Now he had to confront the fact that Lizzy truly was meant to be a doctor. She had all the quick reflexes and right instincts for it. But there was going to be a long road ahead of her before she could allow the kind of distraction that a home and family would bring. What the hell was he supposed to do all those years? Wait here, hoping that when it was over she'd come back to him? He wasn't sure he was capable of that kind of patience.

He was in his office once again when she came back downstairs, wrapped in one of his robes that was miles too big for her. The sleeves had been rolled up a half-dozen times and the belt looped tightly around her waist with most of the material bloused up over it. Even at that, her bare toes barely peeked out beneath the hem. Hank thought she'd never looked more exhausted or more desirable.

"You did good out there," he said quietly. "How're you feeling?"

"More scared now that it's over." She regarded him wistfully. "Do you suppose that's how every trauma-unit doctor feels? Do you think they just act on instinct and then fall apart afterward?"

"I imagine they do. Otherwise they couldn't do their jobs." He studied her intently. "Is that the kind of doctor you're thinking of being?"

She nodded. "It wasn't at first. Remember how I used to talk about my fancy office and my fancy patients? Then when the idea of studying emergency medicine first took hold, I thought maybe it was just watching too much TV, you know. That I'd gotten the excitement and the satisfaction all wrong." She met his gaze. "But I hadn't. That's exactly how it is." Her excitement faded and was replaced by worry. "Have you heard anything from Fort Worth yet?"

"Pete called a minute ago. Billy-Clyde's in surgery. Pete said the doctors there said your quick thinking gave the boy a fighting chance. They're pretty sure they can save him and his leg."

She smiled wearily. "That's good, then."

Before he could ask what was really on his mind,

Mrs. Wyndham bustled in with the promised hot tea, soup and a plate of sandwiches.

"You'll feel better once you've gotten something into your stomach," she told Lizzy. "All that adrenaline pumping through you takes a toll."

Hank shot her a look of gratitude.

"Thank you, Mrs. Wyndham," Lizzy said. "You're an angel."

"Oh, there are some who'd dispute that," she said with a wink. "Including my husband. You call me if you need anything more. I'll have your clothes ready in no time, though I doubt they'll ever be the same again."

When she was gone, Lizzy tackled the sandwiches with enthusiasm. When the color was back in her cheeks and her hand was steadier, Hank decided to broach the subject that had been tormenting him for the past hour.

"Lizzy, what's going on between you and me?"

She gave him a wry look. "Don't you know, cowboy?"

"Okay, I suppose the real question is what does it mean to you?"

She swallowed hard and eventually looked away. "You do ask the tough ones, don't you?"

"I think it's a fair question."

"I can't deny that, but—"

"But what?"

She regarded him with something that might have

been panic in her eyes. "I'm not sure I have an answer, at least not one you want to hear."

"Meaning?"

"I needed to find out something when I came back to Los Piños this time. I needed to discover once and for all if there really was anything between us. For too many years, I dismissed what I was feeling as a silly schoolgirl crush. You seemed to take it the same way."

"So this has been an experiment?" he asked, his tone deadly calm.

"No, of course not." She blinked. "I mean, not really. Hank, you know how I've always felt about you. I know you do, even though you spent a lot of time pretending you didn't."

"Okay, yes, I knew."

"Well, I needed to find out if I'd been imagining the chemistry."

"And now that you know you haven't been imagining it? What now?"

She sighed heavily. "I wish I knew."

"Well, that's just great," he said, unable to curb his rising anger. "Terrific. You've sashayed in here and turned my life upside down to satisfy your curiosity and you don't have a clue about what happens next. Fantastic."

She leveled a look straight at him then, a look full of fire and fury. "Do you?" she asked quietly, clearly struggling to restrain her temper. "Do you have a clue?"

"No, dammit. Not after today, I don't."

His response seemed to confuse her. "Today? What does today have to do with it?"

"I saw you as a doctor for the first time. I finally had to face the fact that you're not just playing a game, that you didn't run off to college just to prove some idiotic point to me."

"Is that what you thought?"

"Yes, dammit."

"And you let me go then because...?"

"Because it was the right thing to do. You were young. You didn't know your own mind, not about me or about school."

"I see. And now that you know different?"

"I don't know," he said miserably. "Nothing I'd meant to do makes sense anymore."

"Nothing you'd meant to do? What does that mean?"

Hank leveled a look straight into her eyes. "It means I was going to ask you to stay," he said quietly. "I was going to ask you to marry me."

Her eyes widened. Her lower lip trembled. "And now you're not?"

Hank met her gaze evenly. "And now I'm not."

Tears spilled over and ran down her cheeks, but Hank couldn't bring himself to go to her. He was too afraid that touching her would only lead to making love. If he held her again, if he felt her body moving beneath his, heard her cries of pleasure, he wasn't sure if he'd be able to let her go the way he knew he must.

Lizzy was in a daze as she left Hank's ranch and drove back to White Pines. Never in her life had she felt more miserable or at a loss. She was the confident one, the one who always knew exactly what she wanted and went about getting it. In fact, that's what she'd done a few days ago. She'd gone after Hank.

Unfortunately, she was also impulsive. She acted without thinking. Now it appeared she was going to have a long time to live with the regrets. Her mother had warned her. She'd told her not to play games, not to start something until she knew precisely how she wanted it to end. Her mother was wrong about one thing, though. She didn't think she'd be bouncing back from pain this deep.

Hank hadn't even given her time to rejoice over his declaration that he'd wanted to marry her before snatching the prospect away from her. There'd been no open door, no chance for her to accept a proposal. In fact, there had never even been a proposal, just the taunting hint that he'd intended to propose.

She'd been tempted to stay and fight him, to try to make him put that offer of marriage on the table, but his expression had been intractable, his tone forbidding. And her mother's warning had finally, too late, begun to echo in her head.

What good would it do to get Hank to propose marriage, when she knew in her heart of hearts that she couldn't say yes, not now, not for a long time? If today's crisis with Billy-Clyde had been a turning point for Hank, it had been one for her, too. It had solidified her resolve to stay the course, to finish med school and become a trauma doctor in some big-city medical center. How could she possibly reconcile the two dreams?

Tears were still tracking down her cheeks when she got back to White Pines. She slipped inside and tried to sneak quietly back to her room to do some long, hard thinking, but her father met her at the top of the steps.

"I heard what happened over at Hank's place," he said, beaming at her with obvious pride. "Everybody says you saved the day."

"I suppose," she said, trying futilely to wipe away the dampness on her cheeks.

Her father's penetrating gaze never left her face. "Then why the tears?"

"I saved that man's life, but I lost Hank in the process."

"Don't be silly," her father said dismissively. "The man's crazy about you."

"I know that, but he figured something out today. He realized how long it's going to be before we can be together, and it was too long to suit him." She couldn't seem to keep the bitterness and hurt out of her voice.

Her father opened his arms, and Lizzy raced into them. "Oh, Daddy, how can love possibly be this cruel? I finally discover Hank really cares about me, only to lose him.''

''You haven't lost him,'' her father reassured her. ''He just needs to get his bearings. He'll wait. When it comes to love, there's no choice.''

Lizzy shook her head. ''You didn't see his face. It's over. He wants a wife now, not years from now.''

Her father chuckled. ''That's what he thinks today, but it won't be long before he figures out that the waiting doesn't matter as long as it's for the right woman.''

Lizzy wished she could believe that.

''You know I believe it's time we had a little party around here,'' her father said, his expression thoughtful. ''Something grand, that'll have the whole state talking.''

''Daddy, you're not up to entertaining.''

''Who says I'm not? Maritza will do all the work with whatever help she needs. All I need to do is show up. If I get tired, I can go to my room for a bit of rest. Besides, what's the good of being rich and powerful and old if you can't make things happen when you want them to?''

No one on earth was better at doing just that, Lizzy thought with amusement. Harlan Adams did love to make things happen.

''Who are you thinking of inviting to this party?'' she asked.

''Never you mind about that. Go get Maritza and

tell her to get up here. If your mama's downstairs, send her up, too.''

The gleam in his eyes was a warning. ''Daddy, what is going on in that devious mind of yours?''

''Nothing you need to concern yourself with. Why don't you go into town and find yourself a pretty new dress? Something that'll knock Hank's socks off.''

''I don't think they have dresses like that in Los Piños.''

''Then call your brother. Tell Jordan to have his pilot fly you to Dallas for a shopping spree first thing in the morning. Take your mama along, too. She needs a break from hovering over me.''

Lizzy regarded him doubtfully. ''You won't try sneaking hot-fudge sundaes and pizza while we're gone?''

''Stop worrying about my diet and go.''

It was only after he'd convinced her and after she and her mother were on their way to Dallas first thing the next morning that Lizzy realized he'd never promised her that he'd behave himself.

''Oh, no,'' she muttered. ''Daddy's probably raiding the refrigerator right now.''

Her mother smiled, her expression surprisingly complacent. ''I don't think so.''

''Why not? What do you know that I don't?''

''You know that padlock we've been joking about?''

Lizzy began to laugh. ''You didn't?''

"Oh, but I did. I had one put on the minute your father started making noises about going back downstairs again."

"Oh, what I wouldn't give to see his expression the first time he sees it."

"I have that covered, too. I left the camera with Maritza."

Laughing, Lizzy suddenly felt better than she had since Hank had tossed her right back out of his life before she'd even gotten a toehold in it.

When the laughter died, she saw her mother studying her worriedly.

"When are you going to tell me what prompted your father's latest matchmaking scheme?"

Though she'd suspected as much, hearing her mother say the word made Lizzy very uneasy. "What makes you think it's a matchmaking scheme?" she asked.

"They usually are with him. Besides, I saw the guest list. Half the eligible bachelors in Texas are being invited to this party. I assume they're either meant to produce a new man for you or they're intended to make Hank jealous. So why is your father taking this drastic measure?"

"Actually, Daddy didn't tell me what he had in mind."

"But you know perfectly well what set him off."

Lizzy sighed and filled her mother in on Hank's decision to end their relationship. Instead of the sympathy she'd expected, her mother frowned.

"I see." She regarded Lizzy intently. "Let me ask you something. If Hank were to change his mind and propose, what would you do?"

"Why, of course, I'd..." Her voice trailed off.

Her mother nodded. "I thought so. Lizzy, didn't I tell you to be careful what you wished for? Hank's always worn his feelings for you on his sleeve, but his actions have been decent and honorable. He's let you go your own way. Now you've come waltzing back into town, led him on, slept with him, I imagine, and in a few days you'll head back to Miami, correct?"

"Yes," she admitted in a small voice.

"Do you really need to have him propose for your own ego?" her mother asked with a hint of impatience. "Or do you honestly want to marry the man?"

"It's not about ego," Lizzy said fiercely. "I care about him. I always have."

"Enough to give up med school?"

"Yes," she said impulsively. Then she hung her head and added miserably, "No."

She met her mother's gaze, expecting more condemnation. Instead, this time she found only sympathy.

"Why does it have to be a choice?" Lizzy asked wistfully. "Why can't I have both?"

"Maybe you can, in time, but not right now, not this minute." She smiled. "You always were impatient and just a little greedy."

"Thanks."

"I'm not blaming you for it," her mother explained, reaching over to squeeze her hand. "Your father always gave you everything you ever wanted. You were an unexpected blessing for both of us. Harlan being Harlan, he spoiled you and I didn't do much to stop him, because he enjoyed it so much. Now he's trying to do it again. You want Hank, so he's doing his level best to make sure you get him. Neither one of you seems to be taking into account Hank's feelings."

"He must love me," Lizzy protested. "He almost proposed yesterday. He admitted that much."

"But he changed his mind and, as he sees it, for a good reason. He didn't want to take medicine away from you by asking you to stay. Maybe this time you're the one who should do the right and noble thing and let him go. Allow him to give you this gift of a career with no distractions or regrets."

Lizzy sighed. "I'm not sure I can. I don't know what I'd do if he went and found someone else. Then I'd live with regrets for the rest of my life."

Her mother reached over and squeezed her hand. "But you'd survive. You're Harlan Adams's daughter and you are every bit as strong as he is. And when it comes to survival, I'm a pretty tough old bird myself. You've got good genes, Lizzy. They'll come through for you."

"But—"

"No, Lizzy, I want you to think about it. If you really love him, think about what's best for Hank."

Lizzy did as her mother asked, which could have turned the shopping expedition into a dismal affair, but she loved clothes a little too much not to get into the spirit of it. With Hank very much on her mind, she picked out a slinky red slip dress beaded with rhinestones for the party.

Then, over her mother's objections, she insisted that her mother pick out something just as sexy for herself. Lizzy just hoped her father's heart was up to the effect of all that bared cleavage.

Not until they were on their way home after dinner in one of their favorite Tex-Mex restaurants did Lizzy allow herself to seriously consider what would happen if she got Hank to change his mind and ask her to marry him, after all.

Could she really give up med school and stay in Los Piños? Would she be content to be a rancher's wife with no career or identity of her own? Hadn't that been the whole point of wanting to be a doctor, to finally make something of herself, something separate from being Harlan Adams's baby daughter? How could she go from being daddy's little girl to being Hank's wife without finding out who she really was along the way?

And then there was medicine itself. She was good at it. She had believed all along that she would be, but yesterday's events had confirmed it. She could be cool in a crisis without losing her sense of compassion. She had always, always wanted to make everyone and everything around her better, from the first injured and abandoned kitten she'd nursed back to health with Dani's help to her parents, whom she'd doctored with chicken soup and cold compresses whenever they caught so much as the sniffles.

At first the idea of taking premed courses had been as impulsive as everything else she'd ever done. By her sophomore year, though, she'd begun to take it seriously as she'd excelled in class after class. Volunteering at the medical center had clinched it. The first time she'd walked through the doors of that bustling facility, it had felt right to her.

Just as right as her feelings for Hank, she thought with a sigh.

She was back full circle. Two dreams, two very divergent dreams. When she finally fell into a restless sleep on the plane, though, it was Hank's face she saw. And the look of yearning on it was enough to make her weep.

She awoke with a start, her cheeks damp with tears. Letting go was going to be a killer, she thought, glancing over to see her mother sleeping peacefully in the opposite seat. For the first time, she realized exactly how Hank must have felt watching her walk away, letting her leave without saying a word that might have enticed her to stay.

And he was doing it again, keeping that proposal silent so that she could go with an easy conscience and no lingering demands to divide her attentions. She owed him the same kind of freedom.

But she clung to something her father had said. If

they were destined to be together, time wouldn't make a difference. Hank would be there when she'd done what she had to do. And if he wasn't, well, she wouldn't be the first woman ever to bury herself in work to hide a broken heart.

they were destined to be together. Time wouldn't make a difference. Hank would be there when she'd done what she had to do. And if the worst befell, she would cope the way women always coped. She would work to mend a broken heart.

Chapter Seven

"What the hell do you mean, you're not coming?" Cody demanded as Hank turned his back and walked away.

Hank sighed and faced the older man. Cody's expression was partly incredulous and partly accusatory. "Which part of that didn't you understand?" he asked, managing somehow to keep his tone even.

"It's a party in Lizzy's honor," Cody protested. "You have to be there."

Clinging stubbornly to his pride and his resolve to let her go once more—this time for good—Hank shook his head. "No law says I have to go."

"What about the fact that you'll be insulting Lizzy and my father if you stay home?"

"That's an exaggeration, and you know it. I doubt your sister is any more anxious to see me than I am to see her. She's not overjoyed with me at the moment," he said in what he considered to be a massive understatement. "She thinks I'm being bullheaded and downright mean, instead of levelheaded and sensible. Lizzy's not the kind of woman who'd want rejection rubbed in her face."

He kept his gaze pinned on Cody, who was beginning to look vaguely uncomfortable at being caught in the middle. "As for your father," Hank continued, "Harlan will get over it. He's described me as antisocial on more than one occasion, when I've turned down his invitations. A family dinner is one thing, but this party is showing all the signs of turning into one of those famous Adams barbecues for the rich and powerful."

"He's kept the guest list down to a couple of dozen. I swear it. He's really counting on you being there. Besides, the whole reason for this party..." Cody said, then winced at the clear implication. "Forget I said that."

Hank's gaze narrowed. "Okay, Cody, what is your daddy up to now?" he asked, as if he didn't know. More matchmaking, most likely. It was Harlan's favorite pastime. Hank wondered, though, if Cody would admit it. He'd always trusted the older man to be straight with him and, when it came to matters of ranching, he was. When it came to family, though, Cody's loyalty was elsewhere.

"Nothing," Cody said, though he couldn't meet Hank's gaze when he said it. "I shouldn't have said anything."

"The words are out now. You can't take them back. If Harlan is up to no good, then that's all the more reason for me to stay as far away from White Pines tonight as possible. Nothing good can come of this, Cody. Trust me. There was only one thing to do under these circumstances, and I've done it."

Cody regarded him slyly. "Lizzy's going back to school in two days. Will you be able to live with yourself if you don't get one last look at her to tide you over till summer?"

"You know, Cody, I would think a big brother would want to keep a man like me as far away from his baby sister as possible."

"Why? No man I know would be a better match for her. You're levelheaded where she's impetuous. She'll be the kind of mother who'll inspire spirited antics. You'll be a terrific, rock-solid father. And you'll give her the moon, if she asks for it. What you're trying to do by staying away from her right now proves that. You're a good man, Hank. The best. Lizzy couldn't do better."

"Thanks for the glowing praise, but right now what Lizzy needs is a mentor in the medical profession, not a husband who'll tie her down."

"Shouldn't you give her the chance to decide that for herself?"

"Not when the deciding will just tear her apart,"

Hank insisted. "Look, Cody, I know she cares about me. Maybe she even fancies herself in love with me, but that doesn't mean she's ready to get married or even to make the choice."

"Why the hell does it have to be a choice?" Cody retorted impatiently.

"Because Miami's a long way away."

"So what? She doesn't have to stay in Miami. She can come back to Texas and go to medical school here. That'll be close enough to make commuting feasible."

"She chose Miami in the first place just because it was far away. She needs to make her own mark on the world, away from the Adams influence."

"Okay, fine. Jordan has his own damned jet. You can commute to Miami."

The same desperate idea had come to Hank in the middle of the night, but he'd resisted it then and he intended to resist it now. "How many days do you get to take off in ranching? Besides, that's not my idea of marriage," he told Cody. "I doubt it's hers, either. Maybe it would work for a few months, even a year, but Lizzy's years away from setting up a medical practice. Until then, she needs her freedom."

"It doesn't sound to me like it's her freedom that matters. Sounds more like you being set in your ways. What's wrong with being flexible, maybe even a little imaginative, if it gets you what you want?" Cody's gaze narrowed. "Or don't you want Lizzy enough to even try?"

Hank turned away. "You don't know anything about what I feel," he muttered.

"Then tell me," Cody argued, sounding combative. "Tell me why my sister was good enough to sleep with, but not good enough to fight for. And don't try denying the two of you have been sleeping together, because I'm not that dumb. She's not creeping into the house at dawn because you two have been off somewhere picking daises in the moonlight."

Hank turned back slowly. "That's what this is really about, isn't it? It sticks in your craw that she and I slept together, even though you practically dared me to see if I could get her into bed." He reached into his pocket and pulled out a roll of bills. He peeled off some twenties and pushed them toward Cody. "You won. Satisfied?"

"Hell, no, I'm not satisfied," Cody said, shoving aside the money. "Far from it."

"Tough. She's a grown woman, Cody. It was her decision to make."

Cody raked his fingers through his hair. "Dammit, I know that. I don't much like it, but I know it. She'd brain me with a skillet if I said otherwise or if I punched you out the way I'm tempted to."

"Well, then, can't you just leave it be?" Once more he held out the money. "Here, take it. You won it fair and square. Lizzy didn't tell me to take a hike, the way I predicted she would. God knows, we'd probably both be better off if she had."

Cody ignored the hundred dollars and shook his

head. "Forget the damned bet." His expression turned sympathetic. "Can I offer a word of advice?"

"Can I stop you?"

"Once upon a time, I took off and hid out, instead of asking the questions I should have asked and demanding straight answers. I'll regret that till the day I die. It cost me a year of my daughter's life, because I didn't even know Melissa was pregnant with Sharon Lynn when I ran."

He gave Hank a beseeching look. "Just come to the party tonight. Talk things through with Lizzy, see if you can't work things out. That's all I ask. What will it be, a couple of hours of your time? Is that so much to ask when your whole future's at stake?"

If that's all it were, no, Hank thought. But it wasn't the time that mattered. It was what seeing Lizzy again was likely to do to his resolve.

"Lizzy and I aren't known for our long-winded, introspective conversations," Hank said.

"You'll be in the midst of a whole throng of people," Cody countered with a wry expression. "There won't be much you can do besides talk."

"I'll think about it," Hank promised. "But don't count on anything."

Cody grinned. "It's not me who's counting on you. It's Daddy and Lizzy. If I were you, I wouldn't want to risk riling either one of them."

Thinking of some of the wicked things Lizzy had done to show her displeasure with him in the past, Hank had to agree. He figured he still had a few hours to weigh that prospect against the danger of seeing Lizzy one last time.

White Pines was crawling with eligible bachelors. Lizzy walked through the downstairs rooms and counted them. There were at least a dozen. Aside from family, it seemed that single males were the only guests. Some were from the state capital. She recognized them as up-and-coming legislators. There were a handful of ranchers from around the state, an oilman pal of Jordan's and a couple of lobbyists from Washington she suspected had been added to the guest list by her cooperative older sister. Jenny had traveled in some powerful circles before she'd decided to come home and teach school.

All in all, her father had outdone himself, she thought with amusement, then sighed.

Only one man was missing, the only one who mattered. Hank couldn't very well be jealous if he never even saw the competition.

"He'll be here," Sharon Lynn promised, arriving at her side and giving her hand a quick squeeze. "I know Daddy had a talk with him this afternoon."

Lizzy frowned. "Cody talked to Hank?"

"Oh, yeah," Sharon Lynn said. "Kyle and I went riding up on the ridge around lunchtime. We could hear Daddy shouting all the way up there."

"Could you hear what they said?" Lizzy asked, even though it was downright embarrassing to be so pitifully eager for information about Hank's state of mind.

"Not really."

Her spirits sank. "Then you don't know if Hank agreed to come tonight or not?"

"No," Sharon Lynn conceded with obvious reluctance.

"Then this whole party is a total waste."

"Not necessarily," Sharon Lynn said. "You could check out the alternatives. Granddaddy has provided a veritable smorgasbord of men for you to choose from. It seems like a shame to waste them. Maybe one of them will be able to take your mind off of Hank."

Lizzy shot her a disgusted look. "Would a total stranger be able to take your mind off Kyle if the two of you were having problems?"

"I suppose not," Sharon Lynn conceded. Her expression brightened. "But if Hank decides to put in an appearance, wouldn't it be better if he walked in and found you engrossed in conversation with some handsome, sexy man, rather than sulking in a corner? Besides, you can't let that dress go to waste. Every male in the room—except Kyle, of course—is practically drooling over you. There's music on the patio. Why not find yourself a partner and go enjoy it?"

Just then, glancing through the French doors, Lizzy could have sworn she'd caught a glimpse of Hank outside in the shadows at the edge of the patio. Her heart lurched. Sharon Lynn's idea began to make a whole lot more sense.

"You know," she said, suddenly more agreeable, "maybe I will go try to persuade one of these men to dance, if you'll have a chat with the band and see if they'll play something nice and slow."

Sharon Lynn regarded her quizzically. "Slow? What are you up to?"

"Never mind. Will you do it?"

"Of course."

Lizzy turned back toward the living room and surveyed the available men. She picked out the tallest, sexiest one there, who also happened to be the oil tycoon. Now, there was a combination that ought to get Hank's attention, as long as he never figured out just how sleazy the man was or how much she disliked him.

She strolled across the room, thoroughly aware of the fact that every male gaze was on her, looked up into Brian Lane's black-as-coal eyes and smiled. "Care to dance?" she asked.

"I'd be honored," he said at once.

He tucked her hand through the crook of his arm and led the way outside. Lizzy didn't miss the triumphant expression on his face as he walked off with the evening's grand prize—her. She would have made him pay for that look, if he hadn't been the perfect choice for the little game she had in mind to torment Hank.

Brian Lane was just over thirty and heir to a family

fortune. A lot of women would have keeled over under the heat of those dark, mysterious, hooded looks he'd perfected. Lizzy had met him at Jordan's on several occasions in the past. She knew how quickly that heated gaze could turn coldly assessing. For all his polite social skills and oodles of money and privilege, Brian Lane was not a very nice man, which was why she'd always declined his invitations to dinner.

But he was exactly the predatory sort of male that drove other men into possessive rages. Even her cool-as-a-cucumber big brother seemed to get a little nervous when Brian began paying a little too much attention to her sister-in-law.

On the patio with the music suddenly and oh-so-conveniently turning slow, he drew Lizzy into his arms just a little too tightly. He would have paid for that, too, had it not suited her purposes. She wondered, as he moved to the music's provocative rhythm, if he had any idea that instead of being swept away by the feel of him, she was busily searching the shadows for a glimpse of another man. She doubted it. Brian was not prone to self-doubts.

"I always knew one day you'd come around," he murmured against her ear.

Lizzy stumbled. "Excuse me?"

"You've been playing hard-to-get since the first time we met at your brother's house," he said. "I figured it couldn't last too much longer. There's always been a chemistry between us. I've sensed it. I know you must have, too."

If he'd been serious, Lizzy would have been nervous, but she'd heard him use the exact same line too many times. She found it laughable but, wisely, she fought that particular reaction. For the moment, she needed him to play the role of ardent suitor.

Brian seemed to take her silence for assent, because he increased the pressure on her back, forcing her even more tightly against him. She felt the first twinge of panic when she realized that he was fully aroused. The second twinge came when he tried to waltz her into the shadows, away from the other dancers.

Well, hell, Lizzy thought. She had not started this game to cause a scene, but Brian was rapidly changing the rules. Just when she was about to chill his amorous intentions with a well-placed and savage kick, the gap between them suddenly widened and Hank moved smoothly in between. No man had ever cut in on another with such tactical precision or such an expression of grim determination.

Hank gave the other man a smile edged with ice. "Thanks for looking after the lady," Hank said in a chilly tone that wasn't nearly as grateful as the words implied. "But I'm here now."

Brian opened his mouth to protest, but Hank's steady, lethal gaze seemed to change his mind. He glanced at Lizzy instead.

"We'll catch up with each other another time."

"I doubt it," Hank said, making it clear that the other man shouldn't even try.

Brian shrugged finally and walked away, but it was

clear from his expression that Hank had just made an enemy. Even so, Lizzy felt relief shimmer through her. Not that she intended to let Hank catch so much as a glimmer of it. She intended to see him suffer for the heartache he'd put her through the past few days.

"Was that some sort of macho ritual I just witnessed?" she inquired lightly, as if she found the study of such behavior fascinating in a purely academic way.

Hank gave her a wry look. "That was me saving you from getting mauled by that creep. Who the hell was he anyway?"

"A business associate of Jordan's."

"Jordan ought to choose his friends more carefully."

"I didn't say they were friends," she began, then shrugged. "Never mind. Did you even stop to consider that maybe I wanted to get mauled?"

His response to that was a hard, silent stare. Lizzy winced and gave up the game. "Okay, maybe I am grateful that you turned up when you did."

He shook his head. "Something tells me you were counting on it. What I can't figure is how you even knew I was around. I haven't even set foot on the patio until now, much less been inside."

"I guess I must have a sixth sense about it when you're around." She grinned at him. "Or maybe you're just not as good at sneaking around and hiding in the bushes as you thought you were."

His cheeks flamed with color. "You saw me?"

"Sure did."

"Then that whole scene was deliberately staged for my benefit?"

"I never said that."

"You didn't have to." He regarded her with amusement. "Give it up, Lizzy. You were trying to make me jealous. That's what this whole charade of a party is about. Your daddy didn't even make a pretense of it being anything else. There's not another single woman here. All those men were meant to be prospective competition for me."

"Okay," she said cheerfully. "Since it worked, I suppose I can admit it. Not that I planned it, of course. This was Daddy's doing."

"I'm sure," he agreed. Then he added softly, "It doesn't change anything."

She refused to accept that. "Of course it does," she insisted. "It proves that you can't just turn your back on me, after all."

"I wasn't turning my back on you," he said wearily. "I was trying to let you go." He studied her intently. "That's still the plan, Lizzy. What just happened doesn't change that."

He tucked a finger under her chin and forced her head up. "If you'll tell the truth, you wouldn't want it any other way, either. You have to go back, darlin'. You know you do."

Tears welled up, but she fought them. "Can't we at least have the next couple of days, then? Please." She waited through the longest silence of her life, then added, "That's as much begging as I'm ever going to do, Hank Robbins, so what is it? Yes or no?"

She saw the torment on his face and the indecision. Finally he sighed. "Yes," he whispered against her cheek. "We'll steal every second that we've got left."

"Can we leave, then?"

"You're the guest of honor," he noted. "It wouldn't be polite."

She'd never regretted her ingrained sense of duty more. "I suppose."

Hank grinned. "Now that the party's served its purpose, you're bored with it, aren't you?"

"I was bored with it before. Now that you're here, I suppose I can make the best of it." She looked up into his eyes. "Hold me a little tighter, cowboy, and let's pretend we're at your place, all alone."

"Oh, no, you don't," he protested, keeping her at arm's length. "Cody's already put me on notice where you're concerned. If I try that right here in plain view, I'll have a whole passel of shotguns aimed straight at my belly. You and I would be standing at an altar before we could blink."

"Would that be so bad?" Lizzy asked wistfully.

Hank stroked his knuckles down her cheek. "You know that's not the way you want it to happen. You don't want the decision taken out of your hands."

"Maybe I do," she said with a touch of defiance.

"A marriage begun like that between the two of us

wouldn't last a month. You'd start resenting me and the situation in the blink of an eye. You know you would.''

If she was being honest, Lizzy couldn't deny it. She wondered, though, about Hank. "What about you? Would you resent me, too?"

He took a long time answering, long enough for her heart to climb into her throat and tears to threaten.

"*Resentment* is the wrong word. I'd just be torn apart knowing how badly you wanted something and that I'd played a role in preventing you from getting it. Starting a marriage with regrets is no way to make it last.''

"You're being noble again, aren't you?"

He grinned at her. "It is a curse, trying to be honorable around you. You make it mighty hard, Mary Elizabeth Adams. Mighty hard.''

Lizzy's spirits brightened. "Then you are tempted, at least?''

"Be patient, darlin'. We ought to be able to sneak away from here by midnight. Then I'll show you just how tempting I find you.''

"Promise?''

"Cross my heart.''

Lizzy sighed contentedly and tucked her head on Hank's shoulder, where she could indulge herself in the feel and scent of him. "Then you know what I'm tempted to do?'' she murmured.

"What's that?''

She looked up and met his gaze. "I am very

tempted to slip inside and start moving every clock in the place forward a couple of hours.''

Hank chuckled. "You'd do it, too, wouldn't you?"

"Oh, yes," she agreed. "But Daddy has gone to a lot of trouble to make tonight happen. I suppose I should make sure he gets his money's worth." She broke free of his embrace. Still holding on to his hand, she led him inside.

"Where are we going?" Hank asked, wondering if she intended to make good on her threat to start moving time forward.

"To show Daddy that his scheming worked one more time."

Hank stopped, forcing her to halt as well. "Bad idea, darlin'."

"Why?"

"Because you'll get his hopes up, and you and I both know that we're not together for good."

"We're not?"

"No," he said emphatically.

"What, then?" she asked, as her heart began to thud dully.

"We're just saying a long goodbye."

Chapter Eight

The goodbye took forty-eight hours and it was the most bittersweet experience of Hank's life.

Once he and Lizzy had slipped away from White Pines and Harlan's smug glances, they had driven to his ranch, raced each other for the front door, stripping away clothes as they'd run. They had made love the first time in an urgent frenzy, right in the foyer, with Lizzy's back braced against the wall, her legs wrapped around Hank's waist.

Later there had been sweet, slow loving in his bed, lingering caresses just because they couldn't stop touching and frantic, uninhibited sex so memorable that just the thought of it could make Hank's blood heat.

For once Lizzy had stayed through the night, awakening in his arms with a sleepy smile and wicked suggestions that had touched off the passion all over again.

This morning, though, her imminent departure had cast a pall over them. They sat at his kitchen table with eggs and toast getting cold on their plates and coffee adding to the acid churning in Hank's stomach.

Finally, he forced his gaze to the clock above the stove. "It's about time, darlin'."

She shot him a shattered look. "Already?"

"Afraid so."

Her lower lip trembled. "I'm not sure I can do it."

"You don't have a choice."

Her chin tilted stubbornly. "Of course I do."

Hank grinned at the flaring of Adams defiance. "Not really."

She regarded him with an unwavering look, then sighed. "I suppose not. I just didn't know it was going to hurt this much." She searched his face. "But you did, didn't you?"

Hank nodded, because he suddenly couldn't speak around the huge lump that was forming in his throat.

"It's worse this time," she whispered. "Much worse."

Again he nodded. "Because now we know for sure. We're good together, Lizzy. Really good. That ought to be the only thing that matters, but we both know it's not."

"We could make it the only thing," she said with grim determination.

"No, we couldn't," he told her, reaching for her hand. "We've been over this a million times, and I've been over it a million more in my head. If I thought there was another way, I'd hold on to you and never let you go, but there's not. You have to go back, and I need to stay right here. I wanted my own place my whole life. I've spent the last few years turning this old wreck into a halfway decent ranching operation. I can't turn my back on it now."

"I know," she admitted. "But I'll only be gone a few weeks and then we'll have the whole summer. We'll just have to concentrate on that."

Obviously, she'd meant it as consolation, but Hank wasn't sure he could bear the thought of summer's torment, having her with him again, only to say goodbye...again. But telling her that now would only make today more difficult, and he wasn't sure he could bear to see any more hurt in her eyes.

"Just a few weeks," he echoed, and left it at that.

"Will you go with me to the airport in Dallas?" she asked. "Jordan's flying me over."

"Are you sure you wouldn't rather say goodbye here, in private?"

"I would, but I also want to hold on to every possible second we can be together."

He thought of all the work that needed doing around the ranch, all the duties he'd already left to his foreman during Lizzy's visit home. What was one more day, though? Pete could manage. He'd be glad to, in fact. The way the man seized responsibility and followed through was one of the reasons he and Hank got along so well. He'd been pushed out of his last job by an employer who thought he'd gotten too old for it. He'd been hell-bent ever since on proving to Hank that he was still up to managing a ranch.

"I'll go with you," he said. "Just let me give Pete a call and tell him I'll be gone for most of the day. Or would you rather I drive you over to White Pines first, so you can have time to say your goodbyes there?"

"That's probably best. I still have a bit of packing to do, too. You can drop me off, then come back around noon. Does that work for you?"

He grinned. "If it works for you, it works for me."

After he'd left her at White Pines, though, he began to imagine turning this into a routine that could last for years yet. Goodbye after goodbye, none of them getting any easier. It would never work, not even with the promise of forever at the end. Neither he nor Lizzy was known for patience. It was the single trait they had in common and the worst one they could have shared under the circumstances.

And yet when he thought about the alternative—never seeing Lizzy again—he couldn't imagine that, either. The very thought made his gut churn. Surely no two people had ever been caught in a more agonizing catch-22, destined to be miserable whatever choice they made.

He remembered what Lizzy had said earlier: summer was right around the corner. Maybe that was soon enough to make the choice, after all. In the meantime, he imagined his long-distance telephone bills were going to be astronomical.

"Daddy, I have to go. Hank's waiting and Jordan's probably already at the airport grumbling about me being late," Lizzy said, giving her father a fierce hug.

"Let 'em wait," he grumbled. "You're my darlin' girl, and I want to know how you're doing before I let you get away from here." He searched her face. "Since you've spent the past couple of days with Hank, does that mean what I think it means? Are you two working things out?"

"We're trying, Daddy."

"Don't make the man wait around too long, Lizzy. No man can put his life on hold forever. You shouldn't, either, for that matter."

"Are you telling me I should give up medicine?"

"I can't tell you that. It's your decision. I'm just saying you need to be sure you have your priorities in order. If Hank's the man you want, then grab on to the love you two have and don't let go. Not for anything." He grinned. "You know, I hear they have a couple of pretty good med schools right up the road a piece. You could choose one closer to home."

Lizzy nodded. "I know."

"And fall would be the perfect time to make a change," he added.

"Daddy, you can't just switch med schools at the drop of a hat," she protested. "Admissions are getting more and more difficult."

"You just say the word, and I'll make it happen," he vowed.

Her mother walked in on them then. "Harlan, are you throwing your weight around again?"

He grinned at his wife. "Threatening to," he admitted. "If it'll get my girl what she wants."

"You know, if you indulge her every whim, she'll never bother figuring out what it is she really wants enough to fight for it. You made the boys stand up for what they wanted and you did okay by them, didn't you?"

"Except for Eric," he said quietly, making a rare reference to the son who'd died in an accident on Luke's ranch. "I tried to make a rancher of him, when he wanted to teach. I like to think I learned from that." He sighed. "I can't help remembering what that cost me, Janet. If it's in my power to make one of my own happy, then I want to do it."

"And your precious Lizzy has you twisted around her little finger," her mother said.

Lizzy grinned and kissed his cheek. "Which is what makes you the most incredible father in the universe, but Mom could be right this time. I have to figure out what I want and then I have to be the one to make it happen."

Her father held up his hands. "Okay, okay, I can't

fight the two of you. Just promise me you'll let me know if you want any help.''

"It's a deal," Lizzy said. She turned and hugged her mother. "Take care of him, you hear."

"She always does," her father said, already slipping an arm around her mother's waist.

When they walked outside, they found Hank waiting beside his pickup, Lizzy's bags already loaded in the back.

"All set?" he asked.

Lizzy forced a smile. "All set."

She gave her parents one last hug, then climbed into the truck. Hank started the engine, then glanced over.

"You okay?"

She gave him a halfhearted smile. "Sure."

He pulled away from the house, watching in the rearview mirror as Harlan and Janet waved goodbye until the truck made the turn in the lane that took it out of sight. He braked then and reached over to brush the tears from Lizzy's cheeks.

"He'll be here when you get home," he promised, even though he had to know it was up to fate, not him.

Lizzy lifted her tear-streaked face to meet his gaze. "What if—?"

"No, darlin', don't even go there. Imagining the worst doesn't help anybody. You saw for yourself that Harlan was getting stronger every day."

"That's what he claimed, anyway."

"He was out of bed the day after you got home," he reminded her. "He danced with your mother at your party. And he just walked down the front steps to say goodbye without even breathing hard. By the time you get back, he'll be out riding again and you two can go chasing over White Pines land the way you used to. I bet he'll even be interrupting our picnics down by the creek."

Lizzy paled at the very idea. "Lordy, I hope not. The shock might give him another heart attack."

"Oh, I think he has a pretty good idea what you and I have been up to."

"Knowing it and stumbling in on it are two very different things," she retorted. "I don't think even Harlan Adams is that broad-minded."

"In that case, no more private picnics by the creek for us," Hank taunted.

"There's always nap-time, I suppose," Lizzy speculated thoughtfully. "Even before the heart attack, Daddy did like his little afternoon catnaps."

"Or maybe we can just put some bells on his horse's bridle."

"He might wonder about that," she said, grinning at last.

"See, there. I made you smile."

"You always could. That's how we met, remember?"

"How could I forget? Whatever happened to that boy who made you cry that day?"

"I believe he ended up in jail for cattle rustling,"

she said, unable to keep the note of satisfaction out of her voice.

"A fitting end for the jerk," Hank declared. "What was it he did to you? You never did tell me that."

Lizzy winced. "Okay, it wasn't all that awful, now that I think back on it, but I was sixteen at the time. Every slight was a mortal wound back then."

"What was it he did?" Hank repeated.

"You're really going to make me say it, aren't you?"

He nodded. "I really am. Something tells me I'm going to enjoy the heck out of whatever you're trying so hard not to say."

"Okay, okay. He refused to carry my tray in the cafeteria. Are you satisfied? It was my first public humiliation."

Hank barely managed to hide the grin tugging at his lips. "Devastating, I'm sure."

"Well, it was. All the other boys were doing it for me. He was the only one who wouldn't."

"Which naturally made him the most attractive," Hank said.

"Of course." Lizzy moaned. "Jeez, I was such an idiot."

"You were a teenage girl," he corrected.

"Maybe idiocy and hormones do go together," she said. "Anyway, you were wonderful. You didn't treat me as if I was sixteen and my problem was nonsense. You listened and then you teased me and you made me smile, just like today. I've never forgotten that."

"Neither have I," he said quietly, glancing over at her as he pulled into the small airport where Jordan was waiting for them. "Neither have I."

"Hank, I—"

She never got to finish the thought because Justin yanked open the door of the pickup, his expression disgruntled. "It's about time you got here. We were supposed to take off a half hour ago."

Lizzy stared at him. "What are you doing here?"

"I'm catching a lift to Dallas, too. I'm checking out the police academy there."

"And Jordan is actually flying you over there?" she asked, incredulous. Her brother's willing participation in Justin's defection from the oil business was astounding. Jordan didn't like losing. It was another of those infamous Adams traits.

Justin shrugged. "He's resigned to it. My hunch is he's hoping I'll flunk out and put an end to what he refers to as 'this utter nonsense.'"

"Now, that sounds more like him," Lizzy said. "Stick to your guns, though, Justin. No pun intended."

Hank groaned. "Hey, Justin, how about giving me a hand with these bags? Lizzy has never grasped the concept of packing light."

"It's not all clothes," she protested. "I have some medical texts in there, and they weigh a ton."

"And how many of those books did you crack while you were home?" Justin teased. "Hank, is that what the two of you were doing over at your place? Studying?''

"Exactly," Lizzy retorted, regarding Hank boldly. "I had a little trouble with my anatomy class. Hank was making sure I got it right.''

"I'll bet," Justin retorted. "My hunch is there was no textbook involved.''

Just then Jordan came around the side of the hangar and glared at all of them. "Is anybody planning to fly to Dallas today?''

"Sorry," Hank said. "Saying goodbye to Harlan took a little longer than we anticipated.''

Jordan's frown eased as he searched Lizzy's face. "He's okay?''

"He's fine. I just got a little crazy when it came time to walk away.''

Her brother nodded sympathetically. "I've had that trouble myself from time to time lately. Now that everybody's here, though, let's get this show on the road. I don't like the looks of that storm that's brewing to the west. I checked with the tower and we're cleared to go, but the window of opportunity won't last forever.''

Lizzy cast a nervous look toward the western horizon. It looked perfectly clear to her, but she knew the unpredictable Texas weather well enough to know that it could change in a heartbeat. "Jordan, are you sure?''

"We'll be fine, if we quit wasting time," he assured her.

"Then let's do it," Hank said.

They climbed aboard Jordan's corporate jet and settled into their seats. Justin, who'd been flying since his sixteenth birthday, took the copilot's seat, which left Lizzy alone with Hank in the main cabin.

The takeoff was smooth, the trip uneventful except for an occasional pocket of turbulence that flipped her stomach upside down. Each time it happened, she reached for Hank's hand and clung to it.

"Lizzy, darlin', your brother is an experienced pilot, and Justin's no slouch himself. We're in good hands."

"I know that," she agreed. "Just in case, though, there's something I want to say to you."

Hank seemed to guess her intention because he reached over and pressed a silencing finger to her lips. "Don't."

"I have to," she insisted. "I have to say it just once."

"Lizzy—"

"I love you, Hank. No matter what happens, I want you to remember that. I love you."

A muscle in his jaw twitched, and his whole body tensed as if she'd slapped him. Eventually, though, he sighed. "I love you, too, darlin'. I truly do."

"Then we'll find some way to make this work," Lizzy promised. "I know we will."

Hank gave her a rueful smile. "I wish I shared your confidence."

She forced her brightest grin in an attempt to overcome his doubts—and her own. "You would if you'd been born an Adams. We believe we can make anything happen. That's Daddy's grandest legacy to us."

"So I've noticed," he said dryly. "There are powerful international leaders who aren't so sure they can sway things to their liking."

"But you've seen it," she persisted. "You have to know we always get what we want."

"Sometimes I've seen you bend what you want to suit what you get."

"That's the pragmatic side of our nature. It comes in handy on those rare occasions when things don't work out quite the way we anticipated."

"Turning lemons into lemonade," Hank suggested.

"Precisely."

"Well, all I can say is, I hope we're not about to drown in the stuff."

"Hank Robbins, you are such a pessimist."

"I'm a realist, and I'd say one of us needs to be."

"Realism is depressing," Lizzy countered. "Want to know what I see for our future?"

Hank grinned. "Sure. Go ahead and entertain me."

"I see me graduating from medical school. Then I see me serving my internship and my residency."

"So far, this seems to be all about you. Where am I while you're making medical history?"

She grinned. "Waiting for me at home like a dutiful husband, maybe getting dinner on the table while I study."

"You do have a vivid imagination, I'll give you that. Who's running my ranch?"

"You are, of course, with Pete's help. You're making the decisions and taking care of the long-range planning, buying the cattle for breeding and studying the futures market for beef. Pete's doing the hands-on work." She regarded Hank hopefully. "He can handle it. You know he can."

"He can," Hank agreed. "But he shouldn't have to. He's a foreman. I'd be a lousy owner if I left all the hard work to him."

"Texas is loaded with rich absentee ranchers."

"I'm not rich and I have no intention of being an absentee anything."

"You haven't even considered the idea," Lizzy protested. "Couldn't you at least give it some thought?"

"I don't have to think about it," Hank said. "It's impossible."

"In other words, if any compromising is going to be done, I'm the one who's going to have to do it. My career automatically has to take a back seat to yours."

Hank scowled. "I never said that."

"You didn't have to say it."

"Do you really want to waste what little time we have left arguing about this ridiculous idea of yours?"

"So, now I'm ridiculous?" she practically shouted.

"I didn't say you were ridiculous, dammit. I said the idea was absurd."

"It's the same thing."

Justin stuck his head into the main cabin. "Hey, you two, do you need a referee back here?"

"No," they shouted in unison, glaring at each other.

"Well, at least you agree on something," Justin said, grinning.

"You are not going to practice negotiating domestic disputes on us," Lizzy muttered.

"Okay, then. Have it your way," Justin said agreeably. "Call me if you change your mind. By the way, Dad says he's thinking of circling the airport until the two of you resolve this. Keep in mind that this plane only holds so much fuel."

"Very amusing," Lizzy retorted. "Now go away."

After he'd gone, she drew in a deep breath and faced Hank. He was staring out the window, his expression enigmatic.

"Hank?"

"Yes," he replied without turning.

"I'm sorry."

He sighed and faced her. "I'm sorry, too, darlin'."

"If I come over there, will you kiss me?"

A slow grin spread across his face. "Only if you lock the cockpit door."

Lizzy was on her feet in a heartbeat. She locked the door, then hurled herself into Hank's waiting arms, only to have the intercom switch on and Jordan advise them they were making their descent into the Dallas–Fort Worth airport.

"Get back into your seat, Mary Elizabeth, and fasten that seat belt," her brother said, his voice laced with amusement. "I am not operating a motel room at twenty thousand feet."

Hank picked up the phone that allowed the passengers to communicate with the pilot. "Too bad, Jordan, because I would pay you a whole lot of money for a couple more uninterrupted hours up here."

"I don't want to hear that," Jordan retorted. "I definitely do not want to hear that."

Without the benefit of a phone of her own, Lizzy simply raised her voice. "You are such a prude, Jordan."

"I think my wife might disagree, little sister."

"And I don't want to hear about *that*," Justin chimed in. "Can't we just get this plane on the ground, please? Lizzy's flight's in an hour, anyway."

Jordan chuckled. "Happy to oblige, son, but something tells me the odds on her making that flight are not real good."

Lizzy's gaze locked with Hank's. "There is a later flight, you know. I checked before we left home."

"Jordan's not going to want to wait around forever," he said with regret.

Apparently, he'd forgotten to disconnect the phone to the cockpit, because Jordan responded, "That weather system's moved in behind us. We're grounded till morning. You're on your own, Hank. I'm sure you can find a way to spend the time."

"Yes," Hank agreed, never taking his gaze from Lizzy's face, "I imagine I can."

Chapter Nine

It was morning before Lizzy finally caught a flight back to Miami. Hank watched her board the plane, then turned and walked away. If he'd stayed, there was a very good chance he'd have bought a ticket and gone to Miami with her. That was the kind of impulsive thing Lizzy might do, but not him. He'd always prided himself on being sensible. Somehow, though, when he got around Lizzy, he lost his head.

When he met Jordan an hour later, Lizzy's brother regarded him sympathetically. "Saying goodbye doesn't get any easier," he said. "I tried it with Kelly for a while. I commuted back and forth to Houston, certain that my company headquarters had to be there. She was just as determined never to set foot in that city again. She'd hated it when she'd lived there with her ex-husband and she'd vowed never to go back. All she ever wanted was to live on her family's ranch in Los Piños.''

It was a sentiment Hank could share, and obviously Jordan saw the connection.

"She turned that ranch around single-handedly," he said with obvious pride. "Did you know that?"

"I'd heard the story," Hank said. He studied Jordan's expression, then asked in a low voice, "Did you ever wish she'd fail?"

Jordan's eyes widened with surprise. "Is that what you're hoping for? That Lizzy will fail at med school?"

Hank sighed. "No, not really, not when she has her heart set on it, but it would make things a hell of a lot easier."

"Easy's not always for the best."

"Another one of those Adams lessons on life?"

"No, just an observation. Daddy's always gone about making life easy for Lizzy," he said without rancor. "It's understandable, her being the youngest and his first girl, if you don't count Jenny, who was already half-grown when Daddy married her mama. Lizzy needs some challenges. She needs to know she can handle them on her own."

His expression turned thoughtful. "The same thing was true with all of us, in one way or another. With Luke and Cody and me, Daddy put every obstacle he could in our way to make us fight for what we wanted. It worked. We're all stronger men because of it. He hasn't done the same with Lizzy. In her case, I think it's going to be up to you to show her what she's made of.''

"And you think I'm up to the challenge?'' Hank inquired.

"Oh, I know you are. So does Daddy. But until you've figured that out for yourself, what we think doesn't matter a tinker's damn.''

Hank laughed despite himself. "One of these days, I'm going to have to ask the women you guys married if the Adams men were worth the trouble they caused.''

"What answer you'll get probably depends on which day you ask. We're not always easy, but Harlan Adams set a high standard for all of us. You'll be getting the best there is, if you can work things out with Lizzy.''

If, Hank thought. For a little, old two-letter word, it had the power to bring a strong man to his knees.

"So, what happened with the hunky rancher?'' Kelsey demanded the minute Lizzy reached the small apartment they shared near the University of Miami med-school campus.

Lizzy's hands stilled on the rumpled clothes she was plucking out of her suitcase. "What makes you think anything happened?''

"Well, if I didn't know it before, your reaction just now confirmed it.'' Kelsey settled down cross-legged in the middle of Lizzy's bed. "Spill it. Did you see Hank? More importantly, did you sleep with him? Is that why you were a day late getting back, because you couldn't bear to leave him?"

Lizzy chuckled. "You know, Kelsey, your imagination is entirely too vivid. I think it's time for you to get a social life of your own. Or maybe to give up medicine and write one of those romance novels you're always reading in your spare time."

"No time," Kelsey replied, waving off the suggestion. "Besides, observing yours is entertainment enough."

"Sorry. You're about to be cut off."

Kelsey blinked. "Cut off? How come? You aren't moving out, are you?"

"No, of course not. Just putting my social life here on ice."

"I knew it," her roommate shouted jubilantly. "You did sleep with him."

Before Lizzy could reply, the phone rang. Grateful for the interruption, she grabbed it. "Hello."

"Hey, darlin', miss me yet?"

"Heavens, no," she lied. "I've barely had time to think, much less miss you." She caught Kelsey observing her with fascination.

"Hold on a sec, will you?" she asked Hank.

"Sure."

She scowled at her roommate. "Kelsey, privacy, please."

"Only if you will swear to fill me in on what went on in Texas," she said, still not budging from the bed.

"How about if I swear to kill you if you don't scoot right this second?"

Kelsey grinned. "That works, too." As she exited the room, she shouted over her shoulder, "Hey, Hank, come see us."

Lizzy grimaced and picked up the phone. "You heard?"

"Indeed. Who was that?"

"My roommate, who has developed a sudden fascination with cowboys. Think I ought to get her one of her own?"

"Possibly. Is she gorgeous?"

"Do you think I'd tell you if she were?"

"Hmm. I'm picturing five-ten, long blond hair and the face of an angel."

"And I'm picturing you dead."

Hank chuckled. "I do love it when you get all possessive on me."

"Must be a guy thing. Women hate jealous men."

"Really? Didn't seem that way when you were kissing up to old Brian at your daddy's party."

"That was different."

"I'd love to hear how."

"It was necessary, part of a larger plan, so to speak."

"And the larger plan was to what? Make me declare my intentions?"

"Something like that."

"So if I mention that I went to Garden City today, that would be okay?"

Lizzy's heart slowed. "You went where?"

"To Garden City," he said, his tone all innocence. "Right after Jordan and I got back."

"I suppose you went to explain why you hadn't been around for the past week or so."

"Something like that."

"Was she forgiving?"

"Always is," he said.

"Then she's dumb as a post," Lizzy countered. "The two of you would never last. You don't need a quiet, accepting woman in your life. You need one who's going to rip your heart out if you stray."

"And that would be you?"

"That would definitely be me," she agreed.

"I'll try and remember that."

"You'd better," she said in a dire tone. "Exactly how much time did you spend in Garden City, anyway?"

"Long enough."

"Long enough to do what?" she demanded.

"What I went there for." He sighed. "Oh, darlin', I do miss you. I wish you were here right this second."

"Then that visit to Garden City must not have been nearly as exciting as the flight to Dallas. What would you do if I were right there beside you?"

"Use your imagination."

"Oh, no. I want you to spell it out for me."

"Now, on the phone?"

"Yep." She settled back against the pillows on her bed and let Hank's low, sexy voice roll over her. It was that voice as much as the wicked suggestions he made that made her pulse race and raised goose bumps.

"No, stop," she whispered in a choked voice when the torment got to be too much.

"Lizzy? What's wrong?"

"Nothing. It's just that I didn't realize how lonely it would make me feel to want you so much and know you're so far away."

"Oh, baby, I know. Believe me, I know."

"Will you call me later?"

"What time? Do you have classes this afternoon?"

"A couple, but I'll be back here by suppertime. Then I'll be studying."

"I'll call you right before I go to bed, then, to say good-night. Okay?"

At least his would be the last voice she heard before falling asleep, Lizzy thought. It would be almost like having him in bed beside her.

"Later, then," she said. "I love you."

Only after she'd put the receiver back in the cradle did she realize that Hank hadn't said he loved her, too. She'd thought she had opened the door to that on the plane, but maybe Hank had only felt obliged to say the words with her staring him in the face. Maybe he'd never meant them at all.

"No," she told herself sternly.

She wasn't going to do this, she vowed. She wasn't going to succumb to doubts on her very first day away from him. If she couldn't trust Hank, if she couldn't believe in their love, then they were doomed and she refused to accept that outcome. They had started something wonderful back in Texas, and she was going to hang on to that with everything she had.

Hank was feeling restless when he got off the phone. The house seemed empty, even though he could hear Mrs. Wyndham bustling around in the kitchen. He had to get out and do something, maybe remind himself why this ranch was so all-fired important to him.

He headed for the barn and saddled his big bay gelding, Uncle Sid, named for a relative of its previous owner who'd apparently been every bit as fractious as the horse. Even now, years later, Uncle Sid danced skittishly as Hank saddled him.

Maybe a hard ride was what he and the horse needed. He could check out some of the downed fence lines Pete had told him about. The foreman suspected they'd been cut through deliberately, possibly by someone hoping the cattle would be put back in that distant pasture and then stray.

It could have been mischief or the first step toward thievery. At the moment, it was a distraction from missing Lizzy, and that was all that mattered.

He urged the horse into a full gallop, hoping the wind would chase away the erotic images he'd meant to stir only for Lizzy. Unfortunately, the game had backfired. It had left him hot and aching, as well.

He hadn't stopped to consider how late in the day it was. Dusk began to fall as he reached the distant fence. He slowed his horse over the uneven terrain. Uncle Sid whinnied nervously.

"It's okay, fella. There's nobody around but us."

Uncle Sid seemed to disagree, fighting the bit in his mouth. It had been a long time since the old bay had acted up this way. Hank gazed through the gathering darkness, searching for movement in the shadows, but seeing nothing. Even so, he was glad he'd thought to bring his gun along.

As he neared the fence line, he spotted the downed barbed wire and broken posts. One could have been split by lightning, but a whole row of them? Not likely. He was about to climb down for a closer look when Uncle Sid turned skittish and danced away from the fence.

At a whizzing sound, the horse shied. Hank clung to the saddle horn, but there was no soothing the frightened animal. Uncle Sid bucked and bolted, heaving the unsuspecting Hank into the air. One foot caught in the stirrup as he fell. He hit the ground with a jarring thud, only to be dragged within inches of pounding hooves as Uncle Sid raced back toward home.

He managed one hoarse shout, but the horse was beyond hearing. Then Hank bounced hard. His head hit something, most likely a rock or fallen tree limb, and the world went black.

Fortunately, the same thud that had knocked him unconscious also jarred his foot free of the stirrup. He was left lying in the dust, alone in a pitch-black night.

He had no idea how long it was before he began to come to. He knew only that the sky was filled with stars and his head ached worse than the worst hangover he'd ever had. He tried to move, then moaned at the pain that shot through him. Bad idea, he concluded and lay still.

The air began to cool as the night deepened. Hank shivered and tried to keep himself awake. Wasn't that the right thing to do with a concussion? If only Lizzy were here, he thought. She would know. She would make the blinding pain go away.

"Supposed to talk to her," he murmured, trying to struggle to his feet once again, only to fall back to the ground with a moan.

He fought sleep, fought to cling to consciousness, only to lose the battle. When he came to again, it was to the sound of hoofbeats and shouts.

"Over here," Cody called out to someone. "He's on the ground over here."

Hank forced his eyes open, only to snap them shut again as the glare of Cody's flashlight fixed on his face.

"Turn that damned thing off," he grumbled.

"Can't be hurt too bad if you're complaining about the rescue," Cody noted.

"How'd you know to come looking for me?" Hank asked.

"You can thank Lizzy for that," Cody said. "When you hadn't called her by midnight, she called me, fussing up a storm with some tale about you being near death."

"Where'd she come up with that?"

"I wondered the same thing. She claimed the only way you wouldn't have called her was if you were half-dead. She insisted I come over to check on you."

Cody grinned. "I tried to explain that a grown man might resent another man checking on him in the middle of the night." He shrugged. "You know Lizzy. She threatened to call Daddy if I wouldn't agree to do it. I couldn't very well let her send him out into the night on a wild-goose chase."

"How'd you know to look out here?"

"A little guesswork and an understanding of your compulsive nature. Your horse was outside the barn with its saddle still on and covered with dust, looking like he'd been ridden hard. I roused Pete, and he told me about the fence. We added up two and two and here we are."

He probed Hank's leg, checking for broken bones. Hank winced but didn't cry out. Cody gave a nod of satisfaction. "Bruised but not broke, I'd say."

"I'd prefer that guess had come from your sister."

"You mean you'd prefer it was Lizzy's hands doing the poking and prodding, more than likely. She's got a gentler touch than I have, no doubt."

"No doubt," Hank agreed with heartfelt sincerity. "Can we get out of here now? I would really like to spend what's left of the night in my own bed."

"Afraid that's out of the question," Cody said. "Lizzy insisted we take you to the hospital to get you checked out. We can go to the one in Garden City. It can't handle major trauma, but something tells me you just need an X ray and maybe a patch or two on a couple of cuts."

"I'm not going to the damned hospital," Hank protested.

"Are you going to be the one to tell Lizzy you refused?" Cody asked. "Because I'm sure as hell not. She'll be on the next plane back from Miami. It'll disrupt her studies and she'll have to take this last quarter over, prolonging her med-school career. I was under the impression you wanted her to finish sooner rather than later."

Hank groaned. "All right, all right. I'll go to the hospital, but I am not checking in. Is that understood?"

"Understood," Cody agreed, then amended, "unless the doc says it's vital to your well-being."

"You are nothing but a damned bully, Cody Adams."

"And I'm a saint, compared to my baby sister. Be glad she's in Miami."

Hank tried to be glad about that. He really did, but a part of him longed to have her there making a fuss over him. It would have irritated the daylights out of him—no doubt about that—but he still wished she were the one doing the fussing.

By the time he'd been X-rayed and bandaged and poked and prodded by the medical experts in Garden City, it was past daybreak. Cody brought him home, filled Mrs. Wyndham in on the doc's instructions and left Hank to grumble about being confined to bed.

Fortunately, when his temper was about to flare into full-fledged rebellion, the phone rang.

"Yes," he barked.

"Ah, I gather the patient is awake and chipper," Lizzy taunted.

Hank's temper cooled at once. "Hey, darlin'."

"Cody told me what happened. Are you really okay?"

"I'm fine. I gather I owe you for calling out the troops last night."

"I knew something was wrong when you didn't call."

"And it never once occurred to you to think I might have forgotten?"

She was silent for a full minute. "Actually, at first that is exactly what I thought. I was ticked about it, too. Then I decided you'd just decided not to call and that made me even madder, so I called you to give you a piece of my mind. I kept calling for an hour. When you didn't answer, I called Cody."

"I could have been in Garden City, you know."

"Not a chance," she insisted.

"Why are you so sure of that?"

"Because I know you. You do not have a death wish."

Hank would have laughed, but it hurt too much. He smiled instead, glad that she couldn't see it.

"You are really okay, aren't you?" she asked, sounding plaintive.

"Bumps and bruises, nothing serious."

"And a concussion," Lizzy corrected. "Cody told me that."

"Cody has a big mouth."

"I wish I were there. I'll bet I could keep you from falling asleep."

"I'll bet you could, too," he agreed.

"Maybe I should come home," she suggested.

"No way. You stay right where you are and finish the school year. I don't want to see you lose time because of me."

"I won't be able to concentrate anyway."

"Who are you kidding? I heard you finished an English exam once with a tornado bearing down on the building," Hank teased.

"I did not. It was a little old thunderstorm. I was twelve, anyway. I thought I was invincible."

"But all the other kids were cowering under their desks," he reminded her. He had always loved that story about Lizzy. To him it epitomized her grit and daring. He glanced at the clock beside his bed. "Shouldn't you be on your way to class now?"

"It's only a ten-minute walk. I'll run," she said.

"Tell me about the fence you went out to check on. Cody says it looks like it was deliberately downed."

"Could be," Hank agreed.

"Why?"

"Somebody after cattle, I imagine. Or just up to no good."

"The same somebody who let that bull loose that gored Billy-Clyde?"

Hank hadn't made the connection before, but he should have. He muttered a harsh oath under his breath.

"Hank? Do you think it's possible the two incidents are linked?"

"It's possible," he said grimly. "I don't know why the thought didn't occur to me before. There was no reason for that bull to be on the loose that day."

"You never said what spooked Uncle Sid last night."

"I'm not sure, to tell the truth." He remembered the whizzing sound just before the horse bolted. It could have been a gunshot with the bullet coming close enough to terrify the horse or even nick him. "I've got to go, darlin', and you need to get to your class. We'll talk later, okay?"

"Hank," Lizzy protested, but he already had the receiver halfway to the cradle.

He hobbled out of bed and yanked on his jeans. The movements were painful, and his head throbbed like a son of a gun, but by heaven he was going to the barn. If that had been a bullet flying last night, it very well could have nicked Uncle Sid and the evidence would be unmistakable. If he found so much as a scratch on that horse's hide, there was going to be hell to pay.

ver, she would have to go back to school and she'd
once, she would be manipulating it the to ...
he's gotten-up-and back to ... both, then he's going to
be out to ...

Chapter Ten

Two weeks after Hank's accident, Lizzy stared at the positive home-pregnancy test she was holding in her hand. For a week, she had blamed her low energy level and queasiness on stress, but the missed period had been a symptom she couldn't ignore. It had taken an act of courage to walk into a pharmacy and buy the pregnancy test. Now she could only stare at the results in dismay.

It couldn't be, she told herself even as she held the clear evidence right in front of her eyes. She couldn't be pregnant.

Well, of course she *could be,* she corrected. No birth-control method was one hundred percent fool-proof. They'd used two, which should have improved the odds, but even then…

Had there been once when Hank had failed to reach for a condom or even once when she'd failed to take her birth-control pill? Or were they just two of the unlucky few whose birth control simply failed?

She wanted desperately to blame that little blue dot on Hank, but there had been two of them in his bed and they'd both been responsible, at least every single time she could recall.

But all it took was once, she reminded herself, one tiny slip. She didn't need a medical textbook to tell her that.

At least she finally knew why she'd been feeling so lousy for the past few days. She hadn't really needed a textbook for that, either. She'd guessed what the nausea, light-headedness and exhaustion added up to. She just hadn't wanted to believe it, because it had the potential to change everything.

She grasped the edge of the sink as a wave of dizziness washed over her. Pregnant. She repeated the word several times in her head, trying to force acceptance. Instead, there was only shock.

A baby. Hank's baby. At any other time, she would have been thrilled beyond belief to be carrying his child. A few years from now, this would be the happiest news she could receive, but now? Now it had her reeling, cursing the impossible timing that threatened years of dreams and planning. This forced their hand in a way she'd never imagined.

How was Hank going to react? she wondered. Would he be stunned? As dismayed as she was? She doubted the latter. Her own father had said that Hank was ready to marry and settle down. Hank himself had broken off with her when he'd finally accepted how long their separation was destined to be. That silly party and the game played with Brian Lane to make him jealous were the only reasons they were still together at all.

Still, even though he was all too determined not to stand in the way of her career, he would be ecstatic at this turn of events. He would book the church and invite the guests before she could blink.

Hank would want her back in Texas permanently. She could just hear him railing on and on until she gave in. He would demand they get married at once and her medical career be damned. Even though he understood her passion for medicine, even though he knew that this was something she had to do, he would fight her for the sake of their child. And as strong as she was under normal conditions, she might not have the strength for this particular battle.

She walked back into her room in a daze and sank onto the bed, huddled against the pillows. When the phone rang, she ignored it. It would be Hank, and she couldn't talk to him right now. He would guess something was wrong and pester her until she told him. Then it would be all too easy to get swept up in the plans he was bound to make.

She listened to the beep on the answering machine, then heard his voice.

"Hey, darlin', just wanted to say hi. I thought

you'd be back from class by now, but I guess you're running late. You'd better not be off on a hot date. Call me when you get in."

The machine chirped another beep, then went silent. Tears tracked down Lizzy's cheeks. She knew she had to tell Hank about the baby. It was not the kind of news she would ever consider keeping from him. But she wasn't ready just yet.

She wasn't ready to make the choices that would have to be made. She wasn't ready to deal with all the pressure, from Hank and everyone else, to come home, get married and settle down as a rancher's wife. She'd been a cowgirl all her life and she'd loved it, but she'd wanted more. So much more.

The only thing she was prepared to admit was that she loved the baby's father and that she would love this baby they'd conceived, no matter how it turned her life upside down.

Kelsey rapped on her door then and called out. "Lizzy, I know you're in there. Is something wrong?"

"I'm fine," she insisted.

"You don't sound fine. Can I come in?"

"Not now," she said, even as the door pushed opened and Kelsey entered anyway, her brow knit with concern.

"You didn't pick up the phone when Hank called."

"How did you know it was Hank?" Lizzy grumbled. "Listening at the keyhole?"

"Ever since he got hurt, he calls at the exact same time every night so you won't worry."

"Oh."

"Why didn't you talk to him? Did you two have a fight?"

"No."

Kelsey clearly wasn't about to let it go. When it came to persistence, she could be an honorary Adams. She plunked herself down beside Lizzy and studied her intently. "Tears, too, I see. Come on, Lizzy, if something's wrong, maybe I can help."

"You can't help," Lizzy told her. "No one can."

With no answers forthcoming from the source, Kelsey glanced around the room. Almost at once her gaze fell on the box the pregnancy test had come in.

"Oh, dear," she murmured, glancing into Lizzy's eyes. "That's it, isn't it? You're pregnant?"

Lizzy nodded miserably.

"The baby's Hank's, isn't it?"

"Of course it's Hank's," Lizzy said indignantly.

"Then that's a good thing, yes?"

"Normally, yes, but now?" she asked plaintively.

"Will he be upset?"

"Never."

"Then this is about you and school and your career," Kelsey guessed.

"Of course."

"Then I don't see the problem. Your family's rich as sin, you can hire a zillion nannies if you have to. You can make it work."

Lizzy regarded her friend ruefully. "I don't think Hank's going to go for nannies raising our baby."

"Well, he'll just have to change his way of thinking. You bend a little, he bends a little and it works. That's all there is to it."

"Thank you, Ann Landers." She sighed. "Hank is not the kind of man who's inclined to bend, even a little."

Kelsey regarded her with a steady look. "What's the alternative? Would you end the pregnancy?"

"Never," Lizzy said, a protective hand on her stomach. "Not in a million years."

"Will you keep the baby a secret?"

That wasn't even a consideration. Even if she didn't believe fiercely in Hank's right to know, she had too many family members who could spill the beans…and would, if they thought it in her best interests. There would be no secrets kept for long in Los Piños, not from Hank or anyone else.

"No," Lizzy said.

"Then I think you'd better have something very specific in mind by the time you tell him or you'll get swept up in his plans."

Lizzy gave her friend a wry look. "Which is exactly why I didn't answer the phone."

Kelsey nodded. "Of course." She was silent for several minutes before she asked, "Any ideas?"

Lizzy sighed. "Unfortunately, not a one."

All she knew for sure was that when she did come up with a plan, it had better be a doozy.

* * *

"Have you talked to Lizzy lately?" Cody asked when Hank ran into him in town.

"Not for a couple of days, actually," Hank admitted. "I've had trouble catching up with her. What about you?"

"No. Nobody at White Pines has been able to reach her, either. You don't suppose something's wrong?"

Hank had wondered that very thing. "What could be wrong?"

Cody shook his head. "I don't have any idea. If it were up to me, I'd just chalk it up to the fact that she's Lizzy and that she's a female, but Daddy doesn't seem inclined to let it go at that. He's getting all worked up over it."

"Maybe you ought to leave a message for her to that effect. You know she'd never intentionally worry Harlan."

Cody nodded. "Good idea. I'll try it later. If you get through to her, let me know what you find out."

Hank nodded. "You do the same."

Up until now, Hank had been making excuses for not being able to reach Lizzy. Surely if something were truly wrong, he would feel it, just as she had known there was a problem the night he hadn't called her as scheduled. The fact that she wasn't talking to anyone at White Pines, either, made him very uneasy.

He walked into Dolan's and approached Sharon Lynn. "Hey, sweetheart, mind if I use your phone? I'll put it on my credit card."

"Help yourself, but if you're going to call Lizzy,

don't bother,'' she said. ''I just tried and got that blasted answering machine again. She can't possibly be in classes or off studying at the library twenty-four hours a day.''

Hank's stomach knotted. ''Then you're worried, too?''

She nodded. ''This isn't like her. Lizzy always stays in touch, especially now.''

''Because of her daddy.''

''Exactly. She never goes more than a day or two without calling. And I'm trying to reach her about the wedding. If I don't get her soon, I'm going to see to it her maid-of-honor dress is chartreuse with lots and lots of ruffles. She'll hate that.''

''Damn,'' Hank muttered. ''What about her room-mate? Does she have a separate phone line?''

Sharon Lynn's expression brightened. ''Of course. Why didn't I think of that? I'll call Kelsey right this second.''

''Mind if I wait while you do?''

Sharon Lynn grinned. ''Any chance I could stop you?''

Hank shrugged. ''Doubtful,'' he said, sliding onto a stool at the counter as she picked up the phone and began to dial. When she'd gotten the roommate's number from Miami information, she dialed again.

''Hello, Kelsey? This is Sharon Lynn Adams, Lizzy's niece.''

To his thorough frustration, Hank couldn't hear what the other woman said. He glanced around to see if he could spot another extension of the store phone and saw one behind the pharmacist's counter. He went over and grabbed it up just in time to hear Kelsey stammering some sort of an excuse about Lizzy being really busy lately.

"Is anything wrong?" she asked Sharon Lynn worriedly. "Nothing's happened to her father, has it?"

"No, but he's worried sick about her. So are the rest of us."

"Wait," Kelsey said. "She just walked in the door. I'll get her for you."

Hank heard her explaining to Lizzy that Sharon Lynn was on the phone. Lizzy's reply was too low for him to catch, but a moment later she came on the line.

"Sharon Lynn? Is everything all right at home?"

"Other than all of us being worried sick about you, yes. What's going on? Nobody's been able to reach you for days."

"School's tough," she said unconvincingly. "I'm spending all my time studying."

"You're sure that's all it is?" Sharon Lynn asked, her skepticism plain.

"Of course," Lizzy said. "What else could it be?"

"I'm glad to hear it. Wait a sec, there's someone else here who'd like to say hi." She gestured toward Hank.

"Hey, darlin'," he said quietly.

"Hank?"

It sounded to him as if her voice trembled. "Yep,

it's me. I just stopped by Dolan's, and Sharon Lynn and I decided to try to track you down."

"I see."

Her dull response, everything about the conversation sounded wrong to Hank. "Lizzy, what's really up with you? And don't try that bull about being too busy studying to call."

"It's the truth. I told you I wasn't doing all that well in my classes before I left for spring break. I'm trying to catch up now."

"And I've got a patch of swamp in the Everglades I'd like to sell you for an amusement park."

"You don't have to be sarcastic."

"I think I do. Come on, Lizzy, talk to me. What's going on?"

"Nothing."

Hank's frustration was escalating by the second. "Is it me? Are you having second thoughts about us?"

She sighed. "No, that's not it."

"But there is something?" he persisted, determined to drag it out of her.

"Hank, I've really got to go."

That distant, cool note was back in her voice, and it was the last straw. "Go where?" he demanded. "You just walked in the damned door."

"And I don't need you yelling at me," she shouted right back. "We'll talk later."

"When?" he asked, but he was talking to air. The phone clicked off in his ear.

Incredulous, he turned to stare at Sharon Lynn. "She hung up on me."

"Something is definitely wrong," Sharon Lynn said. "I heard it in her voice. Now the only question is which one of us is going to go to Miami to find out what it is."

Hank thought of the problems that had been cropping up at his ranch, then dismissed them. Pete would stay on top of things. Lizzy was more important.

"I'll leave first thing tomorrow," he said.

"Jordan could fly you down. Maybe someone from the family should go along anyway."

"No," Hank said adamantly. "Something tells me that whatever's wrong has to do with me. If she intends to dump me, I don't want witnesses."

"Lizzy wouldn't dump you," Sharon Lynn protested. "Not in a million years."

Hank thought of the conversation they'd just had. "Well, she just gave a darned good imitation of it."

Even after she'd hung up on Hank, Lizzy stood frozen in the middle of Kelsey's room.

"Big mistake," she murmured to herself.

Kelsey stared at her. "What was a big mistake?"

"Hanging up on Hank."

"Why?"

"Because he's probably already making reservations to come here."

"I know you probably don't want to hear this, but maybe that's for the best. The two of you can talk about this face-to-face. If you don't settle it, you're going to wind up flunking out of school anyway. You haven't been able to concentrate worth a darn ever since you found out you were pregnant.''

Lizzy sank down on the side of Kelsey's bed. "But I still don't have a plan.''

Kelsey reached for paper and pen. "Then we'll make a list of all the options. We are both very smart women, which is why they admitted us to this med school. I'm sure if we brainstorm, we'll be able to come up with something ingenious.''

Two hours later, they had crossed off everything except "marry Hank'' and "flee to Paris.''

"Okay, we know I am not going to Paris,'' Lizzy said, "tempting though it might be. That leaves us with one choice, to marry Hank and settle down in Los Piños.''

"You say it as if it's a death sentence.''

"It is a death sentence for my medical career.''

"You don't have a medical career, at least not yet.''

Lizzy scowled at her roommate. "Thanks for pointing that out.''

"I'm just trying to be realistic.''

"I could do with a heavy dose of fantasy about now,'' Lizzy said plaintively.

"No, you couldn't. You need real, logical alternatives. I still don't see what's so wrong with transferring back to Texas to attend school. You could take off the next year to have the baby, then start back the following fall.''

"I could,'' Lizzy agreed. "It's just that I'm terrified that once I drop out, I'll never go back again. Hank is very distracting. Add in a baby, and I'm liable to turn into housewife of the year.''

"Then that will tell you something, won't it? It'll tell you that you don't want this career as badly as you think you do.''

"But I do,'' Lizzy protested. "I need to have my own identity and I love medicine. I'm good at it.''

"Then you'll find a way to make it happen,'' Kelsey said with confidence. "Now, go and get some sleep. You don't want Hank to walk in the door and take one look at you and conclude you're deathly ill.''

"I look that bad?''

"Worse, actually, but it's nothing a little sleep and some of those outrageously expensive cosmetics of yours can't fix right up.''

Lizzy started toward her own room on the other side of the apartment, then turned back. "What if I'm wrong? What if he doesn't come, after all?''

Kelsey grinned. "I don't think you need to worry about that. From everything you've told me about Hank Robbins, he is not the kind of man to take a brush-off lightly. He'll be here. If not tomorrow, then the next day.''

And once he heard her news, Hurricane Andrew would seem like a mild weather system compared to the tornado Hank was likely to stir up.

Chapter Eleven

All of Hank's worst fears had been confirmed in that brief conversation with Lizzy. There was something terribly wrong. For a few days now, their talks had been tense, and more often than not she ended them after little more than a hello and goodbye. It had been disconcerting, but not disturbing.

Then she had stopped taking his calls altogether. When she'd cut him off that afternoon practically in midsentence, he'd recognized that their relationship was in serious trouble. What was driving him nuts was why.

One minute, everything between them had been fine. The next minute, she'd been avoiding him and, just as inexplicably, everyone else back home. The latter made no sense at all, not if her problem was with him.

A less self-confident man simply might have interpreted her behavior as a kiss-off and taken the hint, but it only strengthened Hank's resolve to get to the bottom of the change in her. He wasn't walking away from what they'd found together, not without a battle.

He was pretty sure he knew what had happened. With a little space and perspective, she'd gotten scared of the deep emotions they'd discovered. Hell, the feelings had scared the living daylights out of him, too. Their passion was more powerful than anything he'd ever experienced before. But it wasn't something he intended to turn his back on. Instead, he took the first flight he could get to Miami the following morning.

When he got to her apartment building, which was only a few minutes from the airport in the heart of the University of Miami's Jackson Memorial Hospital medical complex, a young, pumped-up security guard stopped him before he could get to the elevator.

"Who are you here to see, sir?" he inquired politely, his accent surprisingly Southern, rather than the Cuban Hank had anticipated with his dark hair and olive complexion.

"Mary Elizabeth Adams," Hank told him. "I know the apartment number. I'll go on up."

"Sorry. Guests need to be announced," he said in a tone meant to cut off options. "Besides, Ms. Adams left for class a few minutes ago."

Hank couldn't hide his frustration. "What about her roommate? Is she there?"

"Nope, they have the same class this morning."

Frustration turned to irritation. This kid couldn't be a day over nineteen, but his uniform gave him a certain amount of smug self-confidence. Hank was not good with authority figures. He never had been, and to make it worse, this one was still wet behind the ears.

"You're awfully damned familiar with their schedule," he accused. "Why is that?"

The guard never even flinched under Hank's penetrating glare. "I make it a point to get to know the tenants. It makes the atmosphere friendly and my job easier. I can spot trouble faster."

Hank still didn't like it, but he backed down at the sensible explanation. "I see."

"You could wait here," the guard suggested. "But I doubt either one of them will be back before lunchtime. I could show you where to go for a cup of coffee."

"Maybe you could show me where their classes are instead. I'll go wait outside the building."

"I'd feel better if you just came back and waited here."

Hank was getting really irritated with the man's zealous protection of Lizzy, but then he thought about it. If the guard wouldn't let him near her, then he wouldn't let anyone else cause her harm, either. And in a city like Miami, that could be a very good thing indeed.

He smiled. "Look, I'm sorry. It's just that I've flown up here from Texas and I'm anxious to see her. I didn't mean to take it out on you. I know you're just doing your job. So where is this coffee you mentioned?"

The young man beamed at him. "You have your choice," he said, and began gesturing toward a variety of hospital cafeterias and fast-food restaurants in the area. "If you've been cooped up in a plane, you might want to take a walk over to Bascom-Palmer. That's the eye institute a couple of blocks east of here. They have a real nice cafeteria. You can get a decent cup of coffee and some nice blueberry muffins there, or there's a deli in the main complex that has those fancy flavored coffees, if you're into that sort of thing."

Hank nodded. "Old-fashioned coffee, black, will do just fine. And you're right, the walk will do me good. Can I bring you anything when I come back?"

The guard's expression brightened. "If you wouldn't mind, one of those muffins would be great. I used to work in that building and I surely do miss them."

"You've got it," Hank said, and took off in the direction the guard had indicated. He walked through the bustling complex with growing astonishment. It was like a small city with the tiny, original, pink stucco Miami City Hospital building—called the Alamo for reasons he couldn't fathom—tucked in its center, surrounded by towering new structures. Patients in hospital gowns and robes, visitors and employees lingered on benches in the parklike setting around it.

He tried to envision Lizzy as a part of this and couldn't. She'd grown up in the wide-open spaces of Texas. Wouldn't all of this concrete make her as claustrophobic as it was making him? He was about to walk between two buildings when he noticed the sign on one declaring it the Rosenstiel Building, headquarters of the University of Miami School of Medicine. Instead of moving on, he found a bench nearby and settled down to watch the door. The protective security guard would just have to wait for his muffin.

With the constant ebb and flow of people around him and the mix of conversations in Spanish and English with an occasional bit of what was probably Creole thrown in, it was impossible to tell when classes might have let out. He kept his gaze glued to the door of the med-school building.

It was the better part of an hour before he finally spotted Lizzy. She was with a group of students, her expression animated as they debated something or other. Her beautiful, long hair was twisted into some kind of a neat knot on top of her head, and she was dressed in linen slacks and a silk blouse. The look was casual, but clearly dressier than what she usually wore on the ranch. She looked—he searched for a word—professional, he decided.

He knew the precise instant when she spotted him. Shock registered for just a moment in the depths of her eyes. Hank stood, but waited where he was, allowing her time to excuse herself from her circle of friends, rather than forcing introductions.

It seemed to take forever before she finally broke free and came his way, her expression wary rather than welcoming.

"This is a surprise," she said.

Her unenthusiastic tone suggested it was anything but a surprise. Hank had the feeling she'd been expecting him and that her guard was already up. "Really?" he asked. "I would have thought you'd know that hanging up on me was practically an invitation for this visit."

Guilt flickered in her eyes. "Okay, yes. I'm sorry about that. You could have just called back, though. You didn't have to fly all the way over here."

"I thought I did."

"Why?"

"I missed you," he said, and let it go at that for now.

"I wish you'd let me know you were coming."

"Why? So you could tell me not to?"

She winced, then lifted her chin. "Yes, as a matter of fact, that is exactly what I would have told you. I have enough pressure with my classes right now. I can't afford any distractions."

Hank bit back an angry retort. With effort, he kept his tone mild. "Is that all I am, a distraction?"

"Here, yes," she said.

He regarded her evenly, trying to guess what was really going on in her head. Her words were deliberately designed to push him away, but there was something in her eyes that contradicted it, a soft yearning perhaps.

Or was that only wishful thinking on his part? Was she so different here? Had this massive medical complex swallowed up his carefree, joyous Lizzy and replaced her with this studious, solemn woman? He was damned well going to find his Lizzy before he left.

"Can you spare time for lunch at least?"

"I only have an hour."

"Fine. I understand there's a good cafeteria at the eye institute. Shall we go there?"

She nodded at once, looking relieved. Had she been afraid he would suggest her apartment? Was she so terribly frightened of being alone with him? Why? Was it because she was not nearly as immune to him as she wanted to be?

If he'd thought she would relax during lunch, he was mistaken. She left the table in a rush twice and came back looking paler each time. Something was terribly wrong, and with a dawning sense of shock, he had a feeling he knew what it was. He recognized all the symptoms, including the mood swings she'd evidenced in their brief conversations. If his guess was correct, he wanted her to be the one to tell him. Confronting her with a demand to know if she was pregnant with his baby would only put her on the defensive and set them up for a royal battle.

"Lizzy," he said quietly. "Talk to me."

She made a feeble attempt to pretend she had no idea what he wanted to know. She quickly switched to small talk, asking about everyone back home, going through the list of relatives one by one.

"You just talked to Sharon Lynn yesterday," he reminded her. "I suspect you probably checked in with your father last night, since she told you he was worrying about you. I know you know all of the news. Let's get back to what's going on with you."

"Classes, studying," she replied evasively. "You know what it's like."

"Actually, I don't. I've been in ranching all my life. I never went after a college degree." All of which she knew, he thought as he watched her face. There was a hint of panic now that she knew the safest topics were exhausted. He reached across the table and grasped her hand in his. Her skin was like ice. Obviously, his plan to draw her out wasn't working. He might as well be direct and damn the consequences.

"Okay, darlin', let's get straight to it. Tell me about the baby," he finally said.

With that, she burst into tears and ran from the cafeteria and the building, straight into a tropical downpour. Hank caught up with her on the sidewalk down the block. He put his hand gently on her shoulder. She turned, her eyes filled with tears, and then she was in his arms, sobbing against his chest.

"I didn't mean for it to happen."

"Well, of course you didn't," he said, surprised that she would believe he might think that of her. Then he realized what she really meant. He looked her straight in the eyes. "Neither did I."

She sighed. "I know."

"Do you really?"

"Yes, it's just that..." She shrugged.

"It's just that you're feeling overwhelmed and scared and mad."

She frowned. "I hate it that you can read my mind."

"No, you don't. It saves time."

Her chin jutted up defiantly. "I can't marry you, you know."

"We'll talk about it," he said.

"I can't."

"I said we'll talk about it. Right now, I'm getting you back to your place. You're soaking wet. You're dead on your feet, and it's not even the middle of the day."

"What about my classes?"

"You can skip them for once. Have you been getting any sleep at all?"

"Enough for me," she insisted, then gave a rueful smile. "Not enough for the baby, apparently."

That afternoon while Lizzy slept, Hank grappled with their dilemma. The woman he loved was going to have his baby. She was also determined not to let that little predicament change her plans for her career. He'd seen that famous Adams stubbornness in her eyes and in the lift of her chin. She'd practically dared him to insist on marriage.

Hank knew better. Not even God Almighty could force an Adams to do something he or she wasn't ready to do. He was going to have to be patient. He was going to have to wear her down or think of a compromise. Not to marriage, of course. He wouldn't compromise on that. He might be willing to adjust the timetable a bit, maybe find some alternatives to the traditional living arrangements, at least for the time being.

Unfortunately, as good as he was at reading Lizzy, there wasn't nearly time enough to come up with answers to all the arguments she was bound to have against their future. His flight back to Texas was booked for that evening. Once again they were going to be separated, only this time he was going to be the one doing the leaving unless he made some quick arrangements so he could stay.

He called Pete first.

"No problems here," the foreman assured him.

"No more downed fence lines? No weird accidents?"

"Nothing. It was probably just kids, nothing to worry about. You stay right where you are as long as you need to. The boys and me will keep this place humming."

"Thanks, Pete. I'll check in with you."

After talking to Pete, he called the airlines and changed his flight. He scheduled it for the next day, then thought about it and made it for the end of the week. He'd never convince Lizzy to do what needed to be done in a matter of hours. It was going to take days, and that was only if she was in an amenable frame of mind.

He was pacing in the living room when her roommate came back. The girl, who appeared years younger than Lizzy though she had to be nearly the same age, blinked at him from behind her thick glasses. He recognized her as one of the students who'd been with Lizzy earlier.

"Oh, my," she murmured. "You must be Hank."

"I am. And you're Kelsey."

"Yes."

He gestured toward a chair. "Have a seat, Kelsey. I think it's time you and I got to know each other."

Kelsey's gaze snapped toward Lizzy's room. "I'm not so sure that…"

"You and Lizzy are friends, right? And Lizzy and I are—" he searched for the right word "—close."

Kelsey watched him silently.

"Which means we both have her best interests at heart," he concluded.

"Sure," she conceded.

"I imagine the two of you have talked about the baby," he said, watching her face intently. Surprise registered at once in her eyes.

"You know?"

"I know."

She regarded him with indignation then. "What are you going to do about it?"

"I'm going to marry her," he said at once. "But that's easier said than done. I need your help."

"What can I do?" She shrugged. "You know how Lizzy is. Once she makes up her mind, it's not so easy to change it."

"No kidding," Hank said with heartfelt agreement. "But you can tell me what she's been thinking since she found out about the baby. If I'm going to come up with a solution, I need to know where her head is."

"Mixed up," Kelsey said succinctly.

Hank nodded. "Scared, too, I'll bet."

Kelsey seemed shocked by the very idea of that. "Lizzy scared? No way."

"Not even of losing out on medical school?"

"Okay, yes," she conceded. "You're right about that. She's really determined to finish."

"Here, I suppose?"

"Actually, I suggested she transfer back to a school closer to home, but she does seem to be set on finishing here. It's like some weird point of honor with her. I have no idea why. I mean, this school is good, but so are lots of others."

Hank nodded. It was every bit as bad as he'd expected. He had his work cut out for him. "Thanks, Kelsey. You've been a big help."

"Really?"

"Really."

She stood up and backed away nervously. "Well, if you're sure everything's okay here, I think I'll just head off to the library to study."

"You don't need to leave on my account."

"Yes, I do," she said firmly, then grinned. "If you and Lizzy are going to discuss this, there won't be much peace and quiet around here for studying."

Hank grinned back, liking her better and better. "You do have a point."

"Will you be here when I get back?"

He glanced toward Lizzy's room and sighed. "That's my plan," he said. "It remains to be seen what Lizzy has in mind. She may decide to kick me out."

Kelsey regarded him doubtfully. "You don't look like the kind of man who'd be kicked out so easily."

"You're right about that. I am a very stubborn guy."

Kelsey gave a little nod of satisfaction. "Then I'd say the two of you are a perfect match."

After Kelsey had gone, Hank settled back in the easy chair by the window and stared out toward the medical complex. Life-and-death decisions were made there every minute, more than likely. People got well. Some died. And babies were born.

As he thought of the latter, an idea came to him. When Lizzy awoke and walked into the living room a few minutes later, he had the beginnings of a plan.

"Come here, darlin'."

She walked toward him, her gaze every bit as wary as when she'd first seen him earlier. "What?"

He beckoned her into his lap. She hesitated for a moment, then settled into his arms with a sigh. When he held her like this, it was almost possible to believe that everything was going to be all right.

"How're you feeling now?" he asked.

"Better."

"Do you feel up to going for a walk?"

She stared at him in surprise. "A walk? Where?"

"You'll see," he said. "Are you game?"

She studied him intently, then finally nodded. "I'll get my purse."

Hank held her still. "Not just yet. First, we have the little matter of a proper greeting."

She regarded him speculatively. "Proper?"

He chuckled. "Okay. Improper." He smoothed the tendrils of hair away from her face, then ran his thumb over her lower lip. Her gaze heated. By the time he tucked his hand behind her head and drew her toward him, he could see the wanting in her eyes. His own body hummed with anticipation.

It seemed like forever since he'd held her like this, even longer since he'd tasted her. Once he'd started, he couldn't seem to stop. The kiss set off a blazing fire that could only lead to one thing.

But even as he scooped her up and headed toward her room, he had second thoughts. Gazing into her face, he asked hesitantly, "Is this okay?"

She nodded. "Yes. It's okay."

"It won't hurt the baby?"

"No. Believe me, I've already read most of the prenatal books in the med-school library."

Still, he was ever so gentle as he placed her on the bed and lay down beside her. He held back the urgency of his own desires to caress slowly and more and more intimately, until she was pleading with him for more.

"Not yet," he whispered, taking his time removing her clothes, trailing his fingers along sensitive flesh, watching the trail of goose bumps left in his wake.

When she was naked, he studied her, looking for changes in her body, running his hand over her belly, trying to envision his child growing inside her. The image was beyond him, but oh, how he wanted to see her body swollen with his baby. And he would. She wouldn't keep him away from sharing in this miracle.

"Hank?"

He blinked and gazed at her. "Yes?"

"Why such a fierce expression?" she asked, smoothing her hand across his brow.

"Just thinking about the months ahead," he said.

"Don't," she pleaded. "Be here, be with me now."

The longing in her voice reached him and forced aside thoughts of the future. He was here with her now and he could use this incredible connection to keep her with him always.

"I'm here," he whispered, his voice husky.

He rose over her and, with his gaze locked with hers, he entered her slowly, sinking into slick, moist heat that was life's most powerful lure. Ever conscious of the baby, he moved with care until Lizzy stole that option from him with a thrust of her hips that demanded more.

Control slipped away, and he was lost to sensation and need—his and hers. Their skin beaded with perspiration, making the glide of each caress exquisite torture. Their movements became more and more frenzied, until at last Lizzy cried out with release. As her body pulsed around him, he, too, exploded with a climax more shattering than any he'd ever felt before.

With a last, shuddering sigh, he rolled onto his back, carrying her with him. He gazed into her eyes. "You okay?"

"I will be when I can breathe again," she said. She grinned. "You?"

"I'm not the one who's pregnant."

For the first time since the topic had first come up, wonder spread across her face. "I am, aren't I? I am actually going to have a baby."

"You're not scared, are you?"

"Of being pregnant? No."

"Just of the changes it will bring," he guessed.

She nodded and tears sprang to her eyes. "It complicates everything."

"And yet you never once considered ending the pregnancy, did you?"

"Never," she said fiercely.

"Because it's ours," he told her, his hand once again resting across her still-flat tummy. "A part of you and me."

"Yes."

"Then we can work out the rest," he promised her.

"I don't see how."

"One day at a time," he told her. "When life throws us a curve, that's the best any of us can do."

"You're not angry?"

"No way. I want this baby, every bit as much as I want you to be my wife."

She opened her mouth to protest, but Hank touched her lips to silence her. This was where the real test of his patience was going to come.

"Not now," he said. "We don't have to decide anything now." He grinned at her. "For one thing, I'm starving. For another, I think we need to get out of here, clear our heads a bit."

"You're not going back tonight?"

Her mixed feelings were totally transparent. "Not tonight," he said. "Disappointed?"

"Of course not, it's just that..." Her voice trailed off guiltily.

"It's just that you're scared you're vulnerable and that I'll talk you into something you don't really want to do," he said.

She frowned. "You're doing it again."

"Doing what?"

"Reading my mind."

He winked at her. "Just think how good I'll be at it when we're eighty."

Chapter Twelve

They were going to be together when they were eighty? Lizzy couldn't think that far ahead. She could barely envision what her life would be like in a few weeks when news of her pregnancy could no longer be concealed. If she thought Hank capable of bullying her into making a decision she would later regret, it was nothing compared to what the combined force of her father and brothers would do. She shuddered at the prospect of withstanding all that testosterone-driven pressure.

"Cold?" Hank asked at once.

She shot him an amused look. "Are you going to be this solicitous when I start pleading for pickles at 3:00 a.m.?"

"Of course," he promised. He studied her carefully. "Am I going to be there when these cravings kick in?"

Lizzy realized belatedly the trap she'd just set for herself. "I don't know," she said honestly. "Isn't that what we need to talk about?"

Hank nodded. "But first food. Where should we go?"

"How about Cuban? We're not that far from Little Havana. I think you'll like the food."

"If that's what you want, it's fine with me."

"Great," she said brightly. "I'll shower and we'll go."

Forty-five minutes later, they were seated in a restaurant that was noisy and jam-packed with a blend of Spanish-speaking families, Anglos and tourists. Versailles on Southwest Eighth Street—Calle Ocho— was one of her favorite places. The decor was bright and featured a lot of etched mirrors on the walls.

Lizzy explained the dishes on the menu, but Hank couldn't seem to focus. She knew exactly what his mind was on. His gaze kept straying to the babies at nearby tables. The expression on his face was a touching blend of awe and fascination.

"Why don't I order?" she said finally.

"Fine."

After the Cuban waitress had taken their order, Lizzy met Hank's gaze. "Okay, what's going on in that head of yours? You're watching those babies as if you've never seen one before."

"Knowing you're going to be a father changes things. I was looking at those babies and wondering if their dads are as terrified of doing the wrong things as I am."

"Hank, you're going to be a wonderful father. You are kind and patient and strong. No man could set a better example for a child."

His jaw set in a way that was all too familiar. "And I will be there to set the example," he said quietly.

"Of course you will."

"I won't settle for being a part-time dad, Lizzy. If things between you and me were different, if we weren't suited at all, then maybe our child would be better off if we weren't together, but that's not the case here, is it?"

"No," she admitted slowly. "We get along great. What's your point?"

"Then there is no reason on earth for us not to get married and give this child the two-parent home he or she deserves," he said, looking directly into her eyes. "Is there?"

Lizzy flinched under that unwavering look. "Hank, it's not that simple."

"Okay, then, let's reduce it to the basics. You love me. I love you. We're having a baby. I want more than anything in this world for that baby to be born with my name, for us to make a home for him or her."

Lizzy regarded him with mounting frustration. "But what about me? What about my dreams?"

"We'll work it out."

"Until you can tell me how, I'm not going to marry you just because it's the easy thing to do."

"What about it being the right thing to do?" he asked quietly. "For one thing, try to imagine what my life expectancy is going to be once Cody and Luke and Jordan find out about the baby."

"Is that what this is all about?" She forced a grin. "No need to panic. I'll protect you."

Hank clearly was not amused. "How? With reason? Your brothers are not reasonable men. They act first and think later. I can't say that I'd blame them in this instance. If you were my sister, I'd kill the man who got you into this fix."

"Nobody is going to get killed, and you did not get me into this 'fix,' as you call it. I had a choice in the matter. What happened between us when I was home was my doing as much as yours."

"But I'm supposed to be the responsible, sensible one," he pointed out.

Lizzy's hackles rose. "And what am I?" she argued indignantly. "The airhead?"

"No, of course not."

"Drop it, Hank. You're just digging a very deep hole for yourself here."

"I'm just saying that I should have answers, but the only one I come up with you seem to be rejecting out of hand."

"Which is?"

"Get married."

"No," she said again.

"Dammit, Lizzy, I love you. You say you love me. We're going to have a baby. We damned well ought to be married," he said with evident frustration.

Lizzy flinched at the mounting anger in his voice. "Be reasonable," she pleaded.

"Me? It seems to me that I am the only one around here who is being reasonable."

That did it. Lizzy stood up. "I knew it," she said, scowling at him. "I knew you were going to try to bully me into marrying you. Well, I'm not going to do it, so you can just get that idea out of your head once and for all."

With that, she turned and marched out of the restaurant, back straight, head held high. She was very much aware of the curious gazes following her and of Hank's muttered oath as he tossed some money on the table and sprinted after her.

"Lizzy," he shouted over the din of voices.

Lizzy was frantically trying to jam the key into her car's lock when Hank caught up with her.

"Lizzy," he said more quietly. "I'm sorry."

"No, you're not. You're like every male in my family. When you don't get your way right off, you turn stubborn and mule headed and sneaky. I wouldn't be a bit surprised if you didn't deliberately sabotage one of those condoms we used."

The silence that fell was so thick she wondered for a moment if she'd gone too far. Finally, she dared a glance into Hank's face. He was staring at her with astonishment and maybe just the tiniest trace of hurt in his eyes.

"If you think for a single minute that I would do something so underhanded," he began quietly, "then we are in serious trouble."

He regarded her steadily until she finally blushed and looked away.

"I'm sorry," she said eventually. "I know this was just one of those zillion-to-one accidents. Neither of us planned it."

"I hope you mean that."

She nodded. "It's just that I panic, and when I panic, I start lashing out. You're an easy target right now."

Hank jammed his hands into the pockets of his jeans as if to keep himself from reaching for her. "You know, darlin', you're not the only one who's been blindsided here. I found out about this today. You've had days to get used to the idea of having a baby, to think about what's best. I'm scrambling for the right answers and I keep locking on the most obvious one. If there's a better alternative, try it on me."

She regarded him miserably. "I don't have one," she confessed unhappily. "Maybe we don't have to have all the answers tonight."

"Maybe not," he agreed.

He opened his arms then, and Lizzy stepped into them and rested her head on his shoulder, breathing in the familiar, reassuring, male scent of him. With all the millions of things she didn't know right now, this was not one of them. This was real and right. Loving Hank was right.

"Do you want to go back in and finish your dinner?" he asked eventually. "I told the waitress not to take anything away, that we might be back."

Even if she weren't very conscious of the baby's need for nourishment, her growling stomach would have answered for her. "Sure," she said, then regarded Hank hopefully. "Do you think they'll bring me extra pickles for the *media noche* sandwich?"

Hank grinned. "If they won't, I'll buy the whole blasted jar."

"Don't go that far," she said. "I'm still not sure I like pickles. I never did before. All of a sudden, though, I just seem to have this craving for them."

"How many more months is this going to go on?" Hank wondered aloud.

Lizzy chuckled at his bewildered expression. "Nine is pretty much standard," she reminded him. "Don't despair, though. You've already missed the first few weeks."

Hank's expression sobered. "I know you meant that as a consolation, darlin', but it's not. It just reinforces my determination not to miss a single second of the next eight months or so."

She heard the grim determination in his voice and realized that she might be able to delay Hank from forcing her into a rash decision, but it would only be postponing the inevitable. He wasn't going to give up on marriage. Not in a million years.

And the pitiful truth was, she wasn't at all certain she wanted him to. That scared her most of all.

It was early evening by the time they got back to Lizzy's apartment and not quite dark. Rather than heading inside, Hank took her hand, tucked it through the crook of his arm and began to stroll toward the main hospital. An idea had struck him earlier in the afternoon, and now seemed like the perfect time to act on it. He sensed that Lizzy's resolve was weakening and he intended to use whatever weapons were at his disposal to assure that she came to see things his way. The ring he'd bought right before leaving Texas had been burning a hole in his pocket. He wanted to give it to her now more than ever.

"Where are we going?" Lizzy asked, but without really balking.

"Just for a stroll," he told her innocently.

"This isn't a neighborhood for strolling," she warned him.

"And we're not going that far."

He led her to the hospital's main entrance, then stepped inside the lobby, which was still bustling with visitors and staff.

"Wait right here," he told Lizzy as he went to talk to a clerk at the information desk.

When he came back, Lizzy regarded him warily. "What on earth are we doing here?"

"Just come with me, okay?"

"Why?"

"Humor me."

Lizzy could have balked then, but not without creating a scene. Hank saw the stirring of her curiosity. In fact, he was counting on it.

"Okay," she said eventually, and followed him to a bank of elevators.

He punched the button for the floor the clerk had indicated and spotted the first glimmer of understanding in Lizzy's eyes. When the doors opened, they were on the huge obstetrical floor, just down the hall from the nursery. Hank turned and led her to the window through which parents could watch their newborns.

A grin spread slowly across her face as she stared at the rows of babies, some of them squalling mightily, others right beside them sound asleep. He watched as her hands slid instinctively to her own belly, then reached over and covered them with his own.

He waited until she looked up at him, before saying quietly, "One of these days we're going to have a little guy or a little girl just like these. It's not a fantasy, Lizzy. It's not going to go away. The baby growing inside you is going to be front and center in our lives. We have to make the best possible decision before that happens. We have to know where we stand with each other and how we're going to cope with this incredible miracle God has given us. We can't keep putting it off and hope time will take care of it, which is why I think we should get married."

He took the jewelry box from his pocket but before he could remove the diamond, she placed her hand over his.

"I understand why you're doing this," she whispered, tears shining in her eyes. "But the decision has to be one we both can live with, Hank. It's not as simple as getting a marriage license and saying the vows. That's over in the blink of an eye. We have to live with everything that comes after."

"It can be as simple or as complicated as we make it," he argued.

"Okay, let me ask you this. Right before I left Texas, you decided not to ask me to marry you because you knew in the end, I would only resent you for making me choose, right?"

"Yes," he conceded, not liking the tack she had taken at all because he could see where it was heading, and it sure as heck wasn't toward the altar. "What's your point?"

"Nothing's changed. Backing me into a corner is no way to start a marriage. The resentment will be a given, just as you predicted it would be."

"There's a baby to consider now. That changes everything." He decided the time had come to hammer home his point. "How will you manage if you don't marry me? Have you considered that? Will you carry the baby to class with you?" he pressed. "What about when you're on duty at the hospital? Will you haul the baby along? Or are you counting on Kelsey being a live-in baby-sitter? She might have other ideas.''

Lizzy looked shaken by the questions. "I don't have all the answers. All I can see is that you're asking me to make a huge sacrifice, to give up medicine, come home and be a wife and mother.''

Hank's temper flared, despite his intentions to stay calm. "Would being my wife and the mother of our child be such a god-awful thing?''

"No, of course not.''

"Then you're just being selfish,'' he accused. "You're being Harlan Adams's baby girl again, believing that you're entitled to everything you want and what's right for everybody else doesn't mean a damned thing. If you think you're turning this baby of mine over to some nanny to raise, you're crazy. I'll fight you for custody first.''

Lizzy visibly reeled under the bitter accusation and the threat. "You won't take this baby away from me, Hank. You can forget that right now. And if you feel that way about me, if I'm such a terrible person and you hold me in such low esteem, why would you want to marry me in the first place?''

"Because I love you, dammit.'' Frustration had him shouting.

"Well, I love you, too,'' she shouted back.

A nurse stepped into the hallway and pressed a finger to her lips. "Shh. This is a hospital. Not a Vegas wedding chapel.''

Hank offered a rueful apology, then turned back to Lizzy.

"We're not going to settle this tonight, are we?" he concluded, awash with regrets for letting the fight escalate and for not having options they could both live with.

"I guess not."

"Then let's go sleep on it. Maybe one of us will come up with a brainstorm before morning. If not tomorrow morning, then the next day."

"Or the next," Lizzy said, sounding fatalistic.

Hank tucked a finger under her chin. "We will work this out, darlin'. I promise you that."

Lizzy didn't look convinced, but she did take his hand when he offered it, and that night, when they crawled into her narrow bed, she trustingly fitted herself to his body and went off to sleep with his arms around her.

Hank was awake for hours, though, trying to untangle the complicated mess they'd made of their lives. He'd meant what he'd said about fighting her for custody before he'd let a stranger raise his child, but that was only a last resort. Surely there were better solutions.

Reduced to its simplest, black-and-white terms, there was only one answer: marriage. But getting Lizzy down the aisle was going to take more ingenuity than he possessed alone.

It was going to require the expertise of a master manipulator like her daddy.

* * *

For the next forty-eight hours, Lizzy did little except eat, go to her classes and talk to Hank. They hashed over their options a thousand times. And by the time he had to leave for Texas, they were no closer to a solution they could live with than they had been when he'd first shown up.

Kelsey had been a saint. She had refereed arguments when asked, but mostly she had stayed away and given them the space they needed to wrestle with the dilemma in which they'd found themselves.

"I'll be home in a month," Lizzy said as Hank distractedly mashed his cornflakes into a sodden mess. "We'll have the whole summer to work this out."

He pushed aside the cereal and lifted his gaze to hers. "In the meantime, is this our secret? Or do you intend to tell your folks?"

Lizzy shook her head at once. "I can't tell Daddy about this now. I don't know how he'll react."

"Oh, I think you do," Hank said dryly. "Harlan can't wait for you to give him another grandbaby. He'll be over the moon about the news."

"Yes, and he'll be on your side about the two of us getting married right away."

"More than likely," Hank agreed, looking as if he considered that an atomic-caliber secret weapon.

"Which is why he is not to know until you and I have reached a decision." She leveled a look straight at him. "Are we clear on that?"

"I will not discuss this with your father," he promised.

She regarded him suspiciously. "Or anyone else in my family."

He grinned. "Okay, darlin'. I will not discuss it with a single living soul. Does that cover enough ground?"

"I suppose." She glanced at the clock. "It's time. Please let me drive you to the airport."

"No. You have a class and I can take a taxi."

Suddenly, she didn't want him to go. Having him here, even though they'd spent most of the time arguing about the future, had been wonderfully reassuring. No matter how things turned out, no matter what decision they eventually reached, they were in this together. And, as she'd known for years, if ever she was in trouble, Hank Robbins was the kind of rock-steady man she'd want in her corner.

"At least let me go downstairs with you, then," she said. "I'll get my books so I can go on to class."

A few minutes later, they stood outside waiting for the taxi. It was a gorgeous spring day with the sky a brilliant blue and the air already thick with the first hint of summer's humidity.

Hank reached over and trailed his thumb along her jaw. "I'm glad I came and I'm glad you told me the truth about the baby."

"I would have told you even if you hadn't come," Lizzy said. "I was just trying to figure things out first."

"We will figure them out, darlin'." He grinned ruefully. "Maybe not on my preferred timetable, but we will figure them out. You can count on that."

A lump formed in her throat. "I can count on you, can't I?"

"Always."

Before she could say more, the cab pulled to the curb. After that, everything was rushed—Hank's kiss, the cab's departure, the wave of loneliness that washed over her.

She realized then how Hank must have felt the times she had walked away. There was one huge difference, though. He had always let her go willingly and with his blessing. For all intents and purposes, she had sent him packing. She only prayed that when she got back to Texas in a few weeks, he would still be there waiting for her with open arms and not a court order demanding custody of their child the minute she gave birth.

464 THE COWBOY & THE UNEXPECTED WEDDING

Chapter Thirteen

The next few weeks were among the longest of Hank's life. He was counting the minutes until Lizzy came home for the summer. His mind kept wandering, imagining her with the legendary inner glow of a mother-to-be. Would her pregnancy be showing by then? Would they have any time at all to work out a plan on their own before the entire Adams clan thrust themselves into the midst of the dilemma and made plans for them?

"Hey, boss? Everything okay?"

Hank's head snapped up at Pete's words. He'd forgotten entirely that the other man was waiting for his decision about whether they needed to hire a private investigator to get to the bottom of the troubling incidents that had been taking place around the ranch. There had been a few more since his return from Miami, mostly minor annoyances, but definitely worrisome in total.

"I'm sorry, Pete. My mind wandered."

"Seems to be doing that a lot lately," the older man noted. "Wouldn't have anything to do with that pretty little doc, would it? When is she coming home?"

Hank grinned. Pete and the men had taken to calling Lizzy "doc" ever since she'd saved Billy-Clyde after that bull had gored him. "A couple of days, I suppose," he said with feigned nonchalance, even though he knew to the precise minute when her flight was due in.

"Don't have it quite calculated down to the second yet?" Pete taunted.

Hank bristled at the accuracy of the man's guesswork. "You know, Pete, you may be a hell of a foreman, but I could do better," he threatened with mock sincerity.

"Not in this lifetime," the old man countered, clearly undaunted. "And not for what you're willing to pay."

"Let's face it, you just stick around for Mrs. Wyndham's cooking."

Pete grinned. "She does make a mighty fine biscuit. If she weren't already a married lady, I do believe I'd court her for those biscuits and her blueberry pie." His gaze narrowed. "Now, back to that private eye. I'm thinking we should bring him in here and put a rest to these little incidents before they get out of hand."

Hank thought of Lizzy and the possible danger to her if he failed to take the mischief seriously enough.

"Do it," he said, vowing to warn her that she was not to go traveling around his property or even her own family's unaccompanied until this was resolved. There was no way in hell he was taking chances on her safety or the baby's.

"Are you going to tell Cody what you're up to?" Pete asked. "He might want to be in on it, too. A couple of things have happened over at White Pines, as well. There's a snake of the human variety sneaking around here, all right. I'd bet my life on it."

"I'll talk to Cody," Hank promised. "I'll ride over there as soon as we're done here. How's Billy-Clyde doing?"

"He should be back to work in a week or so. He's been worried you wouldn't want him back since he won't be up to full speed for a while yet, but I told him we always take care of our own around here and he became one of ours the day you hired him."

"Exactly right," Hank said.

"Could you maybe stop by the bunkhouse and tell him that? It might reassure him."

"I'll do it on my way out," Hank promised. "Okay, then, if that's it, I'll head on over to see Cody."

"I'll fill you in on what happens with the private eye as soon as he agrees to be on the payroll."

Hank gave him a terse nod. It wouldn't be soon enough to suit him.

After a brief visit with Billy-Clyde, he saddled up and rode toward the neighboring ranch, hoping to find Cody in the office, instead of off someplace. But instead of running into Cody in the office at the back of the main house, he found Harlan behind the desk, booted feet resting atop the cluttered mahogany surface, a phone tucked against his ear.

He looked hale and robust for a man of his years and very much back in command. Obviously, his recovery was just about complete. Hank rapped on the door, then waited until Harlan acknowledged him with a beckoning wave.

"Hey, boy, what brings you by?" he said when he got off the phone.

"Looking for Cody, actually, but it's a pleasure to find you up and back in the middle of things."

Harlan grinned. "Doubt Cody would agree with you. He says I'm in here messing up his filing system."

Hank studied the haphazard arrangement of papers, a good number of which had tumbled, helter-skelter onto the floor. "System?" he asked doubtfully.

"My point exactly. The place is a gosh-darned mess. He says all the important stuff is in that danged computer of his anyway. Besides, he claims he's got more-important fish to fry these days." He gave Hank a canny look. "Any idea what he could mean by that?"

Hank's spirits sank. Unfortunately, he suspected he knew exactly what was on Cody's mind and it answered the very question he'd come to ask.

"You do know something, don't you?" Harlan said, immediately picking up on Hank's reaction. "What is it?"

"I can't be sure."

"Then try the guesswork out on me. I'm looking for something I can wrestle with to keep my mind active. The newspapers just get me riled up."

"I'm not sure I should."

Harlan glowered. "Don't you start treating me like an invalid, too. I've had about all I can take of people tiptoeing around me like the least little thing will send me into a relapse. If there's something going on around here, I need to know about it. Until they put me in the ground, White Pines is still my ranch."

Hank understood his frustration. He also understood that even though Harlan had turned the day-to-day operations over to Cody, it was his heart and soul that had taken the run-down family home and turned it into a thriving cattle operation. Harlan Adams had given Hank an example to live by when he'd bought the dilapidated operation up the road.

"Okay, I can only tell you about what's been happening at my place." He elaborated on several incidents.

Harlan's gaze narrowed. "And you think the same sort of thing's been going on around here?"

"I wouldn't be surprised. In fact, that's why I came by this morning. I wanted to talk to Cody about it. See if he wanted to go in with me on hiring an investigator to check things out."

"When exactly did these incidents start?"

"A couple of months back."

Harlan's expression turned pensive. "Around the time you and Lizzy started getting serious," he said thoughtfully.

Hank started at the connection the old man was drawing. "What the hell are you saying?"

"Just that the timing is downright fascinating, don't you think?"

"There's no connection," Hank insisted. "There can't be. The timing's pure coincidence."

"We'll see," Harlan said enigmatically. "You get that private investigator on the job and then send him over to have a chat with me. I don't want to start tossing around accusations without any evidence, but I damned well want him to start looking in the right direction."

Harlan didn't have to say any more. To his deep regret, Hank was suddenly able to follow his unspoken logic. He knew exactly who was implicated—that sleazy oilman who'd been trying his damnedest to seduce Lizzy at that party.

But why? Why would Brian Lane resort to making mischief? Most of the incidents could be dismissed as no more than childish revenge, he supposed, but there had to be more. He met Harlan's gaze directly.

"What do you know about Brian that I don't?" he demanded.

"Enough to know that he's a fool, and a fool with money and a sick soul is dangerous."

"Is this about Lizzy, then?"

"Maybe," Harlan conceded, then surprised Hank by adding, "Maybe not."

"What are you thinking?"

"It could be about the land," Harlan said. "My hunch is that he saw her as a means to get the land around here. You've gotten in his way."

Hank was about to ask about why an oilman would want ranch land, but the answer hit him squarely between the eyes. "Oil," he said softly.

Harlan nodded.

"But if there's oil here, doesn't he know that Jordan would never let it fall into a competitor's hands?"

"He knows that this land is off limits for anyone exploring for oil, even my own son. I haven't spent my whole life building this into a proud cattle empire only to see it pockmarked with a bunch of oil rigs. But if my land is rich with crude, then yours probably is, too. If Brian can drive you off and get Lizzy to marry him, he'll have his foot in the door at both places and he's the kind who'll kick it clean down to get what he wants."

"If he tries getting his blasted toe through the door,

I'll cut the damned thing off for him," Hank said fiercely. "That land is mine and so is Lizzy."

He stopped pacing and noted that Harlan was grinning.

"About time you made yourself clear on that point," the old man said. "I was beginning to wonder if I'd pegged you wrong."

Hank shot him a rueful look. "I'm not the problem, sir. It's your daughter. Unfortunately, she has a mind of her own and a timetable that would drive a teetotaler to drink."

"Then I guess you'd best get busy persuading her that timetables don't mean a danged thing, unless they're for trains or airlines. Human beings ought to be flexible."

"With all due respect, sir, she's an Adams. If the woman's stubborn, she got it from you."

Harlan began to chuckle. "Yes, I suppose she did. Well, you've never struck me as the sort of man to give up just because there's a little roadblock in his path. Or am I wrong?"

"No, sir, you are not wrong," Hank said with grim determination. "Call the caterers, because there's going to be a wedding right here at White Pines before the summer's out, and that's a promise."

Lizzy dreaded going home. She hated the thought of facing her family. Not that they would judge her. She knew better than that. But they would have a thing or two to say about what ought to happen next.

She was relieved when Hank said he would drive over and meet her flight in Dallas. Not that he didn't have his own opinions about the future, but she'd already dealt with him. So far she'd managed to stand up to him just fine.

Of course, he was getting impatient. She'd heard it in his voice the past few times they'd talked. If she didn't give in to his way of thinking soon, he'd be as formidable to deal with as Luke, Jordan, Cody and her father combined.

She spotted him the second she walked off the plane. He was lounging against a railing in the gate area, his booted feet crossed at the ankles, his jeans a snug fit over those long legs and narrow hips, a Stetson pulled low over his brow. There were other men similarly dressed in the waiting area, but nobody on earth personified the cowboy mystique the way this man did. Lizzy could see it in the way every woman who walked past gave him a second look. She wanted to throttle every one of them.

"Okay, cowboy, you can stop posing now," she said. "And don't tell me you weren't aware of the impression you were making."

He regarded her with innocent blue eyes. "Impression?"

"On the ladies. You had them ogling."

"You sound just a smidge jealous, darlin'."

"Do not."

"Do, too," he said, and swept her into a hug and spun her around. He delivered a long, breath-stealing kiss that wiped away every single trace of envy in her body. He stood back and regarded her, his expression smug. "Feel better now?"

"You can't get out of this with a piddly old kiss," she retorted.

"You call that kiss piddly?" he said with pure masculine indignation.

She studied him thoughtfully. "Can you do better?"

He grinned then. "Not in public. Any better and I'd get us arrested."

"Big talk, cowboy."

His expression sobered. "Ah, darlin', it is good to have you home again." He held her at arm's length.

"Hank, what on earth are you doing?"

"Surveying."

"I'm not a piece of land you're thinking of buying," she protested.

"No, you're the mother of my baby. I want to see if it shows." He turned her sideways. "Damn."

"What?"

"You're still downright skinny. Haven't you been eating properly? You can't starve yourself to death. The baby needs sustenance." He held his hand a few inches from her waist. "I expected you to be out to here by now."

Lizzy rolled her eyes. "If this is the way you're going to be for the next few months, I'm getting on a plane back to Miami right this second."

Hank glowered. "Over my dead body."

"Well, then, stop fussing." But even as she uttered the warning, some small part of her blossomed at the concern in his voice and at the possessive way his gaze slid over her. She had always been loved, always been surrounded by people who cared heart and soul for her well-being, but this was different. This was what it felt like to be cherished. How could she turn her back on this?

"Hank?"

"Yes."

"Does anyone at home suspect?"

"Not as far as I know."

"How are we going to tell them?"

"That's up to you. More to the point, what are we going to tell them?" He turned to study her intently. "Are we going to tell them about the baby? Or are we just going to tell them that we can't wait any longer and we're getting married?"

Lizzy sighed. "I've been over this and over it. I'm still no closer to knowing what's right than I was when you left Miami."

Hank's expression turned resigned. "Then I guess we take it one day at a time for now."

"I'm sorry," Lizzy said. "I know that's not what you wanted to hear."

"No," he agreed. "And in a few more weeks, it won't be good enough, not for me and not for anyone in your family. They're going to want answers, Lizzy. We all are."

"Don't you think I want answers, too?" she retorted heatedly. "This isn't exactly a picnic for me, either. I'm just trying to do what's right, Hank, not just for the baby, but for all of us. And I think you can forget having much time before we have to fill my parents in. They're going to figure out something's up by suppertime. They always do."

He slammed the palm of his hand against the steering wheel. "I'll tell you what's right, dammit. The parents of this baby ought to be married. That's what's right."

"Not if we'll be divorced within a year," she flung right back.

There was a hard, unyielding look in Hank's eyes when he met her gaze. "You've got that right. Because once you and I are married, darlin', it's going to be for keeps."

Lizzy trembled under the fire in his eyes. That kind of commitment was something she'd dreamed of all her life. It was the kind of commitment that bound her parents together, the kind she wanted as an example for her own children. And it was what she wanted with Hank, a happily-ever-after, till-death-do-us-part commitment. Just not yet, her head screamed. She needed a few more years to finish her medical training.

But fate wasn't giving her a choice in the matter, it seemed. There was a baby on the way now, and he or she sure as hell wasn't going to wait around for her to finish med school, an internship and a residency before putting in an appearance, not unless she pulled off a pregnancy for the record books.

It would be so easy to say yes to Hank, to simply give in and claim his love and his support, but then what? How long would it be before the resentment kicked in and the little fights over nothing began to eat away at their love?

Hank glanced over. "Lizzy? Are you feeling okay?"

Unless heartsick counted, she was fine. "I'm okay," she said wearily.

"I don't want you worrying about telling your family by yourself," he said. "Whether it's today or a couple of weeks from now, I'll be right there beside you. I want them to know I'm accepting my responsibility."

She grinned halfheartedly at that. "Hank, there would never be a doubt in their minds about that. I'm the one they're going to want to shake some sense into."

"I won't let them do that, either," he promised. "Look, honey, I know this isn't easy. If it were, I'd have dragged you in front of a preacher by now. But there is a solution. We just have to find it."

"Unless you've got one up your sleeve, we're out of luck," she said. "We're only a few miles from White Pines, and one look at my face and Mother and Daddy are going to know something's wrong."

He regarded her with obvious astonishment. "Then you intend to tell them straight out?"

She shrugged. "I might as well. It won't take them long to guess, anyway."

Hank nodded. "Then I'll be right there, too."

"I'm not so sure that's a good idea."

"Well, I am and that's final."

"Okay, if you insist, but I hope you've got your running shoes on, because you might have to make a quick getaway."

"Darlin', one thing you should know about me by now, I never, ever run from a little trouble."

"How about from a whole passel of loaded shotguns?"

Hank paled a bit at that, but his jaw squared and his expression remained resolute. "Not even then."

Oddly enough, now that he'd said it, Lizzy knew that was exactly what she'd been counting on all along. With Hank by her side, she could face anything, even her parents' disappointment and displeasure.

What she wasn't prepared for was finding the whole household in total chaos.

Chapter Fourteen

"There's a fire at Hank's place," Lizzy's mother shouted, waving them down as Lizzy and Hank drove up in front of White Pines. "Hank, you'd better get over there right away."

Hank stared at her as if he couldn't quite comprehend what she was saying. Lizzy jumped in to fill the heavy, shocked silence.

"What happened?" she asked. "Does anyone know yet?"

"Pete says it started in the barn and flared up quick. As dry as the weather's been, they're afraid it could spread to the house," her father explained, his expression filled with sympathy. "Cody and Jordan are on the way, along with Justin and Harlan Patrick and all the men we can spare. Luke's sending whoever he can from his ranch. I've got a helicopter going over to pick them up.''

He reached out and squeezed Hank's shoulder. ''I'm sorry, son. It doesn't look good, but everyone will do what they can. If your place can be saved, we'll do it, and if it can't be, then you can count on all of us to help you rebuild it.''

''Oh, my God,'' Lizzy murmured watching the look of desperation spread over Hank's face. She knew what the ranch meant to him and she wasn't about to let him face this alone. ''I'm coming with you.''

That got his attention. ''No way,'' Hank said, his jaw set stubbornly. ''Get out of the truck, Lizzy. You're staying here.''

She stayed right where she was. ''No, if someone's injured, I can help.''

''She has a point,'' her mother said quietly. ''I'll come, too.''

Hank sent Lizzy a pleading look. ''But the baby…'' he whispered. ''If anything happens to the baby, I'll never forgive myself.''

Oblivious to the shocked looks being exchanged by her parents, Lizzy covered Hank's white-knuckled grip on the steering wheel with her hand. ''It will be okay. I promise we won't get in any danger. Now, stop wasting time and let's go.''

''I'm coming, too,'' her father declared, already moving off toward his pickup.

"Absolutely not," Lizzy and her mother protested in unison.

"I'll stay back with Lizzy," he said, his gaze on his wife steady. "In case she needs me."

"But—" Hank began.

"Just go, dammit. This fire's not going to sit still while we hang around here arguing," her father said, already climbing into his own truck with Janet right on his heels.

Hank threw his truck into gear and took off toward home. In the distance, gray smoke was billowing over the horizon. "I swear to God if that low-down son of a bitch had anything to do with this, he will pay."

As the implication of his words registered, Lizzy stared at him in shock. "You think this fire was deliberately set?"

"I'd bet on it," he said, his expression grim. "Too many things have happened lately for this to be a coincidence."

"But who would do such a thing?" she demanded. Her gaze narrowed as she studied his grim expression. "You think you know that, too, don't you?"

His silence was confirmation enough. His admission that this wasn't the first suspicious incident made her uneasy. Could this be tied in with Hank's accident a few weeks earlier? And how many more little accidents had happened that she knew nothing about?

"Who, Hank? Who's in back of this?"

"Let's just say it's someone who doesn't know when to quit."

By then, it was too late to try to pry answers out of him. He pulled his truck to a stop upwind of the fire in an area that looked for the moment, anyway, to be safe enough. Though smoke was still billowing, it appeared that so far the worst of the blaze had been contained to the barn.

"Lizzy, promise me you won't come any closer," Hank insisted. "And at the first sign that the wind is shifting, you will take the truck and go back to White Pines."

She could see how torn he was about leaving her at all. "Go," she said. "I'll be fine. I'll just get first-aid supplies from the house and come right back here. If anyone's injured, direct them this way."

Hank froze. "You are not to go near the house, dammit. It looks safe enough now, but fire's unpredictable. One little spark and it could flare up all over again. The house could go next."

"No," she said quietly. "You'll have the fire under control long before it gets that far. Look, Hank. Look at the barn. There are very few flames left. It's mostly smoldering now."

"And you and I both know how quickly that could change with the wind whipping around and everything dry as tinder. Stay here, dammit. I'll get whatever supplies you need and send them out here."

She could see there was no arguing with him, so she stayed where she was, relaxing only after he'd gone. Seated on the tailgate of the pickup, her gaze following Hank, she was only dimly aware of her father and mother coming to sit on either side of her.

"It's going to be okay, darlin' girl," her father promised. "It's just a barn. We'll all pitch in and have it rebuilt for him in no time."

"What if I'm wrong, though? What if it does spread and take the house?"

"Then we'll rebuild that, too," he said. "You know how folks around here stick together in a crisis, and Hank's practically family now. We'll do what's right by him."

"You won't be able to rebuild Hank's spirit so easily," she said. "This ranch means the world to him. He's a lot like Luke, Daddy. He could have stayed at home and taken over his father's operation, but he needed to prove he could succeed on his own. You remember what this place was like before he fixed it up. It was a wreck. He's turned it into a home."

"As long as you are safe and his cattle are safe, Hank will have what it takes to start over," her mother said, then gave her a pointed look. "And this baby you're carrying will give him a reason to look forward."

Lizzy was startled that her mother had guessed, then recalled Hank's outburst back at White Pines. She searched her mother's face for signs of anger. "You're not furious with me?"

"You're my daughter. I'll always love you, no matter what. This won't be the first baby that got a jump on its parents' marriage."

Lizzy turned to her father, fearful of the condemnation she might read in his eyes. "And you?"

"Do you even need to ask? All I want is your happiness. Just tell me when the wedding is and I'll be the proudest man in the church."

Tears leaked from her eyes and spilled down her cheeks. "You two are the most incredible parents a woman could ever have." She decided now was not the time to tell them that there was no wedding date just yet or that she was the one holding out. There would be time enough to get into all that when the fire was out and things had settled down again.

Lizzy peered through the increasingly heavy smoke trying to catch sight of Hank, but all she saw were shadows rushing about with hoses and buckets, dousing the new flare-ups, and men with shovels digging a break line to keep the fire from ever reaching the nearby ranch house.

Mrs. Wyndham emerged from the chaos bearing first-aid supplies. "Hank says you may be needing these and that I'm to stay and help."

She was as calm and unflappable as ever. Lizzy had the feeling that it would take a lot more than a fire to rattle Hank's housekeeper.

"Do you have any idea what happened?" Lizzy asked her.

The housekeeper shook her head. "I never saw a thing. Pete was in with me having his supper when we heard a shout from one of the men. Next thing I knew, all hell had broken loose. They had me call over to your place and told me to get what I could out of the house just in case the fire started spreading that way. I've loaded Pete's pickup with all the valuables I could carry and moved it down the lane.''

Her gaze sought out Hank in the distance, and she shook her head. ''That poor boy. Every rancher has a hard life, but Hank's worked harder than most to make a go of this place. He's always had something to prove to himself.''

She glanced at Lizzy. ''As if there was ever any doubt about him measuring up,'' she said fiercely. ''There's not a man around who can hold a candle to him. I don't know what I would have done when C.J. took sick and had to retire, if it weren't for Hank giving me this job. He gave Pete a break when his last employer decided he was too old to work. Hank surely doesn't deserve a thing like this.''

''Were they able to get all the livestock out of the barn?'' Lizzy's father asked.

Mrs. Wyndham nodded. ''Most of the horses were in the corral. The men just turned them loose. I suppose they'll wander back on their own sooner or later.''

''I see,'' her father said, his expression thoughtful.

Lizzy recognized that tone. She could tell from her mother's expression that she did, too.

''Harlan, what are you thinking?'' her mother asked. ''I know that tone of voice.''

''You ever heard of an accidental fire that gets started when it's least likely to harm an animal?''

"There's no accounting for when a short will set off a fire," her mother said.

"It just seems a little too coincidental to me. I'd say someone wanted to do some damage but didn't want to be blamed for taking any lives, not even the horses'."

"Then you're saying this was deliberately set, too," Lizzy said, stunned by her father's confirmation of Hank's own theory, which she'd badly wanted to dismiss as absurd.

"I am and, more than likely, by that same weasel who's been behind all the other mischief around here."

"Who?"

"Brian Lane, of course."

Lizzy's mouth gaped. "What are you saying, Daddy? Surely you don't think Brian would burn down Hank's barn. It doesn't make any sense."

"But that's exactly what I think," he countered. "And if Hank finds out that's who it was, there won't be a place on this earth that man can hide."

"But why?" Lizzy asked, though the sinking sensation in the pit of her stomach told her she already knew some, if not all of it. "It's because of me, isn't it?"

Her father regarded her intently. "Don't you dare go blaming yourself for this. The man had an agenda, that's all. You were an intended victim, same as Hank. It had more to do with oil than love, I can guarantee you that."

"But if Hank loses everything, I'll still be partly to blame," she whispered, staring toward the devastation of the barn.

"You will not," her mother said, taking her firmly by the shoulders and forcing her to meet her gaze. "No one's to blame but Brian." She shot a look at her husband. "*If* this was his doing in the first place. I still say your father is making something out of nothing and that he's going to get sued for slander for dragging the man's name through the mud the way he's been doing the last few hours."

Lizzy forced a smile at the defense of Brian. It was proof of her mother's generous nature. "You always did see the good in people. For an attorney who dealt with her fair share of guilty criminals, it's a pretty amazing trait."

"Yes, well, sometimes you have to look beyond the obvious."

"And sometimes, evil's just plain evil," her father contradicted. "I never liked that man. I told Jordan that, too, on more than one occasion. I suspect that's why Jordan never made him a part of his company, even though Brian hinted at it often enough."

"Daddy, if you felt that way about Brian, why in heaven's name did you even invite him to White Pines?"

He shot her a rueful look. "Because he's the kind of man men tend to take an instant dislike to. Heaven help me, I figured if anyone could get Hank to admit to himself how he felt about you, it would be Brian. Thank goodness that part worked, at least.''

"Oh, Harlan, when will you stop meddling?" her mother whispered with a sigh. "Can't you see that's what set all of this in motion?"

"It also got Lizzy and Hank headed along the right path," he argued, his expression intractable. "And I won't apologize for that."

They were still debating the point when Lizzy slipped away and headed out across Hank's property on the shortcut back to White Pines. The walk would do her good. She needed to think and she needed to be alone to do it. Her mother and Mrs. Wyndham could cope with whatever injuries turned up among the men fighting the blaze at Hank's, and the paramedics had been arriving from neighboring counties for some time now.

None of them had a treatment for what ailed her, though. She doubted there was a medical text available that had a treatment for guilt. No matter what her parents said, she'd set all of this in motion—she and her father—with their games to make Hank jealous.

It was time—way past time, in fact—to grow up and take responsibility for her own actions, to get over the notion that all of her whims would be granted as they had been since childhood. She owed Hank for having set all of this into motion. Now it was payback time. Sometimes there simply were no easy choices or quick fixes. And sometimes love meant sacrificing a dream to do what was right.

By midnight the fire was out and the fatigue had set in. Though the women from the neighboring ranches had brought soup and sandwiches and coffee all during the evening, no one had really had time to sit down and take a break to enjoy them. Now they sat in the beds of pickups and on the ground, waiting to be sure that not a single spark was left to set off a whole new blaze and using the time to catch their collective breath.

"I will never be able to thank you all enough," Hank said to Cody, Luke, Jordan and the other men nearby.

"No thanks necessary," Cody said. "You'd do the same if one of us was in trouble. That's just the way it is."

"My question is how are we going to prove who was behind this?" Jordan asked.

"The truth is we may never know," Luke said bluntly.

"We'll know," Hank said, unwilling to let it rest until they did. "I am going to look that sick son of a bitch straight in the eye and demand an honest answer. I'll know if Brian Lane is lying."

"And then what? Are you going to turn him over to the law?" Cody asked.

"It won't do any good without proof," Justin said as he came up to join them. "You'll need evidence that will stand up in court, not all the suppositions and slander I've heard being tossed around here the past few minutes."

Jordan frowned at his son. "Okay, Justin, you're so dead-set on being a lawman, you find the proof," he challenged. "Then maybe I'll take this notion of yours seriously."

Justin stilled and stared at his father. Hank could feel the tension shimmering in the air between them. Apparently, the others could feel it, too, because Luke said quietly, "Jordan, Justin doesn't need to prove his worth to you. If he wants to be a cop, then he needs your blessing, not a test he has to pass before you'll give it to him. Remember the hoops Daddy made you and me jump through."

"And we were stronger men because of it," Jordan declared, his expression set stubbornly.

"Even so, we both vowed we wouldn't do the same to our own kids," Luke countered. "Not that I did so well taking my own advice where Angela was concerned. My expectations drove her off and kept her away from Jessie and me for years. Learn from my mistakes, too, Jordan."

Jordan sighed. "Okay, you're right," he conceded with obvious reluctance. He faced Justin. "Still and all, catching Brian in his lies ought to guarantee you a place with the sheriff's department right here in Los Piños."

"Tate's eager to retire and run off to Arizona so he can play golf seven days a week. He's already guaranteed me a place,'' Justin retorted with a grin. "But I'll see what I can come up with just the same." He glanced at Hank. "Will you leave it to me for now? I swear to you I won't let Brian Lane get away with this if he's guilty."

Hank didn't want to agree. He wanted to find the other man and beat the truth out of him, but he nodded anyway. "For now," he agreed. He glanced toward the place where he'd left Lizzy hours earlier. His truck was still there, but there was no sign of her. A faint shiver of alarm raced through him when he couldn't spot her. "Has anybody seen Lizzy?"

"Not me," Cody said.

"Haven't seen Janet or Daddy in a while, either," Luke noted. "Their truck's gone. They've probably gone back to White Pines to get some rest. Why don't you give her a call over there, Hank? I'll bet Lizzy is waiting up to hear that everything's okay."

Hank shook his head. If Lizzy had gone home, it was because she needed the sleep. Since he couldn't tell her brothers why rest was so critical for her now, he said simply, "If she's with Harlan and Janet, she's in good hands. I'll catch up with her first thing in the morning. I'm going to get some sleep myself now. You men ought to head on home and do the same."

Cody shook his head. "Send the others home, but I think I'll stick around a little longer, if you don't mind."

"I might as well hang out till morning, too," Luke agreed.

"Count me in," Jordan and Justin said together.

Hank eyed them suspiciously. "Why? You don't think Brian will try again, do you?"

"I wouldn't put anything past that scum," Cody said angrily. "I'd like to get my hands on him myself. We're all here. We might as well keep an eye on things. If he sets foot on the place, one of us will spot him."

Hank gave him a grateful look. "Then you all go on inside and catch whatever sleep you can. I'll have Mrs. Wyndham make me a fresh pot of coffee and I'll take first watch."

The others all agreed and headed for the ranch house, all except Cody, who remained right where he was.

Hank studied him intently. "Something on your mind?"

"You and Lizzy."

"What about us?"

"I haven't heard anything about a wedding date."

"We've had a few other things going on around here since she got home this afternoon," Hank stated.

"Have you set a date or not?" Cody persisted.

Hank gave him a resigned smile. "Not exactly."

"But you've asked her?"

"Till I'm blue in the face," he said with frustration, then shrugged. "She'll come around in her own good time. I'm counting on it."

Cody grinned. "Could be she needs a little nudge. Want me to talk to her? Better yet, I could have Melissa, Sharon Lynn, Jenny and the other women gang up on her.''

"I doubt that would do much good. If there's one thing I've learned about an Adams, they do things in their own sweet time and not even an act of God is going to rush them.''

Cody nodded. "If you know that about us, then I suppose you and Lizzy will get on right well.'' His gaze narrowed. "Just one thing.''

"What's that?''

"Don't follow my example and wait too long. Try to get her to the altar before the baby's born.''

Hank stared at him in shock. "Is there anything you people don't know practically before it happens?''

Cody laughed. "I'm not omniscient, if that's what you're thinking. I had a minute alone with Daddy earlier. He told me you'd let it slip and that Lizzy had confirmed it.''

"Then I'm surprised you didn't toss me in among the dying embers of that blaze.''

"And rob my niece or nephew of a daddy? Not a chance.'' He leveled a steady look at Hank. "But I will hog-tie you and drag you into the church myself if need be.''

"Hey,'' Hank protested. "I'm not the one who needs persuading. You made me an offer not a minute ago. Talk to your sister.''

Cody shuddered, clearly less interested in such a discussion with the stakes escalating by the minute.

"Oh, no, I think I'll leave her to Daddy, after all. She's his little girl. If she's going to listen to anyone, it'll be him."

"That may have been true once," Hank said. "But something tells me Lizzy's marching to her own drummer these days, and the rest of us are just going to have to wait until he starts playing our tune."

Chapter Fifteen

It had been forty-eight hours since the fire, and Hank had been caught up in a whirlwind of decisions. He'd also been beseiged by nosy insurance investigators, to say nothing of trying to round up all the horses that had scattered at the first whiff of smoke. In all the confusion, there had been no sign of Lizzy and no time to go looking for her.

He had a feeling he knew exactly what Lizzy's disappearing act the night of the fire meant. He'd seen the guilt in her eyes when he'd mentioned that Brian Lane might be behind the fire.

He also guessed that she was hiding out at home, trying to distance herself from him and the decisions that had to be made.

By midday of the third day after the fire, things were settling back into a more normal routine. He and Cody and the others agreed that the danger from another fire was slim. Brian—if he was the one responsible—was lying low. Maybe he even knew by now that Justin was looking for clues that would implicate him. It wouldn't stay a secret for long around Los Piños that he was under suspicion for setting the blaze.

"Boss, the men and I were talking," Pete told him when he found Hank staring at the rubble. "We'll get to work on putting up a new barn in our spare time. If you'll get the lumber in here, we'll get started tonight."

Hank was touched by the offer. "That's not necessary," he told the older man. "I can hire a crew to do the job. You all have enough work."

"Yes, it is necessary. You've stood by each of us when we've had our troubles. Just look what you've done by keeping Billy-Clyde on the payroll when he hasn't been able to pull his weight. As for me, I'd be rocking on some porch, bored to tears, if you hadn't given me this job. We figure we owe you."

Hank could see that the offer meant a lot to his foreman. He held out his hand. "Thank you. Tell the men I appreciate what you're doing. I'll have the supplies you'll need here by tomorrow at the latest."

"Boss, one other thing. The men wanted me to tell you how much they appreciated the doc sticking around the other night. She's going to be busy as can be if she sets up practice around here. She's got a real gentle, reassuring way about her."

Hank smiled. She did, indeed. "I'll tell her that."

As soon as Pete had gone, Hank went inside and called the lumber company. They promised he'd have his delivery by morning, along with all the men they could spare, as well.

Mrs. Wyndham appeared in the doorway, hands on hips, her expression grim. "If you don't mind my saying so, you could do with some cleaning up," she chided. "When was the last time you passed under a shower?"

Hank grinned. "Not as many days ago as you're probably thinking, but I imagine I could do with another one."

"Then get on upstairs and take one. I'll have lunch on the table when you get down. Cody said he'd be back around then, and I expect we'll be seeing Luke and the others, as well. This arson business hasn't set well with any of them."

At the mention of arson, Hank's blood began to boil. It had taken all of his willpower to leave matters in Justin's hands, but if he didn't have answers soon, Hank was going after Brian himself. Unless he was made to pay for this, there was no telling what would come next.

By the time he got downstairs, the Adams men were all seated at his dining-room table. They fell silent when Hank walked in. Hank's gaze shot to Justin.

"What have you found out?"

"The fool didn't even have sense enough to buy the gasoline he used in the next county. Carl said he filled up three gallon containers at his pumps the very morning of the fire. Paid with his credit card, too. Now, could be he had a lot of lawn mowers to fill up or it could be he's got an old tractor that doesn't take much gas to operate, but I'm betting that gas came right out here. The insurance-company arson investigator agrees it was gasoline that got things started.''

''Surely the man's not that dumb,'' Hank said. ''If he intended to set a fire, wouldn't he have paid cash at least?''

''You would think so,'' Jordan agreed. ''But the way I figure it, maybe he wanted you to know who was behind it.''

''Why?'' Cody demanded.

''Payback for Lizzy,'' Luke said quietly. ''You stole something he wanted right in plain sight, and now he's done the same to you.''

''What kind of sick logic is that?'' Hank demanded. Then another terrifying thought struck. ''What about Lizzy? Will he go after her, try to claim her?''

Lizzy's brothers exchanged a solemn look that told Hank everything he needed to know. ''I'm going to White Pines.''

''Hank,'' Cody called out. ''Don't worry. He'll have to go through all of us to get to her.''

Hank didn't wait to see if the others intended to follow or not. He saddled his horse and raced for White Pines. Janet met him at the front door. ''Hank, what is it? The fire hasn't started up again, has it?''

''No, it's Lizzy. Is she here? I have to see her.''

''She's upstairs resting.''

''Are you sure?''

She regarded him uneasily. "Of course I'm sure. Where else would she be?"

"I just need to see that for myself. Please."

She stood aside. "Just don't wake her, okay. She's been restless. I don't think she's gotten much sleep the past few days."

Hank barely heard her. He was already sprinting up the stairs. He'd known for years which room Lizzy had. She'd pointed out the window once, hinting that she would scale the tree outside to meet him for a secret rendezvous if he were willing. He'd never taken her up on it, but he'd never forgotten which room it was. Sometimes late at night, he'd sat outside in the dark at his place and imagined he could see the light beckoning from that window.

When he got to the room, he stood silently and forced himself to calm down. He opened the door quietly and eased inside. The drapes were drawn, but even so the sunshine crept through a gap, casting just enough light for him to see that she was safely tucked under the covers. A sigh eased out of him then.

He edged closer and gazed down at her, a lump in his throat. Whatever it took, whatever compromises were necessary, she was going to be his, he vowed. He would not lose her or his baby, not to Brian's sick revenge, not to her own doubts. If that meant making a few sacrifices while she finished her medical studies, then so be it.

Satisfied at last that she was perfectly secure, he slipped out of the room and joined Janet at the foot of the stairs. He shrugged sheepishly at her puzzled expression.

"I got it into my head that Brian could come after her," he said. "Cody and the others were afraid of the same thing."

Janet shook her head. "Which explains why there are pickups barreling up the driveway even as we speak. This has to stop, Hank. Somebody has to deal with Brian, and I know who that someone is going to be."

Hank stared at the grim set of her jaw. "You?"

"She's my daughter, isn't she? I'll lay out a few legal facts for the man. That ought to put the fear of God into him."

Hank grinned at her. "You would, too, wouldn't you?"

"Don't you laugh at me, Hank Robbins. Nobody messes with my family."

Hank put his arm around her. "What about you and me going together?" he suggested.

"Not without the rest of us," Harlan announced, joining them. "I've called Tate. I don't want it to be said that we've turned this into a lynching of an innocent man. The sheriff'll see to it that everything is taken care of nice and legal."

"I could have done that," Janet protested.

Harlan grinned at her. "Who are you kidding? You'd have been the first one to pop the man."

"Somebody has to stay here with Lizzy," Hank said.

"Melissa, Jenny and Sharon Lynn are on their way. Jenny's a heck of a shot if I do say so myself."

"Then we'll go as soon as they get here," Hank said, his expression grim. Come what may, he wanted this over. He wanted to start making plans with Lizzy for what promised to be the most unconventional marriage on record, at least for the next few years with her in Miami and him and their baby in Texas, and all of them chalking up enough frequent-flyer miles for a long honeymoon in Hawaii when it was over.

Lizzy awoke to the sight of her sister sitting at the window with a shotgun in her lap.

"Jenny?"

"Hey, sleepyhead. It's about time you woke up."

"What on earth is going on?"

Jenny glanced down as if surprised by the gun she was holding. "Oh, you mean this. Just a precaution."

Lizzy sat up slowly. "Maybe you'd better explain that."

"To tell you the truth, I'm not sure I understand all the details myself, but Daddy and Hank were convinced you might be in danger, so here I am. Melissa and Sharon Lynn are on guard downstairs."

"And the enemy is?"

"Brian."

Lizzy might have laughed, if it weren't so clear that everyone else was taking this so seriously. "He wouldn't come here."

"I would have said the same thing a few days ago, but then I wouldn't have pegged him as an arsonist, either."

Lizzy's eyes widened. "They know for sure that he set the fire at Hank's?"

"Justin's convinced of it. He's got evidence he

took to Tate and it must be pretty darned convincing because the sheriff's with the rest of them.''

Lizzy moaned softly and covered her face with her hands.

"Lizzy? Sweetie, what is it? Are you okay? Is it the baby?"

"No, but this is all my fault. It started out with that stupid party."

"Don't be ridiculous," Jenny protested. "You are not to blame."

"Of course I am. I had to have my way. I had to make Hank fall in love with me, and look what a mess I've made of it. I'm pregnant and he's off chasing down a lunatic. If anything happens to him, I'll never forgive myself."

"Nothing is going to happen to Hank," Jenny said with confidence. She tilted her head. "So, when's the wedding?"

"Never. I can't marry him. It would be a disaster. I've been nothing but trouble for him."

"I don't think that's the way he sees it. He loves you, sweetie. There's no hiding from it."

Lizzy gave a sigh that was part dismay, part relief and wonder. "He really does, doesn't he?"

Jenny glanced out the window. "And here he comes now, all in one piece. I guess the battle is over and the good guys have won." She leaned down and brushed a kiss across Lizzy's forehead. "I'll give you two some privacy."

Lizzy clutched her hand. "No," she pleaded. "I can't see him yet."

"You don't have a choice. He's heading this way,

and I, for one, am not about to stand in his way. Even with this gun in my hands, I'm no match for a man on a mission like this one.''

Jenny took off just as Lizzy heard Hank taking the stairs two at a time. She heard them exchange a few murmured words in the hall, and then there was a sharp rap on her bedroom door.

''Lizzy? I know you're in there,'' Hank said. ''I'm coming in.''

She sighed and resigned herself to facing him. ''The door's unlocked.''

He opened it slowly and stepped inside. His face was haggard, as if he'd been getting no more sleep than she had been. The temptation to run to him was overwhelming, but she held back. To her dismay, she could already feel the faint stirring of resentment that because of him and their baby she was going to have to give up everything.

He walked over to the bed and sat beside her, not touching, but close enough that she could feel the heat from his body beckoning to her.

''Is everything over with Brian?''

''Tate has taken him in for questioning. There's enough evidence to lock him up.''

''No shots fired?''

''Only one. Your daddy plugged the back tire on Brian's fancy sports car as he tried to get away.''

''I'll bet the sleazeball loved that.''

''He was madder about that than being taken into custody.''

He leveled a look deep into her eyes then that had

her squirming. "What's going on, Lizzy? It's not like you to hide out in your room."

"I had some thinking to do," she said.

Hank nodded. "Me, too."

Unable to stop herself, she reached out and pressed her hand against his stubbled cheek. "It looks as if all that thinking has been keeping you up at night."

He glanced sideways at her. "Doesn't seem to have affected you much. You're more beautiful than ever."

"You would say that even if I looked like something the cat dragged in," she teased. "You're just trying to have your way with me."

He grinned. "What if I am?"

She placed her hand over her belly, which was just showing the first signs of expanding to accommodate the baby growing inside. "Seems to me like you already have."

"Then a time or two more won't make any difference, will it?"

She regarded him indignantly. "A time or two? And then what? Are you planning to get rid of me after that?"

He shook his head. "Not willingly," he said quietly. "Never willingly."

"What then?"

"I'm giving you a gift," he said. "A wedding gift, if you want it."

"I haven't agreed to marry you yet."

"Then think of the gift as a bribe."

Lizzy sighed. "Hank, you don't need to bribe me to marry you. I love you. I want to be your wife."

"Maybe," he agreed. "In due time. But the baby changed the timetable."

"Just one of life's little unexpected surprises," she said, trying to keep her tone light, instead of bitter. "Everyone always said I was the impetuous one. I ought to be able to handle this better than most."

"But you're not handling it, darlin'. You're torn in two. I'm going to make it easy for you."

Lizzy didn't like the sound of that. She didn't like it one little bit. She stood up and scowled at him.

"No," she said heatedly. "You're not going to make it easy for me. That's what Daddy has done my whole life. If I wanted something, he got it for me. If I wanted to get into med school, he made it happen. If I wanted to have this baby on my own and turn it over to him and Janet or a nanny to raise, he'd make that happen too, but that's not the way it's going to be. This baby is my responsibility."

"And mine," Hank reminded her fiercely. "And it's more than a responsibility, Lizzy. This baby is a miracle, our miracle."

The anger went out of her at the wonder in his voice. When he opened his arms, this time she went to him and let herself be held.

"How could I have forgotten that, even for a minute?" she whispered against his neck. "How could I have forgotten what a blessing this is?"

"Because you have something to lose, darlin', something that's important to you. That's here and now, while the baby is still to come. It's harder to weigh them when one doesn't seem quite real yet. As for me, I'm getting the best of the bargain. I'm getting everything I ever dreamed of.''

His gaze swept over her, and his lips curved into a tender smile. ''You know, maybe we've been going about this all wrong. We've been looking at it as if it's an either-or situation. Somebody very wise once told me that the best marriages are based on compromise.''

''Must not have been an Adams,'' Lizzy said dryly.

''Oh, but it was,'' he corrected, and the set to his jaw was every bit as stubborn as any Adams Lizzy had ever known.

''So, I've been thinking,'' he continued. ''We could manage it if you stayed in Miami, but if you would transfer to medical school here in Texas, it'd be just around the corner.''

Lizzy's heart began to fill with hope. ''And what? You'll take care of the baby? Is that what you're saying?''

Hank's chin jutted up a notch. ''Why not?'' he challenged. ''It's better than hiring a nanny, which is what you'd have to do if the baby was with you in Miami. I suppose Mrs. Wyndham and I could manage to change a few diapers, assuming your daddy and Janet would let us near the baby.''

Her spirits began to soar at the possibilities. ''And I could come home and take over on the weekends. And maybe you could even bring the baby up for a few days, if we got an apartment near school with room for a nursery.''

''It would take a lot of patience and flexibility on both our parts,'' Hank warned.

"But we could do it," Lizzy said. "I know we could." She peered into his eyes. "Hank, are you sure? Will you absolutely hate having me gone so much of the time?"

"I would hate it more if I lost you and the baby for good."

Lizzy was beginning to get the idea they could make it work. The prospect of actually marrying Hank without having to give up medicine actually took her breath away.

"We'd have to have a wedding before the end of summer," she said, then added with dismay, "There's not enough time. You know Daddy will want something elaborate."

"Oh, I think I can persuade him that expediency is more important than formality just this once," Hank said with confidence. "A little, old unexpected wedding won't throw him for a minute. As for you, you can just think of it as a surprise party and just show up on time."

Lizzy laughed and settled on his lap. "That gets us through the wedding, but Hank, what about later, after I get out of school?"

He leveled a gaze straight on her. "Now that's the solution you're going to have to come up with. I've done what I could to ease the way through the next few years."

Lizzy sighed and buried her face against his neck. Visions of a medical practice in a major trauma center paled by comparison to images of being with Hank and their child. A smile began to form. If Hank could compromise, so could she.

"Do you think Daddy'd be in the mood to build a hospital in Los Piños?" she asked. "That would be a whole lot nicer than having to go all the way to Garden City to work, especially if I've got a whole passel of kids around the house and a handsome husband I won't ever want to leave."

Hank laughed.

"Darlin', if it'll bring you home where you belong, I can flat out guarantee it. Heck, I'll raise the money for a wing myself." His expression sobered. "Think about it, though, Lizzy. I know you had your heart set on a big-city hospital. Can you be happy back in Los Piños?"

Lizzy gave the question the careful consideration Hank obviously expected. She'd always cared more about medicine than about the money. Maybe she was more like Marcus Welby and less like those *ER* doctors than she'd thought. She might not become a world-renowned trauma doctor in Los Piños, but the past few months had proven that Los Piños had its own share of emergencies. And when it came right down to it, family practice was looking awfully good to her, too.

"To an Adams, Los Piños will always be home," she said. "And you'll be here. And our children. That'll be enough excitement for me." She would make it enough, because Hank was giving her so much in return, not just his love, but his understanding.

"Children?" he was saying now, his expression hopeful.

She grinned at him. "I have a feeling once we get

started, Mr. Robbins, we're not going to want to stop.''

"A whole new dynasty,'' he whispered. "A Robbins dynasty. I think I like the sound of that.''

"Don't tell Daddy that,'' Lizzy warned. "To him every baby in this family is an Adams, no matter what last name they might carry.''

"I won't begrudge him that much,'' Hank said. "After all, he is giving me the woman he thinks of as his own precious miracle.''

"Giving?'' Lizzy repeated. "The man has practically shoved me into your arms.''

"But I was more than ready to catch you, darlin'. And now that I have, I don't intend to ever let you go.''

*   *   *   *   *

NATURAL BORN LAWMAN

Chapter One

Patsy Longhorn held her fussy two-year-old son in her arms and tried to soothe him back to sleep. He was exhausted, feverish and hungry, had been for most of the day, and she was getting desperate. Driving nonstop with a cranky toddler was beginning to take its toll.

She hadn't intended to take another break yet. She'd wanted to put as much distance between herself and Oklahoma as she possibly could today, but she hadn't been able to ignore Billy's whimpers a second longer. She'd pulled into a rest stop and taken him out of his car seat, praying that holding him and rocking him a bit would accomplish what her pitiful repertoire of lullabies hadn't.

So far it wasn't working. Worse, he felt warmer, as if his fever had gone up a little more.

"Come on, sweetie, go to sleep. You'll feel better after you've had a little rest."

At least she prayed that was all it would take. She didn't have money left for medicine and a doctor at this point. Even juice was stretching her tight budget. She'd been giving him sips of cool water and praying that would do the trick.

Billy shifted restlessly, still whimpering, his dark, dark eyes staring back at her, accusing her. Guilt, never far away, washed over her again.

Had she made a mistake leaving Will? Was she crazy to have walked out on her marriage? Walked out with only clothes for the baby and herself and a few hundred dollars from the checking account she had opened several months earlier and had kept secret from her husband?

Though she'd had every right, she hadn't touched a dime in their joint account for fear Will would accuse her of theft. With her name on the account the wild charge wouldn't stick, of course, but she hadn't wanted to give the police any excuses at all to chase after her. It was terrifying enough that Will was likely to go ballistic.

That, she reminded herself staunchly, was exactly the reason she had left. She'd had no choice. Will's temper was out of control. He never talked anymore. He shouted, he threw things. A vase had whizzed past her head, just a few nights ago, only inches from making contact. The violence in his eyes had terrified her. He hadn't hit her or their son yet, but she'd heard enough about abuse to know that it was coming. She wasn't going to stick around and wait for it, not when each scene was already escalating to a more danger-ous level.

Nor was she going to waste time trying to convince Will to seek counseling. His pride and his very visible career would never allow him to admit he needed help. For once in her life, she was doing the smart thing. She was going to cut her losses before tragedy struck.

She hadn't been so smart when she'd impetuously moved to Oklahoma City and almost immediately be-gun an affair with Will Longhorn. Barely nineteen, she'd been so anxious to get away from home and her overly protective parents, to be on her own. The irony was that she'd spent hardly a minute truly on her own before becoming entangled with Will.

He had been her first boss, a twenty-six-year-old attorney in the town's top law firm with a dazzling career ahead of him. Everyone had said so. He was a Native American with the whole world spread out be-fore him. There'd even been talk of a run for political office, first in Oklahoma, then for Congress. Will Longhorn had charisma. He was smart. He had un-blemished integrity, as well, a rarity in politics.

And before too terribly long, he had a beautiful, blond-haired, all-American wife at his side and a baby on the way. The image had been set, the campaign posters all but printed.

At first Patsy had been thrilled to be a part of it all. She'd been caught up in every girl's dream. She had been so proud of her handsome husband, so in love with him.

But all too soon, behind the public displays of affection, behind the jovial smiles for the camera, there had been the private dissension. Even as he showcased his trophy wife and beautiful baby boy, privately Will seemed to resent both Patsy and their son. And because she had given up her job to be a stay-at-home wife and mom, she was totally dependent on Will for everything. It was what he'd wanted, but he'd thrown that back in her face a time or two, as well.

In general the abuse was subtle and mostly verbal, but it was signal enough to her that it was time to go. She might have married in haste, but she had no intention of paying for it for the rest of her life. And no one was going to harm her son. No one.

Protecting Billy became her first priority. Already in his young life, he had heard too much fighting, witnessed too many vicious arguments. If she and Will couldn't live together peacefully, if not lovingly, then it was time to go.

She had fled first to her parents, but Will had followed and the scene he'd caused had terrified all of them. He'd bashed the headlights on her car, dented the hood with a blow of his fists. He'd threatened her, accused her of trying to ruin his career, their future.

He'd threatened her parents, blamed them for harboring his wife when she belonged at home with him. Her parents were just old-fashioned enough to agree that a wife's place was at her husband's side, no matter the circumstances. She had seen the unspoken agreement in their eyes, but still she had balked at leaving.

And then Will had sealed her fate. He had calmly vowed to take Billy away from her if she didn't agree to come home with him.

"You won't even get weekend visitations by the time I'm through. I can do it," he'd said with cool cruelty in his eyes. "You know I can."

She hadn't doubted it for an instant. She had gone with him simply to keep her baby and to get Will away from her frightened family.

Satisfied that he'd gotten his way, Will had promptly gone back on the campaign trail in the mayoral race that was to be the stepping-stone to his entire political future. And the low-key pattern of denigration had begun again—the sarcastic barbs, the ruthless demands, the never-ending criticism. She had taken it for six more humiliating months while she secretly made her plans. And all the while she watched Will, waiting for an explosion of temper that always came.

This time when she'd left, she had known that wherever she went, she was on her own. A local shelter had provided a safe harbor for a day or two. Then she had turned the car toward Texas, hoping that simply crossing the line into another state might offer her some protection. Too many cops, too many judges, too many politicians in Oklahoma owed favors to Will or to the partners' in his law firm. Even though she'd worked there, if it came to a choice between her and Will, she had no doubt which of them would receive the partners' backing.

The memory of that violent explosion in front of her parents' home in full view of the neighbors had kept her on the run for a week now, trying to decide where it would be safe to settle down and begin an anonymous life. While in Oklahoma, she hadn't dared to stay even in a cheap motel for more than a good night's sleep.

As of today, her options were running out. Her pitiful savings were pretty much wiped out and she didn't dare phone her parents for help. For all she knew Will would have bugged their phone. It wasn't beyond him to use the law to his own advantage, especially when her second disappearance at the height of his first campaign for office was no doubt causing him a great deal of public embarrassment.

This time she was truly on her own, for the first time in her life, and the decisions she made were critical not only to her own future, but to the baby's. This was the ultimate test any woman could face. How she handled it would prove what she was made of. So far, she feared, she was falling pitifully short, but she was determined to pull it together. She might be almost out of money and be running low on ideas, but the one thing Patsy Gresham Longhorn had was gumption.

Billy whimpered, reminding her that she was going to have to come to a decision in a hurry. He needed food and, quite possibly, medical attention, though she was pretty sure the fever was little more than a summer cold.

With the two-year-old still cuddled in her arms, she tried awkwardly to unfold the road map she'd picked up at an earlier highway rest stop. Dallas was close, but was a big city the best choice? Wouldn't the police there be on the lookout for her, if Will had spread the word that she was missing?

A small town with more casual, less experienced law enforcement seemed a safer bet. If her logic was faulty, so be it. She felt more at ease with the thought of trying to make a home for herself and Billy someplace quiet and peaceful, someplace where they'd never heard of Will Longhorn. Her gut instincts had gotten her this far. She might as well trust them a little longer.

Staring at the choices on the map, all of them unfamiliar, she finally zeroed in on a tiny speck in the southwestern part of the state: Los Piños. It was only a couple of hundred miles away. The name suggested forests of pine trees, which appealed to her. She craved the serenity such a setting suggested. It reminded her of the town where she'd grown up, the town she'd been in too much of a hurry to leave. Funny, what a difference a few agonizing years could make. She would have given almost anything to be able to go back there now. Since she couldn't, it would have to be Los Piños.

The decision made, she got back on the highway, then took the next exit and stopped at a minimart to buy milk and some cereal for the baby and a ready-made sandwich and soft drink for her. After filling the car with gas, she had ten dollars left, that and whatever change might be buried in the bottom of her purse and in Billy's diaper bag.

Despite the dire circumstances, Patsy felt almost upbeat as she drove into Los Piños a few hours later. She gazed around at the small downtown area with its quaint shops and family-owned restaurants. Though the buildings were old, everything was freshly painted and brightly lit. There was no mistaking that this was a town that took pride in itself. For a second she allowed herself to envision being a part of it, to imagine belonging. For a moment anyway, despair vanished. A feeling of contentment, mixed with a rare smidgen of hope, stole over her.

"We're here, Billy," she whispered to the now-sleeping boy. "We're home." Whatever it took, she would find a way to make that true.

She reached into the back seat and touched his cheek to seal the vow, then drew back in shock. He was burning up with fever. Hope gave way to panic and desperation.

"It'll be okay, baby," she promised. Whatever she had to do, it would be okay.

* * *

"Dadgumit, Justin, if you'd been the law around here when we were kids, I'd have spent my entire teens in jail," Harlan Patrick Adams grumbled, standing on a corner in downtown Los Piños just before dinnertime.

Justin grinned at his cousin. "Probably should have," he said.

"You were no better than me," Harlan Patrick reminded him. "If I belonged in a cell, you surely belonged right there next to me. What happened to you? When did you turn into a saint?"

"Hardly that," Justin said. "It's just that there's right and wrong. Somebody's got to see to it that folks remember the difference."

"Yeah, but that kid you just threatened with jail time threw a gum wrapper on the street. He didn't rob the savings and loan."

"Stop the little crime and you'll have less trouble with the big stuff," Justin retorted. "That's what that mayor up in New York says and it's worked."

"It makes my blood run cold hearing you talk like that," Harlan Patrick taunted. "Guess that means you won't be playing poker with the rest of us out at White Pines later tonight, seeing as how gambling's illegal. Or were you thinking of coming along and arresting Grandpa Harlan when he rakes in his first pot?"

Justin scowled at him. "Very amusing. I'll be there and I intend to take every dime you lay on the table, cowboy."

Harlan Patrick didn't appear unduly worried. "Just as long as you leave that gun locked up at home," he said. "It makes me very nervous to know that you're carrying a weapon. You never could shoot worth a damn."

Justin grinned and fingered his holster. "I'm better now. Want to see?"

Harlan Patrick shuddered. "I think I'll pass, thanks." He gave Justin a mock salute. "Later, cousin."

"Yeah, later."

After all their years of troublemaking, Justin got a kick out of watching Harlan Patrick squirm at the sight of his uniform. No one in the family, least of all his own father, quite understood what had motivated him to become a sheriff's deputy. Jordan Adams had saved a spot in his oil company for Justin and he was mad as hell that his son had turned it down. Justin figured his brother-in-law would settle into the position just fine and sooner or later everyone would get over his defection.

Ironically, it was the family's very own values that had taken root in Justin's heart and made him long to keep the whole community of Los Piños as safe and secure as his family was on their various ranches. In the cutthroat oil business, his father had a straight-arrow reputation for honesty and never cutting corners. Grandpa Harlan's instinctive decency and tough-love brand of justice were as ingrained in Justin as breathing. Even as a kid, when he and Harlan Patrick had played cops and robbers, he'd always, *always* wanted to be the good guy. To him, becoming a cop was less a surprise than a destiny.

He stood on the sidewalk in the middle of town after his cousin had gone and surveyed his domain. Not a bit of trouble in sight. Not even a gum wrapper on the sidewalk, he observed, smiling at the memory of that kid's expression as he'd snatched up the offending piece of paper and thrown it into the litter basket on the corner. His actions had been accompanied by a stern lecture meant to put the fear of God into the boy.

Yep, Justin thought, all was right in his world. Maybe he could actually get fifteen minutes to himself to grab a burger at Dolan's before it closed for the night. He radioed Becky at the station.

"I'll be at Dolan's, if you need me. Want me to bring you anything back?"

"A hamburger, double fries and a milk shake," the very pregnant receptionist said with heartfelt longing.

Coached on her dietary restraints by her worried husband, Justin asked, "How about a tuna on rye and a diet soda?"

Becky sighed. "It'll do."

"Ten-four."

As he walked down the block, he spotted the dusty, expensive car with the out-of-state tags. Los Piños didn't get a lot of tourists. He glanced around for some sign of strangers, but everyone out in the heat of the day was familiar. He shrugged and walked on after making a mental note of the tag number.

Inside the drugstore, he glanced at the counter, expecting to see Harlan Patrick's sister, Sharon Lynn. His cousin had taken over a job once held by her mother and now was thinking of buying out Doc Dolan so he could finally retire. If she actually went through with it, she would hire a new pharmacist and continue running the rest of the store as she had been for the past couple of years anyway.

"Hey, Sharon Lynn, you in here?" he called out, even as he dragged a notebook from his pocket and wrote down the Oklahoma tag number.

"Back here, Justin," she replied from the back of the drugstore. "I'll be with you in a sec."

He'd barely settled on a stool at the counter, when he heard what sounded like a whispered argument. His cop's instincts, already alerted by the out-of-state car, kicked in. Drawing his gun, he moved silently down the aisle in the direction of the voices.

At the end of the row of shelves, he spotted Sharon Lynn and another woman, her blond hair scooped up into a careless ponytail, damp tendrils curling and clinging to her neck. The desperate expression on the stranger's face spelled trouble.

She was talking so fast he couldn't make heads or tails of what she was saying, but he didn't waste time trying to figure it out. While she was distracted, he moved in beside her and laid a restraining hand on her shoulder. Though she was dressed in expensive, tasteful clothes, she was so thin he could feel her bones. At his touch, she jolted as if she'd been shot, her panicked eyes clashing with his. It all added up to the kind of vulnerability that could make a man lose sight of the job he was being paid to do.

Keeping her firmly in his grip, he glanced at Sharon Lynn. "Everything okay?"

The stranger's eyes pleaded with his cousin. Sharon Lynn touched her hand gently.

"It's okay. Justin's my cousin. He's not going to hurt you."

"That all depends," Justin said, contradicting her. "What happened?"

"I needed some children's Tylenol," the woman said in a voice barely above a whisper. "My son's sick."

Sharon Lynn sighed. "I caught her trying to slip them into her purse," she admitted with obvious reluctance.

Justin tried not to react to the tears that were welling up in the woman's eyes, turning them into huge pools of green light, like sunshine reflected in a pond surrounded by tall pines. She was little more than twenty, it seemed to him, and fragile as a bird. He had a feeling if she was shoplifting Tylenol, then she hadn't had much to spend on food lately, either. Just because her clothes were pricey didn't mean she wasn't truly down on her luck. At the thought of the sick child, his rock-solid value system shifted ever so slightly. He felt justice clashing with compassion. Because he had a sudden, uncharacteristic instinct to bend some rules, his next words came out more harshly than he'd intended.

"Where's the boy?" he demanded gruffly.

"In the car."

He fought to hold his temper in check. "You left the baby in the car by himself? As hot as it is out there today?" And why, he wondered, hadn't he spotted the kid if he'd been securely strapped into a car seat as he should have been? He hadn't even checked inside the car. Obviously he was slipping.

"He's okay. I left the windows open a little. He's sound asleep. Besides, I knew I'd only be gone a minute." She stared at him defiantly. "You don't have to tell me all the terrible things that could happen. Believe me, I know. I weighed every one of them and decided he'd be safer there than with me. I didn't want him to cry and draw attention to me." Her shoulders sagged. "It didn't matter. I really am no good at this."

"Get him," Justin said tightly. "Now."

The instant he released her, the woman scooted past him and out the door.

"She'll run," Sharon Lynn said, staring at him in astonishment.

"No, she won't," Justin said.

"How can you be so sure?"

He held up the package. "Not without medicine." He handed his cousin a ten-dollar bill. "Pay for them out of this, okay?"

Sharon Lynn gaped. "Are you all right?"

"Just take the damned money."

She grinned. "Yes, sir."

"And then fix a couple of milk shakes. I'll grab some juice for the baby."

"Uh-oh," Sharon Lynn said. "What did it, Justin? Those big green eyes or the tears?"

"Go to hell."

"You ought to be nicer to me," she taunted. "I can tell this story far and wide by morning. Grandpa Harlan will know every touching detail by the time you get there tonight for the poker game. Your life won't be worth living by the time they finish teasing you about letting a nasty, evil shoplifter off the hook just because she was beautiful."

"You know, Sharon Lynn, there are things about you that old Kyle Mason doesn't know about," he said grimly, referring to her fiancé. "That man's been dangling on the hook for the past fifty million years, it seems like, waiting for you to marry him. Could be I know just the way to cut him loose before the latest wedding date next month."

"You wouldn't dare," she breathed.

He could see her calculating the risks and twisted the knife a little more. "Wouldn't dare tell him that you were the party girl of your senior class at ole Los Piños High? Wouldn't dare mention that you landed in jail on your senior trip?" he taunted. "Try me."

"Kyle knows all that," she said airily. "He loves

me anyway. Besides, you know perfectly well what kind of party girl I was, all talk.''

"So you say.''

Her gaze shifted toward the front window. "If you ask me you'd do a whole lot better to be worrying about why your suspect appears to be about to pull out of the space in front and hightail it out of town.'' She shot him a smug look. "Just the way I predicted she would.''

Justin looked up in time to see a car shoot backward into traffic amid a squeal of tires. As he'd expected, it was the fancy car with the out-of-state tags.

"Well, hell,'' he muttered, and took off running, the carton of juice he'd just grabbed still clutched in his hand.

"If you catch her, tell her I'm not pressing charges,'' Sharon Lynn shouted after him, laughing.

"If I catch her, I'm throwing her in jail,'' he vowed. "You give me a reason, even an itsy-bitsy reason, and you'll be in the cell right next to her.''

Chapter Two

Patsy wasn't sure why she'd run. Obviously she hadn't wanted to be hauled off to jail, something that the sheriff's deputy had seemed perfectly capable of doing. But it was more than that. Fleeing had been instinctive, which told her quite a lot about the damage even a few days on the run had done to her normally assertive personality.

Seeing the judgment in the deputy's eyes, the disdain, ordinarily would have infuriated her enough to make her stand her ground. She was capable of holding her own in an argument, or at least she had been until living with Will had taught her that silence was often the only way to escape from escalating tensions.

One look at the deputy had told her that arguments

would be wasted on him, too. There was an unyielding air about him, the kind of steadfast determination that would be great if he were on your side, not so terrific if he weren't.

She had been startled when he'd released her and sent her after Billy. Grateful for the unexpected opportunity to escape, she had seized it, not pausing to consider just how incensed the deputy might be by her actions.

Maybe the woman in the store could calm him down and keep him from chasing after her, she thought hopefully. Patsy had seen the compassion in the woman's eyes, had known that she was only a hairsbreadth from getting both the medicine and her freedom when the man had turned up. Though she hated taking advantage of anyone's kindness, she had been relieved that Billy would have the medicine he needed. That was all that really mattered.

Now, not only did she not have anything to bring her son's fever down, but she was a criminal, with an attempted shoplifting charge pending if that deputy decided to pursue matters.

For all she knew there were kidnapping charges on file back in Oklahoma, too. Will was perfectly capable of doing something so despicable just to make a point to her, to prove that he was the one with all the power. What would turn up if the deputy happened to catch her tag number and run it through his computer? There was no telling.

She couldn't take any chances that he might find

something damaging. She would just have to drive faster and more cleverly than she ever had before. Suiting her actions to her thoughts, she skidded onto the highway and headed north, back toward Dallas, after all. She would exit a few miles ahead, then take back roads to elude any pursuit.

Though her plight was increasingly desperate, she reminded herself that she still had a bank card with her. Though there was a risk that Will would use any transactions with it to track her, she would use it to get cash if there were no options left to her. She could get enough money to last a few more days, until she could find another town, maybe get a job and find a safe place for herself and Billy. It might even be smarter to abandon the car and fly to another state. If she used cash for the tickets, it would make the job of tracking her more difficult. It was a huge country and Will's reach surely couldn't extend to every corner of it.

When the car sputtered then chugged to a stop barely ten miles outside of Los Piños, she realized that in her rush to get away from the deputy, she'd made a terrible miscalculation. The blasted car was out of gas. It hardly mattered that she had the credit card or a few dollars left in her purse. She hadn't passed a gas station heading out of town. It was impossible to know how far ahead the next one might be.

That was the only reason, she assured herself, that Justin whoever-he-was-lawman caught up with her.

He found her on the side of the road, cursing a blue streak about the gas-guzzling car Will had insisted she have, and rocking the fussy toddler in her arms. His reflective sunglasses prevented her from getting a good look at his eyes, but his I-told-you-so smile said it all. He'd never doubted for a moment that he'd catch up with her and haul her into custody.

"Get in," he ordered, gesturing toward the patrol car.

"You're arresting me?" she asked, as if it were the most ridiculous notion she'd ever heard. Will had been a master of haughty indignation and she had learned by example.

Their gazes clashed, hers defiant, his unreadable.

"No," he said finally with a heavy sigh. "I'm taking you back into town. Unless you'd prefer to stand around here and wait for someone else to come along and offer you a lift. I'll tell you right now, though, that it's a very long way to the next town and hardly anybody uses this particular stretch of road."

Patsy had guessed as much. Not a single car had passed by while she'd been standing beside the car, cursing her lousy luck.

"Sooner or later…" she began, thinking anything would be better than going someplace with this hard, no-nonsense man.

"Are you willing to take that chance? If your son's sick, this heat won't help."

Her resolve wavered. "But the car…"

"Isn't going anywhere," he said. "I'll have some-one bring out some gas and drive it back into town."

"I could wait," she suggested hopefully.

"I don't think so."

"Then you are arresting me."

"Dammit, no. Like I said, I am just trying to get you and the baby out of this blazing heat."

"Oh."

He opened the door to the front seat, which reassured her slightly. If he were arresting her, surely she'd be locked securely in the back. He tossed the bottle of Tylenol over to her, then indicated the carton of juice on the seat. "I brought those along for your boy."

So he did have a heart, after all. Patsy swallowed hard against the tears that threatened. It was enough lure to get her inside. "Thank you."

He closed the door, then went around to the driver's side. When he was behind the wheel, he said, "There's a milk shake in the holder there. You look as if you could use it."

Patsy shook her head, unwilling to be too indebted to this man who so clearly—and justifiably—disapproved of her. "No, thanks."

He rolled his eyes at her deliberate contrariness. "Suit yourself."

The drive into town was made in uncomfortable silence. She waited for another explosion of temper or a stern lecture, but instead he glanced over at Billy, who was belted into the seat with her, no doubt a bending of the rules he was so fond of enforcing. He hadn't argued with her, though, or insisted she get his car seat and put him in the back.

"Is he okay? Are you sure you don't want to get him to a doctor?" he asked. "There's a hospital in Garden City. I could run you over to the emergency room there."

"No," she said in a rush. When he shot a sharp-eyed look at her, she explained, "He'll be fine, once his fever goes down. He's just tired and fussy. I think he's getting a bit of a cold."

"Okay, if you're sure."

"I am."

The same uneasy silence fell again. Billy squirmed in her lap. "Mama?"

"Yes, baby."

Billy stared back at her with fever-bright eyes, then looked over at the man behind the wheel. "Who's that?"

"He's a policeman. He's helping us."

"Nice 'liceman," Billy murmured approvingly and fell back asleep.

Patsy glanced up just in time to catch a fleeting smile at the corners of Justin's mouth.

"At least the boy knows when someone's on his side," he commented.

She regarded him doubtfully. "Are you on my side, Deputy …?"

"Adams," he supplied. "Justin Adams. And as long as you don't break any laws, yes." He gave her a sharp look. "So far you haven't, at least not technically."

"Just because I got caught."

"Be grateful that my cousin has a forgiving nature. She won't press charges."

"Is that the only reason you're letting me off so easy?"

"Yes," he said curtly.

Patsy studied him intently, then shook her head. Her opinion of the man had undergone several drastic shifts since he'd turned up with the juice and medicine. "I don't think so. I think that under that by-the-book exterior beats the heart of a genuinely nice guy."

She was almost convinced he was a man she could trust. Even after he'd caught her stealing, even after she'd fled, he had thought first of her sick child. She could see, though, that the compliment made him uncomfortable. Maybe the leniency didn't fit his own image of himself.

"What's wrong, Deputy? Afraid if word gets out, it'll ruin your reputation?" she asked, daring to tease him, hoping to catch another glimpse of that potentially devastating smile again.

"Something like that," he conceded, unsmiling.

Patsy felt an odd little shock of disappointment, then cursed herself. Was she so desperate for a friend that she was willing to trust this stranger who had the power to give her whereabouts away to her husband? He was clearly a man with a strong sense of right and wrong, a commitment to duty. He would be the worst possible choice for a friend. When it came to a choice between obligation and friendship, there would be no contest. He would choose obligation every time.

She withdrew into silence once again.

"Where are you two heading?" he asked eventually.

The question seemed innocuous enough, no more than casual conversation, except the man was a cop. Patsy hesitated.

He glanced her way and she cursed those reflective sunglasses that prevented her from getting a good look at his eyes.

"Don't you know?" he demanded. "What kind of mother leaves home with a sick baby if she doesn't have to?"

Her temper flared and she clutched Billy a little tighter. "He wasn't sick when we left home."

"When was that?"

"A few days ago," she conceded.

"And the baby's father?"

She'd known the question would come up sooner or later. She'd been praying for later, long enough to have manufactured a believable story. Forced to improvise quickly, she said only, "He's not around."

"I see," Justin said slowly, his expression thoughtful. "You know, if you don't have a place to go, Los Piños isn't a bad little town."

Startled by the suggestion, she stared. "You

wouldn't object? Under the circumstances, I was sure you'd want us as far from your town as possible.''

He glanced over at her. ''You ever stolen anything before?''

''No.''

''Why should I believe you?''

''Because it's the truth,'' she said fiercely. ''If it hadn't been for Billy getting sick, I wouldn't have done it this time. I would have come here, found a place for us to stay, gotten a job. We're looking for a fresh start, Deputy Adams, not trouble and definitely not a handout.''

Even from behind those damnable sunglasses, she could feel his penetrating gaze. It was enough to make a liar squirm. Patsy sat perfectly still and withstood it.

''What's your name?''

''Patsy Gresham,'' she said, resorting to her maiden name. If he checked the car tags, he'd know better, but if not, if luck was on her side, she could preserve the illusion for a little while at least.

He nodded. ''Okay, then, Patsy Gresham. I suppose having you stick around won't be a problem. Just know I'll be keeping an eye on you.''

She could just imagine. He'd probably spread the word from one end of town to the other that Patsy Gresham couldn't be trusted. What kind of life could she make for herself with a cloud of suspicion hanging over her head?

''I won't tell a soul about what happened today, if

that's what's worrying you," he said, his expression softening as if he'd read her mind and wanted to reassure her. "You'll move into town with a clean slate."

"Why are you being so nice?"

Once more, the suggestion that he was anything other than a tough, by-the-book lawman seemed to make him uncomfortable. "Damned if I know," he said eventually. "Just don't make me regret it."

If Patsy had her way, not only wouldn't he regret it, he'd never set eyes on her again. Even in a town the size of Los Piños, it ought to be easy enough to disappear if she wanted to make it happen.

Then she took another long look at the man beside her. Of course, Justin Adams struck her as the kind of stubborn, determined man who could find whomever he set out to find. She'd just have to make darned sure he never had any reason to hunt for her.

Justin was losing it. He knew because there was no way in hell under normal circumstances he would have let a criminal off the way he was letting Patsy Gresham go free, despite what Sharon Lynn wanted.

What was it his cousin had asked? Was it the green eyes or the tears that did it? Neither, he had wanted to shout. Now he wasn't so sure.

Every time he glanced into the woman's sad, wary eyes, he felt some subtle change deep inside him. He wanted to strangle whoever had brought such sorrow into her life. She was entirely too young to look so beaten. And yet there was a surprising strength and feistiness about her. She might be down, but she definitely wasn't out. He found such resilience admirable.

On the way back into town he'd reached a decision. Until he knew more, he wanted Patsy Gresham right where he could keep an eye on her. He could just imagine the kind of razzing he'd take for that. No one in his family would believe for an instant that his motives were altruistic. He could explain from now until every head of Adams cattle was counted that he was being cautious, trying to prevent a more serious crime from taking place, but they wouldn't buy it. Not once they got a look at Patsy, anyway. They'd blame it on his hormones and his good nature and nothing he could say would change their minds.

She was a beautiful woman, all right. Fragile and road weary as she was, there was a delicacy about her that brought a man's protective instincts surging to life. And her mouth, those luscious, sensual lips, well, it was the sort of mouth just made for kissing. Justin's gaze had been drawn to it again and again, wondering what those lips would taste like.

Right. Like he needed to get mixed up with a woman who might be an everyday, common thief. No, what he needed to do was to send Patsy Gresham packing, send her into some other jurisdiction where she'd be another lawman's problem.

The words had been on the tip of his tongue, too. He'd been ready to tell her that the second her car was brought back into town and filled with gas, courtesy of the deputy sheriff, he wanted her gone.

Instead, he'd encouraged her to stay. There were names a whole lot stronger than *fool* for the kind of man that made him. *Jerk* and *idiot* came to mind. It was also pretty clear which part of his anatomy had been doing his thinking.

"Do you have any money at all?" he asked, trying to stay focused.

"No," she admitted after a long hesitation. "At least I won't have any once I buy gas. But I'm willing to work for room and board. I just need a break, that's all. I don't want charity."

To his dismay, he realized what he was going to do the second he crossed into the town limits. A few minutes later he pulled to a stop in front of the house that belonged to his sister, Dani. She still operated her veterinary practice from one side of it, but the living quarters had been empty ever since her marriage. If he asked, Dani would agree in a heartbeat to let Patsy and the baby use the house.

But before taking Patsy Gresham and her baby inside, there were a few more questions he needed answered.

"That car of yours is pretty expensive," he said carefully, watching her intently. "Also, I'm no fashion expert, but I have enough female cousins with expensive taste to know quality when I see it."

Her chin tilted up a notch. "So?"

"The two things combined make me wonder why you appear to be in such dire straits."

"Haven't you heard? Appearances can be deceiving."

"Meaning that those things aren't expensive or meaning that you're not in dire straits? Maybe you didn't need to steal that Tylenol. Maybe you were just doing it for kicks. I've heard there are rich ladies who get their thrills that way."

Indignant color flared in her cheeks. "Of course not. You've seen for yourself. Billy is sick."

"And you don't have the money for the medicine."

"Right."

Her lower lip quivered and she looked as if she were about to cry. Justin really didn't want to deal with a flood of tears, but he had no choice.

"Hand me your purse," he said quietly.

She stared at him. "Why?"

"So I can see for myself what shape you're in financially."

She hugged the white leather bag almost as tightly as she clutched her son. "I don't think so."

"I'm ordering you to."

"And I'm telling you, you'll have to get a search warrant if you want to go poking through my things."

To his regret, she had a point. He had been hoping it wouldn't come to that, that she'd cooperate voluntarily.

"Look, if you'll just get my car back here and loan

me the money for some food, I'll buy my own gas with the money I have left and be on my way. I can see that staying here isn't such a good idea. For all the pretty words, Officer, it's clear you don't really trust me.''

''If you'd let me take a look in your purse, it would go a long way toward changing that,'' he cajoled.

''Not a chance,'' she said, her gaze clashing with his.

Justin debated the meaning of her resistence. She could just be a woman who knew her rights and intended to protect them. Or else she was hiding something. Maybe both. He was going to have to decide quickly whether it would be smarter to encourage her to leave town or to stay right here where he could keep an eye on her until he knew more. He gambled on the latter. It was probably better that he not examine his motives too closely.

''Okay, come with me.''

Her gaze narrowed suspiciously. ''Where?''

''We're going to talk to my sister Dani about using the other half of this house. It's fully furnished and, other than crashing here occasionally after a late night with an injured animal, she doesn't use it.''

There was no mistaking the quick survey she did of the white house with its neat lawn, nor the flaring of hope in her eyes. The house was small and tidy. Something told him it was nothing at all like what she was used to. He waited to see how she'd react.

"Do you really think she'd let me use it for a few days, just until I get on my feet?" she asked eagerly.

Her reaction went a long way toward reassuring him. "If I know Dani, she'll insist on it."

"Maybe you should go ask her first. It'll be easier for her to say no if I'm not standing there with Billy staring her in the face."

Justin grinned. "Which is precisely why I want you to come along. One look at you and the baby and she'll be running out to stock the refrigerator for you. Dani is a very soft touch when it comes to taking in strays. You'll see what I mean when you keep tripping over all the kittens underfoot."

"Kitty?" the boy echoed happily, coming awake again. "Where kitty?"

Justin reached down and took him from his mother's lap. The boy came to him eagerly. Justin grazed his cheek with his knuckles and noted that whatever fever he'd had seemed to have come down. "Inside, son. Want to see?"

His dark eyes regarded Justin somberly, but he nodded at once. "See kitties."

Justin started up the walk, leaving Patsy no choice but to follow.

"Hey, sis, you around here someplace?" Justin called out, striding straight through the crowded waiting room and into the back, where there was a cacophony of sound from the animals being boarded here while families went on summer vacations. A cat promptly wound between his legs, almost tripping him.

"Dani, dammit. Get these cats away from me."

His sister poked her head out of one of the tiny examining rooms. "Justin, why are you raising such a ruckus?" she demanded, then spotted Billy. "Oh, my, isn't he darling? Where'd you find him?"

Justin nodded over his shoulder. "He came with her."

His sister's gaze shifted at once to Patsy. "Ah, yes, I see," she murmured.

Justin regarded her suspiciously. "What does that mean?"

"It means Sharon Lynn mentioned you were hot on the trail of a woman and a baby."

"Sharon Lynn has a big mouth."

"I had to pry it out of her," Dani assured him. "After I'd heard about it from three other people."

Justin sighed. There were no secrets in Los Piños, not when it came to an Adams. "They need a place to stay."

"And you were thinking that they could use this place," she guessed.

He grinned sheepishly. "Well, you're never here. Maybe Patsy could look after the animals for you at night. I'm sure your husband would appreciate having you home all night long for a change."

"An interesting deal." She glanced at Patsy, who was hovering in the doorway. "How do you feel about it?"

Justin waited uneasily. There was no predicting how she would react. Patsy had been surprising him from the second they'd met. So far he'd seen no evidence of uppity, high society ways, but maybe she'd draw the line at caring for a bunch of sick animals. A part of him hoped she would.

In fact, she seemed about to argue, then she glanced his way and sighed. "I'd be grateful," she said with apparent sincerity. "And of course I'd be willing to look after the animals in return, at least until I can get a job and pay you rent."

"No need to worry about that," Dani replied. "We'll try it for a few days and see how it goes." She reached for Patsy's hand. "Come with me. I'll show you around."

Justin would have followed, but Billy patted his cheek. "Want to see kitties," he reminded Justin.

"So you shall," he promised, pausing in the kitchen where several cats were sprawled in patches of sunlight. He hunkered down so Billy could see. The boy's coal black eyes lit up.

"Kitties," he whispered with obvious satisfaction. "Nice kitty?"

Justin nodded and set the boy on his feet. "You can pet them."

Billy toddled to the closest one and bent down until he was practically nose to nose with it. "Kitty," he pronounced, and petted it gently on the head. The cat, used to the comings and goings of Dani's rambunctious stepsons, merely yawned widely and stretched before curling up again with its head resting on its paws.

Billy toddled on unsteady legs toward another and went through the same routine again. Not until he'd greeted every cat in the kitchen did he come back to Justin and hold out his arms to be picked up.

"Mama," he whispered, as if he'd just noticed she was missing. Tears began to well up in his eyes.

"It's okay, fella. Your mama's right here. We'll go find her, okay?"

A thumb went into his mouth and he nodded. "'Kay."

His mother might be all bristly caution, but Billy was so thoroughly trusting it made Justin's heart ache with unexpected longing. He'd never given much thought to marriage and kids. If he wanted to hold a baby, there were plenty to choose from in his family. If he wanted to be surrounded by laughter and love, he could invite himself to dinner at any number of homes.

There was something very different about holding a child that belonged to you, though. He'd seen it in the awed expressions of his cousins' husbands. Something told him that it might feel a whole lot like the sensation rushing over him now.

And that, given how very little he knew about Patsy Gresham and her true circumstances, was a very dangerous reaction.

Chapter Three

Justin saw to it that Patsy Gresham and her baby were settled at Dani's. He made sure her car was filled with gas and parked out front. He even had the Italian restaurant down the block send over dinner.

And then he washed his hands of the entire situation. He'd done his good deed for the week. Maybe even for the whole year. He predicted if word got around that he'd not only let a shoplifter get away, but that he'd taken her under his wing, he'd never hear the end of it.

As it turned out, it didn't take long for word to get around. He was the butt of a fair bit of good-natured teasing from his uncles and cousins at the poker game that night at White Pines. Obviously Sharon Lynn had decided to spill the beans, after all. She must not have taken his threat to have a revealing talk with her fiancé all that seriously.

"Don't pay any attention to them, son," Grandpa Harlan advised, giving him a pat on the shoulder. "They've gotten so old now, they don't recall what it's like to be captivated by a pretty face."

"Except for me, of course," Harlan Patrick said. "I'm younger than Justin."

"And you've never been known to miss a pretty face," Justin retorted. "Is there a woman in this town you haven't chased after at one time or another?"

"Not since I met Laurie," Harlan Patrick said piously. "She'd poke my eyes out if she caught me looking at another woman."

"She just has you thinking she would," Grandpa Harlan corrected. "Laurie is the sweetest little gal you've ever brought around. She has a mighty nice voice, too."

"Yes, indeed," Justin agreed. "One of these days Laurie's going to run off to Nashville and leave Harlan Patrick pining away back here."

His cousin scowled at him. The remark had cut a little too close to Harlan Patrick's greatest fear and Justin knew it.

"How'd we get on my love life, anyway?" Harlan Patrick grumbled. "We were talking about you and the shoplifter."

"Don't call her that," Justin said harshly.

"Why not? Isn't that what you and Sharon Lynn caught her doing?"

"She was desperate," he countered defensively. "Besides, unless a person's tried and convicted, you shouldn't go throwing names around. She could sue you for slander."

"And probably hire my wife to do it," Grandpa Harlan warned. "Janet would just love to get her teeth into a case like that. She hates being retired from her law practice. One of these days she's going to stir up a mess of trouble, just so she can get herself into the thick of it."

"From what I've seen over the years, Daddy, you're all the trouble Janet can cope with," Justin's Uncle Cody said.

Grandpa Harlan scowled. "Watch your tongue, boy. I'm not too old to throw you out of here. Maybe I'll cut you out of the will while I'm at it. White Pines can skip right past you and go straight to Harlan Patrick."

Cody took the good-humored teasing in stride. "Daddy, you've been threatening to take this ranch from me since I can remember. One of these days I'm going to call you on it. I'll hire Janet to contest the will."

"Can't do it," Grandpa Harlan said triumphantly. "It'd be a conflict of interest."

"Is anybody actually going to play poker tonight?" Justin inquired with a wistful glance at the hand he was holding. "I'm feeling lucky."

Harlan Patrick shot him a knowing look. "I'll just bet you are." He tossed some money into the pot. "Okay, let's see those cards you're so proud of."

"Oh, shut up," Justin muttered, and slapped three aces on the table to take the pot from his mouthy cousin.

From that moment on, he tolerated the jokes and proceeded to whip their tails. He walked away from the poker table a good deal richer than he had been when he sat down.

What troubled him, though, was the fact that his first instinct was to give some of his winnings to Patsy Gresham to make sure she got by until she could find a real job.

Obviously he was turning soft, which was why half a dozen people got tickets for minor traffic violations before he stopped for breakfast the next morning.

When he saw who was about to start serving up eggs behind the counter at Dolan's, he wished he'd stayed on the street and given out another dozen citations.

Patsy rose at the crack of dawn, still unable to believe her luck. The tiny house Justin had arranged for her to use was perfect for her and Billy. The furnishings were old, but cheerful with all the chintz upholstery. The rooms were bright and airy.

"I could be happy here," she thought as she stretched and pulled on her robe. It was Dani's doing, of course, and not her own, but the house felt like a home. It wasn't as lavish as the one Will had insisted on buying, but it had a warmth and charm that the house in Oklahoma had lacked no matter how hard she'd tried to turn it into a home.

She checked on Billy, then went into the kitchen where she found cereal, milk and bread, courtesy of Dani, along with a note. "Make yourselves at home. We'll talk later about what you can do to help with the animals. Dani."

A nice woman, she concluded. She'd liked her instantly the day before, just as she'd been drawn to Sharon Lynn at the drugstore. It had been a long time since she'd had girlfriends. Will hadn't encouraged her to have any life at all outside of caring for him and Billy.

Maybe these two women could become real friends in time, she thought wistfully. Maybe there would come a time when she'd be able to confide the truth about her circumstances to them, instead of living this lie. Maybe she could tell them about the fear that had been gnawing at her ever since she'd discovered her husband's violent side.

First, though, she had to make amends to one of them. As soon as she got Billy up and dressed, she postponed breakfast and headed toward the drugstore, determined to get the apology over with. They were there as soon as the doors opened. Relieved that there was no one else around, Patsy faced Sharon Lynn uncertainly.

"I came to apologize and to thank you for not

pressing charges,'' she said. "I would never have done it, not in a million years, if I hadn't been so worried about Billy.''

"I know," Sharon Lynn said, and sounded as if she meant it. She also sounded as if that were the last word she intended to say on the subject. "How about some coffee? I could fix some cereal for Billy, if you like.''

Could it possibly be that easy? Patsy thought in wonder. Still chagrined by her uncharacteristic behavior the day before, Patsy started to refuse, but Sharon Lynn was already pouring the coffee and dumping cereal into a bowl.

"Dry or with milk?" she asked, taking the decision out of Patsy's hands.

"Dry for Billy," Patsy said. "He can eat it with his fingers. Otherwise there's no telling where he's likely to fling it with a spoon.''

Sharon Lynn set the bowl on the counter in front of Billy, then grinned as he grabbed a fistful and shoved it into his mouth.

"His table manners leave something to be desired," Patsy apologized ruefully.

"How old is he?"

"He just turned two."

"Then he's got a few years before people start holding that against him. Besides, once you've been to a family dinner at our place, missile strikes would probably seem tame. There are a lot of kids. We've all been brought up to have endless patience. My grandfather, Harlan Adams, would rather have the chaos than a clean house any day.''

Patsy grinned. ''Maybe he can say that because he's not the one who has to clean it up.''

''Oh, I've seen him on his hands and knees chasing after cornflakes and toys a time or two. Of course, he's in his eighties now and he's not as agile as he once was, but he set a good enough example for his sons that they're pretty decent housekeepers if the need arises. They all married women who see to it the need arises every now and then, just to keep them humble.''

''It must be wonderful to have so much family,'' Patsy said, unable to hide the wistful note in her voice.

''Your own is small?''

''Just me and my parents.''

''And you couldn't go to them for help when things got tough for you and the baby?'' Sharon Lynn asked.

Patsy shook her head. ''No, not this time,'' she said, unable to meet the other woman's gaze for fear all the tears she'd been bottling up would come pouring out.

''I see.'' Sharon Lynn's expression softened. ''I hear Justin arranged for you to stay at Dani's.''

Patsy knew enough about small towns not to be surprised that news had traveled so quickly, especially when it involved family members. ''For the time being anyway.''

Sharon Lynn seemed startled by her reply. ''Why

on earth wouldn't you go on staying there? It's a great house. It's small, but surely it's big enough for just you and Billy.''

"Of course it is, and I'm truly grateful to her for letting us move in on such short notice." Patsy couldn't say that she was afraid she might have to move on, that her husband would discover her whereabouts and come after her. Instead, she said only, "But I need a job, and someone to look after Billy. I haven't even had time to check the want ads yet to see if there are any openings here. I can't stay in Los Piños indefinitely without work."

"Then you have work," Sharon Lynn said with no hesitation at all.

Patsy stared at her. "What?"

"You can work right here. I can use the help. The lunch counter's busier than ever and so's the pharmacy. The pharmacist can't keep up with prescriptions and all the gift sales we're making now that I've expanded that section."

She smiled persuasively. "So, what do you think? Want to give it a try? I can pay you a halfway decent salary and you'll get tips when you work the counter. I know Dani's not going to charge an arm and a leg for the house. No one was using it anyway. And you'll be able to eat here, so you won't have grocery expenses."

It was more than Patsy had ever dreamed of when she'd walked through the door a few minutes earlier. Though she'd trained as a secretary, she'd known she wouldn't be able to find work in that field, not without being able to give references, and she surely couldn't list Will's firm on her résumé. This job was ideal. She didn't have to think twice about it. "I'll take it," she said at once.

"You're sure?" Sharon Lynn asked. "I have to warn you, it gets crazy in here sometimes and I'm going off on a one-week honeymoon at the end of the month. You'll be on your own. Can you cook?"

"If you'll go over the menu with me, I can do it," Patsy assured her. She'd worked in a place just like this back home one summer while she was taking her secretarial training. This job would be a breeze. "And I've run a cash register before. I'm sure I'll pick up the rest in no time."

"You don't have to sell me. I made the offer, remember?"

"I wouldn't want you to regret it."

"I won't," Sharon Lynn said with confidence. "When can you start?"

"What about now?" She glanced over at Billy, who was happily mashing cereal on the counter. "Unless you'd rather I make arrangements for him so he's not in the way."

"He's not in the way. If he gets fussy, you can leave and take him home for a nap. Someone over at Dani's will keep an eye on him for you."

Patsy grinned at her enthusiasm and quick solutions to every possible problem Patsy suggested. "You must be really desperate for help."

"Not today, but given the daze I'm in just thinking about everything that's left to do for the wedding, desperation is not far off." Sharon Lynn grinned ruefully and admitted, "And there are any number of people in town who'll be relieved that someone else is going to help with the cooking in here. I've been a bit absentminded lately. It's given the menu some interesting and not entirely successful twists."

Patsy grinned back at her as she climbed off the stool and started to join Sharon Lynn behind the counter. "What do you want me to do first?"

"Sit back down and eat some breakfast." Before Patsy could protest, Sharon Lynn added, "That's not charity. It's just common sense. You'll be dead on your feet in no time unless you've eaten something. I think scrambled eggs, bacon, hash browns and toast ought to do it," she decided, going to work before Patsy could argue.

Everyone she'd met so far had been so kind Patsy couldn't quite believe her luck. Suddenly she regarded Sharon Lynn suspiciously. "Justin didn't put you up to this, did he?"

"Justin didn't put her up to what?" the very man in question inquired as he came through the door along with a gust of hot, dry air.

"Hiring me," Patsy explained, meeting his gaze for an instant.

For once, with his sunglasses tucked in his pocket, Justin's eyes were visible. She could read the shock

registered there. Even though she knew it was justified, it hurt nonetheless.

"Really?" he asked, regarding his cousin warily.
"Sharon Lynn, could we talk for a minute?" With a
glance in Patsy's direction, he added pointedly, "In
the back."

"No, we cannot," Sharon Lynn told him. "I'm
busy." She flipped Patsy's eggs on the grill, reached
for the toast and buttered it, then placed it all on a
plate and slid it in front of Patsy. "Enjoy. The crowd
will start coming in in about ten minutes."

Patsy nodded. "I'll be finished."

Justin slid onto the stool next to her. She wondered
if he meant to intimidate her, but he merely advised,
"If you gulp that down, you'll have indigestion.
Sharon Lynn doesn't go light on the grease."

She glanced at him. "Worried about my health all
of a sudden?"

"Obviously she's expecting to get a full day's
work out of you. I don't want to see her cheated."
He regarded her meaningfully.

So, there it was, Patsy thought wearily. The trust
he'd promised the day before had barely lasted overnight. She leveled a look straight at him and kept it
steady. "I thought you were going to give me an honest chance to start over."

He sighed. "You're right," he conceded grudgingly. "I was."

"Has something changed since last night?"

"He probably had to answer a lot of questions out

at White Pines last night at the family poker game,'' Sharon Lynn chimed in cheerfully. ''It's made him edgy.''

''I am not edgy,'' he retorted. ''I'm just trying to look out for you. Obviously I'm wasting my time. You think you know it all.''

Sharon Lynn grinned at him. ''When it comes to Patsy, yes, I do think my judgment's better than yours. After all, I am the one who predicted...''

Justin scowled. ''Never mind.''

Patsy stared at the two of them, trying to guess what the unspoken hints were all about. ''Predicted what?''

''Nothing,'' Sharon Lynn soothed. ''Justin's just the family worrywart. Why don't you get back here and fix him some scrambled eggs and a couple of pancakes? I'll pour him some nice strong black coffee. That ought to improve his mood.''

To Patsy's surprise, he didn't argue. Instead he turned his attention to Billy.

''So, young man, what are you up to over there? Has any of that cereal actually made it into your mouth?''

Billy promptly abandoned the mess he was making and reached for Justin. ''Up?'' he pleaded.

Patsy envisioned all the goo on Billy's hands being transferred to Justin's starched uniform shirt and winced. ''No, baby. I don't think so.''

To her amazement, Justin ignored her and accommodated Billy. He scooped him up, apparently oblivious to the mess the baby was bound to make of his clothes. Apparently a whole lot more bonding than she'd been aware of had gone on the day before.

"He's fine where he is. You don't have to do that," she told Justin, eyeing him nervously as Billy patted his cheeks with sticky hands.

"It's not a problem."

"But—"

"I said it's not a problem."

And that, she concluded, was that.

After that, she didn't have time to worry about it. As Sharon Lynn had predicted, the counter began to fill up with regulars eager for a little breakfast and a lot of chitchat over the latest local gossip. Several speculative looks were cast her way. Ignoring them and the gentle banter that ensued, she concentrated on filling orders as quickly as Sharon Lynn passed them to her.

Even though she never once looked back, she was aware of the precise instant that Justin Adams slid off his stool and left. The prickling sensation at the back of her neck vanished and the tension in her shoulders eased.

When the crowd began to thin out, Sharon Lynn introduced her to the handful of remaining customers. At the sight of a burly man in uniform, her nerves jumped.

"This is the sheriff, Tate Owens, Justin's boss. Don't mind the scowl. He looks less fierce once he's had a couple of doughnuts."

"I wish," the man said, casting a longing gaze toward the already depleted display on the counter. "Juice and dry toast for me today. The doc put me on a diet yesterday. He's grumbling about my cholesterol again."

"How about some oatmeal?" Sharon Lynn suggested.

"Not without cream and lots of brown sugar," he lamented. "No, I'll stick with the toast today and some of that blackberry jam, if you have it."

"I keep it back here just for you," Sharon Lynn said.

Patsy noted where Sharon Lynn kept it, so she could supply it on request if she was here alone. She was about to gather up Billy and slip into the back room for a break, when the sheriff spoke directly to her.

"You're new in town."

She met his gaze evenly, fighting the sick sensation in the pit of her stomach. "Yes. My son and I got here yesterday."

"Didn't take you long to find work," he observed.

"No. Sharon Lynn's been very kind."

He nodded. "Welcome to Los Piños, then. You run into any problems, let me know."

The offer was made with such absolute sincerity that for a fleeting instant Patsy had the absurd desire to unburden herself to this man. Who knew, maybe she'd be lucky one more time and he would see what she'd been up against. Maybe he could protect her from Will. She sighed with regret. She couldn't take a chance that it would go the other way.

Instead, she smiled noncommittally. "Thanks. I'll remember that."

"You're from Oklahoma," he noted conversationally. "What part?"

She named her old hometown, rather than Oklahoma City. "I doubt you've ever heard of it. It's tiny, not even as big as Los Piños."

"Must be," he said, his expression thoughtful. "I grew up around Oklahoma City myself and I never heard of it. Of course, my memory's not what it used to be, either. Haven't been home in years, not since my folks died about ten years back."

When he'd mentioned Oklahoma City, Patsy's heart had slammed against her ribs. It hadn't eased back into a normal rhythm until he'd said how long it had been since he'd been back.

Ten years ago Will had been just starting law school. His face—and hers—hadn't been on the front pages of the local papers until much more recently. She doubted that a mayor's race in Oklahoma City would make the local paper here in Los Piños.

"Do you still stay in touch with old friends?" she asked carefully.

"Nope. My friends and family are here now. Haven't heard from a soul back that way. Skipped my high school reunions. Couldn't think of what I'd have to say to people I hadn't seen in years."

"Too bad," she said, though the relief that washed

over her said just the opposite. "It's always sad when we lose touch with old friends."

"What about you? You still have family there?"

"Some," she said.

Thankfully, he let it go at that. Much more poking and prodding, no matter how innocently intended, and she was pretty sure she would have cracked. She just wasn't cut out for this much deception. It was a habit that had started when she and Will were first dating and trying to keep it a secret from their co-workers. She'd been lousy at it then, too. Their relationship had been discovered in no time, which was one reason they'd married in such haste. Will had wanted to quiet the gossip.

Tate Owens drew her attention again. "We'll have to compare notes sometime. It's been my experience that it's a mighty small world. Maybe we'll know some folks in common."

"I doubt that," she said. "Like I said, the town where I grew up was really small."

He nodded. "Okay. Well, I'd better get out of here. If I don't stay on my toes, Justin's going to steal my job right out from under me."

"As if he would ever try," Sharon Lynn chided. "You were his mentor, Tate. And everybody knows you're the best sheriff ever. You'll stay in the job as long as you want it. Besides, something tells me half the town is going to be mad as heck at him this morning."

Tate Owens moaned. "What's he done now?" he asked in a resigned tone.

"Last time I saw him, he was handing out parking tickets all up and down Main Street."

"Damn, I thought I'd broke him of that. The town doesn't need the money, and I don't need the aggravation." He slapped his Stetson on his head and walked out the door.

Patsy watched him go, then turned to Sharon Lynn. "What's with the parking tickets?"

"Tate tends to ignore minor infractions like that. He thought the parking meters were a nuisance in the first place. Justin goes crazy every once in a while and starts handing out tickets. Tate spends the rest of the day soothing ruffled feathers."

Patsy shook her head. "I don't get it. If the people are breaking the law, shouldn't they get tickets?"

"Technically, yes. And Justin is a by-the-book kind of man, especially after he's done something that makes him worry whether he's listening too much to his heart," she said with a look in Patsy's direction.

"Am I supposed to understand that?"

"You're here, aren't you?"

"Yes," she said, still confused.

"And not in a jail cell."

"Oh."

Sharon Lynn grinned. "Oh, indeed. Bottom line, it's my guess that you're the one behind today's rampage with the parking tickets."

Patsy would have chuckled if she hadn't been able

to imagine what everyone in town would have to say if they knew to blame her.

Sharon Lynn's expression turned thoughtful. "Something tells me you're going to be good for him," she said quietly.

"Me? I don't think so," Patsy said at once. If Justin Adams knew the truth about her, he probably wouldn't even blink before tossing her in that jail cell and throwing away the key.

Chapter Four

While Justin had been thoroughly disconcerted by the sight of Patsy Gresham working at Sharon Lynn's that morning, he told himself he'd merely found it troubling that she was becoming so intimately entwined with his family.

What really worried him more, was that quick little shiver of awareness he'd felt when he spotted her. He knew his hormones well enough to recognize a man-woman thing when he felt it, and it was the very last reaction he ought to be having to the woman, not with all those legitimate suspicions he couldn't quite dismiss.

Except for a minor fender bender in midafternoon, the rest of the day had been uneventful. It had taken all of his willpower to keep from wandering into Dolan's a few more times to make sure Patsy's hand wasn't in the till or anywhere else it didn't belong. His conscience had reminded him that he'd promised her an honest chance.

By nightfall, though, he couldn't battle his desire to see how she'd fared. The fact that he chose to get his answers from her, rather than from Sharon Lynn, meant nothing, he assured himself. After all, Patsy was right here in town, while Sharon Lynn was all the way out at the ranch. It was pure logic and convenience that sent him to her doorstep.

Yeah, right.

Dusk was falling by the time he'd showered and changed into jeans and a T-shirt. He strolled up the walkway at Dani's with his mind on the excuse he was going to have to come up with for his visit.

He was about to knock on the front door, when he heard chaos erupt in the veterinary clinic. Muttering under his breath about the fact that he'd left his gun at home, he raced around to the clinic entrance and pounded on the door. It was opened by a frazzled Patsy, backed up by a snarling dog that looked perfectly capable of tearing both of them limb from limb.

"Oh, it's you," she said, and turned back toward the dog, which was straining on its leash. "Punk, hush up. You'll get your food when it's your turn."

Her total lack of concern about the huge dog's barking brought a smile to Justin's lips. He leaned back against the doorway and admired the methodical way she was moving from pen to pen.

"If I were you, I'd take care of Punk first before he decides to turn you into dinner," he observed casually.

She shot him a defiant look that would have been wasted on Punk. "And let him win? I don't think so. He's nothing but a big bully. He'll wait his turn."

Even though she spoke with conviction, he noticed that she skirted carefully just out of the huge dog's reach as she worked. He also noticed that her hands were trembling as she scooped food into the other animals' dishes. Obviously this was some sort of test she was putting herself through. Was it possible that Punk represented another bully in Patsy's life? Perhaps one she hadn't stood up against? Justin couldn't help wondering about all the gaps in her background he hadn't been able to fill in.

"What are you doing here?" she asked as she kept on working.

"I just thought I'd stop by to see how your first day on the job at Dolan's had gone."

A smile broke across her face. "It went great. Everyone is really nice. They were very patient."

"It didn't seem to me they needed much patience. You were a whiz at the grill when I was there, better than Sharon Lynn, in fact. Have you done that sort of work before?"

"Way back," she admitted.

He grinned. "It couldn't have been that long ago. You can't be more than what? Maybe nineteen?"

"Twenty-three, actually." She turned a knowing look on him. "Probing for information again, Deputy?"

He shook his head. "Just making conversation."

"If you don't have anything better to do, maybe you could take Punk for a walk. He could use the exercise."

Justin regarded the dog warily. "You have to take him for a walk? Is Dani crazy?"

She grinned at him. "Don't tell me you're scared of a little ole dog."

"That dog is bigger than I am. He does not have a friendly demeanor."

"He still needs to be walked."

Justin sighed. He knew perfectly well he couldn't go off and leave her to handle the beast. When they found itsy-bitsy pieces of her the next morning, he'd never forgive himself.

"I'll walk him," he agreed grudgingly, "if you'll get Billy and come with me. We'll stop for ice cream."

He could read the temptation in her eyes. How long had it been since she'd had such a simple pleasure, he wondered. How long since her son had been given any kind of treat at all? With money scarce, he doubted there had been many. Patsy struck him as a very practical sort of woman who would put the basics first.

"Where?" she asked cautiously. "Dolan's is closed and I haven't seen any other places for ice cream around town."

He grinned. "But I know the owner at Dolan's and I have a spare key for emergencies."

"Somehow I doubt this qualifies as an emergency."

"True," he agreed. "Actually, though, I wasn't thinking of Dolan's. I just bought a half gallon of rocky road and some cones. I figured we could stop by my place. It's only a few blocks from here."

That all-too-familiar wary expression clouded her eyes. "I don't know."

"Is Billy asleep?"

"No. He's surrounded by kitties and glued to a video Dani left for him. It's one of his favorites. I doubt we'll be able to pry him away from the TV."

"Sure we can. Besides he should get out and get some fresh air, too. A walk will be good for all of us."

"Obviously, you haven't done much walking with a two-year-old. One of us will be carrying him before we get home."

"I can carry him."

"And control Punk?"

"That, too. Consider it a challenge."

Her eyes sparkled at that. It appeared he'd finally made the offer too tempting to resist.

"In that case, I'll get Billy. You're in charge of Punk."

He eyed the beast and wondered if it was too late to reconsider. "Okay," he said, approaching the dog cautiously. "Come on, boy. Let's go for a walk."

Apparently that was the magic word. The dog began pulling at his restraint and barking joyously. As Justin neared, Punk jumped up and put both paws on Justin's shoulders and began trying to lick him to death. Justin managed to pull back just enough to glance at Patsy, who was grinning from ear to ear.

"You knew, didn't you?"

"Dani did mention he really, really liked to walk."

"And that he was a pussycat underneath all that snarling?" he questioned.

"That, too, but I wasn't sure I could believe her on that point."

"So I was the human guinea pig?"

"Something like that."

Justin frowned at her as the dog slobbered all down the front of him. "You'll pay for this, darlin'. I guarantee it."

Even in the face of his threat, she chuckled. "Sorry. I can't help it. You look so..."

"So what?"

"Surprised," she suggested. "Indignant."

"Wait till you see me when I'm flat-out furious," he warned.

Her grin never faltered. "You're forgetting something, Deputy. I've been there, done that."

Justin paused. So she had. And surprisingly, despite the wariness he'd read in her eyes, despite a momen-

tary panic, she hadn't run for cover. Something told
him, though, that they might both be better off if she
had. There were secrets with this woman, secrets and
lies. He didn't doubt it for an instant. When the truth
finally came out, which of them was going to be the
one most hurt by it?

Every instinct she possessed told Patsy to avoid
Justin Adams and yet, when he'd proposed helping
her to walk that huge dog and getting ice cream, she
hadn't been able to resist. For Billy's sake, she reassured herself. It had been a long time since Billy had
an innocent outing, an even longer time since he'd
had one with an adult male who actually seemed to
enjoy his company.

Will hadn't been the kind of father who carted a
messy child off for ice cream unless there was a photo
opportunity in it for him. Then the ice cream had been
little more than a prop and Billy had been handed
back to her the instant the cameras were out of range.

In the living quarters beside the clinic, she'd had
only to mention ice cream and Billy had toddled toward her with his arms upstretched.

"Go," he pleaded, the video forgotten. "Go now."

"We'll go now, but you have to walk. I'm not
going to carry you, okay?"

"'Kay," he agreed, his head bobbing. "Big boy."

She grinned at him. "Yes, you are my big boy."
And the treasure of her life. Everything she was doing, the risk she was taking, starting over in a new

place, all of it was for him. She wouldn't have been able to bear it if he'd been injured—even accidentally—in the cross fire between her and Will.

Justin stuck his head into the room. "All set?"

At the sight of him, Billy ran straight toward him on unsteady legs. "Hi, ya."

"Hi, yourself."

"We go for ice cream," Billy announced.

"I know."

"You, too?"

"Yep, me, too."

"Mama, Justin go, too."

"That's right, baby."

Billy raced for the clinic and passed Punk as if he weren't even there. "Le's go, Mama."

"I'm coming," she assured him. She glanced at Justin. "Are you bringing Punk?"

"Do I have a choice?" he muttered as the dog leaped on him and licked his face. "Down, you beast."

The look of stunned amazement on his face when Punk dutifully sat was priceless. "Dani also mentioned he's very obedient," she said.

"You could have told me that sooner," he grumbled as he headed for the door with the dog heeling on command.

"I wasn't sure I believed her. I figured I'd let you put it to the test."

Justin tightened his hold on the leash and both of them watched with bated breath as Billy marched up to Punk and petted him gently on the nose. "Nice dog."

Punk responded by wagging his tail so hard he shook all over, but he did nothing at all to intimidate his pint-size admirer.

As they started down the block, they passed other families out for an evening stroll. Justin spoke to everyone, but to Patsy's relief he didn't pause to introduce her. Deceiving a handful of people was hard enough. She wasn't ready to put herself to the test with everyone else in town just yet.

Being with Justin like this felt so normal, so ordinary, she couldn't believe it. This was what she'd envisioned her marriage being, the kind of life she'd anticipated with Will. That it had turned out so very differently saddened her more than she could say.

"Hey," Justin said softly. "You okay?"

"Just thinking."

"About?"

"This and that," she equivocated.

"Which made you so sad? This or that?" he inquired lightly.

"What makes you think either one made me sad?"

"There are tears in your eyes."

And now they were spilling down her cheeks, she realized with embarrassment. She brushed them away and forced a smile. "Every now and then I get lost in what might have been."

He regarded her with a troubled expression. "And what might have been makes you sad?"

"No sadder than what was," she admitted and walked quickly on ahead.

"Patsy."

His voice was soft, but something in it commanded her to stop. She hesitated, fought against a fresh batch of tears, then turned back.

"If something's bothering you, you can talk to me. In my line of work, there's not much I haven't seen or heard."

She looked into worried blue eyes and saw the sincere desire to help. As she had said to Tate Owens earlier, she repeated, "Thank you. I'll remember that."

"Something tells me you won't."

"I said I would, didn't I?" she snapped defensively.

"Do you always keep your promises?"

She remembered other promises—vows—she'd made and broken by running off. "When I can," she said quietly.

"What would it take to make you break a promise?" he asked.

"Betrayal," she said without thinking.

There was a quick flash of understanding in his eyes. "Who betrayed you, Patsy?"

"No one," she said hurriedly. "Forget I said that."

His gaze searched her face. She could see there were a hundred questions on the tip of his tongue, but he finally nodded. "For now," he agreed.

Patsy should have felt relieved, but instead the reprieve promised only a temporary solution. Sooner or later, Justin Adams was going to pursue his questioning until he had all the answers he wanted. He was too good a lawman not to. She knew he didn't totally believe a word out of her mouth.

Still she could enjoy tonight. The summer air was dry and stirred by a faint, cooling breeze. The streets of Los Piños were peaceful. The only arguments were between children squabbling over a toy or a game of hopscotch. If there were more serious fights between grown-ups, they were behind closed doors and they weren't her fights. Will Longhorn was far away and, hopefully, nowhere close to finding her. Right this minute she and Billy were safe. They had found a temporary haven, where they could get back on their feet again, where she could rebuild her self-respect.

And even though he represented a very real threat of discovery, Justin Adams also reassured her. She sensed that his quiet strength would never be used against her and, after so many months of fearing for her own safety and Billy's, that was wonderful.

Yet she couldn't help wondering what would happen if Justin knew the truth. Would he feel betrayed because he'd risked believing in her? Would he send her straight back to her husband? Would be believe the lies that Will was bound to tell to discredit her?

Or, as he had with the incident over the Tylenol, would Justin understand that she was only doing what she'd had to do? Would he protect her? Did she even have the right to expect that of him?

As a lawman, yes. It was his sworn duty to keep her safe. Thanks to Sharon Lynn and Tate Owens, she already knew how Justin felt about duty.

But as a man? In less than forty-eight hours she had come to see him as both. Wrong as it was, she had wished, however fleetingly, that she could be loved by a man like Justin Adams. She'd dismissed the thought as ridiculous and hypothetical, not a serious yearning for this particular man. But now, with him beside her, she wondered if the thought had been hypothetical at all, or truly wistful longing?

Forget it, she told herself. It wasn't even something she could afford to consider until she did something about her marital status. At some point, she would have to file for divorce she supposed, but that meant facing Will, dealing with him in a courtroom at the very least. Now she was too fearful of the outcome to risk it. She would live the rest of her life in limbo if she had to.

"Patsy." Justin spoke quietly as if he feared startling her.

Startled anyway, she jerked, then gazed up into those vivid blue eyes again. "Yes?"

His smile was slow and a little sad, perhaps regretful over frightening her. "We're here."

She glanced toward the neatly tended house, a low brick rambler with roses in the yard and a sheriff's car parked in the driveway. The latter was a shock, a reminder that she'd been too ready to drop her guard.

He led the way inside. Punk was eager to explore,

but a soft command to stay had him flopping on the cool marble floor in the foyer.

"The kitchen's this way," Justin said, leading her through a dining room that was empty of furniture.

He spotted her quick look around, then shrugged sheepishly. "I can't decide if I want to use it for a dining room or a family room," he explained. "It seems a little silly to put a fancy table in here, when I never entertain."

He opened a swinging door and gestured inside. "The kitchen's plenty big enough for a table and chairs. Everybody hangs out in here anyway."

Patsy could see why. The antique oak table was huge and it was surrounded by oak chairs with bright cushions on the seats that matched the curtains hanging at the windows. It was a woman's touch and she wondered with a twinge of jealousy who'd been responsible. The appliances appeared to be brand-new, including a state-of-the-art refrigerator that looked big enough to stock a month's supply of food for a family of eight.

When Justin opened the humongous freezer, she had to laugh. Inside there were two half-gallons of ice cream and nothing else, except perhaps some unseen cubes of ice in the automatic ice maker.

"Kind of a waste of space, isn't it?" she teased.

He shrugged. "I eat out a lot."

"Is the other side any better?"

"See for yourself," he said, opening the door to reveal a couple of cans of soda, some sandwich meat, a loaf of bread, a bottle of ketchup, a jar of mayonnaise, and a stick of butter still in its wrapper.

"Interesting diet you have."

"I eat breakfast at Dolan's, lunch wherever it's convenient and dinner with my folks or Grandpa Harlan. This stuff is good enough for a late-night snack or an emergency lunch on my day off."

"No lady friends to cook for you?" she inquired, all too aware of yet another odd little twinge of envy that came automatically with the question.

"Once in a while," he conceded. "No one special."

She could believe it. She could also believe that he didn't entertain them here. The bare necessities weren't meant to impress anyone. And any woman with marriage on her mind would have long since added her own touches to the room and seen to it that the refrigerator was stocked with tempting dishes meant to win his heart. She wouldn't have stopped with the cushions and matching curtains.

Nope, Patsy concluded, this was the home of a dedicated, unattached bachelor, all right. She found that oddly comforting.

"Ice cream," Billy demanded.

Justin hoisted him up and settled him on the counter, then reached into a cupboard and brought out a box of sugar cones. "One scoop or two?" he inquired, the question directed at Billy, but his unsettling gaze fixed on Patsy.

"One," she insisted, overriding Billy's demand for

two. "And prepare for disaster. We probably ought to eat them outside."

"We can take them onto the patio," he said, scooping the rocky road into the cones and handing two to her. When he'd put the carton of ice cream back into the freezer, he picked Billy up and opened the back door to a brick patio and a medium-sized pool that sparkled with underwater lights. Billy clapped his hands in delight.

"Swim, Mama."

"Not now, baby."

She caught Justin's surprised expression.

"He can swim?"

She nodded. "Like a little fish. He had lessons a few months ago. He loves the water." Lessons had been a necessity with the huge pool in their backyard. Even so, she had had safety locks installed on all the doors leading outside to keep Billy from wandering out unattended, lured by the water and oblivious to the potential dangers.

"You'll have to come over sometime and use the pool," Justin said.

"We'll see."

She could see that there were more questions he wanted to ask, such as how a woman who'd been unable to pay for children's Tylenol had afforded swimming lessons or had even had access to a pool. He was probably noting that, right alongside the expensive clothes he'd already commented on and the fancy car, and coming up with a background for her that didn't add up.

"One of these days we're going to have to talk about this," he said, his gaze never leaving hers.

The comment confirmed her worst fears. Patsy sighed and nodded. "One of these days," she conceded.

He nodded slowly, accepting that for now. A plaintive *woof* from inside broke the tension and had them laughing.

"Apparently Punk is tired of being obedient," she noted.

"Should I let him join us or should we head back?"

"We'd better get back," she said reluctantly. "Billy needs to get to sleep. And I have to be up early to get to work."

He gestured behind her. "I don't think Billy's rest is an issue."

She turned and found Billy curled up on a chaise longue sound asleep, his half-eaten ice cream cone melting beside him. Panic spiraled through her at the sight of the mess.

"Oh, dear," she murmured, jumping up at once. "I'll clean it up."

"Stay where you are," he said. "I'll take care of it."

"But—"

"Patsy, it's not a problem. The fabric's washable. Even if it weren't, what would it matter?"

She thought of Will's quick, explosive anger over such minor accidents and wondered at this man who seemed to take the same thing in stride. "Are you sure?" she asked, unable to keep the uneasiness out of her voice.

"Of course, I'm sure," he said, his gaze intent and filled with unspoken curiosity. "Relax. I'll be right back."

Patsy couldn't relax, but she did manage to stay where she was and let Justin deal with the melted ice cream. When it was cleaned up, he hefted Billy into his arms.

"Let's get this guy home and into bed." He glanced at her. "Can you handle Punk?"

"Sure," she said with sheer bravado.

The dog seemed to sense her uncertainty and tested her immediately, but one sharp command from Justin had him behaving.

Back at Dani's Justin took the baby into the bedroom and settled him, then walked back to the front door. He lifted his hand to graze her cheek with his knuckles. Longing shimmered through her, a deep yearning for more than that gentle touch. For now, though—perhaps forever—more was forbidden.

"Thank you," she said, fighting the breathless note in her voice. "I enjoyed the walk and the ice cream."

In fact, she had enjoyed the whole evening entirely too much. It had relaxed her guard around this man. It had made her want things that couldn't be. It would not do to repeat occasions like this too often, for both their sakes.

"We'll have to do it again sometime," he said.

"Sure," she said, but she knew she would have to fight the next invitation.

Tonight had proved beyond any doubt that being around Justin Adams was dangerous. One day soon he wouldn't settle for evasive answers. One day soon he wouldn't settle for the quick brush of his fingertips along her cheek, as he was doing now.

Worse, one day soon, she wouldn't, either. And that could be her downfall.

Chapter Five

Justin had a long and restless night after leaving Patsy. He'd lain awake most of it reciting all the reasons he ought to be fighting his attraction to her for all he was worth. Every instinct he possessed warned him away.

Even without the circumstances of their first meeting still fresh in his mind, he would have known that there were troubling aspects to Patsy Gresham's past. She was too leery of any questions, too skittish around him. He'd noted her easygoing manner with most of the customers in Dolan's the day before and concluded that her nervousness was directed at him. More likely, at his uniform.

There were a couple of obvious reasons for people

to be afraid of a cop. Either they'd committed a crime, or they were trying to hide from someone and feared discovery. He wanted to believe it was the latter in Patsy's case.

But who? And why? He wasn't sure he was going to be thrilled with the answers to those questions, either. That probably explained why he hadn't asked them the night before. If he discovered something in Patsy's background that required reporting, he would be duty-bound to deal with it. For the moment, it seemed to him it might be better not to know.

Looking the other way was totally out of character for him. That he was even in such a position was irritating as the dickens. He left for work in a foul humor, which didn't improve when he walked through the door to be greeted by more questions about Patsy.

"Justin, how much do you know about the Gresham woman?" Tate Owens asked before he'd even had time for a decent cup of coffee.

As riled as he was by the question, Justin had anticipated it. He'd known the sheriff wouldn't let the matter rest ever since Tate had come back from Dolan's the day before. He'd found his conversation with Patsy worrisome. "The woman's in some kind of trouble," he'd said then. "I can feel it in my gut."

Justin hadn't been able to argue with him.

"Justin," Tate prodded now. "What do you know about her?"

"Enough," he said curtly.

"Did you run the tag number?"

"No."

"You're sure it's her car?"

If Justin had been the kind of man who squirmed under pressure, he'd have been doing it now. He knew he should have run the check, but he wasn't sure he wanted the answers it might yield. He hadn't even demanded to see the registration.

"Sure enough," he said curtly.

"I don't suppose you checked the registration, either, did you?"

He scowled at Tate. "No, but—"

The sheriff stared at him. "Justin, you're a better cop than that. The woman shows up here out of the blue, tries to steal from your cousin, and you ignore the obvious way to get a clear picture of what we're dealing with? Why?" Tate studied him closely. "Damn, you've got a thing for her, haven't you?"

"Don't be ridiculous."

"Then give me one good reason for not checking her out."

"I did check. I ran through the stolen vehicle reports," he conceded finally. He'd done even that much reluctantly, praying that he wouldn't find a report on a fancy Oklahoma car in the stack.

Tate was only slightly mollified. "Anything there?"

"Nothing."

"You've spent more time with her than I have. What do you think?"

"I think she's trying her best to start over. Maybe we ought to back off and let her."

"What if whatever trouble she's in follows her here to Los Piños?" Tate inquired. "We should be prepared for it, don't you think? We can't help her, if we don't know what to be on the lookout for."

Justin sighed. He had no argument with his boss's thinking. In law enforcement, especially in a small town with limited resources, it was always better to be prepared.

"We need some answers, son. You know we do."

"I know. I'll see what I can do."

"Don't take too long. Every instinct tells me that it won't be long before all hell breaks loose. A classy woman with a baby and a fancy car, but no money..." He shook his head. "It has all the earmarks of a woman on the run from her husband."

Hearing his own suspicion put into words made Justin's heart sink. Every time a voice in his head had started to shout the possibility, he'd tuned out, refusing to listen. He'd looked for a wedding ring, but she hadn't been wearing one. He'd wanted to believe that meant there was no husband. He was smart enough to know better. Rings would be the first thing she'd hide—or hock.

"Any sign she'd been abused?" Tate asked.

"No bruises, if that's what you mean." He had checked, surreptitiously studying every visible inch of her for fading marks on her pale skin. He'd been relieved by the absence of evidence. "That doesn't mean she wasn't, though."

He thought of the way she'd reacted to Billy's accident with the ice cream the night before. She'd been too quick to leap to her feet, too panicked over such a trivial incident.

"What about the boy?" Tate inquired just as the same thought struck Justin.

"By God, I hope not," he said tightly, consumed with fury at the slightest possibility that that was the explanation for Patsy being on the run. The one good sign was that Billy had shown no fear at all of him. If he'd been harmed by his father, wouldn't he have been wary of men? He clung to that tiny shred of reassurance.

Tate cleared his throat and regarded Justin uneasily. "Son, are you sure you're the best person to be checking into this. Maybe I ought to look into it myself."

"Why?"

"Could be you're too personally involved."

"Involved? I just met the woman."

"Ever heard about lightning bolts?" the sheriff questioned. "They strike without warning. Only takes an instant to change everything."

Justin thought of the way Patsy's skin had felt under his touch the night before, of the way her soft cheek had warmed, of the flicker of desire he'd been so sure he'd seen in her eyes. And then he considered how badly his body had ached the rest of the night with wanting her, with wanting more than that gentle, fleeting brush of skin against skin.

It meant nothing, he assured himself. Just a natural, hormonal reaction to a beautiful woman's proximity.

"My objectivity's not compromised," he insisted, partly because he believed it, mostly because he didn't dare consider the possibility that it could be.

Tate's gaze met his and remained steady. Finally he nodded, accepting Justin's word. "If that changes, let me know. You don't just owe it to me. You owe it to her."

"I will," he promised. If the time ever came when he couldn't do his job, surely he would know it, surely he would do the right thing. He wouldn't let pride and pure cussedness stand in his way.

If he did, if it ever came to that, he would have to reexamine exactly who Justin Adams really was, if he really was the honorable, natural born lawman he'd always thought himself to be. Or if he was like any other man who'd bend the rules when they no longer suited him.

The vivacious woman with the sculpted cheekbones and short black hair beckoned to Patsy, then glanced around furtively.

"Where's Sharon Lynn?" she demanded in a hushed voice.

"She went out to run an errand," Patsy said, dropping her own voice to a whisper in response.

The woman's smile was relieved. "Great. Then we

can talk. I'm Jenny, Sharon Lynn's stepaunt technically, but that's neither here nor there. Dani should be here any minute. We're planning a surprise bridal shower for Sharon Lynn tomorrow. Can you help?''

Patsy grinned, delighted to be asked to be in on the surprise. "Of course. What do you need me to do?"

"Get her there."

"Where? And how on earth can I get her to go anywhere?"

"Well, that's the beauty of it. We thought we'd have it at your place. I understand you've moved into Dani's old house. Sharon Lynn will never suspect that. Maybe you could invite her to dinner or something. We're going to have it right after she closes up here."

Patsy thought about it. "I suppose I could manage that. I owe her a lot for giving me this job. I'll tell her I want to repay her by having her over for dinner."

"That's perfect. Do you mind us having it there? I suppose I should have asked that first thing, but we were already planning it for Dani's and now you're there, so it didn't seem to make sense to move it. In fact, it works out even better this way, if you don't mind, that is."

"Of course not. The house is Dani's, after all. She's been wonderful about letting me and Billy stay there."

"You're invited, of course. No need to bring a present. Sharon Lynn won't expect it."

"You don't need to include me. I'll lure her over and then Billy and I can just go out to eat."

"Absolutely not. Besides, if you're the one dragging her over there, you can't turn right around and leave. And we all want to get to know you better. Seven o'clock, okay? We'll take care of everything."

"I'll have her there," Patsy promised, already looking forward to the chance to pay Sharon Lynn back for her kindness by helping with this surprise.

"Terrific. Dani said we could count on you. Got to run. I'm overdue at home and my husband tends to get restless, especially now that I'm pregnant."

She was out the door before Patsy could blink, another whirlwind Adams entering into her life and drawing her into the family circle.

Weighed down by the assignment just given to her, she was a nervous wreck until Sharon Lynn returned.

Forcing a casual note into her voice, she asked, "Sharon Lynn, do you have plans for tomorrow night?"

A frown of concentration knit her brow. "I don't think so, but let me check my calendar. I can't trust myself to remember anything these days. Why?"

"I'd like to have you over for dinner after we close. Nothing fancy, but I really want to do something special to thank you for being so nice to Billy and me. I know you won't have a spare second once all the wedding plans kick into gear."

"Oh, sweetie, that's not necessary. All I did was give you a job and work you to death."

"But after what happened the first time I came in here, a lot of people wouldn't have been so understanding."

"You've more than made up for that. You've only been here two days and already I can't imagine what I ever did without you. You're fitting right in."

Patsy warmed under the heartfelt praise. It had been a long time since anyone had complimented her. Will's constant carping had eaten away at her self-confidence, eroding it to the point that she hadn't been sure if there was a single thing she could do right at all.

"All I'm doing is scrambling eggs and frying hamburgers," she said quietly.

"It's a lot more than that," Sharon Lynn insisted. "The customers around here can be stingy with praise, but they already love you."

To Patsy's embarrassment, she could feel tears stinging her eyes. "Stop. You're going to make me cry."

Sharon Lynn stared at her. "Just because I'm pointing out the obvious, that you're good at what you do?"

Patsy nodded. "Please," she begged. "Don't ask me to explain."

"I won't," Sharon Lynn agreed, her expression turning fierce. "But if some man has made you feel worthless, then shame on him." She drew in a deep breath, then said more quietly, "If you ever need to talk, I'm a good listener.'' She gave Patsy a pointed look. ''So's Justin.''

''I know,'' Patsy responded. ''But there's nothing to talk about.''

Sharon Lynn seemed about to argue, then she let it go. ''About dinner tomorrow night, if the invitation's still open, I would love to come.''

Mission accomplished, Patsy thought triumphantly, pushing aside all other thoughts to focus on tomorrow's surprise. ''About seven, right after we close?''

''That will be perfect.''

''What will be perfect?'' Justin demanded, walking up to settle on a stool at the counter.

He had a worrisome way of sneaking up on her that constantly caught her off guard. One of these days would he overhear something that would give her away?

''Patsy's invited me to dinner tomorrow night,'' Sharon Lynn explained.

He glanced at her. ''Is that so? What about me?''

Patsy shook her head. ''Sorry. It's a girls-only night.''

''Then maybe I should pick Billy up and take him out for spaghetti with the guys.''

The thought of being separated even for a short time from her son panicked her. ''No, really, he'll be fine with us,'' Patsy said at once.

''Maybe it would be fun for Billy,'' Sharon Lynn said. ''Justin's really good with kids.''

''I know that. It's just that...'' It was just that she

envisioned Will coming to claim him when she wasn't around to prevent it. How could she explain that?

"I'll take good care of him," Justin promised. His gaze locked with hers. "No harm will come to him while he's with me."

It was almost as if he knew, she thought, studying his expression for some clue that would tell her if he'd discovered the truth.

She thought of the real purpose for tomorrow's invitation to Sharon Lynn. The house would be crawling with other women for the shower. It really was no place for a small child. And surely the safest place in the world for Billy to be was with a deputy sheriff.

"Okay," she said at last. "Billy loves spaghetti. Just be aware that he tends to get most of it all over himself and anyone else who's in his path."

Justin grinned. "In that case, maybe I'll invite Harlan Patrick along."

Sharon Lynn laughed.

"Who's Harlan Patrick?" Patsy asked, watching their shared amusement and the conspiratorial wink they exchanged.

"My brother," she explained. "When he's not herding cattle or up to his elbows in muck, he considers himself quite a fashion plate. There's nothing Harlan Patrick likes more than a fancy new outfit that'll impress the ladies. Justin's just imagining how he'd love to have spaghetti spattered all over his best western shirt, especially since his girlfriend will be singing over at the restaurant tomorrow.''

"But that's…" Words failed her.

"Dastardly," Sharon Lynn provided.

"Just plain mean," Patsy said.

"Payback," Justin corrected. "Harlan Patrick and I have a score to settle."

"And you intend to use my son to do it?"

"He and my brother always have a score to settle," Sharon Lynn said. "Goodness knows what it's about this time. Don't worry about it. Just leave them to it. When Harlan Patrick decides to get even, he won't take it out on Billy. All his ire will be directed straight back at Justin."

The idea that a family could engage in teasing and pranks without rancor was so totally alien to the way Patsy had spent the past couple of years that she was enthralled by it. She would almost rather watch Justin get even with his cousin than go through with her role in Sharon Lynn's surprise.

But it was all part of the same cloth, she realized with a sense of wonder. This was a tight-knit, supportive family, the kind she'd always dreamed of being a part of.

"Do you two have any idea how lucky you are?" she asked.

"Of course we do," Sharon Lynn said, clearly grasping her meaning at once. She gave Patsy a tight hug. "You'll see," she promised, glancing toward Justin. "Won't she?"

His gaze caught Patsy's and held. "If I have anything to say about it."

Patsy trembled under the intensity of that look. A fierce longing for what these Adams cousins took for granted rushed over her. Gazing into Justin's eyes she saw what might have been a bold commitment, a promise that was there for the taking if only she could.

If only she could.

She sighed heavily and turned away, busying herself with the last of the day's dishes, which had to be stacked and ready for the morning rush. When she turned again, she realized that Sharon Lynn had silently left, leaving her alone with Justin.

"Come to dinner with me," he suggested. "And before you start making excuses, I've already checked with Dani. She's going to be late at the clinic. She'll look after Billy for another couple of hours. She says he's having the time of his life with the animals. Her boys will be over there soon, too. Billy will be in heaven with all that attention."

"But his dinner…"

"Is taken care of. They shared a fried chicken dinner that I brought them from White Pines."

She regarded him suspiciously. "Something tells me that fried chicken was meant for you. Did you use it to bribe Dani to go along with this scheme of yours?"

He grinned. "What if I did? All it proves is that I

will go to astonishing lengths to grab a few minutes alone with you.''

"Don't," she commanded softly.

"Don't what?"

"Be nice to me."

"Why not?"

"I don't deserve it."

"Darlin', everyone deserves to have someone special be nice to them."

Tears spilled down her cheeks. "No, Justin. This can't be," she whispered, turning away.

She heard his quick movement, felt him behind her, but it was a long while before she felt his hand on her shoulder. It rested there gently, reminding her of his presence, soothing her but asking for nothing. The undemanding reassurance couldn't last forever, though. Sooner or later he would want something in return—answers, at the very least.

"Patsy?"

She sniffed and reached for a napkin to wipe away the dampness on her cheeks. Slowly he turned her to face him, then tucked a finger under her chin and lifted it until their gazes met.

"Tell me," he pleaded.

"I can't."

He brushed the hair back from her face, then lingered to caress her cheek. When he grazed her lower lip with the tip of his finger, the wonder of his gentleness almost shattered her. Slowly, so slowly that she told herself she must be mistaken, he lowered his head until their mouths were a scant hairsbreadth apart.

Hurry, hurry, she wanted to shout. If he rushed, if he simply stole the kiss, she could tell herself forever after that she hadn't wanted it to happen. But this way, there was no denying the pull, no pretending that she didn't want it with every fiber of her being. There was time enough for longing and more than enough time for guilt.

At the last possible second, when she could feel the warmth of his breath fanning over her flesh, honor intruded. She jerked away, moved until the width of the counter was safely between them again. She grasped the cool Formica merely to steady herself, but held so tightly that her knuckles turned white and the edge cut into her hand....

"I'm sorry," he said.

"No," she said adamantly. "You have nothing to be sorry for."

"I do," he insisted. "I knew better. I knew it wasn't what you wanted."

"But I did," she whispered, her voice thick with fresh, unshed tears. "More than anything."

"Why, then?"

Looking into his eyes, she saw that he already knew the answer, that he'd guessed it somehow.

"Who is he, Patsy?"

"Nobody," she said at once. "There's nobody."

Something that might have been pain flared in his

eyes then. His expression turned weary. "You're lying," he said softly.

She turned away because she couldn't bear to see the hurt in his eyes.

"Maybe someday you'll realize you don't have to lie to me," he told her. "Maybe someday you'll trust me with the truth."

And maybe, she thought wistfully, maybe someday there would be angels to look out for women whose hearts had been every bit as battered as their psyches or their bodies.

Chapter Six

Justin cursed himself six ways from Sunday as he walked home after leaving Patsy at her front door. She'd barely said a word to him as she'd closed up Dolan's or as they'd walked up the block to Dani's.

At least he'd been wise enough not to pressure her any more by asking to come in or by walking on into his sister's clinic to say hi to Dani and Billy. No, for once he'd done the smart thing. He'd said good-night, reminded her of his promise to take Billy out for spaghetti the next night and left.

He figured it would be days and not hours before he forgot the wounded look in her eyes when he'd accused her of lying. Even though they both knew the accusation was true, pointing it out hadn't helped anything. Now she would only be more wary of him than ever. He regretted that almost as deeply as he regretted not getting to steal that kiss.

Of course, that had been a mistake, too. Had he forgotten so quickly Tate's warning to maintain his objectivity or, if he found he couldn't, to turn the unofficial investigation into Patsy's background over to Tate himself? He'd come damned close to blowing everything. For a man who prided himself on not crossing lines, he was virtually doing a hundred-yard dash across this one.

Distracted by his dark thoughts, he was halfway up the walk at home before he realized that someone was waiting in the shadows. Regretting that he didn't have his gun, he was preparing to launch himself at the intruder, when Harlan Patrick stepped into the light cast by the streetlight on the corner.

"Hey, Justin. You're late getting home."

"Damn you, do you know how close you came to getting tackled?" Justin muttered as he brushed past his cousin and unlocked his door. "You have a key. Why didn't you go inside to wait for me?"

"Because I just got here," he explained with exaggerated patience. "I saw you coming and waited out here. What the devil's wrong with you, anyway? Why are you so jumpy? This is Los Piños, not Dallas. How many criminals wait in shadows around here? For that matter, how many bad guys have you arrested lately, not counting those sickos who dared to let their parking meters run out?"

Harlan Patrick gave Justin a knowing look. "Wait. Forget I asked that. You let the last genuine law-breaker go free, didn't you, and it's still stuck in your craw. This does have something to do with the mysterious stranger, doesn't it?"

"It's none of your business." Justin pushed past him and went into the kitchen, where he grabbed a soda from the almost barren refrigerator. "Want one?"

"Sure."

He tossed that can to his cousin, then grabbed another and popped the top. A long, cold drink did nothing to soothe his frayed temper.

"Justin?"

"Yeah."

"Is there a problem?"

"I wish to hell I knew for sure."

"What does that mean?"

"It means every instinct tells me there is, but I can't get a handle on it."

"Or do you just not like the answers you're coming up with?"

He sighed. "That, too," he admitted.

"Want to talk about it?"

"Not especially."

"I have tremendous insight into the female mind," Harlan Patrick claimed.

Justin hooted at that. "If playing the field counts for anything, I'm sure that's true. I'm just not so sure

I want to take advice from a man who doesn't know the meaning of settling down."

"I am settling down. I haven't dated anyone but Laurie for months now."

"Really? Months? That must be some kind of record."

"I'd make it permanent if she'd hear of it, but she still has this crazy idea about going to Nashville as soon as she gets some money together."

"Maybe you ought to loan her the money," Justin suggested. "Let her get it out of her system."

"No way," Harlan Patrick said. "I'm not going to help set her up for heartache."

"She'll do it on her own, then. You know she will. And in the meantime, you'll be waiting around."

Harlan Patrick shook his head. "No way. She'll wake up one of these days and realize that it's only a foolish dream. Then we'll get married and raise a family out at White Pines. She'll switch from singing country to lullabies."

Justin had only spent a few evenings with Laurie Jensen, but even he could see that his cousin had a blind spot when it came to Laurie's commitment to her music. "If you believe that, then you don't know your lady half as well as you think you do," he warned. "Where is she tonight?"

"Over in Garden City, singing at a club."

"And what's she doing tomorrow?"

Harlan Patrick scowled. "Singing here in town."

"And you don't think that means anything?"

"Sure, it does. I don't object if she wants to sing every once in a while around here."

"That's mighty big of you. When was the last time Laurie asked your permission?"

Harlan Patrick's disgruntled expression was answer enough. "Never mind," Justin said. "Wake up, cousin. The woman has the voice of an angel, a way with words and the ambition it takes to make her dream come true. Either help her or get out of her way."

"Who asked for your advice?"

"Consider it a gift from someone who's older and wiser."

"You can't be that wise, if you can't make heads or tails of what's going on with the town's newest resident. I thought cops had all sorts of ways to get answers if they wanted them badly enough."

That was the trouble, of course. Justin wasn't one bit sure he was ready to hear the answers, not from that computer down at the station, not even from Patsy's own lips.

Billy's cheeks were flushed, his straight black hair a damp fringe around his face. He smelled like talcum powder and baby.

"Which bedtime story tonight?" Patsy asked him, holding up the two books she'd taken from his shelves when they'd left home. There had been dozens more she'd left behind, but these two were Billy's favorites.

Bathing Billy had soothed her jangled nerves after that near kiss from Justin. That and the story were a familiar routine, one that had been repeated for so long, no matter where they were, that she could almost convince herself that their lives were normal.

Billy popped his thumb into his mouth and studied the covers of the books as intently as if it were the first time he'd ever seen them. "Two stories," he pleaded finally.

"No, sweet pea. Only one."

A mutinous expression crossed his face. "Two."

"Choose or there will be no story at all." She moved to put the books away.

"No, Mama. Read rabbit story."

She grinned. Forced to choose, *The Velveteen Rabbit* was always the one he picked. "You must know it by heart."

"Don't care. Read it," he commanded with the same authoritative manner as his father.

"Please," she prompted.

"Please, Mama."

As she began reading the familiar words, Billy began to drift off. She was even more surprised, then, when he murmured, "Mama, where's Daddy?"

It was the first time he'd mentioned his father since they'd left home. She'd wondered more than once if that was because Will was so often away from home that Billy was used to not seeing him or if it was because he preferred this quiet, peaceful life without his father around.

"Daddy's at home in Oklahoma."

"Wanna see him."

Patsy sat back and tried to control the shaking that began deep inside. She hadn't wanted to believe that Billy would ever miss his daddy. She'd almost convinced herself that the disruption in their lives she'd brought on by running away hadn't fazed Billy at all. After all, he and his father had spent precious little time together bonding. Obviously, though, what time they had shared had had a profound impact, one that weeks of separation hadn't dimmed.

Before she could think of anything at all to say, Billy crawled into her lap. "Please, Mama."

Patsy hugged him tightly. "Oh, baby, I know you miss your daddy, but it's not possible to see him right now."

"Please."

"Daddy's far away. He can't come visit."

"Wanna see him," Billy protested, tears welling up in his eyes.

Patsy rocked him. "Shh, baby. It's going to be okay," she promised.

How? a voice inside her head demanded. How was she going to make this right? She couldn't explain to a two-year-old that his daddy was a potential threat to both of them. For almost the first time since she'd left home, doubts began to crowd in.

Maybe she should call Will. Maybe by now he would have gotten the message that she wouldn't tolerate his behavior. Maybe he'd reform.

And maybe pigs would fly, she thought sarcastically. She knew better. How many women fell into that trap? How many convinced themselves that their husbands were truly sorry, that the psychological abuse or battering would never happen again? She wasn't going to delude herself that way. She wasn't going to wait for Will to actually slam his fist into her rather than an inanimate object.

Still she could take a drive one day, call Will from a public phone and let Billy talk to him. If she made the call far from Los Piños and kept it brief, surely he wouldn't be able to trace it, wouldn't be able to find them. Didn't she owe Billy that much at least?

She glanced down and saw that her son was finally asleep, his thumb tucked securely in his mouth. She shifted him into position on his bed, then pulled a sheet up over him. He'd kick it off in no time, but at least he could start the night covered up.

She stood for a long time, gazing down at him, then bent over and pressed a kiss to his flushed cheek. "I love you, angel. More than anything."

After she left him, she took her own bath, sinking into a sea of fragrant bubbles and trying to let her mind drift. Unfortunately, every time it did, an image of Justin Adams floated into view. Even the memory of his fingers against her cheek made her nipples hard. Recalling the exact instant when she'd known he was going to kiss her made her flesh heat. As the cooling bathwater lapped against her overheated flesh, she moaned softly.

Next time she might not be so strong. Next time she might accept the tenderness he was offering, the promise of even a few moments of gentle loving.

No. She brought herself back sharply from the provocative image. Stepping out of the tub, she toweled herself dry with rough strokes, then yanked on her robe. She didn't dare even begin to think that way about Justin. She was still married, if only in name. She was no doubt in a heap of trouble with Will, if not with the authorities. She couldn't drag Justin into the middle of all that.

Nor could she turn to a man to solve her problems. All her life, she had been relying on other people. First it had been her parents who'd set the rules and protected her from harm. She had left her hometown to prove that she could stand on her own two feet, only to fall in love with Will and let him take over the control of her life just as her parents had before him.

This time was going to be different. She was going to solve her own problems. She would settle this mess with Will, establish a solid, respectable future for herself and her son and then…well, then, if Justin was still interested, if the attraction hadn't died, maybe there could be something between them. Not if she needed his protection, though. Only if she could come to him as an equal, a woman every bit as strong and capable as he was.

"You're getting a little ahead of yourself," she

chided herself aloud. "The man tried to kiss you. He didn't propose marriage."

But something told her that a man as honorable as Justin Adams had proved himself to be took even his kisses seriously and that she would be very wise to remember that.

Patsy barely had the door at Dolan's open in the morning when Justin came in. She switched on the lights and watched warily as he crossed to the counter and settled on a stool. If he brought up that almost kiss, she wasn't sure what she was going to say to him.

"I guess the coffee's not ready yet, is it?" he asked, his manner nothing more than friendly.

Patsy let out a sigh of relief. Apparently last night was forgotten. "I'm just about to put it on. It won't take a minute. Can I get you something else?"

"Take your time. I know it's not really opening time yet. I wanted to catch you alone."

Panic, never far away, choked her. "Why?" she asked, barely managing to get the single word out.

He seemed amused by the question. "To talk."

"About?"

"It can wait. Whenever you're set, I'll take eggs, bacon, toast."

She already knew he liked his eggs over easy, his bacon crisp and his toast the same color as his coffee—or so he claimed. She'd thought he was only being polite when she accidentally burned the first batch she ever made for him, but he swore burnt toast reminded him of home. She noticed, though, that he scraped away most of the black before eating it.

She was about to turn away to start his breakfast, when he snagged her hand.

"Patsy."

Her gaze met his, then skittered away. "Yes?"

"Maybe we should get this out of the way. I'm sorry about last night."

"There's nothing to be sorry for."

"I pushed."

"You've already apologized. It wasn't necessary then. It isn't now."

"But—"

"Justin, please," she pleaded. "Drop it."

His gaze locked with hers, questioning her even without any accompanying words. She held her breath, waiting for something, an explosion maybe. Will would have gone into a rage if she'd dared to cut him off.

Finally, to her relief, Justin simply nodded.

"For now."

It had become a refrain between them, a subtle warning that one day she would pay for all the silences. One day the questions would intensify and there would be no holding back. He would demand to know everything.

"I'll get your breakfast," she said, and hurried away.

By the time she'd fixed his eggs and bacon, Sharon

Lynn had arrived and there were more customers. From then on Patsy was so busy she didn't have time to take a deep breath, much less worry about Justin and his unanswered questions.

If was well after nine before she got a real break.

"Sit for a minute," Sharon Lynn ordered. "I'll bring you a cup of coffee."

"You must be as beat as I am. Why should you wait on me?"

"Because you opened up this morning and Justin was right on your heels so I know perfectly well you haven't had a spare second since." She gave Patsy a curious look. "Everything okay between you and my cousin?"

"Of course," Patsy said a little too quickly. "Why wouldn't it be?"

"I just thought there might be some residual suspiciousness because of that incident when you first arrived. Justin's like a dog with a bone when things don't add up to him."

Patsy's hand stilled with the coffee halfway to her mouth. She regarded Sharon Lynn warily. "And you think things don't add up with me?"

"I didn't say that."

"But you believe Justin has doubts."

"He's a cop. Doubts are second nature to him. It doesn't mean I think he's right."

Fear streaked through her. What if Justin hadn't let things rest, after all? What if he'd dug up something? What if he knew all about her past and was waiting for her to open up and admit the trouble she was in? What if…?

"Has he said something?" she asked cautiously.

"No, but I've watched him around you. One second he looks like a man who's falling hard for a woman, the next he gets this wary expression in his eyes."

Patsy couldn't deny Sharon Lynn's perception. She'd seen the same reactions all too often herself.

"I'm sorry," Sharon Lynn said. "I shouldn't have said anything. I didn't mean to upset you. I don't want you to be on your guard every time he's around."

"I'm not upset. I can't blame Justin for the way he feels. I was shoplifting when he first saw me. I offered to move on, to leave Los Piños. He assured me he could forget what happened, but maybe he can't. Maybe I should go."

Sharon Lynn looked thunderstruck. "No, absolutely not. Where would you go?"

"I don't know," Patsy admitted.

"Then put that idea right out of your head. Nobody wants you to leave."

"Leave? Who's leaving?" Justin demanded, walking up behind them.

Patsy turned slowly. "I thought maybe it would be for the best if I did."

"Well, it wouldn't," he said succinctly.

His sharp response hung in the air. For the longest time no one said anything.

"I'll be in the back if anyone needs me," Sharon

Lynn said finally, but neither Justin nor Patsy spared her a glance.

"Are you sure you don't want me to go?" she asked, searching his face.

"Yes, I'm sure. I just wish…" His voice trailed off.

"Wish what?"

"That you felt you could be honest with me."

Patsy wished that, too, more than she could say. She knew, too, that he could get most of the answers he craved just by running her license tag number. Obviously he hadn't, or he'd want to know why she'd lied about her name being Gresham, not Longhorn. Either he was waiting for her to come to him with the truth on her own or he was afraid of it.

"I can't," she said simply. "I wish I could, but I can't."

"Will you tell me one thing?"

"If I can."

"Have you broken any laws?"

"No," she said honestly. Not unless Will had manufactured a crime out of her leaving with their son.

Relief washed some of the tension out of his expression. "Then we'll leave it at that."

She grinned. "For now."

He chuckled at her repetition of his favorite warning. "Who knows? Maybe I'll just drop it for good. Maybe I'll just take it on faith that you'll tell me the whole story when you feel you can."

Patsy regarded him skeptically. "Can you do that?"

He started to answer, then sighed. "Probably not," he admitted regretfully.

"That's what makes you a good cop, Deputy."

"Maybe it doesn't make me such a terrific man. I ought to trust you. I want to."

"I've given you plenty of cause not to."

He lifted his hand, hesitated, then, looking as if he wanted to do so much more, he gently grazed her cheek with his knuckles. "You know what I wish more than anything?"

Dazed by the look of pure longing in his eyes, Patsy shook her head.

"I wish that I knew whether I had any right at all to kiss you."

She shuddered with a longing that was equal to his, then finally looked away.

Justin sighed. "That pretty much answers my question, doesn't it?"

With her eyes squeezed tightly shut to keep the tears from falling, she said softly, "Yes, I suppose it does."

It was only a tiny hint at the whole truth, but it was enough to put a bleak expression on Justin's face and send him striding out of Dolan's without a backward glance.

It was also more than enough to break Patsy's heart in two.

Chapter Seven

With Justin gone, Patsy was left all alone to battle tears and guilt and shame. How could she go on deceiving a man who had been nothing but kind to her, a man who'd already put aside his own convictions about right and wrong to give her a break? She was still wrestling with that when Sharon Lynn came out of the back.

Patsy hastily wiped her eyes and forced a smile. She didn't want this compassionate woman to be caught in the middle. It was too soon to test the strength of their friendship, especially when Justin was part of her family. She knew enough about the Adamses by now to know that they were bound tight by love and loyalty.

"Everything okay?" Sharon Lynn asked, concern etched on her face.

"Fine."

"You don't look fine. You look as if you've been crying." Her expression turned indignant. "If that cousin of mine has done anything to upset you, I'll tear him limb from limb."

The fierce promise startled Patsy, then left her chuckling. "Don't you think it would be a bit of a mismatch?" she asked.

"Hey, I grew up playing with him and my brother. I'm as tough as they are. I had to be." Sharon Lynn winked. "I'm also a better shot."

Patsy shuddered at the teasing suggestion. "Please, you don't need to prove it on my account. I don't think there will be any need to resort to guns. Justin didn't deliberately upset me. I'm the one responsible for him taking off in such a foul humor. It was all my fault."

She deliberately pushed her own concerns over Justin aside. Now seemed like a really good time to change the subject and focus on that night's surprise bridal shower before Sharon Lynn wanted to know exactly what she'd done that was so terrible.

"Don't forget we're having dinner tonight," she reminded Sharon Lynn.

For a moment Sharon Lynn seemed startled by the abrupt shift in topic. "Patsy, don't you want to talk about what just happened here?"

"No," she said honestly. "I'd rather think about

the pleasant evening we're going to have. It's been a long time since I've invited company over. You haven't forgotten, have you?''

''No, of course not, but there's no reason you should cook after standing in front of the grill here all day. Why don't we go out?'' she suggested. ''We can let somebody else cook for both of us for a change.''

Patsy thought of all the people who'd be waiting in her living room and almost panicked. ''Absolutely not,'' she said hurriedly and began improvising. ''I already have everything ready. It won't take a minute to get dinner on the table.''

''But you must not get a chance to go out with friends very often because of Billy. Since he'll be with Justin, it would be the perfect time to get out and kick up your heels a little.''

''Believe me, the last thing I want to do is kick up my heels,'' she said with heartfelt sincerity.

Patsy studied her intently, then nodded. ''If you're sure…''

''I am.''

The rest of the afternoon was so busy the only words they had time to exchange were about orders. By the time they closed up, both of them were dead on their feet. Even so, Patsy couldn't help feeling excited as she and Sharon Lynn headed for her place and the waiting bridal shower. She was grateful she'd been asked to play even a minor role in the surprise. It made her feel as if she belonged, as if she had a contribution to make, something she hadn't felt in a very long time.

When they reached the house, she was taken aback by its deserted look. Not even Dani's car was in the driveway, and there were no extra cars parked along the block. Where was everyone? Had she gotten it wrong, after all? If she had, the big surprise for Sharon Lynn was going to be the fact that there was no dinner waiting in the fridge.

Taking it on faith that there was a surprise party waiting inside, she unlocked the door, then led the way into the living room. It wasn't dark yet, but the room was filled with shadows. Just as she was about to reach for a light switch, someone else turned on the overhead light and the room erupted with noise. People burst in from the clinic, where they'd obviously been hiding. All the shouts of "Surprise!" set off the animals. The dogs began howling and the cats scurried for cover.

In the midst of the chaos, Sharon Lynn stared around at all of her friends and family, then burst into tears.

"Oh, dear," Patsy murmured, stunned by the reaction. She put an arm around her. "What's wrong? Please, don't cry."

Sharon Lynn waved off the sympathy. "I'm okay. It's just…"

"It's just that she's never gotten this far before," Jenny said, coming over to envelop her in a hug. "It's only a little over a week and counting to the big day."

Sharon Lynn mopped at her eyes. "I'm actually beginning to believe it's going to happen this time." She turned to Patsy and said with mock severity, "As for you, you are a very sneaky lady. I had no idea what you were up to. No wonder you turned down my offer to go out for dinner."

"Thank goodness you didn't insist on it. I'm not sure what I would have come up with to get you over here. As for the rest, I didn't really do anything," Patsy said. "Jenny and Dani did all the planning and the work. I was just brought in at the last second to deliver you. I still think I ought to get Billy and go out to eat, while you all celebrate."

"Absolutely not," Dani said, joining them. "Besides, Justin already has Billy. The boy has my brother wound around his little finger. I believe they were going to stop at the toy store on the way to dinner. Justin saw a remote control police car in there he wanted to check out."

"Oh, dear," Patsy murmured. "Maybe I should—"

"You should relax and enjoy yourself," Jenny told her. "Let Justin spend a little of his money for a change. It'll do him good to hang out in a toy store. Maybe he'll rediscover the kid inside. He's not even thirty and already he's turned into a straitlaced old man."

"You've got that right," Sharon Lynn said. "When I think of how much mischief he and Harlan

Patrick used to get into, it's hard to believe it's the same person."

"Come on, ladies," an older woman with the same dark hair as Jenny said. "I'm starving and you know your grandfather will start worrying if I'm out too late. Next thing you know he'll use it as an excuse to come looking for me. As it is, he's very put out that he wasn't invited to the shower. Just give him the slightest excuse and he'll race into town."

"Maybe it would be worth it," Dani said with a wicked twinkle in her eyes. "I can just see Grandpa Harlan's expression when Sharon Lynn starts opening packages filled with slinky lingerie."

"If Mom's half the woman I know she is, it won't be anything he hasn't seen before," Jenny teased, bringing a blush to the older woman's cheeks.

"Patsy, have you met Janet yet?" Dani asked. "She's married to Grandpa Harlan and she claims to give him a run for his money, but as you just heard, the man has the original feminist in the family on a short leash."

Janet winked. "I just let him think that. Now that I've closed my law practice, I do my level best to drive him crazy. It's the only thing I have to look forward to."

Patsy regarded her intently. "You're a lawyer?"

"One of the best in the business," Jenny said proudly. "She was also a real activist for Native American rights. If you ever have a legal problem, you couldn't find anyone in town to give you better advice.''

Patsy tucked that piece of information away for another time. Could this woman with the wise face and kind eyes be the answer to her prayers? If she knew a lot about Native American affairs, wouldn't she also know if Patsy's position would be weakened in a custody battle because she wasn't Native American? The fear that tribal law would come into play had been nagging at her from the moment she decided to run. She had been terrified that that was the unspoken threat Will would use to take her baby away.

"Hey, why so solemn?" Jenny asked, studying her worriedly.

Patsy forced a smile. "Sorry. Don't let my mood spoil the party.''

"She and Justin had a little set-to earlier," Sharon Lynn explained.

"Oh, really?" Janet said, her expression thoughtful. "I haven't seen Justin riled up much. He's always been a pretty even-tempered guy.''

"Put him in a room with Patsy for ten minutes and watch the fireworks," Sharon Lynn suggested.

"Interesting," Janet said.

"Okay, enough of this. Forget Justin. He's just a man. Nothing is going to ruin this shower," Jenny said adamantly. "It's been too long coming, right, Sharon Lynn?''

"Way too long," Sharon Lynn replied fervently. She beckoned to Patsy. "Come with me. I hear there's a huge Tex-Mex buffet in the dining room and the word is that the housekeeper at White Pines made the food. Maritza's enchiladas are to die for.''

From that moment on, everyone made a deliberate effort to include Patsy in the celebration. By the time it was over, she had pushed aside the words she had exchanged with Justin and her worries over a custody battle for Billy. For a couple of hours, she actually managed to live in the moment. More than being accepted as a stranger in their midst, she felt as if she were part of this large extended family.

If only it were true, she thought wistfully as the last of them left. Surrounded by their strength, she was pretty sure she could face just about anything.

As she helped Sharon Lynn pile the last of the packages into the back of her car, Justin came up the walk, carrying a sleeping Billy in his arms. He grinned at Sharon Lynn.

''Looks like you picked up a lot of loot. Any sexy lingerie in there?''

''None that you'll ever see,'' Sharon Lynn told him. ''You find your own woman and your own sexy lingerie.''

Justin's gaze shifted instantly to Patsy. She could feel her cheeks burning as he studied her thoughtfully. To cover her rush of embarrassment, she reached for her son.

''I'll take Billy.''

''No need,'' Justin countered, his expression turning stubborn. "I'll carry him in to bed." He held out a huge sack. "You can take this, though."

She reached for the bag and almost dropped it. "What on earth?"

"Billy and I did a little shopping."

Remembering what Jenny had said earlier, she asked, "For yourself or for him?"

He grinned. "He's promised to let me come over and play with his new toys every now and then."

"Justin, you really shouldn't have."

"Of course I should. I haven't had so much fun in years. Wait till you see this really nifty police car. It even has a siren."

Sharon Lynn regarded him with amusement. "I thought you had your own police car with a siren."

The comment didn't seem to faze him. "Yeah, but Billy didn't," he said matter-of-factly.

As far as Patsy knew, Billy had never expressed any interest in having a remote control car. As Jenny had suggested earlier, she suspected the toy really was for Justin, bought under the guise of a gift. She hefted the bag, which weighed a ton.

"There's more than a car in here, isn't there?"

"We saw a basketball set that was pretty snazzy, too."

Patsy stared. "Basketball? Billy's two. It'll be a long time before he can even hold a basketball, much less play hoops with someone your size."

"This is a toddler basketball set. The net's only as

high as my waist and the ball weighs about five ounces. It's not exactly regulation.''

''I see. Anything else?''

''A surprise for you. Billy picked it out.''

''At the toy store?''

''Yep.''

Sharon Lynn regarded them both with tolerant amusement. ''Looks like it's your turn for surprises, Patsy. I'll just run along now and leave you to it.''

''Don't go,'' she said in a rush. She didn't want to be left alone with this man whose every action charmed her and reminded her of how long it had been since anyone at all had given a thought to what might make her happy.

''I have a long drive,'' Sharon Lynn said, ignoring the plea and getting into her car. ''See you two in the morning.'' She blew a kiss in Patsy's direction. ''Thanks again for everything.''

After she'd gone, Patsy seemed to be rooted to the spot. It was Justin who finally said, ''I think maybe I ought to get Billy into bed before he wakes up.''

Flustered, she murmured, ''Yes, of course.''

Inside, she followed him into Billy's room. She took off Billy's shoes and socks, then stripped off his shorts. She left his spaghetti-stained T-shirt on, fearful that removing it would awaken him. He settled onto his tummy, his thumb going instinctively into his mouth.

She glanced up and caught an odd expression on

Justin's face, something that might have been long-ing.

"He's a terrific kid," he said softly.

"He's the light of my life," she said. "I don't know what I'd ever do if something happened to him."

Justin's gaze shifted to her. "What could happen?"

Realizing that she'd almost given her very real fears away, she said, "You know, any of the million and one things that can happen to a kid."

Justin shook his head. "You sounded as if you had something very specific in mind," he said, seizing on her slip of the tongue.

"No," she protested. "Just the usual worries any parent has."

His piercing gaze was unrelenting. "Why don't I believe you?"

"Because not believing me has become second na-ture to you."

He continued to study her intently, then finally sighed and relaxed. "Okay, maybe my cop's instincts have been on overdrive since we met. I'll try to let up."

Patsy recognized it for the futile promise it was. Rather than debating it with him again, she poked at the bag she'd dropped on the floor. "Okay, where's my surprise?"

Justin picked up the sack and carried it into the living room. "Close your eyes."

She did as she was told and waited with as much

anticipation as she might have the promise of a kiss. Her heart skipped a beat. Her pulse pounded.

"Hold out your hands."

She held them out in front of her. A second later she felt something soft and fluffy being placed in her hands. She opened her eyes and saw a toy dog that looked so real she was certain it would begin to bark at any second. The terrier look-alike was caramel colored and had a pink tongue so real looking she expected him to lick her fingers.

"He's wonderful," she said, hugging him to her.

"Billy said you liked dogs. I figured I shouldn't try getting you a real one without discussing it with you, but this looked like the next best thing."

"He feels real," she said, running her fingers through the curling plush hair. "And look at these eyes. He's staring right at me."

"Have you ever had a dog?"

She shook her head. "My parents both worked. They didn't think it was right to leave a dog home alone all day." And Will hadn't wanted anything that might mess up the house and spoil his image if a reporter happened to drop by unexpectedly.

"You could have one now," Justin suggested.

She gestured toward the cats that were curled hither and yon in the living room. "What about them?"

"They're used to every kind of animal under the sun. Dani's a vet, remember? She's spent her whole life taking in every stray that wandered by. She might have one next door even as we speak."

"Several," she conceded, thinking of the cacophony of sound they'd set off earlier. She grinned. "There's always Punk."

"That's not a dog. That's a beast."

"He has his own home, anyway. His owners are due back any day now."

"You sound sad about it."

"I've gotten used to him. Punk and I have an understanding. I sneak him treats and he doesn't lick me to death."

Justin grinned. "See what I mean? You're a natural pet owner. Think about it," he encouraged.

Getting a dog of her own would make a statement of sorts, she realized, if only to herself. It would mean that she intended to stay right here, that she was beginning to put down roots. It would also finalize her decision never to return to Will.

"I'll think about it," she said, then stroked the toy dog in her lap. "In the meantime, Chester here will do just fine."

"Chester?"

She shrugged. "I have no idea why. The name just came to me."

He grinned. "Don't expect me to argue with divine inspiration." He stood and headed for the door, then paused. "I'm glad you like the surprise."

"I *love* the surprise," she said emphatically. It was the very best one she could remember.

With Sharon Lynn's wedding only a few days away, the burden for running Dolan's fell on Patsy's shoulders. She was grateful for the responsibility. It kept her so busy she didn't have time to think about how much longer she could continue with this charade before Justin found out the rest of the truth.

"You're sure you can handle things if I'm gone today?" Sharon Lynn asked for the umpteenth time.

"I can handle it," Patsy repeated, also for the umpteenth time.

"You remember how Mrs. Jenkins likes her eggs?"

"Scrambled moist," Patsy dutifully recited.

"And Tate prefers—"

"Rye toast, not plain."

"What about Doc Dolan?"

"He likes egg salad on white for lunch with a scoop of potato salad on the plate."

Sharon Lynn nodded. "Yes, perfect." She started for the door, then turned back. "I won't be back from Dallas before seven. I've got the fitting for the wedding dress, then a meeting with the florist and a late lunch with two of my bridesmaids, women I went to high school with who're living in Dallas now."

"I can close up," Patsy reassured her. "I'll leave the day's deposit in the night drop at the bank. You've shown me what to do."

"I know. I just hate dumping all this on you."

"You're not dumping anything on me. You told me, when you hired me, you were getting married and that I'd have extra work. Stop worrying and get going before you miss your final fitting.''

"Given the number of times Kyle and I almost made it to the altar in the past, you'd think I'd have this down to a science by now.''

"Well, this time's the charm. It's less than a week till the wedding and everything's going smoothly, right?''

"I suppose.''

Patsy studied her intently. "Sharon Lynn, is there something else worrying you?''

"Not really. I suppose it's just panic. There's been one crisis or another every time the wedding date got close. I'm afraid we're jinxed.''

"I don't believe in jinxes. Now go, before your uncle Jordan pitches a fit. He is flying you over, isn't he?''

"Yes, and you're right. He's always in a rush. I'll call you later just to see if anything's come up.''

"If you call, I'll be insulted.''

Sharon Lynn grinned. "Okay, okay.'' She paused to hug Patsy. "Thank you. You've been a godsend.''

"So have you,'' Patsy replied quietly. "More than you know.''

Sharon Lynn gave her an odd little look, but she let whatever questions she had die on her lips. Finally she smiled and said again, "Thanks.''

"Go.''

"Let me check—''

"Sharon Lynn!''

"Okay, I'm out of here."

Justin met her in the doorway. "It's a good thing," he said. "I just got a call from Dad. He's at the airport and he's getting really irritated. You were supposed to be there a half hour ago. He has a business meeting he's going to miss if you don't hit the road right this second."

"Why didn't he call me?"

"Because apparently your phone is dead or off the hook."

"Oh, my God," she murmured as the color drained from her face. She raced into the back room.

Patsy and Justin exchanged an amused look, then followed. They caught Sharon Lynn putting the receiver back into place.

"I laid it down to look for my wedding checklist while I was talking to Mom," she explained sheepishly. "I guess I got distracted."

Justin shook his head. "Which explains why I had a call from your mother, as well," he said with tolerant amusement. "Maybe I'd better drive you to the airport."

Sharon Lynn looked oddly relieved. "Would you? You're a doll."

Justin turned and winked at Patsy. "Remember that, would you?"

"No need," she said. "I already knew it."

He seemed startled by her reply. He hesitated as if there were something more on his mind, but Sharon Lynn clutched his arm and dragged him away.

"I'll be back," he promised. "And I won't forget what you said."

Patsy's heart skipped a beat. He was making far too big a thing out of a casual admission, she thought. Had she known he would? Was that why she'd said it?

Of course not, she consoled herself. It had just been a teasing response to his own deliberate taunt. It had been so long since she'd engaged in even the most innocent flirting, she'd forgotten that it could be taken seriously. She hadn't meant to light that fire in his eyes. Surely she hadn't meant to undo all she'd done to keep him at a distance. Justin had simply read too much into it.

The fact remained that he was going to be back here in no time and he was going to have expectations of one sort or another. And she was going to have to think of yet another lie to push him away, when all she really wanted was for him to sweep her into his arms and never let go.

Was that why she'd tempted fate just now? Had she wanted him to take the decision out of her hands at last? Had she deliberately prompted him into making a move so that she wouldn't have to hold herself accountable? Was that the kind of woman she'd become?

She was still debating with herself and not liking any of the answers she came up with, when a man with white hair and the impish grin of every Adams she'd ever run across walked in and sauntered up to the counter. He settled on a stool, then looked her over with blatant fascination.

"Can I help you?" she said, trying not to flinch under that penetrating scrutiny.

"That depends. Are you Patsy Gresham?"

She nodded.

"I'm Harlan Adams. Since no one's seen fit to bring you by the ranch to meet me, I figured it was up to me to perform the introductions. I'm Justin's granddaddy."

"Yes, sir."

His gaze never wavered. "And you're the woman who's managed to tie that boy into knots." Another grin broke across his face. "Congratulations!"

Patsy swallowed hard. "Sir, I don't know what you've heard, but I think you've got it all wrong. Justin and I are just friends. Acquaintances, really."

"Girl, I don't care what you call it, as long as you bring some joy into his life."

She was stunned by his analysis. "Actually, all I've brought into his life so far is aggravation," she said, to set the record straight.

He chuckled at that. "So much the better. Now I want you to come to White Pines for dinner tomorrow night. Bring that little one of yours, too. The place will be crawling with my grandbabies. One more won't make a bit of difference. In fact, the whole family will be there."

"Then won't I be out of place?"

"I invited you, didn't I? Besides, it's a little get-together in Sharon Lynn's honor. You belong there."

"Yes, but—"

He got off the stool and headed for the door. "Seven o'clock sharp. Maritza gets downright testy if her food gets cold."

He was gone before Patsy could argue. One thing his visit had proved, though. The Adams men were bossy as the very dickens and she was pretty sure most of them always got their own way. It was one more thing she needed to keep in mind when she was dealing with Justin.

Chapter Eight

Justin's day went from bad to worse. After he dropped Sharon Lynn off at the small local airport, he got a call about a prowler at the home of an elderly woman. More than likely it was her overly vivid imagination, but he couldn't ignore the call. Once Letty Jane got to talking, though, it took an act of God to get him away from the place. Literally.

A late morning thunderstorm rolled in with unexpected force, toppling a line of trees. Everyone vowed it hadn't been a twister, but Justin couldn't prove that by the damage the wind had done. It had upended a trailer on an acre of isolated property on the opposite side of town from Letty Jane's. He spent all day running to and fro, from one crisis to the next, never settling in one place long enough even to call Patsy and explain why he hadn't gotten back.

Not that she was likely to mind, he conceded. He'd seen the quick flaring of panic in her eyes when he'd promised to return. He'd known he was pushing again, but he hadn't been able to help it. There was something between them and he intended to do whatever it took to force her to admit she felt it, too.

After that, they could worry together about the consequences, assuming there was anything that needed worrying about.

Which he still didn't know, he reminded himself with a weary sigh.

As he drove back into town he told himself it was only natural to be going down Main Street just to see that all was right with his little world, even though a shortcut would have gotten him home more quickly. It didn't have anything at all to do with hoping to catch a glimpse of Patsy, either at Dolan's or at her own place.

Unfortunately, the drugstore was locked up tight, the only light the red glow of the exit sign inside the door. Patsy's was just as dark. He tried to tell himself it was just as well. He was exhausted and filthy. Even if she'd opened her arms and invited him in, he was too damned tired to do much about it. He satisfied himself with just knowing that she was all tucked in for the night.

He drove on to the sheriff's office. He could get a cup of coffee there, do his paperwork and head on home for a shower and a good night's sleep. Tomorrow would be soon enough to pursue things with Patsy. Tomorrow or the next day.

Or the day after that, if she had her way.

"My, my, you're a pretty sight," Tate Owens observed when Justin dragged into the station.

"Fortunately, you're not paying me according to my appearance," he retorted. "This is what happens when you slog around in a foot of mud for a few hours chasing down a woman's belongings."

"It surely was a mess out there," Tate agreed.

"I noticed you didn't linger long enough to muss the crease in your trousers," Justin commented good-naturedly. They both knew that Tate wasn't above getting filthy if there was a need for it. Today Justin had had things under control without his help.

Despite the jest, Tate's expression turned serious. "Becky called. Something came in over the wire she thought I ought to see."

A solemn note in Tate's voice alerted Justin that it was something he needed to see as well. "About Patsy Gresham?"

The sheriff nodded and handed over a flyer. "Her name's Longhorn," he said. "And she's got a husband over in Oklahoma who's been looking for her for a while now. Seems like she's been gone since just a little before she showed up here."

Justin stared blankly at the missing persons flyer. The picture was a family portrait—Patsy, Billy and a man who had to be her husband, Will Longhorn, according to the information at the bottom. For some reason that picture reminded him of a damned campaign poster. Even though the three of them were at some sort of outdoor picnic, there was a posed quality to it, a perfection to the lighting that suggested it had been taken by a professional, rather than some family member or a cooperative stranger.

"They look happy enough, don't they?" Tate said, his tone gentle.

Justin told himself it was his boss's tone, the hint of pity, that made him want to start throwing things. It had nothing to do with the gut-sick feeling in the pit of his stomach at the sight of Patsy with another man.

"You going to talk to her about this or am I?" Tate asked.

Justin stared at him in surprise. "You haven't reported her to the Oklahoma authorities yet?"

"Hell, no," Tate declared. "I figure she's a grown-up woman. If she's here, instead of there, there must be a reason for it. I'm not turning her over to them until I know a hell of a lot more than I do right now. You see anything on there about a crime? No. She's just a missing person. And while I think her family probably has a right to know she's safe, I don't think it's my place to go about giving her away until I hear her side of it." His gaze was steady. "Or until you do."

"I'll talk to her," Justin said, his heart aching. The poster in his hands was proof that Patsy Gresham—

Patsy Longhorn—was more out of his reach than ever. "How much time do I have?"

"I can bury that poster on my desk. Given the amount of paperwork piled up, it could take me a mighty long time to find it again. On the other hand, my conscience says a week at the outside."

Justin nodded. It was more than he'd hoped for. "I'll get the answers we need," he said grimly. "You can count on it."

Patsy had never met anyone like the Adams clan. They stuck together. And while there seemed to be a whole crowd of them, there was always room for a stranger in their midst.

The dinner she'd been invited to at White Pines had been a revelation. Harlan Adams's ranch was bigger by far than the ostentatious house Will had insisted they buy, yet White Pines was a home. There was no mistaking the warmth and love in every single room.

To her amazement, though, there had been no sign of Justin by dinnertime. No one had made excuses for him, either. When he'd appeared just in time for dessert, everyone had accepted his arrival without question.

If he'd been surprised to see her, he hadn't shown it. But he'd also seemed to be avoiding her the past few days, making her wonder if he was angry about her inclusion in the family event. Maybe she'd misread his intentions toward her, or maybe they'd just changed.

It was obvious he'd been startled again today when she'd walked into the wedding reception for Sharon Lynn. She hadn't made it to the church, because she'd filled in at Dolan's in the morning so everyone else could go to the service. But Sharon Lynn and Doc Dolan had insisted she close up and come to the reception. Neither of them had taken no for an answer.

"I intend to toss my bouquet straight at you, so you'd better be prepared," Sharon Lynn had told her.

The teasing remark had brought tears and a fresh bout of guilt she hadn't been able to explain.

The dance music was just starting when she walked into the huge tent that had been set up on the lawn at the ranch. Justin had been laughing with his cousins, but the laughter had died when he'd spotted her. This time, though, it seemed he didn't intend to avoid her. He made his way across the room and ended up at her side.

"What a wonderful party," she said, forcing a smile to go along with the lighthearted small talk. "Sharon Lynn looks radiant. And Kyle looks dazed."

"I don't think he can believe it's finally happened. It took them a long time to make this trip down the aisle. They deserve to be happy." His gaze locked with hers. "Everyone does."

She sensed at once that there was a deeper meaning behind his words, but for the life of her she couldn't imagine what it was. There was a vague hint of the old suspicion, the old caution, back in his expression, too.

Rather than ignoring the undercurrents as she once would have done, she addressed them directly. "Justin, are you upset that I came?"

He looked vaguely guilty at the pointed question. "No, of course not."

"Are you sure? I know there's nothing between us."

"Not for lack of trying on my part," he said.

She persisted, determined to apologize for intruding where she didn't belong. "I'm sorry if finding me at all these family functions the past few days is making you uncomfortable. Your grandfather and Sharon Lynn, they insisted I come."

"I'm sure," he said ruefully. He shook his head. "No, I'm the one who should be apologizing. We're a family of meddlers. With Sharon Lynn married off tonight, I'm the next logical target. Next week or next month it'll be Harlan Patrick's turn. I'm sorry you got caught in the cross fire."

"I don't mind," she confessed with a catch in her voice, uncertain what sort of reaction the admission might draw.

He regarded her with surprise. "Really? Now that is a change."

"It's true."

In fact, if the truth were known, she liked being linked to this strong, decent man whose temper never seemed to get the better of him. She'd seen his patience tested to the limits—by her, in fact—but he'd never once raised his voice. It was a welcome relief after Will.

If things were different, if she were free, a man like Justin Adams would be the kind of man she'd like in her life.

If she were free...

But she wasn't, and because she wasn't, she turned and hurried away, ignoring Justin's commands for her to stop. She didn't slow until she was locked in a bathroom upstairs, far from the crowd of well-wishers.

She should leave, not just White Pines, but Los Piños. There was something different about Justin tonight, something that warned her away, told her that she'd stayed too long, tempting fate.

But if she took even a second to look into her heart, she knew that no matter the consequences, she couldn't go. The time for running was over.

"Getting any ideas, son?" Grandpa Harlan asked Justin as Sharon Lynn and Kyle moved into each other's arms for the first dance at the reception.

The question's timing couldn't have been worse, because he was getting ideas, had had them for a long time now, but he now knew for a fact they would never be. That poster on Tate's desk was evidence of that. Patsy belonged to another man. He'd guessed it weeks ago, but the proof had torn him apart.

"Don't you start, old man," he said, trying to take the sting out of his words.

His grandfather was made of hearty stuff. The order didn't faze him.

"I've seen the way you look at that pretty little gal from Oklahoma," he said, casting a sly look across the room to where Patsy was standing all alone. "You've got a thing for her. Why not admit it?"

Justin sighed. "Because there are things you don't know, Grandpa Harlan, things I'm not even sure about. Seems like we just weren't meant to be."

"Such as?"

Justin hesitated, then decided that his grandfather might be the one person on earth who could give him the kind of levelheaded advice he desperately needed right now. "I think she's on the run."

His grandfather took that news in stride. "From the law?" he demanded indignantly. "I don't believe it. If that girl's some sort of criminal, then I'm no judge of character."

"Maybe not from the law," Justin conceded. "More likely from a man, possibly her husband."

That did raise his grandfather's eyebrows ever so slightly. "She's married? You know that for a fact?"

There was the missing persons report, but that was only one side of the story, just as Tate had suggested. "Not exactly," he said eventually.

"Well, if you suspect it's the case, why the dickens haven't you asked her? From what I've seen, both of you have a lot riding on the truth."

"I'm not sure she'd tell me the truth," Justin admitted. "I see how skittish she is around me whenever I'm wearing my uniform. Tate flat out terrifies her. If she's going to open up, it might not be to one of us."

What if she knew about the poster, guessed they'd seen it? he wondered. Would she run again? Was she that desperate to get away from her husband? He sighed. He couldn't get into that with his grandfather. He'd probably told him more than he should as it was.

"I keep hoping she'll explain on her own and let me help."

His grandfather regarded him with sympathy. "I think I see the position you're in. There's your duty as a sworn lawman. And, then, there's your duty to a woman you care about."

"Which one's more important?" Justin asked, aware that the question sounded a little plaintive. "I always thought for sure I knew. The law's the law."

"It's a delicate balancing act, all right," his grandfather said. "Maybe there's a way for both to be the same."

"How?"

"You won't know until you know all the truth. Talk to her, son. Do it now, tonight, before your courage fails you and before the answers can cut too deep."

"Too late for that," Justin said. "I'm already in way over my head."

"Then you'll find a way to make things right," his

grandfather said with absolute confidence. "For both of you."

"I hope you're right."

"Well, of course I am," his grandfather said with exaggerated indignation. "You don't get to be my age without learning a thing or two. Now, go along. Talk to her. Unless I miss my guess, she's as torn up inside as you are."

Justin knew his grandfather was right. There was no way around it. This was one time he couldn't afford to be endlessly patient. Lives and futures were at stake. Patsy's and Billy's, maybe. His own for sure.

He weaved through the crowd, his gaze locked on the woman who stood all alone on the fringes. She looked more fragile than ever in a pale blue slip dress that skimmed over her body in a silken caress. The dress was the epitome of costly simplicity. It practically had designer stamped all over it. The cop in him had wanted to check for a label and demand explanations once again for the inconsistencies in her lifestyle. The man simply wanted to slide it over her head and run callused hands over the woman beneath.

If he listened to the throbbing in his veins, that dress would be merely an inconvenience. If he listened to his head, he would escort her somewhere very public for the conversation that had been too long coming. By the time he reached her side, he still wasn't sure which side had won the mental debate.

"Everything okay?" he asked, his tone cautious.

"Of course," she said, a little too brightly.

"Where'd you run off to?"

"The ladies' room."

"I thought maybe you were running away?"

Alarm flared in her eyes, but she quickly hid it. "From what?"

"Me."

"You don't scare me."

"I should."

"Why?"

"Because I want you."

She swallowed hard at the bold assertion. "I know."

"Any objections?"

Her hesitation—combined with the pure desire written all over her face—was enough to tell him as much as he needed to know. She wanted him all right, but she was going to do the honorable thing—the *wifely* thing—and say yes. She was going to tell him to take a hike.

Before she could say anything, he said quietly, "Let's go somewhere for coffee."

She blinked in surprise. "Coffee?"

"Don't argue. You don't want the alternative."

Her gaze locked with his. "I didn't say that."

His smile was forced. "You didn't have to. Come on, darlin', before I change my mind. Sharon Lynn and Kyle will be leaving any minute now, anyway."

Before she could object, he clasped her hand and dragged her along behind him, nodding politely to everyone they passed. It was a neat trick to get away from White Pines without being subjected to a million and one questions, but he managed it.

As he headed for his car, Patsy began to voice her first objection. "My car—"

He refused to relinquish his grip on her. "I'll have someone drive it into town in the morning."

Only after they were in his car with the radio playing at top volume to drown out any need for conversation did she speak again. Raising her voice to be heard, she asked, "Justin, what's going on?"

"We'll talk when we get into town."

"What's wrong with here?"

"I can't concentrate on you and the road at the same time."

He thought he caught the beginnings of a smile at that.

"Ever heard of small talk?"

"That's the last thing I want to engage in with you." To make his point, he reached for the volume and turned it up another notch. Now there was nothing in the car but the sound of George Strait and a sizzling tension for which there would be no relief.

In town, he parked in front of the Italian restaurant, knowing that it would be virtually empty at this hour, especially with half the folks in town out at White Pines at the wedding reception. The coffee was strong enough to keep them both wide-awake until they'd hashed this mess through from beginning to end.

He led the way to a booth with Patsy trailing along behind, silently fuming. He could practically feel the anger radiating from her. He couldn't say he blamed her, but he wasn't exactly dancing with joy tonight himself.

"Two coffees," he told the waitress in a tone that warned her not to linger.

"Sure, Justin." She left without asking about the wedding, returned with two cups and a whole pot of coffee, then retreated all the way into the kitchen.

"Look," Patsy began, scowling at him, "I don't know what has you in such a snit tonight, but you don't have any business taking it out on her, or on me, for that matter."

Justin sighed. "You're right."

"Then what's this all about?"

He looked into her eyes and saw the beginnings of wariness again. "Same old thing," he said, trying to make light of it.

"You think I'm hiding something."

"I *know* you're hiding something," he corrected.

She began twisting the napkin she was holding into a tight knot. She looked everywhere in the restaurant except at him. When the napkin shredded, she stared at it in dismay.

"Patsy, please, can't you tell me the truth after all this time? Maybe I can help."

The tears welling up in her eyes were almost his undoing. He wanted to take back all the questions. He wanted to promise that he would never pry into her past again, but it was too late for that. If he didn't, Tate would. It was better if he did it, if the truth was something shared between them, instead of a barrier they could never overcome.

"You can't," she whispered finally. "You can't help."

"I can try."

She shook her head. "This isn't the kind of problem you can fix with a screwdriver or even a hankie," she said, accepting the one he offered with a rueful smile.

"Neither of us will really know that until you tell me." He looked directly into her eyes then, willing her to begin at the beginning and tell him everything.

She opened her mouth, about to speak, when his beeper went off. He ignored it, but it went off again and then again.

"Damn," he muttered. "I've got to call the station. I'll be back in a second."

Relief washed over her face at the reprieve.

"I will be back, though, and we will finish this conversation," he vowed as he went toward the pay phone to call the station.

Justin quickly placed a call to the station. "Justin, I'm sorry to call you, but I thought you'd want to know," the late-night dispatcher said.

"What? Couldn't it wait until morning?" he asked impatiently.

"There's been an accident on the highway coming into town from White Pines. It's Sharon Lynn and Kyle."

Cold dread settled in the pit of his stomach. "Are they okay?"

"It's bad, Justin. Real bad. I think you'd better get out there."

He slammed the phone down and walked slowly back to the table. "I have to go," he said, his voice cracking on a sob he hadn't even known was bottled up inside.

Patsy jumped up and followed him. "Justin? What is it? You're white as a ghost."

"An accident," he said. "Sharon Lynn and Kyle."

All of the color drained out of her face, too. "I'm coming with you."

"No. There's no need. I can drop you at your place."

Her chin shot up. "I'm coming with you," she repeated. "Are you going to waste time standing here arguing?"

He realized then how desperately he wanted her with him, how very badly he would need her to hang on to if the news was as grim as the dispatcher had made it sound.

"Buckle up, then," he said grimly as she climbed into the car and shot him a look that dared him to argue.

"You won't help anyone by getting killed en route," she said softly as he took the corner on two wheels and shot down Main Street.

He slowed, but only to the point of reason and well in excess of the speed limit. He'd done enough training and high-speed chases to know precisely what his own limits were on the road. He drove with total concentration, allowing his mind to wander only long enough to utter a few fervent prayers that Sharon Lynn and her new husband would be all right.

What in God's name had happened? Kyle was a good driver, the roads were practically deserted this time of night and he'd bet the ranch that neither of them had had more than a glass of champagne during the reception.

"I see the flashing lights up ahead," Patsy murmured, fear in her voice. "It looks as if there's a lot of them."

"That just means they're getting all the help they need. Nothing to panic over." He said it as much for his own benefit as hers.

They arrived just as an ambulance sped off toward Garden City in the opposite direction, siren blaring. There were two more on the scene and paramedics seemed to be everywhere, most of them volunteers who'd come scrambling in pickups, lights flashing on their dashboards and casting an eerie glow in the dark.

A huge spotlight was shining on the twisted wreckage of Kyle's car, guiding him through the maze of rescue vehicles, police cars and ambulances. One glimpse was enough to make Justin want to retch. He heard Patsy's gasp beside him at the sight of the crushed passenger compartment.

"Get back into the car," he said. "There's nothing you can do to help. I'll find out what's happening."

"Sharon Lynn," she began in a whisper every bit as tormented as his own thoughts.

"Shh, don't think the worst. Let me get some answers."

He herded her back toward his car, then moved again through the tangle of debris and people. He saw the expressions of sympathy and knew then that the news wasn't going to be good.

Swallowing hard, he forced himself to face the deputy in charge. "My cousin," he began. It was all he could say without falling apart.

"Sharon Lynn's badly injured, but she's going to make it," Dusty assured him. "She's unconscious, but her vital signs were good. She's already on her way to the hospital."

Justin's gaze was drawn back to the collapsed mass of metal on the passenger side. "But how?"

"She was driving," Dusty said succinctly. "The air bag saved her. Kyle took the brunt of the impact." He looked as if he wanted to cry, too. "He...he wasn't so lucky, Justin. There was a faint pulse when we got here, but we couldn't get him out in time to save him. The guys did everything they could."

Justin felt the world begin to spin. Sheer will kept him upright. "Do you know what happened?"

"A drunk crossed the center line. It looked as if Sharon Lynn tried to get out of his way, but with no shoulders and those deep ditches, there was no place to go."

"Is he dead?"

Dusty looked startled that he cared. "The drunk driver?"

Justin nodded.

"No, he's over there. Some minor cuts and bruises. He'll walk away."

Pure rage made Justin see red. He turned in the direction the deputy had indicated, ignoring Dusty's commands to stop, to let it go. He had to see for himself, had to look into the face of the man who'd murdered his cousin's husband, who'd almost killed her, as well.

And then he might very well beat that face into a bloody pulp.

Chapter Nine

Patsy saw Justin walking toward the side of the highway. There was something about his jerky, dazed progress that brought her scrambling from the car and heading straight for him. She reached him just as a deputy she recognized as Dusty Patterson got to his side and clamped a hand on his shoulder.

"Get away from me," Justin demanded, his voice like ice.

"Don't do this," Dusty pleaded. "You're not thinking straight."

Anger radiated from Justin in palpable waves. Even without knowing what was going on, Patsy sensed that he was about to do something he would come to regret. Instinctively she stepped in front of the two men.

"Justin?"

When he didn't even glance at her, she spoke his name again, more sharply this time. As if he'd been drawn out of some distant hell, his gaze finally shifted to clash with hers. The sight of the tears streaking down his cheeks was almost her undoing. There was no doubt in her mind now that something truly terrible had happened to Sharon Lynn and Kyle. What else could create such despair in such a strong man?

She reached up and touched his face. "Come with me, please," she begged.

For the longest time, she wasn't sure he would agree. He seemed torn between anger and a distress so deep and heart wrenching, she could only fear its cause. At last, he turned away and went with her.

He got into the car and leaned forward, his head resting on the steering wheel. Quiet sobs shook his shoulders. Patsy scrambled across the seat and put her arms around him. As desperately as she wanted to know what had happened, how badly Kyle and Sharon Lynn were injured, she kept silent, letting Justin do his grieving in silence while she fought her own fears.

It seemed they remained like that forever, but in truth it was no more than a minute or two, she realized, before he drew in a shuddering breath and faced her.

"We have to go to the hospital."

"Sharon Lynn and Kyle are there?"

He shook his head. "Only Sharon Lynn."

The implication of that tore through her. "Oh, my God. Kyle?"

"Didn't make it." He looked so shattered that all she wanted to do was reach over and hold him again, but he was already starting the engine. The grim set of his mouth told her he wouldn't appreciate a show of sympathy right now, that he'd only tolerated the first display because he'd been nearly oblivious to it. All she could do was stay with him, be there when he needed someone and be there for Sharon Lynn, whose world had just come crashing down around her head. She thought of Sharon Lynn's terrible premonition that her future with Kyle was jinxed and realized the enormity of what lay ahead for her.

At the hospital, they found the rest of the family already gathered, most of them still in the clothes they'd worn to the wedding. Patsy faded into the background once she was certain that Justin was being taken care of by his family.

She wandered from the emergency room waiting area and went in search of a chapel. When she found it off the main lobby, she went inside and found Janet Adams already there, her face damp with tears.

Patsy started to tiptoe out again, but the older woman spotted her and held out her hand. "Come, sit with me. I just came to tell God how grateful we are for sparing Sharon Lynn."

"What about how angry we are that Kyle was taken from her?" Patsy asked, unable to hide her own bitterness on her friend's behalf. "How could this happen to someone as decent and kind as Sharon Lynn?"

"God never gives us any pain he doesn't think will make us stronger."

Patsy wondered about that. Then she thought of her own life up until now. When she'd been caught up in Will's web of snide remarks and psychological abuse, she'd thought only about the terrible sense of failure he was instilling in her. When she'd run, she'd felt more like a victim than ever and she'd cursed him for that, hating him every bit as much as if he'd hit her.

But she was stronger now and her strength had come out of that pain. Would the same be true for Sharon Lynn? She could only pray that Janet was right.

They sat quietly side by side, lost in their own thoughts, taking comfort from each other's presence. It was a long time before she looked up and saw Justin standing hesitantly in the doorway. "I heard this was where you'd gone," he said, still not coming into the quiet, dimly lit chapel.

Janet regarded him with sympathy. "I'm sorry you had to be there tonight. It must have been terrible for you."

Anger flashed in his eyes. "I'm not the one who needs your pity. Save it for Sharon Lynn. I only wish I could have killed the man responsible when I had the chance."

"You don't mean that," Janet said gently. "The

courts will hand down justice. It wasn't up to you. You know that's the way it has to be."

"Do I?" he asked bitterly. His gaze shifted to Patsy. "There's nothing more we can do here tonight. I'll take you home."

She nodded and squeezed Janet's hand. "Thank you for what you said. It meant a lot to me. If there's anything I can do for any of you, let me know."

Janet glanced toward the doorway. "Stay with Justin," she said, her expression worried. "He's going to need you. You heard him just now. This doesn't fit with his sense of justice at all. It won't be easy for him to reconcile it." She sighed. "If I'm being totally honest, no matter what I said before, even I know it won't be easy for any of us."

The next few days went by in a terrible haze. Patsy did the only thing she could think of to do that might help. She kept the lunch counter at Dolan's running smoothly from dawn to dusk. The news on Sharon Lynn was more positive each day and by the beginning of the following week she had been released from the hospital. Patsy went to visit her at the ranch, where the whole family was hovering over her. When she went into Sharon Lynn's room, she was horrified by what she found.

Though Sharon Lynn's injuries were healing nicely and the bruises had begun to fade, she was lying in bed staring dully at the ceiling. When Patsy had walked into the room, her friend had not even glanced in her direction.

"Hey," Patsy said softly. "I'm so relieved to see you safe at home again."

Sharon Lynn nodded, her expression blank. "Thanks," she murmured with no emotion in her voice at all.

"Everyone at Dolan's misses you like crazy. They're asking when you'll be back."

No response. Patsy tried again.

"What is the doctor saying about getting back on your feet again?"

"Not much."

Patsy didn't know too much about clinical depression, but it seemed to her that Sharon Lynn was sinking into the kind of dark despair that needed quick attention. She wondered if anyone had broached the subject with her, then wondered if she dared do it herself. She was still debating whether she had any right or even an obligation to say something, when Sharon Lynn spoke.

"I killed him, you know." She whispered it matter-of-factly.

Patsy reacted angrily. "Don't be absurd. Kyle was killed by a drunk driver. Don't you ever think otherwise."

"But I was driving our car. I should have done…" Her voice trailed off before she finally added forlornly, "Something. I should have done something."

Patsy reached for her hand. It was ice-cold and

limp. "There was nothing you could have done, no place you could turn," she insisted. "The road's narrow, and there are deep ditches on either side. The only person responsible for this tragedy was the other driver."

The door to the room opened just as she spoke.

"Damn right!" Justin said fiercely. He came over to the bed and reached down for Sharon Lynn's hand. "Don't you dare blame yourself. The slime who did this should be locked up for a long, long time. The sheriff will see that he is."

Sharon Lynn retreated visibly, staring back up at the ceiling again, her expression blank. Patsy beckoned to Justin and led him from the room. It was the first time she'd seen him in days as well. He looked only marginally better than his cousin. She wanted to throw her arms around him and hold him. It was a strange feeling to think of herself as the strong one after so many years of believing herself to be weak.

"Are you okay?" she asked quietly.

A ghost of a smile came and went. "Better now that I've seen you."

"You don't look as if you've slept a wink in days."

"You mean I'm not as handsome as ever?" he asked, a twinkle bringing a momentary light to his eyes.

"Oh, you'll always be handsome enough, Justin Adams, but right now you're pale and drawn. Haven't you been eating? You haven't been by Dolan's since this happened."

He did smile at that. "Did you miss me?"

"Of course not. I just worried that the thieves were going to start getting ideas now that there hasn't been a lawman parked at the counter for days."

"So it's my badge you've been missing," he teased. "I'm surprised. I always had the feeling it made you nervous."

Patsy's pulse thudded dully at the taunt. It was too close to being squarely on the mark.

"I don't hear you denying it," he said.

"Because it's so ridiculous it doesn't deserve a reply," she said, trying to brazen it out. She met his gaze unblinkingly.

Eventually he grinned. "If you say so, darlin'."

"Can we talk about Sharon Lynn for a minute?" she asked.

She knew it was a topic that would fully capture his attention and get the glare of the spotlight off her for a bit. As she'd anticipated, a worried frown creased his brow.

"What about her?"

"I think maybe she's going to need some help getting through this."

"She's getting help. We're all here. All she has to do is say the word and any one of us will get her whatever she needs."

"I'm not talking about soup or some custard when

she says she's hungry. I'm talking about professional help.''

''A shrink?''

She nodded.

''That's crazy,'' he said indignantly. ''Anyone would be upset after a tragedy like this. Sharon Lynn's strong. She's an Adams. She'll pull herself together in time.''

Patsy was doubtful. ''Will she? She's eaten up with guilt. She told me she killed Kyle. You heard her yourself.''

''That's the grief talking. She'll put this into perspective. Once the other driver is convicted and locked away, she'll see it wasn't her fault.''

Patsy remained silent in response. Finally Justin said, ''You don't believe that, do you?''

''No, I don't. There's something about the way she's staring off into space, as if she's slowly disconnecting from the world. It worries me. Maybe it's just grief, but it seems to me it goes deeper than that. It's not just that she's lost Kyle.'' She struggled to put it into words. ''It's as if she's lost her reason for living.''

''And you got all that from a five-minute visit?'' Justin asked, his expression incredulous.

Patsy refused to back down, even in the face of his blatant skepticism. ''Okay, it's just my opinion and I'm not an expert. I'm just saying an expert would be able to say once and for all if she needs some counseling. Don't trust my judgment, just ask yourself if you want to take the chance that I'm right.''

Justin sighed and ran his fingers through his close-cropped hair. ''Hell, I suppose you could be right. It's just that Adamses solve their own problems.''

''Sometimes the solution is asking for help,'' Patsy said.

''I'll mention it to the family and see what they think,'' Justin promised. He reached over and tucked a stray curl behind her ear. ''By the way, has anyone thanked you for pitching in and taking over at Dolan's?''

''I don't need to be thanked. It's my job. Dani's staff has been great about helping with Billy so I could be there longer hours.''

''Don't work yourself to a frazzle,'' he warned. ''You need to look after yourself, too.''

She gazed into his eyes and saw genuine concern there. It was the first time in as long as she could remember that anyone had been truly worried about her well-being. It had mattered to Will only as far as her ability to campaign on his behalf.

''I'm fine,'' she reassured Justin. ''But I'd better be getting back into town. With the hours I'm putting in at Dolan's, I don't like to leave Billy with a sitter in the evenings, too.''

''Mind if I come along?'' Justin asked. ''I promised him I'd be by to play with those toys we bought. I haven't had a chance up until now. Frankly, I could use a break from all this.''

"He'd like that."

"And you? Would you like that, too?"

She knew what he was really asking, but she wasn't sure she entirely trusted his motives. Did it really matter to him whether she was beginning to care for him or was he simply trying to test her again? Even though it had been days since their last talk and despite all that had happened, she doubted Justin had forgotten all the questions he had about her past.

"Of course," she said cheerily. "If you haven't eaten yet, you can share a pizza with us."

"Why don't I pick it up on my way and meet you at the house?"

"I can do it."

"Why should you when I can and you can get home to Billy that much sooner?"

She grinned. "Okay, when you put it like that, how can I argue? But I insist on paying for it."

"We'll discuss that later."

"Justin!" She took a twenty from her purse and tried to press it into his hands. He jammed his hands into his pockets and defied her to follow with the money. She was tempted to do just that, but the prospect of finding her own hand trapped between his and his body with only a layer of denim in between rattled her too badly. That jittery temptation was proof enough that she had no business getting in any kind of intimate contact with him.

She sighed. "Okay, you win. We'll discuss it later."

He grinned. "It's nice to see that you can compromise."

"Is that what you call it?"

"Sure, darlin'. I have it on the best authority that compromise is very important in any relationship."

Patsy didn't know whether to cheer or turn tail and run at the mention of the word *relationship*. She and Justin weren't having a relationship. It was impossible.

But, oh, how she wished it weren't.

"Patsy?"

Startled, she glanced up and met Justin's worried frown.

"Everything okay?"

"Sure," she lied. "Just trying to remember how big a mess the house is in. I'd hate for you to walk in and wonder if a tornado blew through. After all, it is your sister's place. I'd hate to have her evict me."

"There's no chance of that," he assured her. "And don't worry about the state of your housekeeping. With all the nieces and nephews running around in this family, no one knows the meaning of tidy anymore."

"Not even you? You live alone and, as I recall, your place was spotless the one time I came over."

"That's because I'm never there. And it's not tidy. It's sterile. Give me chaos any day. It's what makes the difference between a house and a home."

"Maybe I should let Billy come and visit for an

afternoon. The resulting mess ought to send you into raptures.''

''I'd love it,'' he said, much to her amazement. ''In the meantime, let's get into town. Suddenly I'm starved for the first time in days.''

The gleam in his eyes was a reminder that food was not the only thing a man could be starved for. Patsy was drawn to that look, wanted desperately to respond to it, but decency prevented it.

She had the whole long drive into town to wonder how long she could allow this marital limbo to drag on. It was unfair to Billy and to her. Maybe even to Will. Most of all, though, it was unfair to Justin, because he didn't even know what he was up against.

How was she going to resolve it? Could she simply file for divorce long-distance and pray that Will went along with it? Thinking he would was a foolish idea. He was a very possessive man. Even though she knew he no longer loved her—if he ever had—he would fight the divorce if only because he would fear the damage to his image if he let her go. He would demand custody of Billy for the same reason.

Her feet were dragging as she walked into the house, not just from exhaustion, but from despair. How could she ever truly move on with her life, build a real future for herself and her son, unless she resolved things with Will? She'd been crazy to think that simply running away would solve all of her problems. It had removed her and Billy from harm's way, but it had created a whole new set of problems.

Still the thought of seeing Will again under any circumstances terrified her. She had weathered a lot in the past couple of months. She was far stronger than she'd been when she'd run from Oklahoma, but was she strong enough for the battle that was likely to ensue?

Before she could reach any conclusion at all about that, Billy came running toward her, arms held high, a piece of paper clutched in one tiny hand.

"Mama, Mama, Mama," he chanted. "Me drew picture for you. See?"

She took the paper and looked at the colorful scribbles. They were meaningless to her, but clearly not to her son. She hunkered down beside him. "This is beautiful," she said admiringly. "Tell me about it."

"I drewed us. We're a family. See?" He pointed to the littlest batch of swirls and lines. "That's me. And that's you."

"Ah," she said, seeing the relative difference in sizes, if not the identifying details. "And this?"

"That's Daddy." There was a mulish lift to his chin when he said it, then added, "Want to see Daddy."

"Daddy's far away," she reminded him.

"Want to see him."

"Maybe we can call him later."

"Now," Billy demanded. "Call now."

Patsy sighed. She had promised him days ago that they would call his daddy, but there had never been time to take a trip to some out-of-the-way pay phone that couldn't be traced. Obviously she would have to make the time.

"Tomorrow," she promised. She would get one of the women who'd volunteered to help out at Dolan's in Sharon Lynn's absence to fill in long enough for her to take Billy to make the phone call. "Now why don't we get you cleaned up? Justin's coming over and he's bringing pizza."

The mention of his favorite food—to say nothing of his favorite grown-up playmate—was enough to distract him. She went into the living room where Flo Bartle was waiting. Flo lived next door and, since the accident, had taken over baby-sitting duty when Dani's staff left for the day.

"Flo, I can't thank you enough for looking out for Billy for me."

"No problem. He's an angel. You do whatever you need to do to help out Sharon Lynn. There are plenty of us who can pitch in and help with Billy. All I'd be doing at home is watching my husband snooze through the national news. Believe me, I'd rather be here."

"Justin's bringing a pizza by. Would you like to stay?"

"No, indeed. I'd have heartburn the rest of the night." She winked. "Besides, I doubt Justin's coming by so he can look at an old lady across the table."

"It would be fine," Patsy insisted. "Justin and I are just friends."

"If you say so, dear. Just remember there are friends and then there are *friends*."

"Hey, Mrs. B.," Justin called out as he came up the walk carrying a huge pizza box. "You get more beautiful every time I see you."

"Then your eyesight's going, boy, or else you're as full of blarney as every other male in your family."

He dropped a kiss on her cheek. "I'm a deputy sheriff, Mrs. B. I'm sworn to uphold the law and to tell the truth, so help me God."

The teasing comment put a sparkle in her neighbor's eyes, but it sent a shiver down Patsy's spine. Once again she'd been reminded of the position she'd been putting Justin in since the day they'd met. It had to stop.

Tomorrow, she vowed to herself as she had to Billy earlier. Tomorrow, when she called Will, she would test the waters and see if there was any way to put an end to all the lies and deception or whether she was doomed to a life in limbo.

Chapter Ten

It was the first time since the night of the accident that Justin had let himself relax. He was stretched out on the floor in Patsy's living room, his back braced against the sofa, the empty pizza box off to one side, as he watched Billy struggle to build a tower with a new set of blocks.

One block, two, then eventually six, stacked in a way that virtually assured disaster. With awkward fingers Billy tried to put the seventh block on top, only to set the whole stack to teetering dangerously. Justin reached over and steadied it, but balance was elusive. It toppled over, sending Billy into fits of giggles.

"Again," he insisted, putting the first block into place.

"Maybe it needs a bigger base," Justin suggested idly.

"What's a base?" Billy demanded.

"More blocks on the bottom." He reached over and set four of the colorful plastic blocks into a square, then stacked two on top of that. "See, like this."

"Won't fall down?" Billy asked skeptically.

"Nope."

"'Kay," Billy agreed, and added another block to the pile, then another.

When it all teetered and fell again, he stared at it with a look of such betrayal in his eyes that Justin felt like a heel. This time tears, rather than giggles, accompanied the architectural disaster.

"Maybe I'm not as good an engineer as I thought," he apologized.

"Or maybe your work crew isn't past the apprentice stage yet," Patsy suggested, grinning at them. "It's Billy's bedtime, anyway."

"No," Billy said at once, even though his eyelids had been drooping for the past half hour.

"I'll put you to bed and tell you a story," Justin offered.

Billy's eyes widened. "You will?"

"Indeed, I will. I'll tell you the story about a girl named Little Red Riding Hood and this big, bad wolf."

"No. Want rabbit story."

Justin shrugged. "Then the rabbit story it will be,

but I gotta tell you, kid, the big, bad wolf is much more of a guy thing.''

"He might be a little young for guy things," Patsy said, her expression amused. "And you won't be the one left to deal with the nightmares."

"Okay, Mom. I bow to your superior knowledge on the subject," he said, scooping Billy up and tickling him until he giggled. The sound was pure delight, so he kept it up. It reminded him of things like innocence and simple pleasures. It reminded him of all the things he wanted and that were out of reach.

"You realize, of course, that if you do that much more he'll never get to sleep," Patsy observed.

Justin shook his head and gave Billy a sympathetic look. "Moms just don't get it, do they?"

Billy shook his head. "Don't get it."

He carried Billy into his room and helped him into his pj's, then settled him in bed. He'd done the same thing a hundred times with his nieces and nephews, but there was something different about putting Billy to bed. The kids in his family all had adoring dads of their own. He was just a welcome variance in their routine. With Billy he sensed that having a man put him to bed was a whole new experience. He seemed wide-eyed that Justin would want to, and pitifully eager to prolong the storytelling as long as possible.

"Read it again," he begged, even though he could barely hold his eyes open after the second time.

"Close your eyes and go to sleep," Justin countered. "I'll read for five more minutes, but you'd better be snoozing when I'm done."

Billy smiled contentedly and snuggled down beneath the covers. He dutifully closed his eyes. As Justin had expected, he was sound asleep before Justin had finished reading the first page. Justin sat for a moment longer and stared at the boy, amazed by the sense of yearning that came over him.

Why had he waited so long before claiming nights like this for himself? He'd been dating forever—maybe not as extensively as Harlan Patrick, but enthusiastically. The idea of settling down had never once crossed his mind until now.

He sighed heavily. It would have to be a woman with secrets and a boy with coal black eyes who drew him. Something told him that down that path lay heartache. The new report that had landed on Tate's desk today confirmed it. Will Longhorn was now claiming that Patsy had kidnapped their son. The stakes had escalated way past his own needs and longings.

He was still sitting there when he sensed Patsy behind him. He jolted when her hand came to rest on his shoulder. The touch was as light and tentative as the flutter of a bird's wings, but he felt as if it were the most intimate caress he'd ever shared.

"You guys finish your story?" she whispered.

"Twice," he admitted.

"Dani was right. He does have you wound around

his little finger. I thought you were made of tougher stuff than that.''

"He gets to me.''

"Why?''

He shrugged. "I'm not sure. Is it possible for a man to feel an instinctive bond with a child who's not his own?''

"Adoptive dads do that all the time.''

"True.'' He glanced over his shoulder into her eyes. "Maybe I'm just getting to a time in my life when I'm thinking about a family and wondering when I'll have one of my own.''

"You will when you want to,'' she said. "You come from a long line of men who go after whatever they want. They're all family men, with deep roots. You're no different.''

"What happens if I pick the wrong woman?'' he inquired softly, meeting her gaze evenly. "What if I pick someone who's not free to love me back?''

He saw the flare of alarm in her eyes, the sudden rush of dismay that stripped the color from her cheeks.

"What are you saying?'' she asked, her voice shaky.

He refused to look away or to yield to her obvious panic. "I'm just wondering, hypothetically, what would happen to my dreams if I fell in love with a woman who's not available? Where would that leave me?''

Rather than answer, she whirled and left the room.

Justin followed slowly. He found her on the front porch, staring out at the night sky. He walked up behind her and rested his hands on her shoulders, much as she had done to him earlier. He could feel her trembling, felt the buck of her pulse where his thumb rested against her neck.

And then he felt the hot splash of a tear on his hand. It almost brought him to his knees. He hadn't meant for her to cry, hadn't meant to shake her so badly that she would run from him. He'd just wanted to prod her into opening up at last. Maybe a direct, straightforward question would have been better, after all.

He turned her gently, then pulled her into his arms. She resisted for no more than a heartbeat, then rested her head against his shoulder.

"I'm sorry," he apologized.

"For what?"

"Pushing again."

"It's not that."

"What then?"

She drew in a deep, shuddering breath, then whispered, "You know, don't you? I've sensed it for days now."

His own breath caught in his throat. At last, he thought. At last there would be truth between them.

And then what? he wondered to himself. What the hell would he do when the truth was out? There would be no turning back, then. What if it started them both down a path that destroyed any hope of the future he'd been envisioning just a short time before?

"Know what?" he asked, because he had to, because it was the only thing to do. The kidnapping charge was too serious to be ignored, no matter how ridiculous he might believe it to be. "About me." She drew in a deep breath, then blurted, "That I'm married."

He sighed. He'd hoped, prayed, that he'd been wrong about that, that she was divorced at least, but the report on Tate's desk hadn't lied. Will Longhorn was still her husband. What was the rest of the truth, though? Were they in the process of getting a divorce? Was there a battle for custody? Had she kidnapped their son to avoid losing him to her husband? Justin didn't believe that, even though it would explain the skittishness, the use of her maiden name, rather than her husband's. He would lay odds that she had every right to have that boy with her.

"Maybe I'm the wrong person for you to talk to about this," he said finally.

She regarded him incredulously. "You forced this into the open and now you don't want to talk about it?"

He touched a silencing finger to her lips. "It's not that I don't want to hear everything. I just think maybe it would be best if you talked to Janet."

"Why?"

"Because she's an attorney and a damned fine one.

If you're in trouble, she can help. She'll want to, you know that. You won't go wrong listening to her.''

"Who says I need an attorney?"

"I do," he said, a gentle hand on her cheek. "Listen to me. Talk to Janet."

"Justin, how much do you know?"

"Not everything," he admitted. "I know that your husband is looking for you."

She sighed. "I thought he might be. What else?"

"He's accusing you of kidnapping your baby."

She stared at him in shock. "Kidnapping? That's absurd. Billy is mine as much as he is Will's. There's been no divorce, no custody battle. There's no way he could accuse me of kidnapping my own son." She regarded him with a panicky expression. "Could he?"

He rushed to reassure her. "He can make all the accusations he wants, but it remains to be seen if any of them will stand up in court. That's why I think you should talk to Janet."

"I can't," she whispered. "What if she says I have to go back? What if she tells me he can take Billy away from me, that I have to give up my son?"

He studied her intently, recognizing the genuine fear in her eyes. "Has Will Longhorn ever hurt you?"

His heart was in his throat as he waited what seemed to be a lifetime for her to slowly shake her head.

"Not physically, no. He's come close. His temper

gets out of control. He's threatened me, my parents. It was terrifyingly real.''

And then she burst into tears and buried her face in her hands. All Justin could do was wait out the storm, his arms around her, his shirt growing damp with her tears. Eventually, when the sobs subsided, he handed her a handkerchief. She blotted her eyes and scrubbed away the dampness on her cheeks.

''I'm sorry.''

''There's nothing to apologize for,'' he insisted.

Patsy sighed heavily. ''I knew I should have dealt with this straight on, but I was so afraid, Justin. I was afraid he'd take my baby. That's what he threatened to do.''

Once the words were out, it was as if a dam had burst. She told him everything, about meeting the attractive, ambitious young attorney, about working for him and falling in love, about marrying him and joining him in his political rise, only to have their home life disintegrate.

''I was his trophy wife, the all-American girl. I know it wasn't true, but sometimes I wondered if he hadn't married me because his political advisers told him to. He resented me that much.''

Justin heard pain and confusion in her voice, but not the bitterness he'd expected. That was a surprise. He touched a hand to her cheek. ''Are you still in love with him?''

She stared at him in shock. ''In love with Will?

No. He killed whatever love there was between us a long time ago.''

Relief washed over him. He'd had to be sure. If there was even a lingering trace of love for the man back in Oklahoma, then his advice might have been different. Instead, he advised one more time. "Talk to Janet. She will tell you what your legal options are.''

"I'll think about it," she promised.

"Do it," he said more sharply than he'd intended. He sighed. "Sorry. It's just that I can't bury these notices forever and neither can Tate.''

She stared at him, her expression horrified. "Tate knows?"

Justin nodded. "He found the first report. He's left it up to me to take care of this for the moment, but it can't wait forever. Earlier today it escalated from a simple missing persons report to a kidnapping charge. It sounds as if your husband's getting desperate.''

"I've put you in a terrible position, haven't I?"

He noticed that she put concern for him ahead of concern for her husband. That was something to hold on to in the days ahead. There was no question it was going to get messy. Any man who would threaten his wife with violence as Will Longhorn had was dangerous. He was also a lawyer with political connections. It was impossible to tell what lengths he might go to before everything was sorted out in a courtroom.

"I want you to think about moving out to White Pines," he said carefully. "Billy will have a wonderful time on the ranch and there will be people around.''

"You think this is going to get ugly, don't you?''

"Hasn't it already?'' he asked dryly.

"But I can't involve your family. It's bad enough that you're in the middle of this.''

"I made the choice,'' he said. "I could have called the Oklahoma authorities the second I knew who you were. So could Tate.''

"Why didn't you?''

His mouth curved slowly. "Darlin', if you don't know that, then you're not half as quick as I've been giving you credit for being.''

A faint smile touched her lips, then faded just as quickly. "And Tate?''

"Tate's a lot like Grandpa Harlan. He's the kind of a man who trusts his gut instincts. And when it comes to a choice between that and a piece of paper coming in over a fax machine, he'll go with his gut every time. He likes you. He believes there's more to the story than what's on those papers and until his back's to the wall, he'll do everything he can to protect you. In the meantime, I'd feel a whole lot better if you were out at White Pines.''

"I can't impose like that, especially not if things start getting ugly.''

"That's exactly why you need to be there. Grandpa Harlan will stand up to the devil himself to protect those he loves. Cody's there and Harlan Patrick, not that I want you seeing too much of him.''

"No," she said, that familiar stubborn tilt to her chin. "This is my fight, not your family's."

He regarded her soberly. "I'm making it mine."

"No," she said again, though a little less forcefully.

Justin grinned. "Yes. Don't fight me on this, darlin'. My mind's made up and nobody on earth's more stubborn than an Adams."

"We could debate that," she teased, her expression brightening for the first time since the conversation began. "I'm not exactly a pushover."

"No, you are anything but a pushover," he agreed, amused. "Let's just say you've met your match."

He'd made the remark lightly, but the words hung in the air and set off a sizzling tension. Patsy's gaze locked with his.

"Yes," she said very quietly. "I think maybe I have."

After that soft-spoken admission, it took every last bit of willpower Justin possessed to walk away from her and go back to his own place. It was late. He was exhausted. Stress piled on top of stress for days now had left him thoroughly drained. And yet he knew he wouldn't sleep.

He was a man who liked to control his own destiny and too much of his future hinged now on other people. For the first time since he'd put on a badge he regretted it. It kept him from being able to track down Will Longhorn and bloody his nose for the hell he'd put Patsy through and the likely anguish that was yet to come.

Even with right on her side, there was no way to be sure that things wouldn't get twisted around in a courtroom with Patsy coming out the loser. That was why she needed Janet at the moment, even more than she needed him. He could love her—and God knows he'd finally recognized that he did—but he couldn't protect her from the fallout of her own impetuous decision to run. Not that he blamed her for not wanting to square off against her husband when all the odds were stacked in his favor.

That, at least, was no longer true. With the considerable force of the Adams name behind her now, Patsy stood a better than even chance in a legal battle.

But what if she lost? He had to consider that possibility. Nothing was certain when it came to the whims of judges. He'd seen too many black-and-white cases dismissed on a technicality. He had to believe, though, that she would win. If she didn't, then nothing he worked for as a law enforcement officer was worth anything.

If the legal system went awry, what then? What if he was forced to choose between a misguided legal decision and what he saw as Patsy's God-given right to have her son? God help him, what would he do? Encourage her to take Billy and run again? Go with them, leaving behind his family, his principles?

It won't come to that, he reassured himself time and again. It would be too cruel.

But fate could take cruel twists. Just ask Sharon Lynn. She'd waited for years to finally marry the man she loved, only to lose him on her wedding night. Where was the justice in that?

He thought back to those few brief hours earlier in the evening when he'd actually felt at ease for the first time in days. Why the devil had he insisted on opening up this whole blasted can of worms? Maybe ignorance really was bliss. A few hours ago he'd only suspected the tangle of problems facing Patsy. Now he knew for sure what was ahead of her, ahead of both of them.

How could he possibly seize control of this before things got out of hand? Other than pounding some sense into Will Longhorn, that is? Longhorn held the answers, though. And Justin was a cop with all sorts of investigative skills at his command.

His spirits brightened. Maybe he couldn't do anything officially, but unofficially? Yes, indeed, he could find out if there was so much as a parking violation outstanding in the man's past. If there was anything, anything at all, he would hand it to Patsy and Janet as ammunition for the battle ahead.

With something concrete he could do to help Patsy, his mind eased and he finally fell into a deep sleep. Unfortunately, it lasted little more than half an hour before the alarm was going off and the phone was ringing.

"Justin, I'm sorry to wake you," Becky apologized. "But you'd better get over to Dolan's right away."

He struggled to shake the cobwebs from his mind. "Dolan's? Why? What's happened?"

"Patsy just called. She was too upset for me to make much sense of it, but I think she said someone's trying to break down the front door."

He glanced at the clock. Patsy wasn't due at work for another half hour. "She's there?"

"Locked in the back room is what she said. I could hear the glass breaking."

"I'm on my way. Have you called Tate?"

"Not yet. I got Dusty rolling first. He was just coming back into town from a patrol on the highway. He's on his way. Should be there any second now."

"I'm on my way," he said, and hung up. He was still pulling on his clothes as he ran out of the house. He had his service revolver tucked into his waistband.

It took him less than five minutes to reach Main Street. He could hear the commotion as he made the turn. Glass was shattering and someone was laying into whatever remained of the front of the store with something heavy, more than likely a crowbar or tire iron. Dusty was shouting commands that were being ignored. Instead, more debris flew, amid a flurry of curses and threats.

Justin made the turn on two wheels, then slammed to a stop behind Dusty's patrol car. He stared at the mess in disbelief.

"What the hell's going on?"

Dusty turned, his expression shaken. "Beats the hell out of me. Looks like the guy just lost it. Either he's got a grudge against Doc or he's a junkie out of his mind and desperate for drugs. Do you recognize him?"

Justin surveyed the man, from his pitch-dark black hair to his sculpted cheekbones, angled jaw and well-tailored suit. This was no thug or drifter. In fact, he concluded with a sinking heart, he would bet the ranch that this was Will Longhorn. He glanced up and down the block until he spotted a very fancy car that was almost exactly like Patsy's, just shiny black to her white one.

"Can you see the tags on that car?" he asked Dusty, who had a better angle on them.

"Oklahoma."

"Damn."

"What the hell is going on here?" Tate demanded, joining them.

"Unless I miss my guess, we're about to meet Will Longhorn," Justin said.

Tate's eyebrows rose. "Patsy's husband?"

"The one and only. It appears he's come calling, though I have to say his courting leaves a little something to be desired."

The sheriff's expression cheered considerably. "Well, well, well. It will surely be my pleasure to lock him up." He glanced at Justin and Dusty. "Shall we?"

"Oh, yeah," Justin said grimly.

Tate gave him a sharp look. "You don't lay a hand on him. Understood?"

Justin grimaced, then sighed. "Yes, sir."

"Then let's do it," Tate said.

It was an uneven fight, three against one with the three armed, as well. Tate had slapped handcuffs on the man before he even realized he was being taken into custody. When he heard the click and felt the cold metal around his wrists, he whirled on Tate.

"What the hell do you think you're doing?"

"Arresting you," Tate said evenly. "We can start with destruction of property and go from there." He began reading him his rights.

"Do you know who I am?"

"I don't give a damn if you're the governor or the president of the U.S. of A., nobody pulls a stunt like this in my town," Tate retorted.

Justin didn't waste time listening to the rest of the exchange. He stepped over glass shards and broken toys from the window displays, then used his own key to the drugstore. As he went inside, he called out to Patsy. The door to the back room cracked open.

"Justin?"

"It's me," he said, and opened his arms.

Patsy ran straight into them and clung. "Oh, my God, did you see him? He's lost his mind. He must have."

"I take it that's Will."

Her head bobbed against his chest.

"It's okay, darlin'. Tate has him in custody. He won't hurt you."

"But this place," she murmured, gazing around in horror. "Look what he's done."

"As long as you're all right, it doesn't matter. We'll have it cleaned up in no time."

"I can't believe this. It's all my fault."

"It is not your fault," Justin said. "He's an adult. He's responsible for his own actions, and believe me, this is not going to look good when you go into court and ask for your divorce. You have three cops as witnesses to the violence he's capable of. You can't get any better than that."

Patsy regarded him sadly. "It won't be that easy. He won't let it be."

"I know. But I'll be right here with you." He tilted her chin up and gazed into her eyes. "Believe it or not, this is a good thing."

She stared at the broken glass and demolished displays. "You'll pardon me if I can't quite see it that way."

"Darlin', I think I could forgive you just about anything. Now get a couple of brooms and let's get busy."

"Don't you have to go down to the station?"

"Not yet. Tate can handle your husband. When things settle down a bit, you and I can go down there and you can press formal charges against him. Doc Dolan can press whatever charges he wants to for the damage to the store. Then you can see Janet and we'll find out just what kind of a case she can put together for you.'' He brushed a wayward curl from her cheek. ''It's almost over, Patsy. I guarantee it.''

But, of course, it was just beginning.

Chapter Eleven

The last place on earth Patsy wanted to be was the sheriff's office. Even with Justin by her side, she dreaded confronting Will after the scene and destruction he'd caused. She was thoroughly embarrassed, not only for herself, but for him. He'd always been such a proud person. She didn't like thinking that she was to blame for him being reduced to this out-of-control mockery of a man.

"Want me to come in with you?" Justin asked as she hesitated at the doorway to the cell block.

Overcome with a sense of foreboding and trepidation, she almost agreed. It would be so easy to rely on his strength, to accept his protection. Then she thought better of it. She squared her shoulders and shook her head.

"No," she said. "It would only outrage him."

"So what?" Justin retorted with a touch of defiance. "Let him be outraged. Let him take a swing at me and give us one more thing to charge him with."

"No," she repeated, certain now that this was a confrontation she had to face alone. "I'll be safe enough."

Despite her claim, though, she was grateful that the cell door between them would be locked. Today's scene had proved her worst fears about Will's temper.

After taking one last look at Justin, she drew in a deep breath and went to see her husband, all the while trying to remember that this was a man she had once loved with all her heart.

Since she'd seen him being led away from Dolan's, all of the fight had drained out of him. He was sitting on the cot in his cell looking dazed, as if he weren't quite sure how he'd gotten there. He looked surprisingly chastened.

In the months since she'd last seen him, he'd aged. There were even premature hints of gray in his straight, coal black hair. There were shadows under his eyes and lines of weariness etched on his face. And yet, despite the obvious exhaustion, he was as handsome as ever, his clothes perfectly tailored, if badly mussed from his rampage at Dolan's. He would hate it when he realized how filthy and wrinkled he was.

"Will," she said softly.

His head jerked up and for a brief instant she saw

the hint of vulnerability, the flash of a boyish smile that had made her fall in love with him when they'd first met. Then, as if he suddenly remembered the circumstances, his expression hardened and the light in his eyes died.

"You'll pay for this, Patsy," he said coldly.

"No," she said, refusing to cower under the threat. "You brought this on yourself. I wasn't the one smashing things up at Dolan's."

"If you'd opened the damn door..."

"You were out of control," she reminded him patiently.

"Because of you. You took my son. You ran away from our marriage and you did it when it would hurt me the most, right in the middle of a campaign. You deliberately humiliated me."

"You're wrong," she said, and met his gaze evenly. "I wasn't even thinking of you."

"There, you see. It didn't matter a damn to you that your leaving could cost me the election."

"No, it didn't. I was only thinking about saving myself and Billy."

He gazed at her incredulously. "From me?"

"Yes, from you. You'd turned our house into a war zone. I left you once because of it, but rather than change, you just threatened me and my parents. You virtually blackmailed me into coming back. This time I just made sure there was nobody else involved and I came to a place I prayed you'd never find me. Obviously it wasn't far enough."

His expression turned triumphant. "You should have known better than that. I have the resources to find you no matter where you try to hide. It would be wise of you to remember that if you ever get a crazy idea about leaving again."

Patsy wrapped her arms around her middle and forced herself not to show how terrified she was that he might try to make her go home with him again.

"I'm not coming back to Oklahoma, Will, and neither is Billy." She said it firmly, her gaze fixed on his face as she waited for the explosion of temper likely to follow. To her amazement—and fear—there was no explosion, just a cold, cruel look.

"I guess we'll see about that," he said in a soft, lethal tone. "Have you noticed that this cell has a window? It has a perfectly fascinating view of Main Street. I saw you and your boyfriend."

Patsy barely contained a gasp of dismay. Surely he wouldn't drag Justin into the middle of their fight. She stared into his unrelenting eyes and sighed. Of course, he would.

"He is not my boyfriend," she said, hoping to persuade him.

"Oh, I'm sure I can find folks who'd say otherwise."

"Pay them to, you mean."

"If necessary."

"It won't hold up, Will."

"Are you willing to risk that? Is he worth losing Billy?"

Fury outdistanced fear. "You will never take my son. *Never!*"

"Try me."

"You won't win."

"Oh, but I will. I have money and power and influential friends. I can give Billy everything. He's half Native American. That'll work in my favor, too. Living with you would rob him of his heritage, keep him from understanding his father's culture. Tribal law—"

She cut him off. "Since when are you so concerned with your culture?" she snapped. "The only time it's mattered to you is when it can be exploited for your own political gain. Beyond that, you've turned your back on your people. When was the last time you spent even five minutes with your parents on the reservation? When did you ever give a damn about the customs of your people?"

As soon as the words were out of her mouth, she knew she'd made a mistake. She had touched a raw nerve. In fact, she suspected that most of her own problems with her husband arose from the fact that he knew in his heart that marrying her had been a betrayal of his roots, the final slap in the face of his family. He'd been proud of winning her love, only to resent the fact that he'd needed her by his side to become a more acceptable candidate for office.

"Then the best way to make amends will be to insure that my son is raised by his Native American family," he retorted. "It will happen, Patsy. Count on it."

"Will," she began, ready to beg. Then she caught herself. That was what he wanted. He wanted to see the fear in her eyes, wanted to hear it in her voice. She wouldn't give him the satisfaction, even though she was quaking inside. Instead, she said quietly, "I'm sorry it's come to this. I really am. There was a time when I truly loved and respected you."

For a moment he seemed taken aback, but Patsy didn't wait to see what he might say next. She had to get away from him before she made things worse than she already had. Head held high, she walked out of the cell block. Only when she was back in the lobby with the door firmly closed behind her did she sag against it. Justin was there at once, concern written on his face as he led her to a seat beside his desk.

"What can I get you? Want some coffee? It's foul, but the caffeine might jolt some color back into your cheeks."

"No, thanks."

"What happened in there? What did he say to you?"

"The same old thing," she said wearily. "He's going to take Billy from me."

"Over my dead body," Justin said fiercely. "That is the one thing that will never happen."

"You can't guarantee that."

"Okay, maybe I can't," he conceded, "but Janet

can.'' He tucked a hand under her elbow and hauled her to her feet. "Come on."

All Patsy wanted to do was go home and hold her baby, then crawl under the covers and hide for a month. But that was what the old Patsy would have done. She was stronger now. She had to keep reminding herself of that.

"Where are we going?" she asked as Justin half dragged her from the station.

"To see Janet. I've already called. She'll meet us at her office."

"I thought she'd retired."

"There's retired and then there's Janet's version of retired. She's giving it lip service for Grandpa Harlan's sake, but, believe me, she can't wait to find a case she can get her teeth into."

He grinned. "That's why she never quite got around to putting her office on the market, much less moving out her desk and files and law books. Personally, I think she sneaks into town and hides out there after telling Grandpa Harlan she's gone shopping, but I can't prove it. I've never caught her there. Then, again, I've never seen her carrying a lot of packages to her car, either."

"I don't want to be responsible for the two of them fussing with each other," Patsy said, still reluctant.

"Oh, Grandpa may bluster some, but he knows deep down that Janet loves being a lawyer too much ever to walk away from it entirely. At least he's gotten her to slow down, and he thoroughly enjoys letting her think she's putting something over on him.''

Patsy sighed enviously. "They have a wonderful marriage, don't they?''

"The best. It's set a great example for the rest of us. As I understand it, my grandmother Mary adored my grandfather. She was the epitome of the traditional wife. She devoted herself to him, almost to the exclusion of their sons. When she died in a riding accident, Grandpa was devastated.''

He chuckled. "Then, thanks to Jenny stealing his car, he met Janet.''

Patsy stared at him, flabbergasted. "Jenny stole his car?''

"Oh, yeah. She was fourteen at the time. She crashed it into a tree.''

"I'll bet that got his relationship with her mother off to a rocky start.''

"You could say that. Janet was definitely not the kind of woman Grandpa was used to. For one thing she didn't bow to his every whim. I was pretty little when they met, but the stories are legendary about their courtship. Best of all, the sparks are still there. You can feel it whenever they're in the same room.''

He met her gaze. "Just like us,'' he added softly.

Patsy had always wanted to believe that a relationship like that was possible. Her own parents had been married for years, but it was as much habit as love that kept them together. There was none of the warmth and tenderness she had witnessed between Janet and Harlan Adams. Theirs was the kind of relationship she'd always dreamed of, the kind she could almost imagine having with Justin if things were different. Maybe someday, though, as soon as this mess was straightened out once and for all.

They reached Janet's office and paused on the sidewalk out front.

"You ready?" Justin asked, tucking a finger under her chin to tilt her face up so he could study it.

Thinking of Will's view of the street, she backed away, ignoring the flash of hurt in Justin's eyes. "I don't have any choice, do I?"

"Not unless you're willing to go back to Oklahoma with him and go through the same thing all over again."

"Never," she said adamantly.

"Then let's do it." He held open the door.

Inside, Janet rose to greet them. She gave Justin a kiss on the cheek, then enfolded Patsy in a hug.

"Justin's filled me in on the basics. It's going to be okay," she promised, her expression radiating a quiet serenity.

And for the first time in months, Patsy actually felt as if it might be.

Before Patsy realized what was happening, Janet was ushering a protesting Justin out the door.

"He can stay," she said, responding to the indignation on his face.

"No," Janet countered. "It will be best if we have this conversation in private."

"But—" Justin began, only to be cut off again.

"Go," Janet said. "You've done your part by bringing her here. Now, go away and have a cup of coffee or something."

Justin's gaze sought Patsy's. "You're okay with this?"

Patsy nodded. "Thanks to you, I'm in good hands."

"Well, of course. That's not the issue."

Janet smiled tolerantly. "Justin, go," she commanded softly.

He bent and brushed a kiss across Patsy's forehead. "I'll be at the office if you need me."

After he'd gone, Janet turned a thoughtful look on Patsy. "He's very protective of you, isn't he?"

"That's just his nature. It's probably why he became a cop."

"Sweetie, I don't think this has anything to do with his job. Whether he knows it or not, he's falling in love with you."

Patsy stared at her in shocked disbelief. "You're wrong. I mean, I know he cares about me and Billy, but love? No, it can't be."

"Why not? Because you don't love him?"

"I never said that."

Janet grinned. "Good, then we won't be starting out with any lies and half-truths between us."

Patsy studied her intently. "You tricked me, didn't you?"

"I suppose. I just wanted to be sure where things

stood. I don't want Justin to be hurt. He has a tender heart.'' She shuffled some papers on her desk and got out a pen. "Now, tell me about you and Will Longhorn. From the beginning.''

An hour later Patsy was still talking. She told Janet every single thing she could recall about their relationship, from the moment she'd gone to work in Will's office until she had run away and sought refuge for herself and her son in Los Piños.

Janet rarely interrupted and then only to ask very pointed questions about something Patsy had said. When Patsy was finished, she regarded Janet evenly. "It's not a very pretty story, is it?''

"I've heard worse. How much of this does Justin know?''

"All of it.'' She hesitated, then said, "There is one more thing you should probably know. Will saw me with Justin earlier. He's threatened to drag him into it.''

To her surprise, Janet chuckled.

"That will certainly make his day,'' she said. "He's already spoiling for a fight with this man. Heaven help Will Longhorn if he gives Justin an excuse.''

"Justin can't be involved,'' Patsy said fiercely. "He's already paid a price for keeping silent rather than reporting me to the Oklahoma authorities. I know he struggled with his conscience every day over that.''

"Justin knew you were wanted for kidnapping your son?" Janet asked, clearly surprised.

Patsy nodded. "It put him in a terrible position."

"Did you ask him to keep silent?"

"No, of course not. I didn't even realize how much he knew until yesterday. That's when he admitted that both he and Tate knew all about Will's claim. I guess Tate had buried the paperwork."

"Well, well, well," Janet murmured. "I've always known that Tate Owens was a good man, but to tell you the truth I've wondered when Justin would get the perspective he needs to do that job right."

Patsy was startled by the implied criticism. She rushed to Justin's defense. "Justin is an excellent lawman. You have to know that. He believes so fiercely in right and wrong."

"Exactly," Janet said. "Up until now it's been black-and-white with him. You're either obeying the law or you're breaking it, in spirit or in deed. Apparently he's finally discovered that there are some actual gray areas in life. It will make him a better policeman. Maybe he'll even find a way to forgive the man who hurt Sharon Lynn and killed Kyle."

"Has Sharon Lynn been able to do that?"

Janet looked deeply troubled by the question. "I'm not sure she ever thinks of him at all. She's still blaming herself."

"I was afraid of that. Do you think she needs to see a psychologist?"

"It doesn't matter what I think," Janet responded.

"Sharon Lynn has to want to move on and right now she's too consumed with guilt to think about the future."

"Is she better physically?"

"She's getting stronger every day. She needs to start getting up and getting out."

Patsy gave that some thought. "I have an idea."

Janet's expression brightened. "Tell me."

"I know she'd been thinking about buying Dolan's. What if she were to think that Doc was about to leave and the rest of us were going to be out of jobs. She loves that place. Would she be able to bear the thought of it closing down?"

Janet pondered the idea, then nodded slowly. "It just might work. Particularly if you were the one to tell her, maybe lay it on really thick about how important the job is to you, especially now with the custody fight and your very expensive lawyer." She added the last with a grin.

"How expensive?" Patsy asked. "Are you really going to help me? Do we have a case?"

"Don't worry about my fee. We'll work something out. I'm grateful to have a case that my husband can't possibly disapprove of my taking. As for winning it, there's something you need to understand about me. I have never accepted losing as a possibility. That doesn't mean I haven't lost a time or two, but I always fight to win."

"But the system—"

"The system requires a fair fight. With all due

modesty, with me on your side, the fight will be more than fair. I know how to handle the Will Longhorns of the world.'' She met Patsy's gaze evenly. ''Tell me this, what are you most afraid of?''

''That Will will try to take the baby, insist on him being raised by the tribe. Isn't that what's happening with babies who are part Native American?''

''They won't take the baby from its natural mother. I promise. And given what you've told me about your husband, I doubt he'll fight the divorce or even whatever custody arrangements we want, not if he wants to run for political office,'' she said grimly. ''He won't want all the details of his abuse made public.''

''But—''

''No buts. Even if he tries to claim that the charges are false, he'll never be able to wash away all the mud on his reputation,'' Janet said with confidence. ''If he's smart and his advisers truly believe in him, they'll convince him to settle this quietly and with as little publicity as possible. From everything you've said about him, I doubt Will Longhorn will be vindictive enough to throw away everything he's ever wanted just to get even with you.''

For the first time since she'd fled, Patsy began to hope that she could finally stop running. Relief coursed through her. ''Will I have to go back to Oklahoma?''

''No. We'll file the divorce papers right here. I'll have him served before he even gets out of jail.'' She came around the side of her desk and clasped Patsy's icy hands. "You and Billy will be fine, and you *will* be together. Trust me."

"He'll be furious when he gets the papers." She thought of his temper. "What if he comes to the house?"

"I'll ask for a restraining order."

Relieved, Patsy was ready to grasp at the option and then she thought of Billy. He wanted so badly to see his daddy. Could she keep them apart? Or did she owe it to Billy to let him maintain some sort of relationship with his father, however carefully guarded?

Finally she voiced her concerns out loud. "Billy's been asking to see his father. With Will right here, what should I do?"

Janet considered the question for some time. "We can work it out, if it's what you want. It might be for the best, prove how reasonable we intend to be."

"Not alone, though," Patsy said hurriedly. "I don't want Will alone with him. He might take him and run."

"A supervised visit, then. I think I know of a sheriff's deputy who'd be happy to hang out with the two of them or all three of you, if that's what you'd prefer."

"Yes," Patsy said at once, thinking of the likely need for a buffer between the two men. Will was going to resent Justin's right to be there, and Justin was clearly itching for an excuse to slug him. "I'd better be there."

"Then when Will's released, we'll arrange for him to come to the house to see his son."

"Thank you," Patsy said. "For everything."

"No need. I'm doing this as much for Justin as I am for you. You're good for him."

"I've brought him nothing but trouble."

"No," Janet corrected. "You've opened up his heart."

Chapter Twelve

When Patsy emerged from Janet's office into the bright sunlight, she couldn't help comparing it to emerging from the darkness of the nightmare Will had put her through these past few years. At last, though, the future was bright again. The debt she owed to the Adamses was enormous, beginning way back with Sharon Lynn.

Instead of heading directly to Justin's office, she went to Dolan's and found the elderly pharmacist filling prescriptions as methodically as ever, evidently unconcerned about the mess in the front of the store.

"Doc, I'm truly sorry about all of this. I'll pay for fixing it."

He peered at her over his reading glasses. "You didn't do it, did you?"

702 NATURAL BORN LAWMAN

"Well, no, but—"

"Then I'm not laying the blame on you. It'll get fixed up. The glass cutter's already been here. Justin saw to it."

"But I should be the one—"

He grinned. "You're wasting your time arguing with me, young lady. If you disagree with the plan, you'll have to talk to Justin."

Patsy sighed. He was doing it again. He was fixing things for her. On the one hand, she was grateful. On the other, it was a reminder of too many years of weakness and dependence on other people.

"I'll speak to him," she said grimly.

The older man grinned. "Let me know how it turns out. It's been my experience that once an Adams makes up his mind, there's not much use in fighting him."

"We'll just see about that," Patsy retorted. "Before I go to see Justin, there's something else I want to discuss with you." She explained her idea for lighting a fire under Sharon Lynn and hopefully jolting her out of her depression. She didn't mention that the plot was helping her to keep her own mind off whatever was going on with Will down at the sheriff's office.

"Are you sure you're not an Adams?" he asked when she'd finished. "You're sneaky just like they are."

"You disapprove?"

"No, indeed. Not if it'll get the job done. I'll go

along with anything that'll get that pretty little gal out of her bed and back among the living. I've just been putting off my retirement until she made up her mind whether she wanted to take this place off my hands.''

Impulsively Patsy hugged him. ''Thank you. Since the lunch counter's already covered, I'm going out to White Pines now, if you don't mind.''

''Go. Be sure to let me know how it turns out.''

''If I go about this right, you won't need me to tell you. Sharon Lynn will be busting down the door before the afternoon's over with.''

''Lordy, I hope not,'' he said with mock horror. ''One busted door in a day is about all an old man can cope with.''

''You know perfectly well what I mean.''

''Yes, I do. Now, get along with you.''

When she arrived at the ranch, she went straight up to Sharon Lynn's room in the main house. She found her friend still in bed, still gazing blankly at the ceiling.

''Hey, sweetie, how're you feeling?'' she asked, pulling a chair up beside the bed.

Sharon Lynn cast a distracted look her way, then gazed off in the distance again.

''I have some news,'' she said, deliberately injecting a somber note into her voice.

The statement drew no response.

''It's about Dolan's.''

There was a flicker of interest in Sharon Lynn's eyes, but nothing more.

"The Doc told me today that he intends to close it down."

Sharon Lynn blinked rapidly at that, then turned slowly to face Patsy. "He's closing it?"

"Well, you know he's been thinking of retiring for some time. You told me that yourself. I guess he's decided it's time."

Sharon Lynn frowned. "But he knew I was thinking about buying it."

"I guess he figured since the accident and all, you wouldn't be interested, and he didn't want to wait around until another buyer showed up. I guess he's anxious to move on down to the Gulf Coast and go fishing."

The news clearly agitated her friend. Sharon Lynn began to fiddle with the pretty flowered comforter that was drawn up to her chin.

"This couldn't have come at a worse time," Patsy said sorrowfully.

"What do you mean?"

"I guess you haven't heard. My husband, Will, he showed up in town today and bashed down the door at Dolan's." Her shudder at the memory was only slightly exaggerated for Sharon Lynn's benefit. "Maybe that was the final straw for Doc. I don't know. Anyway, Will's in jail, and Janet's about to file divorce and custody papers. It's going to be expensive, and I'm out of a job again."

"You don't need to worry about that. Janet won't take your money anyway."

"Of course she will. I'm not accepting charity. It's important to me to prove I can stand on my own two feet. I'm sure you can understand that. Dolan's has always represented a certain amount of independence to you, too, hasn't it?"

"Yes, I suppose it has. I've never thought about it that way before. I just knew I liked working there. It gave me my own identity away from the family's ranching. Plus I was following in my mother's footsteps. She and Daddy did most of their courting in that place while she ran the lunch counter."

"There, you see?" Patsy said brightly. "I knew you'd understand." Then she sighed heavily. "Of course, I can probably find another job in another town."

Sharon Lynn appeared genuinely shocked by the suggestion. "And leave Justin? You would do that to him?"

"Well, I wouldn't want to, but—"

The next thing she knew, Sharon Lynn had tossed off the comforter and was climbing out of bed. She brushed past Patsy.

"Oh, for heaven's sake, get out of my way."

Patsy barely contained a hoot of triumph. "Why? Where are you going? Should you be out of bed?"

"I should have been out of bed days ago. As for where I'm going, you know perfectly well, I'm going to have a talk with Doc Dolan. I will not let Dolan's be closed down, and if anybody's going to buy that place, it's going to be me."

Patsy regarded her innocently. "If you're sure..."

"I'm sure."

Patsy kept up a steady barrage of doubts all the way to the front door, right past a gaping Harlan Adams. After they'd waltzed past him, Patsy turned around and caught his wink. Obviously Janet had filled him in on the plan, though he was clearly stunned to see it had worked.

"I really don't know if you should be going all the way into town your first day out of bed," Patsy said, along with half a dozen other protests designed to keep Sharon Lynn just irritated enough not to back down.

"Oh, will you just shut up," Sharon Lynn finally snapped. "I'm going and that's final."

"If you say so."

"Well, I do."

Outside, though, Sharon Lynn came to an abrupt halt. Patsy regarded her worriedly. "What is it? Is something wrong? Are you feeling faint?"

"I don't have a car," she whispered, her voice cracking. "And even if I did, I couldn't...I don't think I can ever drive again."

Patsy reached for her hand and squeezed. "Then isn't it a good thing that my car is here? I'll drive you into town, if that's what you want."

For a moment, Sharon Lynn looked as if she might back down, but then she squared her shoulders. "Perfect. I'm sure Justin or someone in the family will be coming out this way later. I can hitch a ride home with them.''

"Or I'll bring you back. It's not a problem.''

"Whatever.'' She walked over to Patsy's car and reached for the handle of the passenger door, then faltered. She swallowed hard. "I'm not sure...''

Patsy sensed that Sharon Lynn had to do this today or she might never try again. "You'll be fine. I'll drive very carefully.''

"Of course you will. It's not that.''

"Let me ask you something. Have you ever fallen off a horse?''

Sharon Lynn regarded her impatiently. "I grew up on a ranch. What do you think?''

"And what did your dad or grandfather tell you?''

"To get up and get back on.''

"Same thing after an accident,'' Patsy said lightly, praying that she was giving the right advice.

"I'll never get behind the wheel of a car again,'' Sharon Lynn said fiercely, her expression anguished.

"You don't have to drive, if you don't want to, but you're bound to want to go places. How will you get into town every day, if someone doesn't bring you?''

"I'll move to town.''

"Then how will you get back out here for family dinners and holidays?'' Patsy asked reasonably.

"Oh, for heaven's sake,'' Sharon Lynn finally grumbled, and opened the door. "Let's just go and get it over with.''

She maintained a white-knuckled grip on the edge

of the seat all the way into town, but she didn't utter another protest. Still there was no question she was relieved when Patsy parked in front of the drugstore. She rushed out of the car as if she'd just been advised there was a bomb under the hood.

Thankfully, the glass cutter had been busy while Patsy had been at the ranch. Though the window displays hadn't been redone, at least there were shiny new windows in place. Sharon Lynn viewed the residue of the disaster with lifted brows, then walked inside. Heads turned as she sailed past the lunch counter and straight to Doc Dolan's place behind the prescription counter.

"We need to talk," she said in a no-nonsense tone.

"As soon as I finish getting Mrs. Phelps's pills ready for her," the pharmacist said without looking up.

"Now!" Sharon Lynn said fiercely.

"Sounds like she's back to her old self," Justin observed, coming up behind Patsy.

"Not yet, but I think she's getting there."

He rested his hands on her shoulders and turned her to face him. "You're a good friend, maybe even a bit of a miracle worker."

"There were no miracles involved. I just thought of a reason for her to get out of that bed. Thank God, it was the right one." Satisfied that everything had been set into motion at the back of the store, she met Justin's gaze. "Anything happen at the jail I should know about?"

"Your husband got the divorce papers."

Stunned by the speed with which Janet had worked, she asked, "Is the building still standing?"

"It was when I left. He's demanding a conference with Janet."

"Oh, dear."

"Not to worry. Janet was sitting in Tate's office waiting. She'd anticipated the request. She looked downright eager to have a little face-to-face with him."

"Did she tell you about the visitation with Billy?"

"I'll be there," he said softly. "Don't worry about it."

She regarded him worriedly. "You won't be looking for an excuse to shoot him, will you?" she asked, only partially in jest.

He grinned. "Not as long as he keeps his temper in check and Billy's glad to see him."

"Any idea when he'll be free to come over?"

He nodded. "That's why I came looking for you. He's going to be released right after his meeting with Janet. I thought you might want to go home to prepare Billy."

Patsy's knees turned weak at the prospect. She hadn't expected it to happen so soon, not on a day that had already been a roller coaster of emotional ups and downs. "Tonight?"

"Yes. Then with any luck he'll leave town. That's the deal for his release. Doc Dolan won't press charges if Will heads back to Oklahoma and never sets foot in Los Piños again except for liberal court-approved visits with his son." He stroked a finger down her cheek. "It's going to be over, Patsy. By this time tomorrow, it's finally going to be over."

She wanted to believe that, but she couldn't. Not yet. Not until she saw Will actually get in his car and drive away. Maybe not even then. Maybe not until he'd been gone for weeks or months and there'd been no attempts at payback.

The first step to insuring that Will would stick to their bargain and leave was to let him see Billy tonight. Needing Justin's strength, she reached for his hand and said in an unsteady voice, "Let's go home."

"I'll walk you over, then head back to the station," Justin said. "I'm going to escort him officially to your place after his release. After that, he'll stay overnight at a motel, then if all the details are ironed out in the morning and all the papers are signed to Janet's satisfaction, you can say goodbye once and for all."

If only it would go that smoothly, Patsy thought wistfully, but this was Will they were talking about. He didn't give up anything he considered to be his that easily.

Justin stood idly by as Will Longhorn signed himself out of jail. Tate made it a point to remind the lawyer of his agreement to be gone by the next day. For a brief instant, the man's arrogance threatened to erupt, but he finally set his jaw and nodded.

"If you're ready, I'll take you by Patsy's," Justin said when the last paper was signed.

"I can get there on my own," Will said, dismissing him.

Justin stood his ground. "Afraid not."

"More rules?" Will demanded sarcastically, but he followed Justin to the waiting patrol car. "What kind of town is this? Do you all just make up these regulations as you go along? Or are you taking particular pleasure in tormenting me?"

"We believe in the kind of justice it takes to get the job done," Justin said evenly as he drove the few blocks to Patsy's and pulled up to the curb in front. "If it requires a little creativity, so much the better."

Will glared at him. "Believe me, I know exactly what your agenda is. You think you're so smart, don't you? You think you've won."

"Where you're concerned, I don't have to win. This is all about your wife and son and what's right for them. If you've got a shred of decency in you, you'll set them free."

"It's not up to you."

Justin feared prolonging the debate would only make the other man's hackles rise. He was clearly spoiling for a fight and Justin was a handy target. If Justin thought about accommodating him, it might be enough to cause him to back out on whatever deal he'd agreed to with Janet. To prevent that from happening Justin remained tight-lipped.

"Nothing to say to that?" Will taunted.

"Maybe you should stop worrying about me and concentrate on your boy," Justin said mildly, gesturing toward the window where Billy was watching for them.

Even as they looked, Billy scrambled down and raced out the front door.

"Daddy, Daddy," he shouted as he toddled unsteadily down the walk.

To Justin's surprise, Will Longhorn bolted from the car, knelt down on the sidewalk and scooped his son into his arms. There were tears in his eyes as Billy's arms locked around his neck.

"I missed you, Daddy. I missed you lots."

"I missed you more," Will murmured, his voice thick with tears.

Justin felt his throat squeeze tight as he watched the two of them. The sight had shaken him more than he cared to admit. It was yet another reminder that not everything was as black-and-white as he'd always believed. His view of Will Longhorn had been colored by what he knew of the man's shabby treatment of Patsy. Now, seeing him with his son, he realized that whatever his faults, Will Longhorn loved his son and Billy returned that love. It wasn't a bond that could be broken lightly.

He glanced up and saw that Patsy was watching the scene with tears in her eyes. He went past the man and boy to stand beside her.

"How can I do it?" she wondered aloud. "How

can I keep them apart? Billy still brings out the good in him.''

''That's a heavy burden for a two-year-old. Will needs to find the good in himself some other way.''

She sighed. ''I know you're right, but—''

''No, darlin'. You're doing the right thing. I suspect if he's honest with himself, even Will sees that.''

''I hope you're right,'' she said as Will stood up with Billy in his arms and started toward the house. Despite whatever trepidations she might be having, she managed a smile for them. Justin had never been prouder of her.

''Daddy's going to stay for dinner,'' Billy announced. ''S'ghetti.''

''That's right, munchkin. Your favorite.''

Justin hid a smile. He'd seen the damage Billy could do to the surrounding area with a plate of spaghetti. He wondered how Will would feel when it wound up splashed all over his fancy clothes, even if they were a little the worse for wear.

He was in for a surprise on that score, too. Will never batted an eye when sauce splattered off Billy's exuberantly wielded fork. Patsy started out of her chair at the sight of the red stain, but Will waved her off.

''It's a suit,'' he said mildly. ''It'll clean, or I'll get another one.''

She stared at him in blatant amazement. Even Will grinned at her reaction.

''Okay, so I'm mellowing. Maybe I've finally

started getting my priorities in order." He regarded her wearily. "Too bad it's too late, isn't it?"

"Yes," she said softly. "Yes, it is." And then she turned and gazed at Justin.

There was no mistaking the message in her eyes, and Will didn't pretend not to get it. He rose from the table and picked up his son. "I'll give Billy his bath and put him to bed, if you two don't mind. Then I'll be on my way."

"Fine," Patsy agreed, watching as he left the room and headed toward the bathroom with Billy pointing the way.

After he'd gone, she gazed at Justin. "He's changed."

With an odd, cold sensation in his chest, Justin stared at her evenly. "Enough?"

"No," she said, reaching out to lay a hand against his cheek. "It can never be enough."

Relief swept over him then. They weren't at the end of her troubles yet, but they were getting there. And when they did, Justin vowed that he would be waiting.

When it was time to escort Will to his motel, Patsy beckoned Justin back inside for a moment. He studied her expression, trying to guess what was on her mind.

"Second thoughts?"

"About Will and the divorce? No. I just wanted to ask you if you could come to dinner tomorrow night, alone, just the two of us?"

Justin's heart lurched and his blood began to pump

a little faster. He had a thousand questions begging to be asked, but with Will waiting, there was no time. "Seven o'clock?" he asked.

She nodded. "That will be perfect."

"I'll be here."

Back outside he glanced at his watch and noted that it was already after nine. Less than twenty-two hours until he could return and by then Patsy Longhorn would be well on her way to becoming a free woman. He wondered if she could possibly be looking forward to that any more than he was.

Chapter Thirteen

Justin couldn't seem to make himself wait until dinnertime before catching a glimpse of Patsy. He strolled into Dolan's first thing in the morning and was stunned to find Sharon Lynn at work behind the counter. Even though he'd seen her talking to Doc Dolan the day before, he hadn't expected her to return full-time anytime soon.

"Hey, sweetheart, what are you doing here?"

She gave him a wry look. "I work here, or had you forgotten?"

Her tone suggested she didn't want to get into anything connected to her absence. Justin followed her lead. "Seems to me I do recall seeing you here a time or two. You cook a mean hamburger."

"I'm glad you approve, because I just bought the place."

Justin stared. This was a wrinkle he hadn't really anticipated. He knew she'd been toying with the idea, but to actually do it, especially considering her recent state of mind. He prayed she hadn't been pushed into making a hasty decision she would come to regret.

"You bought it?" he repeated slowly.

"Yesterday. Doc will stick around for a few more months until he's sure I understand how his part runs and until I find a replacement pharmacist, but it's all mine as soon as the bank works out the financing."

"Are you sure you're ready to take this on?"

She met his gaze evenly and her chin jutted stubbornly in typical Adams style. "I need it, Justin. Now more than ever. I couldn't lose it, too. Not after..." Her voice trailed off.

"Not after Kyle?" he asked gently.

She shook her head, blinking back tears. "He was my..."

"I know, sweetheart. Kyle was your world." He went around behind the counter and hugged her fiercely. "Do you know how proud I am of you?"

"Me? I haven't done anything."

"Sure you have. You've taken the first step toward getting on with your life. That's the hardest one. I guess for a minute there I was just surprised you'd taken such a big one."

"You can thank Patsy for that. She's a very clever woman."

He grinned. "I've noticed."

Sharon Lynn snagged a handkerchief from his pocket, brushed away tears and gave him a penetrating look. "Speaking of Patsy, I hear I'm not the only one who's getting on with her life."

"I have no idea what you're talking about," he claimed innocently.

"Yeah, right."

"By the way, where is she this morning?"

Sharon Lynn shot him a look of triumph that could have rivaled one of Grandpa Harlan's. "So much for the innocent act. And here I thought you'd stopped by just to visit with me."

"Just tell me where she is."

"Meeting with Janet and Will." She surveyed him knowingly. "Then she's taking the rest of the day off to get ready for her big date."

"Oh, you've heard about that, too, have you? The grapevine must be in really top form these days."

"No need to worry about that. She just discussed it with me to arrange for the time off."

"And you haven't been burning up the phone lines out to White Pines?"

"Not a peep," she swore.

"I would be eternally grateful if that remained true," he said.

She feigned disappointment. "For how long?"

"How about the next year?" He grinned at her shock. "Okay, at least until tomorrow."

Sharon Lynn nodded. "I can do that."

Justin slid onto a stool. "Now what does a guy have to do to get a cup of coffee around here?"

"Begging would be a good start."

"How about if I ask nicely and leave a big tip?"

"That would work, too."

Patsy was a nervous wreck. In a few minutes she was going to walk into Janet's office and the details of her divorce agreement with Will were going to be finalized. It would be over. Oh, there would be a wait for the final decree, but with Will not contesting, she would be free to move on with her life. Once the wheels had been set into motion, it had all happened so quickly her head was spinning. She could thank Justin and Janet Adams for that.

Janet claimed that dueling wits with Will Longhorn had been sheer pleasure and that no thanks were necessary, but Patsy intended to offer a more personal sort of thanks to Justin that night. She was going to show him how very grateful she was for everything he had done for her, from giving her a break on her first day in town, to arranging for Janet to intercede with Will.

In the meantime, though, there was one more thing she had to do. She had to talk to Will and try one last time to understand where everything in their marriage had gone so wrong. How much of it had been her fault? For too long she'd been willing to shoulder most of the blame, but she knew better now. Will was the one who'd changed and made their lives into a hell.

On the sidewalk outside of Janet's office, she drew in a deep breath, then turned the doorknob and walked in. She crossed the empty reception area and rapped on the office door even though it was wide-open. Janet and Will looked up at her knock.

"Good, there you are," Janet said, giving her a reassuring smile and beckoning her inside. "We were just going over the last little details."

"Everything's okay, isn't it?" she asked, the question directed at Janet but her gaze on Will.

He gave her a rueful smile. "I suppose that depends on your point of view, but in general everything is just fine. I'm not fighting you on anything. You've been generous with the visitation schedule, probably more generous than I deserve."

"Thank you for not fighting me."

"Don't thank me. I figure I owe you, and your lawyer has seen to it that I remember that."

"I don't want your money, Will." She turned to Janet. "I thought I made that clear."

"We've only asked for child support," Janet reassured her. "Billy deserves that."

"And I insist on it," Will said, his expression defiant.

"Yes, you're right," she said, backing down. "Of course there should be money for Billy. I can put it into a college fund."

Janet slid the papers across her desk. "Then let's

get the last of these signed and everything will be official. I can file it with the court this afternoon."

Will cast one last look at Patsy, then turned back and signed the papers. Patsy followed with her own signature wherever Janet indicated.

"That's that, then," Janet said. She glanced at Patsy. "Would you two like a little time alone?"

Patsy nodded. "Please."

"I'll be in the next room, if you need me for anything."

After she'd gone, Will said, "An amazing woman, isn't she?"

"Yes, she is."

"I'd heard about her, of course, but the stories didn't do her justice. Seeing her in action reminded me of what being a good lawyer is all about." He met Patsy's gaze. "She's very protective of you, too. Is that because of Justin?"

"It's because she's a good lawyer, just as you said."

He shrugged. "I suppose."

"Can I ask you something, Will?"

"Why not?"

"What went wrong?"

He sighed heavily. "I wish I could begin to understand that. I certainly never meant to hurt you or Billy. I guess I didn't even realize how deeply words could cut or the kind of scars they could leave. I'm sorry,"

There was a raw anguish in his expression that

Patsy had never seen before. "Can you just explain why you seemed to hate me so? Was it because I'm not Native American?"

"Amazing," he said, clearly startled by the question. "I wonder if you hadn't figured that out long before I did. I began dating you, married you, for all the wrong reasons. You fit the image I thought I needed to go someplace. All those advisers I had around me concurred. They were ecstatic about our relationship. One day I just woke up and saw it as a betrayal of who I was. I blamed you for it, when the fault was my own." For the first time he looked directly into her eyes. "Can you forgive me?"

Patsy thought of Justin, a man whose self-esteem was so strong, whose sense of family had never been tested. He would never struggle with who he was as Will had. And he was able to share his family and his strength with her. She'd never thought it possible, but she actually pitied Will for struggling to find a place in two sometimes incompatible worlds.

"Of course, I can forgive you," she said eventually. "More important, though, can you forgive yourself?"

His smile was a mere ghost of the trademark Longhorn smile, the one that lit up his campaign posters and would no doubt seduce thousands of voters. "I'm working on it." He moved closer and gently touched her cheek, his expression turning unbearably sad. "See you around, Patsy."

"Yeah. See you around."

And then he was gone and in the blink of an eye she was on her own again. This time, she vowed, she was going to make sure she got it right.

Justin got through the rest of the day cruising on automatic. His mind certainly wasn't on work. It was fortunate for everyone that it was a quiet day. Everybody parked where they were supposed to and no one violated so much as the speed limit, much less any more serious laws. He spent most of the day catching up on paperwork.

"You still here?" Tate asked at six o'clock when he found Justin at his desk.

"Just killing a little time."

"Until your date with Patsy?"

"How the hell did you know about that?"

"My wife saw her picking up a couple of steaks at the supermarket. Plus she wasn't at work today and I saw Dani leaving the house a few minutes ago with Billy." He grinned. "Doesn't take a genius to add all that up, and I am a highly qualified sheriff. I make deductions a whole lot trickier than that all the time."

"You're also entirely too smug for your own good."

"So why aren't you at home getting ready?"

"How long can it take to shower and change?"

"What about stopping off to buy some flowers, maybe a box of candy? Women like those little touches. Trust me."

"When I want advice on my love life, I'll go to

Grandpa Harlan. You may be a good cop, but he's a grand master at mapping out a courtship strategy. Of course, he rarely bothers with notifying the principals of his intentions where they're concerned. I'm just grateful he's left Patsy and me pretty much on our own.''

''Once his wife mentions that those divorce papers got filed in court today, he might not be so reticent. I'd suggest you take advantage of the time left to you before he starts meddling.''

Justin nodded. ''Good point. I'm out of here.'' He glanced at the clock and muttered a curse. It was after six.

Tate grinned and said innocently, ''By the way, I told Millie at the florist's you might be by for a bouquet of flowers. She's staying open till you get there.''

''Remind me to thank you one of these days.''

''Just make sure I get an invitation to the wedding.''

Justin was halfway down the block before Tate's words sank in. Who'd said anything about a wedding? Certainly not him. To be perfectly technical, this would be his very first date with Patsy. No one proposed on a first date, not when the ink wasn't even dry on the woman's divorce petition. Even with all the tricks at Janet's command it could be weeks or even months before the decree was final.

Still he couldn't seem to shake the idea once it had been planted. Wasn't that what the past few months had been leading up to? There wasn't a doubt in his head about how he felt about Patsy. Like all the Adams men, he might be a little slow at recognizing love when it was staring him in the face, but once he did, he couldn't see a whole lot of reasons for delaying the inevitable. Patsy, however, might not be quite so anxious to plunge into another marriage.

He was still reminding himself of that when he rang her doorbell promptly at seven, a huge bouquet of daffodils and bluebonnets in his hand. When she opened the door, she took his breath away.

She was wearing a pale yellow sundress that bared just enough of her shoulders and cleavage to make his mouth go dry. Her hair fell in waves to her shoulders, and moist color on her lips had turned her shy smile sexy. He swallowed hard.

"You look beautiful," he finally managed to say.

"So do you," she said, then blushed furiously. "I meant the flowers. They're lovely."

He shoved them into her hands, then cursed the fact that he suddenly felt like an awkward adolescent on his very first blind date ever, instead of an experienced man having dinner with an attractive woman he'd known for months.

"Dinner will be ready in a few minutes," she said, turning and leading the way through the dining room.

"Steaks," he said even before they reached the kitchen.

She glanced over her shoulder. "How did you know?"

He winced at the slip of the tongue. He absolutely

refused to tell her that half the town probably knew. "I can smell the charcoal," he improvised. "Want me to throw them on the grill?"

"Would you mind? I'll finish up the salad."

Justin almost chuckled at her eagerness to get him out onto the patio and out of her way. It was clear she was every bit as nervous as he was. He found that as endearing as everything else about her.

He had the steaks on a plate and was about to come back inside just as she came through the screen door. They were standing toe to toe, gazes locked.

"I was just coming to check…"

"The steaks are done. I was just coming back in to…"

She covered her face and turned away. "Oh, God, I can't do this."

Justin stared at her, appalled. "Can't do what?"

"Nothing."

He brushed past her and set the platter of meat on the kitchen table, then turned to draw her into his arms.

"What's going on here?" he asked.

"I wanted everything to be perfect."

He was still confused. "It is perfect."

"No, it's not," she mumbled with a sniff. "I've ruined it."

"How? We haven't even sat down at the table yet."

"I don't mean the dinner."

Now he was more confused than ever. "What then?"

She gazed up at him with tear-filled eyes. "Justin, would you do something for me?"

"Anything."

"Kiss me, please."

He stared at her for no more than a heartbeat, before murmuring, "Now, darlin', that would be my pleasure."

He lowered his head and brushed his lips across hers, tasting the salty dampness of tears on her skin. It was the first tentative hint of a kiss, no more, but it might as well have been the most passionate one he had ever shared. Heat and yearning and desire slammed through him. He wound his fingers through her silky hair and stilled her head beneath his as he continued to explore the exquisite texture and taste of her mouth.

She moaned softly and opened her mouth to his tongue. Her body molded itself to his, every curve fitting snugly against the hard planes of his body. The intimate contact sent images streaking through his mind of the two of them tangled together in his bed.

"We have to stop," he said on a ragged breath, pulling away.

"Why?"

"Because this is happening too fast. It's all wrong."

"It's not wrong," she insisted. "Not if we both want it."

Holding her at arm's length, gazing into her eyes, he admitted to himself for the first time without reservations that he had fallen deeply in love with this fragile yet brave woman. Whether she loved him, though, was another matter. What he saw in her eyes was nothing more than gratitude, mixed in perhaps with a whole lot of lust.

"Is this what tonight was about?" he asked gently. "Did you ask me over so you could seduce me?"

"You want me," she said. "I know you do."

"That's not the issue."

"What else is there?"

He smiled ruefully. "If you have to ask that, then we really are on the wrong wavelength."

"I want you to make love to me, Justin."

He heard the urgency in her voice, but it wasn't the urgency of desire. It was, he was sure, the need to settle a debt and it broke his heart.

"Not like this," he admonished her softly.

"Like what?"

"This isn't the way to say thanks, Patsy. Dinner will do for that just fine."

She started as if he'd slapped her. "You think I was offering myself to you out of gratitude?" she demanded.

"Weren't you?"

The question hung in the air, adding to the already high tension. Her expression faltered under his steady gaze.

"Okay, yes," she said finally. Eyes blazing she met

his gaze. "But it was more than that. It is more than that."

"Tell me, then."

Her temper died slowly and only then did she murmur in a voice so low he could barely hear it, "I think I'm falling in love with you. It scares me to death, but there it is," she said with a defiant tilt to her chin.

Justin's heart flipped over. With some other woman maybes might have been enough. Not with this woman. With Patsy he wanted it all. He wanted love, commitment, permanence. He wanted a family and forever, with no doubts at all.

He bent his head and touched his lips to hers, then headed for the door because he knew he didn't dare stay. He glanced back, saw her shattered expression and almost changed his mind, but something warned him that it would be the worst mistake of his life.

After taking one last look at this woman who'd stolen his heart, he sighed, then said, "Let me know when you're sure."

He almost made it out the door, but her softly whispered cry of his name stopped him. He turned slowly back.

"I know now," she said, her eyes bright.

He smiled. "So fast?"

She nodded. "Because you were willing to walk out of here when I know you didn't want to. I knew in that instant."

He wanted desperately to believe her.

She held out her hand. "Please stay. Just for dinner, if that's all you're interested in."

"You know better than that."

"Please stay," she repeated.

Still wondering if he could trust himself, he grinned. "No hanky-panky?"

"Absolutely not." She sketched an X across her heart, then regarded him innocently. "Unless you change your mind."

"The steaks are probably ruined," he noted.

"We probably shouldn't be eating meat, anyway."

"Don't ever say that out at White Pines," he warned. "Grandpa Harlan will surely take offense. He does run a cattle empire, you know."

"I'll remember that." She tilted her head. "So was that a yes? Are you going to stay?"

He considered the question for some time, debating the wisdom of his decision, weighing desire against reason. Finally he nodded.

"Against my better judgment."

She laughed at his somber tone. "What's the matter, Deputy? Don't you trust yourself around me?"

"You've got that right."

"I'll do my best to see that you don't go against any of those important principles of yours."

"There's only one principle that applies to this particular situation," he told her.

"What's that?"

"I don't want to do anything that either one of us is going to regret in the morning."

She stepped up close then, deliberately crowding him, and rested her hand against his cheek. His skin heated under her touch. "There is nothing we could do, Justin, *nothing,* that I would ever regret."

She said it so fiercely, with so much passion that Justin's only choice was to kiss her. He moved quickly, before he could think, before second thoughts could come roaring back. And when he claimed her lips this time, he knew there would be no turning back.

Until the very instant when Justin's mouth had come crushing down on hers again, Patsy had been terrified that he would walk out the door. She had also been very much afraid that she would never again have the courage to go after him. It had been a long time since she'd taken an emotional risk. Her confidence was shaky.

She had been astonished earlier when he'd read her so easily, when he'd guessed that she'd wanted to give herself to him out of gratitude. Men weren't supposed to be so perceptive. Then, again, this wasn't most men they were talking about. This was Justin. He'd always struck her as a cut above the rest and tonight he had proved it.

She wanted him so desperately. She wanted the physical connection, knowing that it would come with the emotional commitment. She had been so sure that she was doomed to a life of solitude, a life on the run, an unending marital limbo. Because of Justin, all that had changed. He had given her back her life, given her back her heart. So, yes, she was grateful.

She was also wildly, passionately in love with him. There wasn't a doubt in her mind about that now. She had told him the honest-to-God truth about that. She had known, though, that he was really asking more than that. He was asking not just about her feelings, but about her readiness to face the future, a future with him very much in the middle of it. Could she answer that question as easily? Truthfully, no. She'd made so many resolutions about standing on her own two feet. It was important to keep them.

But with Justin's mouth covering hers, with his hands dancing over her skin and setting off wildfires in the wake of his touches, the only answer she could give was with her body and she gave it eagerly.

Clothes were shed in a frenzy, his, hers, flying through the air and landing who knew where. His heated gaze was as seductive as his caresses, lingering on every inch of bared flesh, stirring her.

He slowly slid his hand along her belly toward the hook of her bra. He flicked it open, then slowly brushed away the scraps of lace. She watched the muscle in his jaw work as he stared at her breasts.

"You are so beautiful," he whispered for the second time that night, his breathing ragged. "I want to make love to you right here, right now."

"In the kitchen?" she said on a gasp that was as much pure pleasure as shock as he skimmed his finger across an already hardened nipple.

"You'll never prepare a meal in here again without remembering," he teased.

"I'm not sure my heart will be able to take it."

"Now, see, there's something I didn't know about you. You're very traditional."

Patsy glanced at the counter, then considered that they were both already mostly undressed. "I can change," she said thoughtfully. "It could be fascinating."

He chuckled. "You've turned daring now? In the blink of an eye?"

She felt laughter bubbling up. "It's been that kind of day."

"Come here then," he suggested, stealing away the last scraps of clothes she was wearing and hoisting her onto the counter. The tiles were cold, a startling contrast to the fire burning inside her.

When he lowered his head to take her breast in his mouth, she rocked back, stunned by the sheer magic of it. He shucked off his jeans and briefs, guided her legs around his waist and then he paused. Anticipation had her ready to plead with him, but then she saw that he was only reaching for a foil packet in his pocket.

And then, before the heat had cooled even so much as a degree, he was inside her and it was building again. So much heat, so much urgency. Patsy was trembling from the inside out, straining toward an elusive goal that promised release. She kept thinking about the magic of it, the wonder of being touched by a man who was totally, thoroughly dedicated to her pleasure.

And then she wasn't thinking at all, just feeling as Justin's thrusts went deeper, as tension coiled in her belly, then sent shock waves ricocheting wildly through her. The intensity of it shattered her, leaving her panting and sated and awed by the wonder that was Justin.

Chapter Fourteen

It was morning before Justin was finally able to force himself to leave Patsy's bed. They had finally made their way into it long after midnight. In the meantime, they had used Patsy's newfound daring to make love in several spots along the way.

Gazing at her with the morning sun splashed across her body, he was struck anew by what a remarkable woman she was. Definitely full of surprises, that was for sure.

He dressed quickly and paused beside the bed for one last, lingering look. She stirred as if she'd felt his gaze. She came awake slowly, stretching like a sinuous cat and setting his blood to roaring through his veins all over again. When her eyes finally focused on him, she blinked.

"You're already dressed."

"I need to get to work and I have to stop by the house first to change into my uniform."

She glanced at the clock. "Oh my gosh, I'm going to be late, too."

"Take your time. I've got an in with your boss."

She scowled. "Which you are not to use. Getting there on time is my responsibility. I'm supposed to open up. Sharon Lynn's not ready to be back full-time yet." She yawned.

"The impression I got is that she's anxious to be busy."

"I'm going in," she repeated emphatically.

Justin decided he'd better not argue with her. He'd seen evidence of this stubborn streak before, and after growing up with a whole clan of control freaks, he knew better than to take her on over the inconsequential stuff.

"Just don't burn the coffee."

"You can't burn coffee."

"You can if you forget to put any water in the pot. Ask Sharon Lynn. She has firsthand experience."

"When she was distracted by the wedding preparations?"

"Oh, yeah. And that was just the tip of the iceberg. Suffice it to say, you will always be regarded as something of a savior of the public health in this town."

She tilted her head. "Is that how you think of me?"

"No way, darlin'." He leaned down and whispered

in her ear, chuckling when her cheeks turned bright red. "That's how I will think of you from now on."

"Well, I certainly hope you're the only one who feels *that* way."

"I'd better be," he concurred. He leaned down and delivered a hard, quick kiss that made up in intent what it lacked in passion. It was meant as a final reminder that she was his now. The dazed look in her eyes suggested he'd gotten his message across.

"See you in a while," he said.

"Justin, we are going to keep quiet about this, aren't we? For now, at least?"

He grinned, knowing the futility of it. "We can try."

She sighed. "I was afraid you were going to say that."

The whole blasted town was jumping to conclusions. Patsy realized it when half a dozen people asked very pointed questions that morning about her dinner with Justin and none of them had even witnessed the warm, personal greeting he gave her when he stopped by for a quick cup of coffee just before nine. Nor had most of them seen the way she'd brightened at his entrance. No, indeed, their probing had been sparked by something else entirely.

Thoroughly embarrassed at having her private life made public, she mumbled evasive answers to the prying questions and retreated to the back room at Dolan's every chance she got. Obviously Justin had known what he was talking about. There hadn't been a chance in hell of keeping anything secret in this town. It was all too reminiscent of being the wife of a promising political candidate.

"Hiding out again?" Sharon Lynn inquired, peeking through the partially opened door.

"I am not hiding out."

"Sure you are. Can't say I blame you. The folks in Los Piños do like their breakfast served up with gossip."

Patsy sighed. "What I can't figure out is how they even knew Justin and I were having dinner last night."

"That's a no-brainer."

"Explain."

"Did you shop at the grocery store?"

"Of course."

"Enough food for two, maybe something a little special, like thick steaks?"

She began to see where this was heading. "Yes."

"Did he bring you flowers?"

"Yes, but—"

"Did I cover for you in here yesterday afternoon?"

She got the picture. "Oh, good grief," she muttered impatiently. "Am I going to have to buy food in the next town before I invite him over again?"

Sharon Lynn grinned. "It won't help. We have sources there, too." She sat down on a stack of boxes. "So, tell me, how did it go?"

"We had a great time."

"Did you sleep with him?"

"Sharon Lynn!"

Her friend—and his cousin, she must never forget that—grinned impudently. "Never mind. I think you've just answered that question."

"I did not."

"That bright pink color in your cheeks did."

"Maybe I was just embarrassed that you would even think such a thing."

"If you're trying to persuade me I'm wrong, it's not working. Justin couldn't look me in the eye and give me a straight answer, either."

"You asked him, too?"

"Well, of course I did. I love both of you. I want this to work out."

"Then maybe you should just leave us alone. Knowing there's a fascinated audience panting for a play-by-play won't help."

"If you think I'm nosy, wait until you run into Grandpa Harlan."

"Did I hear somebody mention my name?" the very man in question called out. "Where the dickens are you, girl? You hiding in the broom closet like your mama and Cody used to do?"

Patsy sent a panicked glance toward the door. "I am absolutely not going out there."

"Of course you are," Sharon Lynn said, clearly eager to throw her to the wolves—or one wolf in particular, at least. "Your break's over. Mine's just beginning."

Before Patsy could argue that point, the door pushed open and Harlan Adams poked his head in. He was evidently tired of waiting for either of them to appear.

"I knew it," he gloated. "What is it about this room that lures everybody back here?"

"Maybe they're hoping for a little privacy," Sharon Lynn teased, going over to give him a kiss on the cheek.

He seemed fascinated by the explanation. "You two indulging in a little girl talk? Mind if an old man sits in?" He glanced at Patsy. "I have a few questions about you and my grandson."

"Sorry, sir. You'll have to get those answers from Justin," Patsy said, slipping past him with the finesse and speed of a very crafty running back.

"Dadgumit, he wouldn't tell me a blasted thing, either," he grumbled irritably.

"Bless his heart," Patsy murmured.

"What was that?" Harlan Adams asked.

"She said he's a wise man, Grandpa. What she had the good grace not to say was that you're being a nosy old man."

He scowled at her. "Like you haven't been poking at her all morning long."

Sharon Lynn shrugged. "I'm her friend. I'm entitled."

His gaze narrowed. "Did she tell you anything?"

"No, I did not," Patsy said, giving Sharon Lynn a

warning look. "Some people just enjoy making assumptions."

"How the devil is a man supposed to plan a wedding, if nobody will tell him anything."

Patsy halted in her tracks. A wedding? Who the hell had said anything about a wedding? Sharon Lynn shot her a sympathetic albeit an I-told-you-so look.

"Maybe you should let the people involved make their own wedding plans, Grandpa, if there are any to be made."

He stared hard at Patsy. "That what you want?"

"I think it would be best," she agreed, then relented just a little at his look of disappointment. "I will tell you one thing, though. If and when Justin and I talk about getting married, you will be the first to know."

He gave a little nod of satisfaction. "Good enough." He bent down and kissed Sharon Lynn's cheek, then Patsy's. "I'd best be getting back to White Pines. Janet's been moping around out there this morning because she doesn't have a case to work on. I've got to come up with something to keep her occupied or she'll be back here in town practicing law full-time before I can blink. That case of yours sparked her hunger to work again."

Sharon Lynn winked at Patsy. "Maybe you should compromise, Grandpa. Let her take on a case now and then."

"She is a very good lawyer," Patsy offered. "It's

a shame not to take advantage of all that legal knowledge.''

''You two are just too danged liberated for your own good. Her place is home with me. It's taken me too darn long to get her there as it is.''

''She'll be happier if she's feeling fulfilled professionally,'' Sharon Lynn said.

''Which means she will be very, very grateful to you for suggesting that she go back to work part-time,'' Patsy said slyly. She did not mention just what form that gratitude might take, even though she had some very recent experience with it.

He regarded Patsy with a twinkle in his eyes. ''I do like the way you think, girl. I hope you and my grandson hurry up and get this show on the road.''

''Why don't you forget about Justin and Patsy and pester Harlan Patrick,'' Sharon Lynn suggested. ''Now there is a man just ripe for matrimony.''

''Never you mind your brother. He's right on track with Laurie Jensen, as far as I can tell.''

''And you would know, I'm sure,'' Sharon Lynn teased.

He scowled at her. ''I have to see to it that all my babies are settled, don't I?''

''You think you do, anyway,'' she agreed.

Harlan Adams's expression sobered. ''What about you, darlin' girl? You doing okay?''

The smile on Sharon Lynn's face faded faster than the sun dipping below the horizon. Patsy gave her hand a squeeze.

"She's doing fine," Patsy said, trying to bring a quick end to the subject. She was all too aware that Sharon Lynn's tears were too close to the surface and that the slightest reminder of Kyle could bring them coursing down her cheeks again. She'd dashed into this back room a few times herself today, when a customer's sincere expression of sympathy had gotten to be too much for her.

Thankfully, Harlan Adams glanced at Sharon Lynn and took Patsy's hint. He rose to his feet, again kissed his granddaughter on the cheek, then pressed another kiss on Patsy's cheek.

"I'll be getting on home now. As for you two, you might want to come out of this broom closet every now and again. It looks to me like there are some impatient folks sitting out here wondering what happened to the help."

"I'll go," Patsy said at once, brushing past him to discover that the only impatient person in the store was Justin. Her heartbeat accelerated. She forced herself to walk slowly back to the counter, pausing to grab a cup and the coffeepot on her way to where he sat.

"Back so soon?" she asked.

"Had to get my hourly fix of the prettiest woman in Los Piños," he teased.

"Sharon Lynn, get out here," Patsy called. "Justin's looking for you."

He grinned. "Very funny."

He looked past her just then and spotted his grandfather. To Patsy's amusement, he regarded him suspiciously.

"What are you doing here?" he asked.

"Do you think you're the only one in the world who appreciates a beautiful woman?" his grandfather asked.

"Go find your own. This one's mine," Justin said.

"Says who?" Patsy inquired.

"Whooee," his grandfather said, grinning. "I like this girl."

Justin turned his gaze from his grandfather to Patsy. His expression sobered. "So do I, Grandpa. So do I."

"Then I'll just run along and leave you to see what you can do about getting her to change her mind about you."

After he'd gone, Justin focused on Patsy. "So, what about it? Can I change your mind?"

"About?"

"Being mine."

Something in his tone told her the question wasn't being asked in jest. And as desperately as one part of her wanted to say yes, another part reminded her that once before she'd been too eager to jump into a relationship. She hadn't even fully extricated herself from that mistake yet.

"Maybe one of these days," she said. She glanced around to make sure they were unobserved, then leaned across the counter to brush a kiss across his lips. "You are awfully cute."

When she would have drawn away, Justin tucked

his hand around the back of her neck and held her still long enough to deepen the kiss into something wild and sweet.

"Have dinner with me tonight," he suggested when he released her.

"Two nights running. People will talk," she teased.

"Darlin', I'm beginning to think it's our civic duty to give them something fascinating to talk about."

"That sounds a little too self-serving to me."

He grinned. "I was going for noble. What about it, though? Will you have dinner with me? We'll go someplace quiet and romantic."

Patsy had been to most of the restaurants in town. None she knew qualified. "Where?"

"You'll see."

"Justin, I really think you ought to tell me. I have a son to consider."

"Taken care of. He's going out to the ranch to spend the night. Janet says she can't wait."

Once again, he was taking over, smoothing things out to get his own way. Maybe under other circumstances she would have found the gesture touching. Instead, it rankled.

"Don't you think you should have consulted me before making arrangements for my son?" she asked testily.

"The plans aren't cast in stone," he replied, his tone reasonable. "If you have a problem with them, we'll change them."

"That's not the point."

"Then what is the point?" he asked patiently.

"I don't need somebody to run my life for me, Justin. I've been there, done that, and I didn't like it."

He nodded slowly. "I see."

"Do you really?"

"I think so. Will pretty much set the agenda for your lives and expected you to fall in line. How am I doing so far?"

There was that perception of his kicking in again to surprise her. "On the money," she admitted.

"I'll try to be more sensitive to that in the future," he promised.

She shrugged, not entirely trusting an easily made and easily broken promise. The proof would have to come over time.

He gave her one of his crooked, endearing smiles. "Can we start this conversation over again?"

She hesitated, then grinned back, unable to resist him in the end. "What the heck, give it a try."

"Patsy, would you care to have dinner with me tonight?"

"I'd be delighted," she said, because she could recognize the stupidity of turning down a date with a man she loved just to make a point.

"What about a baby-sitter for Billy? Need any help in making arrangements?"

"I'll volunteer," Sharon Lynn offered, joining them.

It was impossible to tell how much of the earlier conversation she'd overheard, but Patsy was grateful for the offer. "Are you sure you won't mind?"

"Heavens, no. It'll be fun. I can even stay over at your place. That way I won't have to have someone from the ranch come into town to pick me up tonight and you won't have to rush back home." She grinned. "In fact, you could stay out all night if you wanted to."

Patsy almost laughed at the hopeful expression on Justin's face. "Okay, it's a deal," she said. "Thank you."

"No," Sharon Lynn said softly. "You're the one doing me a favor."

Her expression was so sad that Patsy was taken aback. She had seen firsthand how getting into a car had panicked Sharon Lynn. Now she realized just what a toll the trips into town and home again were taking. Suddenly she knew that if she weren't staying in Dani's old place, Sharon Lynn would have snatched it up for herself to rid herself of the frightening commute.

Before she could second-guess herself, she said casually, "You know, Sharon Lynn, if you wanted to, you could stay with Billy and me for a while."

The suggestion startled both Justin and Sharon Lynn, but Sharon Lynn seized on it with such a look of relief that Patsy knew she'd done the right thing.

"Are you sure you wouldn't mind? It would save

me..." She hesitated, then sighed, not quite meeting Patsy's gaze. "It would save a lot of time."

Patsy met her gaze evenly. "I understand, and it would be fine with me. And I have no intention of thinking of you as a built-in baby-sitter. I'll enjoy the company."

"What about my company?" Justin demanded irritably.

"You, cousin dear, are an entirely different kind of company," Sharon Lynn teased. "And I'm sure she enjoys that, too."

"I do," Patsy assured him.

"Then we're on for dinner?"

"We are definitely on for dinner."

He grinned. "And after?"

"Don't push your luck, lawman. We'll negotiate the details over dinner."

He touched a finger to his Stetson in a mock salute as he put it back on. "I'll be looking forward to it, ma'am. What time shall I pick you up?"

"Why don't I pick you up?" she suggested, as a perfectly fascinating idea occurred to her.

"Why not? I'm a flexible kind of guy."

"That'll be the day," Sharon Lynn taunted.

He scowled at his cousin, then said to Patsy, "Don't listen to a thing she says about me. She's never forgiven me for laughing when she fell off a horse in front of..." The teasing light in his eyes died. "Oh, God, I'm sorry, sweetie."

Tears welled up in Sharon Lynn's eyes, but she

reached over and touched Justin's lips. "Don't be sorry. Don't ever be sorry for reminding me of the good times. It's just that…"

"It's just that the wound is still raw," Justin said. "But you're going to be okay, you know that, don't you?"

"Sure," she said, forcing a wobbly smile. "We Adamses are made of tough stuff."

"The toughest," Justin concurred.

But looking at the tenderness in Justin's expression as he watched Sharon Lynn, Patsy knew he was wrong. Justin Adams, at least, had the softest heart she'd ever seen.

Justin had no idea why it had been so important to Patsy to pick him up that night, but he was going nuts waiting for her. Was this how women felt all the time waiting for their dates to arrive? No wonder some of them were itching to turn into control freaks.

Oh, he'd recognized what that whole discussion at Dolan's had been about that afternoon. Will Longhorn had dictated every aspect of his wife's life and she didn't intend to let it happen again. He had to wonder, though, how long these bids for independence were likely to go on. Would she refuse to marry him just to prove she could get along on her own? Or could he persuade her that it was possible to be half of a whole without losing her own identity? Tonight would be a fascinating test of his theory that she needed to know that at least some of the decisions in their relationship were hers to make.

When the doorbell rang at last, he bolted to answer it. To his astonishment, in spite of the humid evening air and clear skies, Patsy was wearing a raincoat.

"Expecting a storm?" he inquired lightly.

She gave him an enigmatic look. "In a manner of speaking. May I come in?"

He stepped aside. "Be my guest."

She sailed past him in a cloud of very seductive perfume. By the time he could recover from that and had closed the door, she had disappeared.

"Patsy?"

"Back here," she said in a tone that could have lured ships to crash into rocky cliffs.

There was no question that her voice was coming from the bedroom, his bedroom, unless he missed his guess. He swallowed hard. Something told him that dinner was going to be very late and was going to consist of whatever was in his freezer.

When he got to the door to his room and glanced inside, his mouth gaped. Patsy was standing in the middle of the room in a black negligee so scanty he thought for sure his heart would slam to a stop if he stared at her too long.

"Won't you get cold at the restaurant?" he asked when he could find his voice.

Her confident expression faltered just a little. "You still want to go out?"

He barely held back a grin at her wistful tone. "Not if you don't."

"I thought I was making myself pretty clear."

"It wouldn't be the first time we've gotten our signals crossed."

"Justin, you will never make sheriff if you can't read a clue this obvious."

He grinned. "Okay, let me try." He paused thoughtfully. "You are less interested in dinner than you are in seduction."

She stepped toward him and nodded. "Very good," she praised.

She slid her arms around his neck. "And this?"

"No waiting?"

"Oh, yes," she murmured just before she stood on tiptoe and kissed him with an enthusiasm that left not a single doubt in either of their minds about how they were going to spend the rest of the evening.

Chapter Fifteen

Patsy was very proud of the way she'd managed to render Justin Adams totally speechless. Lying next to him in his bed, she felt as if she'd finally come home, finally met a man who thought of her as an equal, a partner. Maybe she was being a fool for setting some artificial time constraint on the relationship.

"Satisfied?" he asked, regarding her with an amused look.

"Oh, my, yes," she said.

"What happens now?" he asked.

Her expression faltered. "I guess that depends on you."

"Oh, no, you don't, Patsy Gresham Longhorn. For the past twenty-four hours you've been telling me every way you knew how that you are capable of making your own decisions, capable of taking the initiative, capable of standing on your own two feet, that you *insist* on standing on your own two feet, come what may.''

''There are still some things that are a man's prerogative,'' she admitted unwillingly.

''Such as?''

She was not going to put these words into his mouth. Nor was she quite brave enough to demand that he marry her and make an honest woman of her. Maybe if neither of them could put the question into words, there was a reason for it. Maybe it really was too soon after Will.

Even if she did absolutely adore being in his bed, with his arms around her and her head resting against his chest.

She sighed, rolled over and stood up. Justin regarded her with surprise.

''Where are you going?''

''You promised me dinner.''

''Sorry, darlin'. The cupboard's practically bare.'' He grinned. ''We could order in. That would certainly make Angie's day over at the Italian restaurant. Or we could call Rosa and ask her to deliver some Mexican. Of course, she is related to the housekeeper at White Pines, which means there would be more talk.''

''Are you saying there is not one tiny little scrap of food in this house?''

''Not even a cracker.'' He surveyed her thoroughly.

"And you're not exactly dressed to go to the restaurant I had in mind." He beckoned to her. "Maybe if you climb back into bed I can make you forget all about your growling tummy."

"I'm sure you could," she agreed. "But without food neither of us will survive another round of really energetic sex."

"Then we'll take it nice and slow," he said in a provocative way that set her blood to pumping furiously.

She was still standing there debating the wisdom of that when Justin's beeper went off. In an instant, he was all cop. He grabbed the beeper from his nightstand, reaching for the phone at the same time.

"What is it?" he demanded, even as he scrambled to find clothes. His expression sobered. "I see. Okay, I'm on my way."

He slammed the phone down, pulled on his shirt and unlocked the drawer to get his gun. Patsy watched him and shivered. It was a full minute before he glanced her way and noticed her expression.

"I'm sorry," he said.

"No, it's okay. Of course, you have to go. What's happened?"

"We've got a high speed chase on the interstate heading this way. Tate wants me to set up a roadblock."

Patsy's blood ran cold as images of Sharon Lynn's wrecked car came whirling back.

He touched a finger to her cheek. "Don't worry. I know what I'm doing."

"I know. It's just that…"

"The accident," he said succinctly. "I'll be fine, Patsy. We have important things left to finish here tonight. I'll make sure I get back before you even miss me."

"Not possible," she told him softly. He wasn't out the door and she missed him already.

The instant he was gone, panic began to set in. What if he never came back? What if something happened and she'd never told him just how desperately she loved him? What if she'd wasted precious time while trying to declare her independence? Would it be worth it?

Maybe, she told herself as she sat huddled in a blanket on the sofa waiting for him, maybe when something was so clearly right, only a fool would take a chance on throwing it away.

When the clock ticked on slowly and still Justin hadn't returned, Patsy could no longer sit still. Despite his earlier claims that there was no food in the place, she went into the kitchen in search of something to eat.

When that proved fruitless, she went back to the bedroom and began straightening up. It didn't take long. Justin was invariably neat. Only the clothes they'd worn earlier were scattered about. Her negligee and raincoat seemed ludicrous now, when she'd been reduced to wearing one of his shirts. Why hadn't she at least tucked an overnight bag with a change of clothes into the back of the car? Had she planned on leaving here in broad daylight wearing virtually nothing? The truth was, she hadn't thought about leaving at all, only about getting here and stunning him speechless.

She picked up his slacks and when she did, something dropped out of the pocket, then rolled under the bed. She scrambled after it. When her hand closed around it, she realized it was a small velvet box. Her heart stood still.

She rocked back on her heels and stared at the red velvet in wonder. This was what he'd had in mind for tonight, she realized. A romantic dinner and then this. With fingers that trembled, she flipped open the lid and gazed at a stunning solitaire diamond on a wide gold band. Even though the stone was large, there was nothing ostentatious about it. It was elegant and simple, a declaration not just of love, but of understanding.

"He knew," she murmured as tears began to build. He had understood that all of Will's gestures had been for show—the gaudiest diamond, fanciest car, biggest house. This ring just said that Justin Adams loved her and nothing more.

"Oh, Justin," she whispered, her throat tight.

What if she never got to say yes? What if the divorce dragged on, for some reason? What if…? She couldn't bear to say it, not even to think it. Instead, she slid the ring onto her finger. Somehow, she thought, somehow he would know her answer, no matter what. When the decree was final—when Justin was safe— they would start to plan their future.

It was nearly daybreak when she heard the front door open, then close quietly. In a heartbeat, she was on her feet and racing toward the living room. She skidded to a stop at the sight of him. He looked as if he'd been mauled by a particularly cantankerous bull. There were cuts and gashes and dirt. His uniform was in tatters, but he was alive, she told herself. He was blessedly alive.

He glanced up and saw her then and the exhaustion vanished. His eyes lit up.

Patsy moved toward him, then hesitated, all too aware of the state he was in. "How badly are you hurt?"

"Just a few bumps and bruises. The guy took exception to being arrested. I had to chase him down and wrestle around with him near a barbed wire fence. The fence won."

"And you? Did you get your man?"

"Of course," he said, his expression smug. "The good guys always win." He reached for her gingerly, then searched her face. "Don't they?"

"Depends on what they're after, I suppose."

"You know what I'm after," he said. "Are you ready for me to spell it out?"

She held out her hand. "Does it have anything to do with this?"

He stared at the ring in surprise. "You found it?"

"I was straightening up. It fell out of your pocket."

He grinned. "And you assumed it was meant for you?"

She scowled. "And who else would it have been meant for?"

"Maybe some woman who knows her own mind."

"I know my own mind."

"Do you?"

"Always have." She circled his waist with her arms and held on, relishing the sense of security that swept over her. "It just took me a while to figure out I could trust my own judgment. I have had reason to question it, you know."

"You can trust yourself this time, darlin'. I will love you till my dying breath, Patsy Longhorn. I will never hurt you. I will treat Billy as if he were my own and I will make absolutely sure that we have a house crawling with brothers and sisters for him, if that's what you want."

"Oh, it is definitely what I want," she assured him. She gazed into his eyes. "No doubt about it."

He lifted her hand and admired the ring that fit perfectly. "You stole my thunder. I was going to ask you last night," he said. "But you had other plans for the evening."

"I didn't hear any complaints at the time."

"No way. Now, though, I want your full attention. No funny business, okay?"

"Okay."

He surveyed her from the open collar of his shirt

to her bare thighs. She could feel the heat of his gaze everywhere it touched.

"Maybe you ought to get dressed."

She grinned. "My choices are pretty limited. It's this shirt, the negligee or the raincoat."

He groaned. "Never mind. I'll just have to concentrate a little harder."

"Can't remember what you had in mind?" She waved the ring under his nose, then dropped it into his palm. "Does it have anything to do with this?"

Justin looked as if he'd never seen the diamond engagement ring before in his life. "This? Yeah."

His reaction, his inability to focus on anything but her couldn't have pleased her more. Will had always acted as if half his attention was on a speech he had to make later in the day.

"How about the future?" she coached. "Does it have anything to do with that?"

"You're beautiful, you know that."

"The future, together, you and me," she persisted, refusing to allow him to distract her, too.

"Mmm-hmm," he said, and reached for her.

Sometime later, Justin finally managed to get out the words and get the ring on her finger, but the moment was almost anticlimactic. She'd given him her answer long before, in his arms, when she'd murmured yes over and over in his ear. And one day soon, when her divorce was final, the whole world would know, too.

* * *

The wedding plans had been taken completely out of her hands the very instant the divorce decree was final, but for once Patsy wasn't feeling the least bit defensive about losing control over her life. It gave her more time to spend with Justin and Billy, more time to indulge in the incredible romantic fantasy her life had become.

Watching her son with his prospective stepdaddy always brought a lump to her throat. And listening to Will explain to Billy that he would always be his daddy, but that it was okay with him if Billy loved Justin did bring tears to her eyes.

"Thank you," she told Will as he walked to his car after his visit.

"You deserve to be happy. Your being happy will insure that Billy's happy, too. How could I want anything less for my son?" He gazed into her eyes. "There's something I need to thank you for, too."

"What's that?"

"For snapping me back to reality and for agreeing to let Billy spend time with me and my family while you're on your honeymoon. I think it's time both of us learned something about our roots."

"You've always known who you were, Will. You just got lost for a little while."

He grinned sheepishly. "Well, that's one way of looking at it, I suppose." He gave her a peck on the cheek. "Good luck, sweetheart. I think you're getting a better deal this time around."

Patsy didn't say it, but she knew she was. Her gaze

lifted just in time to see Justin coming toward them. Will turned slowly and met Justin's gaze steadily.

"Make her happy," he said.

"I intend to."

"Okay, then, I'll see you two tomorrow night, right after the wedding reception."

"Are you sure you don't want to come?" Patsy said.

"You'd be welcome," Justin added.

Will seemed startled by the sincerity of the gesture. "No, but thanks. Patsy ought to start her new life without a reminder from her old one staring her in the face."

He got into his car then and drove away, leaving Patsy staring after him, her expression thoughtful. "Maybe he's not such a bad person, after all. Maybe it was just the circumstances and the timing."

"I don't know about that," Justin said. "The only timing I'm concerned about now is seeing to it you make it to the church on time tomorrow."

"Sharon Lynn is staying with me. Janet has a time-table posted on the refrigerator door. There's no way I'll be late," she promised.

Of course, she hadn't counted on getting stopped for speeding halfway to the chapel. Even as she hit the brakes, she glanced at the speedometer and noted that she was barely exceeding the posted speed limit.

Ready for an argument, she glanced up into Tate's amused eyes.

"Going somewhere in a hurry, aren't you?"

"You do realize if you keep me out here on the side of the road, I will be late and Justin will worry and the whole family will get in on the act?"

He grinned. "Which is why I decided to be your escort. I don't want any other law enforcement officer coming along and delaying this wedding."

She regarded him curiously. "Why is my marrying Justin so important to you?"

"Because the second you get back from your honeymoon, I'm going to follow Doc Dolan down to the Gulf Coast and spend the rest of my days fishing. Already have my place picked out and my wife's chomping at the bit to get going."

"Which means what for Justin?"

"That he'll be sheriff, if he wants the job."

"Have you told him that?"

"Nope. It's my wedding present. I'll tell him at the reception."

Patsy grinned. "It's better than another blender, I'll give you that."

"Come on, then, girl. We're wasting time. If you're late, Harlan Adams will have the state troopers, the Texas Rangers and Lord knows who else out here looking for you."

When they reached the church, Justin was indeed pacing around outside, with his grandfather right on his heels. The pair of them glared at Tate, who wisely scooted inside without getting dragged into a discussion over his role in her delayed arrival.

"You can go on in now, Grandpa. The wedding's about to start," Justin said, his relief evident.

When they were alone, he scowled at her. "I ought to have you arrested, you know."

"For what? I haven't done anything."

"Sure you have. You stole my heart."

Patsy reached up and cupped his face in her hands. "For a lawman, you sure do have a way with words."

And then she kissed him, which is why, forever after, everyone in Los Piños would talk about the fact that Justin Adams kissed his bride before the wedding and almost never made it to the chapel at all.

* * * * *

Every day is

A Mother's Day

in this heartwarming anthology
celebrating motherhood and romance!

Featuring the classic story "Nobody's Child" by Emilie Richard
He had come to a child's rescue, and now Officer Farrell Riley was
suddenly sharing parenthood with beautiful Gemma Hancock.
But would their ready-made family last forever?

Plus two brand-new romances:

"Baby on the Way" by Marie Ferrarella

Single and pregnant, Madeline Reed found the perfect husband in the
handsome cop who helped bring her infant son into the world. But did his
dutiful role in the surprise delivery make J. T. Walker a daddy?

"A Daddy for Her Daughters" by Elizabeth Bevarly

When confronted with spirited Naomi Carmichael and her brood of girls,
bachelor Sloan Sullivan realized he had a lot to learn about women!
Especially if he hoped to win this sexy single mom's heart....

Available this April from Silhouette Books!

Where love comes alive™

Visit Silhouette at www.eHarlequin.com

PSAMD

These New York Times *bestselling authors*
have created stories to capture the hearts and minds
of women everywhere.
Here are three classic tales about the power of love—
and the wonder of discovering the place
where you belong....

FINDING HOME

DUNCAN'S BRIDE
by
LINDA HOWARD

CHAIN LIGHTNING
by
ELIZABETH LOWELL

POPCORN AND KISSES
by
KASEY MICHAELS

Available only from Silhouette
at your favorite retail outlet.

Where love comes alive™

Coming in May 2002

**Three Bravo men marry for convenience—
but will they love in leisure? Find out in
Christine Rimmer's *Bravo Family Ties!***

Cash—for stealing a young woman's innocence, and to
give their baby a name, in *The Nine-Month Marriage*

Nate—for the sake of a codicil in his beloved
grandfather's will, in *Marriage by Necessity*

Zach—for the unlucky-in-love rancher's chance to
have a marriage—even of convenience—
with the woman he *really* loves!

BRAVO
FAMILY TIES

Silhouette®
Where love comes alive™

Visit Silhouette at www.eHarlequin.com

BR3BFT